How Deep the Ocean

Gloria Lucas

For Kris
And for our sons, Christian and Cayden

Never forget the stories about your father. You are his most precious of
legacies. There is not a part of you that would not make him proud.

The reality is that you will grieve forever. You will not 'get over' the loss of a loved one; you'll learn to live with it. You will heal and you will rebuild yourself around the loss you have suffered. You will be whole again but you will never be the same. Nor should you be the same nor would you want to.
ELIZABETH KUBLER-ROSS AND DAVID KESSLER,
ON GRIEF AND GRIEVING

-Chapter 1-

T he dream dissipated like fog encountering the morning sun. Mia's throat was thick with emotion, and when she opened her eyes, one fat tear escaped, quickly making its way down past her temple and into the dip of her ear. She hated the feeling, but didn't move to wipe it. Light filtered in through the bedroom curtains, painting the room gold. For a moment, she thought she picked up the scent of her husband's woodsy, floral cologne. The weight of loss sat squarely on her chest. Her hand stretched out across the coolness of the bed, her breath catching as it glided against fabric and found nothing.

Even after so much time had passed—a whole year!—the emptiness startled her. Periodically, she'd walk into the living room, expecting to see Austin relaxing on the couch watching his favorite show. Instead, she found emptiness, the television's black screen a dark mirror. There were times she envisioned herself ripping it off the wall, throwing it across the room, watching stoically as the screen exploded into a thousand tiny shards. The rage scared her, and she would wait at the edge of the room until the impulse passed.

There were times in the shower, eyes closed, rinsing her hair, when she would brace for his surprise arrival. "I got Isaiah down for his nap. You got room in there for me?" Her stomach would jump in anticipation, a flutter of desire and regret.

But he did none of those things. Not anymore.

The only times he visited were in her nightmares; mercifully, those were rare. Days typically ended with the meeting of body to bed, the exhaustion of survival clinging to her skin, which meant most nights were spent in the abyss of unconsciousness.

She found his appearances in troubled dreams ironic. Before, if she ever woke from a bad dream, she'd wake him too. Half-asleep, he'd pull her close and murmur that she was safe, he'd keep them safe. He knew some of what haunted her as she knew some of what haunted him. They were broken children, trying their best to smooth over the jagged pieces. As he held her, she'd smile and press her face against his chest, breathing him in.

Those were the only promises that made her feel better. Looking back, she wasn't sure why. It wasn't that he never lied. Nor was she trusting by nature. Maybe it was the vulnerable state she'd wake in, the magical window between asleep and awake, the sacred space that allowed monsters to scare adults and promises to mean something. In it, she was a child again, and as much as she hated to admit it, she wanted someone to protect her. She wanted to drop her guard, her constant vigilance.

Perhaps that's why, a whole year later, she still reached for him.

She knew now that loss was not abstract. Loss was the vacuum left after someone died, the loneliness that followed her. It constricted her heart, pressed in on her ribs, made it harder to breathe.

A memory came then, unbidden. *Laughter.*

He had worked late into the evening, well past Isaiah's bedtime. Annoyed, she went to bed as soon as their son was down and took up as much of the bed as possible. Her body was cocooned in pillows and bedding, partially because she knew he'd have to wake her to join her in bed and partially because without him, she felt cold.

When he walked into the bedroom, she heard a laugh. Then, a heavy thud as he jumped onto the bed, his body perpendicular to hers.

She hadn't been sleeping, but she protested anyway. "Hey! Can't a girl get some sleep?"

He giggled. "I see you, bed hog."

"It's not hogging if you're not here. I'm just taking advantage of the bed."

"Oh," he said. "You want to take advantage of the bed, huh?" He righted himself and kissed her nose and her cheek, then met her mouth as he worked the covers down.

It was funny, though; now that the bed was completely hers, she never dared trespass onto his side. It was as if his death had left a negative space that took up all the vacancies within their home.

A noise in the bathroom brought her back to the present. The smell of cologne wasn't a memory. She threw the covers off her body and bolted to the source. A small shadow stood frozen near the closet, caught. She flicked on the lights.

"Isaiah!" Too late, she realized she had shouted.

Two worried brown eyes met hers. Her son sank to a crouch in the master bathroom, his hands wrapped around the cologne bottle. His face was a childish reflection of hers—the high cheekbones and wide nose, a smattering of freckles decorating his face—but his eyes and brow were those of his father.

Mia closed her eyes and took a deep breath; her hands were balled into fists. Anger coursed through her body. It came so easily these days. She tried to keep her voice even. "What are you doing?"

As she opened her eyes, she willed her hands to relax. She paused to let him talk, but he remained frozen, staring.

"What are you doing?" She fought the urge to cross the room and yank the bottle from his grip.

"I..." he faltered. The corners of his lips tugged downward. He stood, drew a shaky breath, and held out the cologne bottle. "I'm sorry."

Mia crossed the short space and accepted the bottle. She took another even breath. "I'm not asking for an apology. I'm asking, 'What are you doing?'"

"I wasn't making a mess. I—I thought it was Daddy's."

Whenever Mia reflected on the weeks leading up to Austin's death, it astounded her that everything had felt normal. Had he known this would be the last cologne bottle he'd buy? It was strange how quickly the mundane had turned special. He had bought many cologne bottles throughout their relationship. This one, however, was now sacred. On nights when insomnia held her hostage, she would mist a small amount over the sheets. After a few minutes, she'd wrap herself in them, careful to stay on her side of the bed, and hope the mix of her sweaty skin against the fresh scent would bring him back to her.

She dreaded the day it would run out. She knew, of course, that she could buy another. But that would be a bottle she bought, not him. It was a matter of semantics, she supposed, but it mattered.

Isaiah's eyes brimmed with tears. Six years old and already navigating the loss of a parent. Most kids were introduced to death when their goldfish died. Mia was barely keeping it together, yet she realized she was expecting her son to be on his best behavior. It made sense he would be clinging to the relics of their old life as much as she was.

She felt like shit.

Why'd you leave me alone, Austin? she thought. *This is so hard.*

She pressed her lips into what she hoped was a reassuring smile.

"It's okay, mi vida. It's okay. This is Daddy's. But that's why we have to be careful with it. Please ask next time. Wait till I'm awake. Okay?"

He looked at the floor and nodded.

"I miss Daddy, too," Mia said.

He shrugged.

She relocated the bottle of cologne to a high corner of the bathroom closet and made a mental note to hide it elsewhere once Isaiah wasn't around. Though she was willing to share, especially if he asked, it was highly probable he'd simply scale the closet and avoid requesting permission. He didn't listen to her as well as she would like. Not anymore.

She picked him up and squeezed. "I'm sorry I yelled."

Isaiah's stiff body melted enough to allow the embrace, and he laid his head on her shoulder.

"You smell just like Daddy," she said.

She felt him smile. "Really?" His breath was warm against her neck.

"Mm-hmm. But we don't want to waste it. So, let's be careful, yes?" She kissed his cheek.

His body stiffened again. "Okay."

She set him down and changed the subject. "Breakfast?"

∞ ∞ ∞

"Mia."

She didn't look up and instead rifled through the papers on the kitchen counter, gathering the forms she had been instructed to bring on her first day. "I'm going to be late."

"You're going to be early. You have plenty of time."

"Not true. You know how traffic can be. I have to go soon."

"Mia."

She kicked herself for not getting everything ready the night before. Once identified, she stacked the papers together and slid them into a folder. "Austin." She didn't look up when she replied, instead stuffing the folder into her oversized bag.

"Mi amor." He dragged out the 'r' in an American accent, knowing it would annoy her.

She sighed and shot him a look. "You're being a little bit annoying."

Austin sighed, too, but he was smiling. "You're being dramatic."

"I'm not being dramatic. Estoy nerviosa." She held the 'a,' and it came out in a bit of a whine, which made her feel childish and increased her anxiety.

"Stop stressing. Eat some breakfast so you don't end up passing out on your first day of work. Or worse, get all hangry."

She snorted and stuck her tongue out at him.

The gesture eased some tension, and he walked up behind her, rubbing her shoulders in a slow methodical motion.

She relaxed and shook him off. "I really am going to be late if I don't hurry."

"Only because you're being mean and refusing my amazing spread. Look. Omelets and stone fruit salad." He wiggled his eyebrows. "Sounds fancy, but that just means there's plums in it. And you could have eaten by now."

She laughed and conceded. "Okay, okay, okay. But I have to be quick about it."

He nodded. "Fair enough." He piled her plate high with salad and pulled the oversized omelet off the pan. "Bon appétit."

She kissed him lightly on the lips. "You didn't have to do this, you know."

"I know. I gotta contribute somehow."

The words dropped like heavy stones in a pond. Tension filled the space between them, and Mia felt obligated to finish her plate. Austin had been laid off a year prior and had yet to find a job. Though she hadn't needed to worry about her position, she applied elsewhere for a higher paying one. To her delight—and horror—she had been accepted.

When she broke the news to Austin, her tone was apologetic, as if she were confessing a sin.

She hated the feeling, hated how Austin had seemed to feel better only when she'd started making excuses about why it was easier for her to find something. She understood the bruised ego. But goddammit, she wanted to believe he was above all that. She had thought they were beyond the stereotype of the man being the breadwinner.

Mia understood gender role expectations. After she had been born, her mother, Gabriela, had taken a year off work to stay home with her. Gabriela's mother, Teresa, had misinterpreted the sabbatical as a decision to become a stay-at-home mother. When Gabriela returned to work as a teacher in their county's school district, Teresa was shocked and disappointed. Mia still remembered the passive-aggressive comments her grandmother would say when discussing mothers in the workforce.

Gabriela's father, José, would come to her rescue when Teresa would fuss too much. "Así es aquí en los estados." *That's how it is here in the states.*

And yet, even with a career, Gabriela didn't escape the impact of her upbringing, and she ensured that dinner was ready by the time her husband, David, arrived home. She served him first and often ate the beginning of her meal standing up as she tended to Mia.

For her part, Mia absorbed the lessons on keeping a happy home but did her best to reject the dogma of traditional gender roles. And she believed Austin did, too. Until he lost his job. Then, as weeks stretched into months, a darkness settled onto him, a darkness he tried his best to hide from her—or perhaps himself—by burying himself in other work.

He didn't just cook dinner; he came up with elaborate new recipes. Numerous areas of the house suddenly required repair or improvements. Mia offered to help cover costs, but Austin insisted on using the money in his savings account. When she questioned the complexity of house projects, he boasted it was a learning opportunity for himself and their son.

"That's the beauty of owning a house!" he'd explain. "We can tailor it to our own wants and needs."

And so, the study had been half-constructed into a mess of a library-in-progress, the walls sometimes changed colors, and Mia would fuss over the occasional tool that was left within arm's reach of Isaiah. Which seemed acceptable and normal, until dinner didn't come out as anticipated or a house project grew too complex to finish alone. Those instances felt laced with danger, and Mia found herself tiptoeing around a house that didn't quite feel like home.

If she found Austin brooding or looking guilty, she'd wrap her arms around his waist, rest her head against his back. *It's fine,* she'd say. She wouldn't elaborate, because they both knew what she meant. He'd allow her to hug him for a moment and then pull away. *I know, I know.*

But maybe it wasn't fine. She had looked for a higher paying position, hadn't she? As if she knew Austin would never find another job. As if she knew it wouldn't be fine. As if deep inside, she knew to prepare for the storm that was coming.

She smiled at him. "Thank you for breakfast, babe. It's lovely."

Once in the kitchen, Mia turned to Isaiah. "Do you want French toast or chorizo con huevo, little man?"

He considered. "French toast!"

"You got it."

"Can I help, Mama?"

"Claro, mi vida."

Mia dragged a chair over to the kitchen island. She remembered the days when they had been so careful not to scratch the new wooden floor. Now, the blonde wood showed evidence of neglect and busy days.

She pulled out eggs, milk, spices, and a loaf of bread. Isaiah was getting better at cracking eggs into the bowl, but she still had to scoop out a few small pieces of shell. Together, they poured the milk. She added a splash of vanilla, but let him generously add the rest.

Austin used to tell her the reason he loved her was because she added spice to everything. Even her French toast couldn't be the common blend of vanilla and cinnamon. She liked to add allspice or nutmeg or star anise or hazelnut extract—or all of it. They had been happy once upon a time, hadn't they?

"Can I help dip it?" Isaiah asked.

Mia imagined the mess he would create, and the idea exhausted her. "Uh... maybe I'll do the dipping."

His shoulders slumped. "Oh. Okay."

She hated herself. After a beat, she thought of a compromise. "Well, you know... I do need a taste tester!"

"With syrup?"

"Well, of course, silly!"

"I'll grab all of them!" He hopped off the chair and ran to the pantry.

She frowned. Did they have more than one kind? She said a small prayer to the god of petty problems as she dipped the bread and placed them on the heated skillet.

Isaiah came back grunting, trying his best to hug his haul securely in his arms. He had found maple syrup, chocolate ice cream topping, and a small jar of plum jam.

"I found some," he said. He plopped them onto the table.

Thank you, petty god. "Oh, great!"

Internally, she counted the number of carbs and simple sugars the taste testing and final breakfast plate would offer. "Should I make some scrambled eggs, too?"

Isaiah looked confused. "French toast has eggs."

The guilt remained, but she took the out.

"Good point. Well, eat up! We're going to visit Camille and Luca in a bit."

He lit up. "Really? Yeah!"

Mia wondered when everyday tasks wouldn't feel so burdensome. She knew half the reason she made decent meals were for Isaiah's sake.

Motherhood both drained and motivated her.

Sometimes she'd wonder how Isaiah would remember her as an adult. Did he pick up on her exasperation? Her own mother seemed to have had boundless patience, especially in regard to cooking. As she began to brew coffee for herself, her thoughts wandered to the lessons her mother had tried to instill in her through food.

"You didn't grow up in Mexico, mija," Gabriela had said, "but that's why you can't ever forget your Spanish. And why you need to learn how to cook! Food is culture, princesa."

Mia, hardly Isaiah's age, didn't understand what culture really was, let alone how food was tied into it, but her mother had promised she could help with making masa for tamales and the idea of jamming her hands into the dough sounded amazing. She shook her head furiously, eyes bright with excitement. She was cooking for her dad and her family, basically a grown up.

Gabriela would tell her stories while modeling how to make perfectly round tortillas, her hands working the dough with a soft pat-pat-pat as the tortilla was moved from hand to hand. Together they would make frijoles borrachos and champurrado while her father grilled carne asada. She remembered stealing bits of homemade cookie batter, giggling when her mother batted her hand away.

Maybe Isaiah would only have memories of easy-made meals and takeout. There were a lot of days, too many days, that made her feel like all she could do was place one foot in front of the other and stumble forward. Everyone promised it would get easier. They praised her strength. But a year had passed, and she didn't feel strong. She felt tired. Endlessly tired.

The smell of coffee brought her back to the present and she fixed herself a cup. She took a careful sip and glanced at Isaiah. He was greedily shoveling French toast into his mouth.

"Woah, little man! Hold your horses. There's no hurry. They'll wait for us."

"But," he said, mouth still full, "I wanna hurry, because then we get more play time."

"We'll have plenty of play time, okay? Plus, you don't want to choke, do you?"

He set his fork down and worked on chewing. "Because then I'll be dead like Daddy?"

Mia felt herself flush. "Choking doesn't mean dying. People—not everyone who chokes—well, anyway, let's just not be a little piggy about it, yes?"

She forced herself to smile, but it didn't matter. He wasn't paying attention to her. He was busy dipping a piece of French toast into a puddle of chocolate topping. Whatever bothered her about her son nonchalantly talking about a breakfast-related fatality clearly didn't have the same effect on him.

She felt as if she had swallowed a stone. She forced more coffee down.

Maybe this is a good sign, she thought, *being able to talk about death.*

Isaiah went to therapy every other week. His provider, Lucy, had gently cautioned that death became less abstract to children at around age six. "You can expect new questions or more of the same questions you thought you had already discussed."

Mia had smiled weakly at the news, wondering how she would stomach another difficult milestone. For months after Austin's death, Isaiah would ask when his father was coming back home. Even after Mia explained he had died. Even after the funeral. Even when day after day without him proved he wasn't coming back.

Every time, it was a knife in the gut.

After breakfast, Mia wiped off his face and helped him wash his hands. He bounced with excitement on the way out to the car.

She wondered if she scheduled enough time for Isaiah to play with other children. Rarely, she'd get together with her friends Lori or Rochelle. Lack of time and overly busy schedules prevented a lot of possible interactions. She was fairly certain that the last time they had all seen each other was at the beginning of summer, when they had scheduled a trip to the zoo. She felt a touch of guilt for not reaching out more often.

"Mo-om," whined Isaiah. "Are we going?" He had already buckled himself into his booster seat.

Mia blinked. She had been staring at the empty spot in their driveway. "Yeah. Yeah, buddy. We're going."

-Chapter 2 -

August 2016

T he playground was a quick drive from their house. Mia parked in the
gravel lot, and Isaiah scrambled from the car the moment she turned it
off. "Wait a minute!" she yelled, snatching her purse from the passenger seat.
Her son continued, unperturbed.

"Luca!" Isaiah ran toward the playground, arms waving. It took Mia a
second to locate her son's friend. He hung upside down from the monkey
bars. He swung his body gently back and forth, hands outstretched, as a little
girl in a sundress jumped and tried to slap her hand against his.

"Mia!"

She turned toward her name and spotted her best friend, Camille, sitting
under a cluster of trees. A giant, colorful boho bag took up the space next to
her, a visual sign that the spot was taken. The park was full of people and
most of the other benches and tables were taken by other adults idly chatting
with one another. A birthday party was in full swing under a gazebo.

The day was cloudless and warm. A gentle breeze stirred the leaves in the
trees above Camille's blonde head, the mild rustling barely audible above the
whoops and screams of playing children.

A dragonfly flitted close to Camille's face, eliciting a surprised gasp and a
quick fan of her hand. The bug got the hint and flew off.

"Hey." Mia walked over and sat heavily next to her friend.

Camille looked her up and down. "Not enough coffee?"

"No, enough. I'm just—eh, I'm fine." Mia pressed her lips into what she hoped was a smile. Camille raised an eyebrow, but after so many years, she knew not to press for answers. Their friendship had started in high school and had lasted through some of the scariest, darkest times of their lives. When she was ready, Mia would talk.

Camille was one of the first phone calls Mia had made when she found Austin, second only to the police. Her voice was probably just as frantic both times, but unlike the operator, Camille hadn't asked her to slow down or repeat herself. She had simply responded with, "I'm on my way."

The image of Austin, body slouched over in the garage, thick lines of crimson blood trailing from his nostrils and mouth and soaking his shirt, still haunted Mia. It flashed in her mind's eye abruptly and without warning when she sat too long at a red light, went over the day's to-do list, or visited her friends at the park.

Camille nodded. "Okay, chica. How's Isaiah?"

"He's great. I essentially fed him pure sugar this morning."

"Nice! Now he gets to run it off at the park."

They took a moment to locate their children. Luca's vivid red hair always made finding them easy. He was the spitting image of his father, Keegan, which sometimes annoyed Camille. *I did all the work, and Keegan gets all the credit.*

She and Keegan had gone through a whirlwind of a romance. The passion was hot and fiery, but like all things that burned brightly, it fizzled out with an abruptness that left a chill. Shortly after the breakup, Camille found out she was pregnant. Devastated, she called Mia.

They spent the weekend together and ran through every option. Initially, Camille had leaned toward an abortion. She scheduled the initial appointment, and Mia promised to go along. But in the end, she cancelled.

"Am I making a mistake?" she had asked. "Last time... it was different, I think. I'm just—I'm older, I'm established at work. There's plenty of moms there. Some single moms, too! This just isn't how I expected to start a family and..." Her lip quivered.

Mia smiled empathetically and hugged her. "You don't have to explain anything to me. You know I want the best for you. And if having the baby is what you want, then I'm with you. If you change your mind, I'm there every step."

This had brought up the issue of telling Keegan. Camille had been terrified to tell him. An abortion at least meant she could entertain keeping it a secret.

"This is technically a city," Mia had said, "but it's not that big. And who knows? He might surprise you."

In the end, Keegan had surprised even himself. He was ecstatic to find out he was going to be a father, though both knew it wasn't a sign to get back together. By Camille's eighth month of pregnancy, he had moved into a small house in her neighborhood.

The only person more excited than him was his mother, Aislinn. She had thrown what was likely the largest baby shower anyone in the town had seen, because as a successful realtor, she seemed to know everyone. And as a mother to an only child, who—as she explained to everyone—insisted he'd never have children, the announcement of a future grandchild was akin to a miracle.

"This needs the celebration of a lifetime!" she had asserted shortly after Camille had given her permission to tell everyone.

The turnout was impressive.

"We need the Guinness world record guys out here," Mia had joked to Camille.

Camille laughed and rubbed her belly. Her blonde hair was swept back and pinned, cascading down her back like a waterfall of curls. She was always beautiful, with intelligent blue eyes, a sharp jawline, and deep dimples, but even when pregnancy rounded out her cheeks and shoulders, she simply looked more regal.

"I can't wait to meet him," Mia said, referencing her future godson. "I wonder what he'll look like."

"Hopefully me!" Camille had joked, her eyes shining.

Mia smiled at the memory. Her own shower was much smaller, with only close friends and family, but it suited her.

Their children were about three months apart, which meant when she visited Camille in the hospital, her own belly was starting to swell. Mia had remembered Camille's wishful thinking when she saw Keegan holding his son. Baby Luca barely had any hair, but the bit of fuzz on his head shone red like his father's. The button nose and tiny lips mirrored the adult version above him.

Keegan passed the baby the Mia after she dutifully washed her hands, and she gazed down at the baby, already in love with her godson. Impatience to hold her own child swept through her.

Mia shot her friend an amused look.

Camille read it in an instant and laughed. "You'd think after I spent nine months building all of him…"

Keegan snickered. "I had something to do with it, too, y'know."

Camille rolled her eyes, but she grinned. "Yeah. Okay, you get a little credit. I'm just saying, it's unfair that it looks like you just pushed him out."

"I mean, I think he has your feet," Keegan said.

Camille shifted in the hospital bed. "Really?"

"Yeah. Poor little thing. That weird little toe longer than his big toe! On the plus side, he'll probably save a lot money if he wants to go skiing."

"Aislinn! Smack your child for me!" Camille yelped.

Mia couldn't help but laugh along with Keegan while Aislinn fussed at them both for not recognizing the perfection of her grandchild.

She watched the boys, now six-years-old, running after each other. In a sense, they had known each other since before they were born. She sometimes wondered if they'd ever drift apart. She hoped not, but for now, as evidenced by their shrieky little laughs, they loved each other.

"So," said Camille, "I got it all covered. Babysitter, drinks, friends, location." Her smile was wide.

Mia sighed.

"No. No. No. I know that sigh. You are not flaking out on me." Camille grabbed Mia's wrist as if to prevent her from running away.

"I just..."

"You just what? You are tired and burnt out and way too hard on yourself. I'm serious! You need this. We need this. When's the last time we went out? Like, really went out. No kids involved." She released Mia and crossed her arms, her face a challenge.

Mia slumped back into the park bench.

"Ha! See? There. You know it. I know it. You need this. Alcohol. No kids. Men. Bad decisions. Maybe some sex? God, when's the last time you got laid? Don't answer that. I'm just saying." Camille squealed and gave her friend a squeeze. "It's going to be so much fun!"

Despite herself, Mia laughed. "You're right. You're right."

"I know I'm right. I'm always right. And as your very smart friend, I also see that you're overstressing yourself trying to fill up everything in Isaiah's life," Camille said.

Mia bristled.

Sensing the shift, she smiled gently and searched her friend's eyes. "You're an amazing mom, Mia. You're who I look up to. Everything seems to come so naturally for you. I'm like the PTA flunky."

"You're not part of the PTA."

"I know! See? That's how bad it is!"

Mia laughed.

"You're a great mom," Camille repeated, emphasizing each word. "I know you guys have gone through a lot. And I can only imagine what it's like trying to explain all this to him, but be kind to yourself. You need some time living!"

Mia looked down and picked at a hangnail.

"Girl, you really need a manicure." Camille slapped Mia's hand, her own nails a perfectly manicured robin's egg blue. "I know nails are dead last to kicking ass at work and raising people, but a manicure has never killed anyone. Neither has going out, for that matter."

"I know." Mia sighed. "But I've been swamped at work lately. And I don't get extra points for sparkly nails."

Camille rolled her eyes at the sarcasm and then grinned. "Speaking of work. How'd it go?"

Mia relaxed at the question. "I got the promotion."

Camille screamed and clapped her hands. A few people startled and turned toward them.

"Shh. You're scaring people, but yes! I'm so excited."

"CFO, here you come!"

"Well," Mia said, "I think there's a few more stops along the way between senior financial analyst and CFO, but I'm happy."

"Even more of a reason to celebrate. My bestie is a badass. See? It's a sign. You need to go out!"

Mia shrugged, but couldn't help smiling with pride. "Well, anyway, any news from you?"

A guilty look flashed over Camille's face, and she bit her lip.

Mia narrowed her eyes. "What?"

"I don't know if this is news. Or a secret. Or both."

"What? How are we going to be old lady roommates one day if you're keeping secrets?"

Camille winced. "I know! I didn't want to say anything because it's nothing. Also, because it's a little weird. Though, in my defense, it kinda started as nothing, but now it's evolved into something. What something exactly? I'm not sure. I'm undecided. It's not like there's no history there. There is. But it's sort of complicated. Like, who do I tell? Is it Facebook status worthy? Is it—"

"Christ, Camille. Spit it out!"

Camille lowered her head and mumbled words so quickly it sounded nonsensical.

"What?"

"I'm sleeping with Keegan." Camille's voice was barely above a whisper, but she paused between each word.

"What!" It was Mia's turn to startle people.

"Shh!" Camille hissed. "We've gotten together before, you know, like between people and when we're just feeling—well, anyway, it's happened before." She waved her hand as if brushing away a fly. "But rarely, and now it's more like this weird, regular, not-actually-weird-kind-of-nice way that makes me miss him sometimes." She sighed a little and then smiled sheepishly.

"Wow. Well, that's some news. But not super surprising. You guys did very well in the beginning. And you have a kid together," Mia said.

"Oh, ugh, please don't pull the kid card thing. Yes, we have a kid together, but that's not why. I'm not a stay-together-for-the-kids type of person."

"I know. I'm just saying you have history. And a connection."

Camille took a second to locate their children and then shot Mia a sideways look. "Either way, it kind of came out of nowhere. He came over because—oh, God, this sounds so lame—but he came over to help me with my washer."

Mia burst out laughing. "Did you tell him you didn't have any money to pay?"

Camille shoved her, and Mia laughed harder. "Screw you," she hissed. "No, that's not how it happened. If anything, I paid him with dinner. I—stop laughing—we have dinner every now and again. He stayed to put Luca to bed, which isn't out of the ordinary. Except that time, I don't know. One thing led to another, I guess."

She paused, remembering. "It was a little funny, though, because I ended up pushing him out of bed at about four a.m. like some sort of walk of shame. I didn't—goddammit, woman, stop laughing at me—I didn't want Luca to see him leaving the house. I thought it'd be weird or make him think... I don't even know. Is that messed up? That I don't want our kid to know we're together?"

Mia wiped the tears from her eyes and sighed. "I needed that laugh. No, I don't think it's weird. I mean, maybe a little, but I get it. So, you're together, then?"

Camille's eyebrows shot up. "I did say together, didn't I? I don't know. Are we officially together?" She looked over at Luca. "Maybe."

"Well, just be careful. Go slowly."

She smiled. "Yeah. It's nice, whatever this is."

Mia grabbed her hand and squeezed. They smiled at each other and continued talking about the little things. Mia spoke about Isaiah's most recent accomplishments in school, and Camille reciprocated.

They took turns watching for their children. Mia responded to their call for adult help when they decided to play on the merry-go-round. She stuck her tongue out on her walk back to the bench, mimicking a panting dog. "You think you're in shape until you have to run in a circle pushing them a thousand times."

Later, Camille played a game of tag that turned into a game of dragon killer, in which both boys were heroes and Camille was dubbed the dragon. She died honorably several times on the patch of grass next to the playground equipment and then announced a dragon could only die so many times before needing a break.

The boys made a noise of protest but immediately ran back toward the monkey bars.

Camille walked back to the bench picking bits of grass out of her hair. "It's amazing how energetic they are."

"I think they tap it directly from our soul," Mia said, laughing.

A couple hours after they had arrived, Camille announced she had to go.

Mia nodded in agreement. She dog-eared a page in the book she was reading.

"Why don't you ever use bookmarks? That seems so cruel and unusual."

"Because Isaiah likes to lose them. I don't know what possesses that kid to do some of the stuff he does, but apparently bookmarks both intrigue and bore him. I used to find them everywhere except in my books. So, I stopped. Plus, this gives books a little bit of character, don't you think?"

Camille sniffed. "I think it's book abuse. But I get you. Luca likes to pick some of the flowers from the flower beds. Drives me insane, because it makes the flower pots look all ratty, but then he turns around and gives them to me. Like, 'Here you go, I went out of my way to pick this beautiful flower for my mama!'" She sighed. "Pisses me off. But, also, it's cute. Boys are so infuriating. What are you gonna do, right?"

"I vote for selling them to the circus. Then, we'll have money for more books and plants."

They laughed.

The boys ran by.

"Five minutes!" yelled Camille.

They turned and frowned. Their cheeks were flushed, but Luca's shone brighter against his pale skin.

"Nooo," Luca whined, his eyebrows furrowed. Isaiah mimicked the look and added crossed arms.

"We've been here forever, Isaiah," said Mia.

"Nuh-uh. We've been here like, uh, one hour," he replied, his lips in a pout.

"Yeah, one hour!" Luca clasped his hands together like he was praying.

Camille pressed her lips together. "We leave now or in five minutes. Your choice, Luca."

The boys groaned in unison. "Slides one more time?" asked Luca, giving his best smile.

Mia conceded. "You guys can each go down the slide two times and then it's time to go."

"Okay!" They ran off.

"What's the chance they do that and come right back?" asked Camille.

"Zero."

The women picked up their belongings and walked over to the slides. As predicted, there were more protests from the boys when their mothers took their hands.

"We're still on for spaghetti night next Thursday?" Mia asked.

"Of course! I'll bring a red."

"Perfect."

"And don't forget next Saturday! And be excited!"

The idea of people packed together in a bar, music blaring, made Mia's stomach tie into a knot. Her steps felt heavier. "I'm excited," she said weakly.

"Thatta girl! See you later!"

-Chapter 3-

Spring 2003

Normally, new kids fit in as well as a mismatched puzzle piece. Especially in high school. Especially in towns where kids had known each other for the majority of their school lives.

Not Camille.

She was a palpable energy in every room she occupied. She might not have been part of the popular elite, but overall, she was liked by the majority. Mia was the opposite, both physically and in personality. She had dark hair and eyes, someone who melted into the shadows, but she enjoyed being the wallflower, preferred keeping her group of friends small.

When Camille joined the school, Mia registered her arrival and promptly ignored her, not maliciously, but simply because she had no reason to speak to her. It wasn't until they both joined the debate club that a friendship began to form.

"It's so funny," said Camille, her eyes probing Mia's. "You're so quiet in class and then rock during debates. Why don't you speak up more?"

They were sitting on the school's concrete divider between the sidewalk and grassy hill that rolled gently up to the building. The evening's practice debate was over, and they were waiting for their parents to pick them up.

Mia straightened her form and considered the question. She shrugged.

Camille grinned, her lips shining brightly with the bubble gum pink lip gloss she liked wearing. "I wonder if it's because you want to blindside everyone when you stand up. Keep them underestimating you so they're not prepared." Mia began to protest, but Camille waved it away. "It's cool, your secret's safe with me."

Soon, they were inseparable, passing notes back and forth whenever they could, sad they only shared two classes together. After school, Mia found herself eating dinner most nights with Camille and her family.

She loved the easygoing nature they had. Her father, Raphael, a muscular man that approached 6'4 was as close to the idea of a gentle giant as Mia could imagine. His honey brown eyes would sparkle with amusement right before he told a cheesy joke. Camille would groan and roll her eyes. *You're so lame, Dad.* She'd cut her eyes at Mia like an apology.

Her parents would kiss deeply in front of anyone. Sometimes Raphael would work late and arrive halfway through dinner prep. He would theatrically sneak into the kitchen, pausing to wink at the girls. Still in his suit, he'd scoop up his wife, Eloise, kiss her, and spin her around once. She'd giggle, and Camille would call them embarrassing and pretend to gag while Mia fell more in love with them.

Once, Camille asked why they never went to Mia's house. She had just shrugged.

"My dad doesn't really know how to cook."

Truthfully, her house seemed so devoid of everything Camille's naturally had. When Mia's mother had died, she had taken the only spark that existed. The rooms felt darker, colder, emptier. And yet, at a time when she and her father should have leaned on each other for warmth, they crept to separate spaces. Their home felt vacant.

Camille's home, on the other hand, was full of life. She was the youngest of six and obviously the baby. She had four older brothers and one sister. Her sister was a senior in their school and stressing over colleges. Her brothers were all moved out, either in college or working or both, but they visited often.

Mia had had a major crush on Camille's oldest brother, Noel, which she, embarrassingly enough, confessed to Camille during a sleepover. Camille screamed and then collapsed on her bed in a fit of giggles.

"Wait till he finds out!" she gasped.

Mia felt her face grow hot. "Don't. You. Dare!"

"Mia and Noel, sitting in a tree. K-I—"

A pillow was thrown. "Shut up! You're such a jerk. I—"

"K-I-S—stop!" Camille tossed the pillow away, "I'm trying to sing. I'm just —okay, okay, okay. I'm done. I was just kidding." A pause, then louder, "Oh my God, you have to name your babies after me!"

"Stop! Ugh, I swear to God, I will murder you in your sleep and hide your body."

Camille cackled in delighted. "You are so embarrassed. This is, like, the best, though. We'd be sisters-in-law or whatever."

Mia pulled a pillow over her head. "You're the worst friend."

"I'm the best."

And she was.

In her senior year, perhaps due to the approaching freedom of adulthood, Mia accepted invites to house parties. She assumed her invitations came as a plus one to Camille's, but she didn't mind.

She was also hopelessly in love—from afar—with Jesse McKenzie. Star football player, in as serious a relationship with the head cheerleader as was possible in high school, and appeared completely oblivious to her presence. It was cliché and awful, but she couldn't help the attraction. He was smart, funny, and aesthetically perfect.

"He's not actually that funny, Mia," Camille said.

"You have to admit he's beautiful. He even has dimples. His smile is—"

"He's alright, I guess."

Mia didn't understand how Camille could roll her eyes at him. But then, Camille had a line of guys falling over themselves.

One night, she was at a party Camille couldn't attend, and Jesse walked over to her.

"Hey," he said, two drinks in hand.

"H-hi," she stuttered. She felt blood rush to her cheeks.

"Mia, right?" he asked, and she thought she was going to faint. He knew her name.

She nodded and smiled, afraid to say anything.

"You drinking?"

She wasn't, but nodded again.

"You don't have a cup in your hand."

She looked down at her hands as if she had just found out she had them. She felt like an idiot. "Oh, uh, I-I was, but now I'm not."

He laughed like she had made a joke, and she smiled, unsure of herself.

"Here, I have an extra," he said.

She was holding the drink before she realized she had accepted it.

He drank from his, and she mimicked, careful to only sip a little. She hated alcohol, hated the smell of beer emanating from her father every evening, hated the hangovers he complained of on Sunday mornings.

"It's kind of awesome that Bella's parents go away so much, huh?" he said.

She nodded again and realized she probably looked like some kind of ridiculous bobblehead, so she quickly added, "Yeah. It's cool." A pause. "I don't normally come to these parties, but I guess I was a little bored with my normal evening routine of nothing." She laughed awkwardly.

He smiled politely and let a beat pass.

What am I doing? she thought.

"I'm glad you came."

Her stomach filled with butterflies. "Really?" she asked, breathless.

He smiled so genuinely, she felt she could die. His hazel eyes gazed into hers. "Yeah. You're always so serious in class. I'm glad this gives us a chance to talk."

Once again, the idea that he was aware of her presence elated her.

He took another drink, and she parroted the action. The alcohol burned on its way down, but she found she didn't mind as long as he was with her.

"Oh, I just—I'm a bit of a nerd, I guess," she laughed.

He grinned. "I like that, though. The smart girl."

More butterflies.

For the next hour, they talked about anything and everything. It was magical. She felt herself loosening up, the alcohol went down easier, and she was glad she had come out even if Camille hadn't been able to attend. Maybe even glad Camille was absent. Would he have approached her if she hadn't been alone?

A few drinks later, she found herself in an upstairs bedroom alone with him. They sat on the bed, and when the conversation lulled to silence, he touched her face and pulled her in for a kiss. It was gentle, with a bit of heat that she felt in her chest.

She gazed at him afterwards, a little tipsy, wide-eyed.

He smiled and kissed her again, this time with some tongue. For a moment, Mia was euphoric. She couldn't wait to tell Camille everything the next day. *He knows me! He kissed me! He likes me!*

Abruptly, the kisses demanded more, and she found she couldn't meet them. He kissed down her jaw and neck while his hands started to wander. Dread washed over her body when she realized he expected more of her than she was willing to give. She felt like a liar. She tensed and pushed his hands away, trying in vain to keep her own from shaking.

"Hey, hey," he breathed. "It's okay." And he kissed her more.

"No, I'm just—I don't—I can't—" He kissed her mouth as she spoke, interrupting her protests.

"Just relax. You're just so beautiful. You know you're beautiful, right?" Jesse caressed her face and smiled.

"I—" Mia didn't know what to say. She wanted him to like her, but wanted this to stop.

"I like you a lot."

"I like you, too," she said. He smiled and went for another kiss, but she leaned backward. "But—I thought you had a girlfriend?"

He dropped his hands into his lap and dipped his head. "It's—it's a little bit complicated. I'm breaking up with her next week. She's just—she's great, but —she's not, like, I don't know, what I really want, you know? She's just this shallow, crazy thing who is so jealous all the time."

Mia opened her mouth but nothing came out. She had no retort. Any other day she would have been happy to hear he was leaving his girlfriend, but right now he was spoken for and trying to fool around with another girl. She was out of her depth, a girl who had yearned for the ocean but found she belonged in a lake.

"Sometimes it's hard to let people down, you know? I don't know. Maybe I just want to start listening to me, not other people," he said and kissed her. "And right now, I'm thinking I'm really lucky that you came to this party."

Mia regretted the drinks. Her head felt like it was two steps behind. Each movement felt sluggish, each thought delayed.

For a few minutes, she let him do as he wanted, but when his hands started to wander too far, she pushed back.

"Jesse," she warned.

"Mia," he whispered and pressed himself onto her. They were lying down on the bed.

"No, I'm—I'm serious, I can't. I don't know what—"

He shushed her and pulled her dress up. He slipped her underwear down to her knees.

Too late, she realized how strong he was. She stopped struggling and turned her head to find the window. The night was clear enough to see a tree, the moon, and a scattering of stars. She wondered if there were any birds nested in the branches. Maybe there was a mama bird, sitting gently on tiny eggs, days away from hatching.

She wished she were a bird. If she were a bird, she would be soaring miles above the earth. She wondered what it would be like to fly free, unburdened, to feel the wind against her face. When he finished and stood up, saying something about how he hated when girls pretended to play hard to get, she watched him, distracted, confused, thinking of all the types of birds she knew.

He disappeared back into the party. She walked home, snuck into her house, and stayed in the shower for an hour. Afterward, she threw her clothes into the outside bin, wondering if her father would question why loose clothing was dumped on top of bagged trash.

She was both relieved and upset he didn't notice. Or maybe he did and didn't care. Either way, trash day came, and everything was dumped into the back of the rusty, green vehicle, never to be seen again.

At school, two days after the party, a cheerleader slammed her shoulder into Mia while she walked by.

"Oops," she said, glaring. Her friends laughed, and they sauntered away, leaving Mia, heart racing, to pick up her belongings.

The next week, they cornered Mia in the bathroom.

Jesse's girlfriend, Miranda, stood front and center, hands on her hips, her eyes flashing with rage. "You fucking slut, can't even get your own man."

Mia blanched. "What? I didn't—I... I..."

"I... I... I..." Miranda mimicked, her voice thick with fury. "You're a fucking whore. Stay away from Jesse, or I will beat your ass. Do you hear me?"

Mia started to stammer a response.

The girls started laughing.

One of Miranda's friends stepped forward, her lips curled into a cruel smile. "What, you don't know English? You live in this country, you gotta learn it, babe. Otherwise, they deport you. Or is that why you're trying to steal someone else's man? A green card?"

The girls dissolved into a fit of laughter. Mia was too shocked to be angry.

Another cheerleader shoved her roughly away. "Bitch," she said simply, and they walked away, still muttering insults. Mia left the bathroom shaking. She skipped the rest of the day.

The following Friday, a tampon was taped to her locker with the word 'slut' written in red nail polish underneath. She would find out later that Jesse had disclosed the encounter, somehow bragging about it to all the guys while spreading the word that she had laid it all heavy on him. They had been drinking, so he wasn't acting like himself. Otherwise, he would have said no, of course. Especially when discovering she was on her period.

Mia skipped as much school as she could and avoided everyone, including Camille until the locker display. Camille pulled her aside before she fled for the school day. The locker destroyed her ability to deny anything, and she told Camille the story, sobbing the entire time. They stole acetone from the art room and wiped it clean.

The next day, Camille stayed after school. She walked into the locker room as the cheerleaders were getting ready for practice.

"Hi, Miranda."

Camille surprised her with a heavy backpack to the face. As Miranda's friends flocked over to her, Camille took the opportunity to run away. She marched onto the football field and slapped Jesse hard on the face. Stunned, he stared at her, and she took the opportunity to kick him in the groin.

"You fucking rapist!" she screeched and started clawing at his face. The coach quickly separated them and promised Camille an immediate suspension.

The threat was carried out.

The next school day, Mia was called into the office and told to wait for her father. As she sat outside of the principal's office, she texted Camille, her knee bouncing frantically. David, Camille, and Raphael arrived within minutes of each other.

In the office, Mia's face burned with humiliation. When questions were directed at her, she made noncommittal noises. She could feel her father's eyes on her. She trained her gaze on the carpet, not daring to look up, trying her best not to let the tears fall. She thought of birds. *It's fine. I'm soaring in the clouds. I'm not here.*

Initially, Raphael did most of the talking. Camille's suspension was lifted when he reminded the principal of the school's no tolerance bullying policy and upcoming football games. Technically, Mia would be able to press charges against Jesse for rape and Miranda and her friends for intimidation and physical threats. Camille was happy to report second hand accounts about threats and physical violence directed toward Mia. A game without cheerleaders would seem odd.

The principal swallowed hard.

Mia said she didn't want to press formal charges, so David demanded Jesse be expelled. The principal shook his head, trying his best to deescalate the situation. "It sounds like bad decisions were made by all parties," said the principal. "You said you guys were at a party? Was there alcohol involved?"

Mia looked down into her lap, and her father erupted. "With all due respect, but what the fuck are you talking about?"

She looked up sharply and saw the principal had paled. "I-I'm just saying that young people tend to do things they regret—"

"Listen, I drink from time to time, and I know that I have never raped anybody, drunk or not. Are you blaming my daughter for getting raped?" David yelled. He stood on the last word, his dark brown eyes flashing in fury.

The principal looked green and waved his hand in a downward motion, trying to deescalate the situation. "Mr. Hernandez, Mr.—I did not mean—"

"You're blaming my daughter—"

"I'm just—"

"You're just fucking what?"

"If I could—I don't know if we should call it—"

"Call it what?" David's voice was so loud Mia wondered if the whole school could hear. "Rape? That's what it is. It's RAPE. SAY THE FUCKING WORD."

"I-I think that it's terrible, what happened, and I'm not giving anyone a free pass—I just—"

"What's terrible?" asked David. "What's terrible? What is it you're talking about? You can't even say the word, can you? Rape. He RAPED her."

Mia thought she was going to die. She wanted the ground to open up and swallow her whole. She hadn't thought of it as rape, either. She didn't know what she thought of it, just that she wanted to forget it. Perhaps in another universe, she had declined the invitation to the party.

"Dad," she said, so softly she wasn't sure if he would hear her.

He stopped yelling and looked at her for a moment. "I'm taking her home. She'll be absent tomorrow."

Raphael spoke next. "I think that if that boy is allowed to remain in this school, which I strongly disagree with, and charges aren't filed, neither girl should be in classes with him. Further, their schedules need to be arranged so the girls are together throughout the day. Because, frankly, from what I'm hearing from everyone, there are a lot of people who are on the rapist's side, including you, and no one on Mia's."

The principal frowned. "No, no, no. I want what's best for everyone. I think that's unwarranted—"

"I disagree," Raphael said.

"Well, it's a little difficult to arrange. I mean, we only have a few months left—"

"And that's plenty of time for Mia to get harassed. You know how high school kids are. Mia has a right to feel safe while she's finishing her education."

The principal said nothing.

"Great, I'll expect that they'll have new schedules by tomorrow." He stood to leave. "Alright, Camille, let's go."

David looked over at Raphael and nodded his head once in thanks. Raphael smiled sadly in reply.

As they walked out of the school, Camille held Mia's hand firmly.

"Do you want to come over?" she asked.

Mia looked over at her father. The lines on his forehead and around his eyes looked deeper, giving her a glimpse of what he'd look like as an old man. It dawned on her that, in a sense, her mother would be young forever. "No, that's okay. I think maybe I'll go straight home today."

Camille gave her a hug and kissed her cheek. "It'll get better."

The drive home was silent, the weight of unspoken emotions pressing heavily against her heart.

When they arrived, David turned off the car, sat for a moment, and then turned toward her. He cleared his throat. "You know—you know you can talk to me. About anything."

Mia looked at him and tried to smile. "I know." Her face crumpled, and she started to cry.

Her father gripped her hand and sat with her while she sobbed. When the tears ran out, she scrubbed her face hard and sighed, suddenly tired.

"I'm sorry," she whispered. She knew he tried, but he was not the type of father who gave frequent hugs or spoke much about what was on his mind. She had thought him more and more uncaring since her mother's passing. The outburst at the school had both shocked her and reminded her they were still a family, albeit a broken one. After that moment, the distance between them lessened; even so, David still found the bottle too often, and Mia still sought the refuge of Camille's home.

Mia couldn't wait to shake free of the shame that accompanied her last few months of high school. The cheerleaders didn't bother her anymore, but the school had turned into halls of whispers and icy stares. It was bewildering to know Jesse was the one that had forced himself on top of her, inside of her, and the one who had walked away the victim.

No longer the wallflower, she was now the center of attention. She felt them stealing glances at her, the exaggerated avoidance, the fear of associating with someone that had dared sin as she had. Not the sex, of course, but rather the reporting of a rape against the star football player with perfect grades, a perfect girlfriend, and the perfect life. In response, she wrapped herself in baggy layers of clothing and tried her hardest to hide in plain sight.

Even as summer approached, she walked around with an oversized sweater and bulky jeans. She rushed through the halls, staring at the ground, Camille right next to her glaring anyone who looked over.

"Forget them," Camille often said. She broke ties with anyone who didn't think Jesse was complete garbage. "They're not worth it."

-Chapter 4-

August 2016

M ia felt too lazy to cook. On the way home from the park, she swung by a McDonald's and ordered herself a large fry and Isaiah a Happy Meal with chicken nuggets.

Isaiah only ate two before falling asleep. She kept checking her rearview mirror to make sure he was sleeping and not somehow choking on a nugget. She tried to remember whether this paranoia was new or if she had always felt this worried about him. She wanted to think there was a time frame when life hadn't felt so fragile, when she took it for granted and assumed everyone would be fine day after day.

Of course, every parent knows the anxiety of bringing new life into the world. At least, Mia hoped so, because she remembered how worried she was in the beginning. On their return trip from the hospital, she couldn't sit in the front passenger seat for long; she felt miles away from her precious baby. The tiny mirror they had fixed on the back seat to reflect their son's image seemed like a good idea in theory, but it had turned out inadequate in application. Yes, she could see him. Yes, she thought his skin reflected a pink hue. But was he really okay? Was he breathing?

On their way home from the hospital, she made Austin pull over after a mile and moved back to sit in the middle seat, her belly soft and empty, her heart full. She placed her finger underneath his nose and felt a whisper of an exhale. She exhaled with her baby and informed Austin he could start driving again.

Isaiah had been so small, barely six pounds, born just one day after her 38th week, a birth day that contradicted her obstetrician's guestimate.

∞∞∞

Mia was at what Camille had dubbed the "vagina swab" visit. Her doctor had explained that around 36 weeks pregnant, women are screened for GBS, a type of bacteria that usually did nothing to the mom but could be devastating to the baby. She admitted that she had been looking up worst-case scenarios on Google. Dr. Barnes had smiled knowingly and reassured her a positive result would only mean she needed an antibiotic administered through an IV during labor.

She wondered why it seemed like so much could go wrong.

"You think it'll be soon?" she had asked, hopeful that she'd give birth before her due date.

He chuckled. "Well, you never really know, but probably not soon enough. I know it's hard to be patient, but most first-time moms go past their due dates. I usually wait a few days, and assuming everything goes well, which I'm confident it will, we can talk about inducing at the 41-week mark."

Mia had tried hard not to glare at him. What did an old man know about patience during pregnancy?

When she returned home, tears began to fall. She couldn't imagine another month of the same. She was tired of waking up pregnant. She was tired of not being able to see her feet, of the insomnia, of the nausea. Isaiah, as if aware of his mother's distress, began to kick. She rubbed her belly and apologized.

"I just want you to be healthy and happy. Stay in there a week or five. I don't care. Just be healthy and happy. I love you."

But it was a lie. She *did* care. She wanted him healthy and out of her body. So, she cried again. She splashed cold water on her face before Austin got home to lessen the puffiness around her eyes, but when he walked through the door, she burst into tears again.

Alarmed, he rushed to her and asked what was wrong.

She was crying so hard she could barely speak. She wanted to tell him how tired she was of sharing her body with another person. She wanted to explain the fatigue of late pregnancy, how every night she had to wedge pillows around her heavy belly, between her knees, behind her back, and lie just right so sleep could find her, only to get the urge to pee. She wanted to complain about the so-called morning sickness no one warned her would return at the end. She wanted to pass along the frustration of swollen ankles and irregular bathroom habits.

Instead, all she could get out was, "I'm pregnant."

Austin had swallowed a laugh. "What?"

"No," she sobbed and shook her head. He didn't get it. "I'm still pregnant."

Two weeks later, she delivered her son.

Labor started unremarkably. The contractions initially felt like menstrual cramps that made her belly feel tight. Austin had just finished making dinner when Mia walked into the kitchen, took a bite of chicken, and announced she was in labor.

Austin was every stereotypical father that night. He ran around the kitchen twice before grabbing her hand, asking, "Are you sure?" Then, he was off, leaving her to labor alone in the kitchen while he installed the car seat and tried to remember the locations of all the items they needed for the hospital trip.

Between contractions, she shouted out locations of her birth bag, his wallet, her purse, and his keys. "It's fine, babe. It's really mild, and the doctor said it'll probably take a while. I think you can calm down."

Halfway to the hospital, she was the one on the verge of panic. By the time they arrived, she was screaming.

The nurses met her in the emergency room lobby and tried to get her to sit in a wheelchair. As soon as she sat, a contraction came, and she wailed. She stood up when it was over.

"I'll walk."

The two nurses exchanged a glance and tried to coax her back into the wheelchair. "It's policy because it's safer. Plus, we'll get you up there faster."

"When I sit, I feel like I'm going to break in half! I'm walking!"

It was a short trip to labor and delivery, but it felt like an eternity. The room felt chaotic. She climbed onto the bed on all fours. The nurse announced she was crowning.

"Don't push! Breathe!" said a nurse. "Breathe!"

Another nurse instructed to lay on her back.

Mia ignored her as another contraction hit. She roared.

"Babe, maybe listen to the nurse?" said Austin.

She glared at him and bore down as another contraction wracked her body. She heard the nurses fussing about something, but she couldn't decipher what they were saying nor did she care.

Isaiah's head slipped out. His body tumbled out afterward, and Mia was shocked to see her obstetrician standing nearby. Apparently, a nurse had stood by as the head was delivered, and the doctor had caught the rest of Isaiah.

Her baby had arrived with a loud cry, and Austin helped her turn over onto her back. The doctor laughed as he placed Mia's son on her chest.

"He was in a hurry, wasn't he?"

Mia looked down at her son and took a second to breathe. She was surprised to find him alert and staring at her. His little mouth opened and closed. His hand reached out into the air and returned back to his side. His little movements were nothing extraordinary, but she was fascinated, mesmerized.

She had a son. A small stab of sorrow caught her in the chest. He would never know his grandmother.

She looked over at Austin and grinned. His eyes were on the baby with a look of wonder that matched her thoughts.

"You want to hold him?"

"Uh, I... I don't know—"

Years prior, when Mia was holding a friend's baby, she had offered him to Austin. He had blanched and shaken his head. *No, thanks. Babies make me nervous.*

One of the nurses sensed his hesitation and smiled. She helped with the transfer and had him sit down.

While they took care of Mia, Austin sat, staring, sometimes smiling, at his newborn son.

"I'm so proud of you," he whispered.

Somehow, all of them—mother, father, and baby—were brand new that day; they were new versions of themselves, and Mia couldn't imagine being happier.

She was eager to go home, but when she crossed the threshold with her son, she realized she wasn't sure what came next. The two days spent in the hospital were a series of tasks and checklists: baby's first bath, shower for mom, baby's assessment, hearing test, PKU test, birth certificate. Nurses bustled in and out to check vitals and look over the breastfeeding chart.

"If he doesn't nurse enough, we'll have to give him a bottle," warned one of the nurses after reviewing the breastfeeding log.

Mia frowned. "He's nursed more than what we wrote down. It's just busy in here."

The nurse clucked her tongue. "Well, you have to write it down, or we can't tell if he's eaten, and then he has to get formula."

She wanted to argue, but she found she didn't have the energy.

Austin stood up. "I'll make sure to mark it." The nurse seemed satisfied. When she had finished logging vitals and entering her notes, she left the room.

Mia rolled her eyes at Austin. "Ugh. I can't wait to get out of here."

He smiled and walked to her bedside. He kissed the top of her head and placed his hand on top of his son's head. Isaiah was sleeping, wrapped in a loose swaddle, his face toward Mia's naked chest. His eyes danced under his eyelids, and he sighed.

"You think he's dreaming?" asked Austin.

She pulled Isaiah up a little, kissed her son's lips. "Probably."

"What do you think he's dreaming about?"

She tilted her head, studying their newborn. "Maybe about heartbeats and milk."

"Maybe about a traumatizing bright light—"

Mia snorted. "Oh, go away."

"I'm serious!" he laughed. "I'm just saying, that was crazy to watch. What an entrance. All he's known is—are their eyes open in the womb?"

Mia nodded.

"Okay, so all he's known is red light at best and murmur-y voices. Then, bam! Bright lights and fabric and a shot! Yeesh. What a welcome. Sorry, buddy."

"I didn't even think about that. Well, now he's with his mama, so it's fine. We'll be home. No more hospital stuff."

But then they were home, and she didn't know what to do.

What's the first step of parenting? she thought. She looked to Austin for help, but he assumed she had built-in instincts.

So, she did the only thing she could think of: she showed him the whole house, describing the different rooms and what he would do in them one day. Austin had followed, amused. When she arrived at the nursery, she changed his diaper and sat in the rocking chair.

"I guess I'll nurse him," she announced.

Mia glanced into the rearview mirror and studied his sleeping form. *And now he's six*, she thought. *Austin is missing all of this.*

She pulled into her driveway and parked.

"Mama?" said Isaiah. His voice was full of sleep.

She looked into the rearview and smiled. "We're home."

"Oh. I thought we were getting something to eat." He stretched.

"We did, remember? You have chicken nuggets."

He looked around and frowned. "It's on the floor."

She swallowed a sigh. "That's okay. It picks up just fine."

She got out of the car and helped her son out after picking up his lunch. She passed over the Happy Meal. "Hold onto this and let's get inside."

That night, after she tucked him into bed, she barely made it to her pillow before sleep swallowed her.

Mia was in the garage, staring at the floor near the workbench. As she watched, a pool of blood formed, then grew. She looked down at her feet and saw she was barefoot. The blood advanced menacingly, and the thought of the blood reaching and staining her skin frightened her. She took a step back and looked up.

The blood was gone, and in its place was Austin, head lowered. He looked like he was sleeping.

She rushed to him, falling to her knees when she reached his body. "Austin!"

His head snapped up, eyes dark. He was furious.

Suddenly, she was in bed, unable to move. Austin's dark form stood next to her. She couldn't see his features, but she knew his silhouette. His anger resonated through the room like a pulse. It pressed down onto her body like a heavy blanket.

She was suffocating.

Mia gasped awake. The room was full of shadows. A dark form near the foot of her bed shifted slightly. Her heart jumped into her throat. The shape ran toward her.

"Isaiah!" she said. "Oh, man, don't scare me like that!"

He threw his arms around her neck.

"What's wrong, baby?"

"I had a bad dream."

Welcome to the club. "Oh no! What was it about?" She pulled him into the bed and threw the comforter over him. As he started to talk, she drew him in close to her.

"There was a big spider. And it was trying to bite me. And then it ran, and I tried to run away, but I couldn't. And then it almost bit me!"

"Bite you!" she said. "Like this?" She planted kisses around his face.

He giggled. "No! Like this!" He pretended to bite her shoulder.

"Oh! Like this!" She pretended to take giant bites of his chin and neck and shoulder.

He dissolved into a fit of giggles.

She smiled. "Well, don't worry. Dream spiders can't hurt you." She thought back to her own nightmare. *Dream ghosts can't hurt you.*

"Can I sleep with you?"

She hesitated. He was a fitful sleeper. "Sure, mi vida. But let's go to sleep now." She glanced at the clock. Four a.m. "It's late, and you have school in the morning. And I have work."

Isaiah yawned. "I'm not tired."

Mia stroked his head, her fingers combing through his hair. "That's okay. Then, you don't have to sleep. Just lie there. And close your eyes. Are they closed? Yes? Okay, good."

A few minutes later, he was fast asleep. She willed herself to join him, trying her best to match her son's breathing. But all she found was restlessness. Weariness finally hit her minutes before her alarm sounded.

-*Chapter 5*-

August 2016

Mia sat in her home office working on end-of-quarter financial reports. They weren't due until Friday, but she liked to meet her deadlines at least a day early.

After a night of bad dreams, the day had started a little rocky. Isaiah was very hard to rouse for school, though her lack of patience hadn't helped the situation. He had protested every little thing that morning. He didn't want to change his shirt, he didn't want to brush his teeth, breakfast was yucky, his favorite socks were in the wash. By the end, she had practically shoved him into the car and peeled out of the driveway. She was ready for the breathing room school provided.

It made her feel guilty, but she tried her best to push it away.

Her cell rang, and she glanced at the Caller ID. 'Dad' flashed on the screen. She let it go to voicemail. *I'll text him later.* If she wrapped up the reports within the next hour, she'd have a full hour and a half to relax before she needed to go pick Isaiah up. Her employer had a rule stating that employees who had worked there for at least a year could work remotely twice a week. Company culture, however, frowned upon those who dipped into the policy. After her rough morning, Mia didn't care.

She chewed on her nail as she skimmed the documents. The phone rang again.

She answered without looking. "Why do you never text?"

There was a pause.

"Uh, hello? Ms. Strouse?" a thin, reedy voice inquired.

It was the school counselor, Mrs. Ramos.

"This is Mia, yes, hi, it's me. What's going on?" She sat up straighter, her heartbeat quickening.

"Good afternoon, Ms. Strouse. It's Mrs. Ramos. Well, first, I want to say everything is fine and under control."

What an unnecessary phrase, she thought. Phone calls from school counselors never occurred when everything was fine and under control, but she said nothing.

"Isaiah is doing great, but he's taking a little bit of a time out in the nurse's office. Not that he's sick! He's fine. He just, well... he had a hard time for a little bit there. He got very upset during a spelling test today. He refused to do it and ended up tearing it up. Mr. Leonhardt said he wasn't really acting like he usually does, so he sent him my way. We talked a bit, and he said he wanted to go home and that his tummy hurt.

"I know that a lot of times when children are upset, there are complaints of upset stomachs. We did some breathing exercises, and he said he felt better, but he didn't feel up to going back to class. He might feel a little embarrassed over the episode. So, I told him if he liked, he could go to the nurse and lie there until it was time to go home."

Mia stacked her notes together. "Do I need to come get him now?"

"Oh, no," said Mrs. Ramos. "It's almost the end of the day. It's fine for him to stay there until you normally come pick up. I just wanted you to know what happened and where you'll go to pick up. I know..." A pause. "I know that he's going through some hard times. It's very difficult to lose a parent at such a young age."

Mia picked at a stray thread on her shirt.

Mrs. Ramos continued, "But I'm really proud of him for advocating for himself."

"I'll wrap up here and be over to pick him up in a bit."

"Oh, okay, that's no problem, either."

Mia hung up and bit her lip. *Maybe I'm being rash.*

She mulled over the idea of letting him hang out with the nurse to get alone time that didn't involve work or errands. Guilt won.

When she arrived at the school, she signed Isaiah out and was led to the nurse's station. The little room housed two exam tables that doubled as beds. No one was there besides the nurse, who looked up as she arrived, and Isaiah. He sat in a seat next to the nurse, engrossed in a drawing.

Mia watched him for a moment and smiled. She loved him so much and so fiercely sometimes it felt like her heart would break. She just wished love translated into patience and saying the right things at the right time.

Her own mother was the embodiment of patience. As a child, whenever Mia was hurt, she would cry out for her mother. The response was always the same. *It's okay, mi amor. It's okay. I am here.* Maybe in that respect, Mia had turned out more like her father.

"Hey, little man. Heard you had a bit of a rough day."

Isaiah looked up and broke out into a smile. "Mommy!" He ran to her. "Mommy, Mommy, Mommy!" He wrapped his arms around her waist.

Mia glanced at the nurse to dismiss him. "I'm picking him up a bit early."

"Okay, sounds good. I hope he feels better! Have a great one, Isaiah."

"Thank you! Can I take my drawing?"

The nurse smiled. "Of course."

Isaiah ran back to the table and snatched the paper. "I'm ready!"

∞ ∞ ∞

"Isaiah?" Lucy, his therapist, walked into the waiting area.

Isaiah's face brightened. "Hi, Miss Lucy!"

After Mia had brought Isaiah home early, she'd called his therapist for an urgent appointment. Lucy had had an evening slot available the next day, and Mia had gratefully accepted.

As always, Lucy pulled Isaiah back for a partial solo session. Mia was always invited the latter half of the appointment. Initially, she attended the entire session, but after trust was earned, she agreed that Isaiah deserved private time with his therapist.

The urgent appointment was technically scheduled after hours, which meant no one else was in the waiting area. Mia pulled out her phone and mindlessly played a game.

'Dad' flashed on her screen as an incoming call. She had forgotten to call him back.

"Hey, Apá."

"Hey, princesa."

As a child, he always called her by her name, or at most, mija. *My daughter.* Now, as an adult, he chose to give her pet names. Maybe that's what regret did, made people pretend things could be redone.

"What's going on?" she asked.

"I was just checking in. I found this really cool toy truck at an estate sale. I thought Isaiah might like it."

"That's really nice. I'm sure he will."

Her father was a homebody, happier working on his vehicles than doing anything in the company of others. However, one pastime he found enjoyable was hunting through estate sales for rare or eclectic items. A few times, he had found valuable collector's items nice enough to sell. The families had either not realized or not cared how much the items were truly worth. David always called Mia excited to report the find and subsequent sale.

She was happy for him, but she found the whole idea depressing. A person's entire existence, a lifetime of memories and moments and interests, gone in a weekend. The items sold quickly and were then added to the collections of other mortals who would one day be nothing but vague memories, sorted into piles to be either trashed or sold.

"How are you doing?"

Mia paused for a second. "I'm good. A little tired, but you know how it is."

Her father grunted in agreement. "Well, I can swing by and drop it off. It's been a while since I've been over, and I'm still driving."

"Oh," she said. "We're at the therapist's office."

There was disagreement in the brief silence. Her father hated psychology, and he hated the idea that his grandson needed a so-called shrink even more.

"He had an incident at school." She kicked herself for wanting to justify her parenting.

"An incident? Is he okay? What happened?"

She sighed. "It's—he's fine. He just had a hard day."

"I don't know if a hard day at school is a reason for—cómo se dice?—psicoterapia." David's voice was gruff.

Her jaw worked. "It's more than just a difficult school day, Apá. I'm not talking about being upset because the teacher chastised him for speaking out of turn. He's missing his dad, you know. He doesn't even know how—he misses his dad. Austin's not here, and it's just me, and I'm trying my best." Her voice broke, which infuriated her. She blinked back tears.

Her father's voice softened. "I'm not saying you're not doing your best, mija. I just—diablos—what do I know? I know it's my fault that we weren't that close. Especially after your mom died. She was the glue to the family, and without her, all I could do was feel sorry for myself and hate that some asshole took her from me. From us... Pues, anyway." He cleared his throat. "Therapy seems—just like a lot for six. But your mother was the one who would have known more about that kinda stuff than me."

Silence enveloped the waiting room.

Mia extended an olive branch. "Why don't you come over Sunday? You can give Isaiah the truck in person. I'll make dinner."

"Okay," he said. "I'd like that."

The door to the waiting room opened, and Lucy stuck her head through it. "Mia?"

"I gotta go, Dad. They're calling me back. I'll see you later."

Isaiah was making a tower out of foam blocks when Mia walked into the therapy room. Lucy's work space was huge. It had a seating area, a desk, and beyond that, a playing area with puppets, dolls, trains, blocks, and art supplies. One of Isaiah's favorite things to do was to stack the blocks as high as he could and then push them over.

"Look how high I can make this, Mom!"

"I'm looking," she said.

She joined Lucy in the sitting area, and they both watched him play for a few minutes.

Lucy turned toward her and smiled. "I think he's processing well. There will be bumps in the road, of course, but grief is not straightforward. This time, he brought up his dad right away, which is great because it means he's getting more comfortable talking about him. And it's good for him to explore the feelings he has regarding life without his father. Essentially, that's what the drawing at school is about. He didn't bring it up, but he did talk about how he's learning to read. He wants his father to be proud of him."

The backs of Mia's eyes burned, and she tried to blink the tears away. Lucy noticed and handed her a tissue. Mia accepted and balled it in her fist.

Lucy continued, "Milestones are hard. It's okay if they feel a bit rough, for you and Isaiah. Grief is a journey. And for Isaiah, it may get a little complicated soon, because he's understanding more and more what dying means."

"Mom, watch, I'm going to smash it!" Isaiah yelled.

They turned and watched him. The tower fell, and he laughed. Mia clapped.

Lucy smiled and walked to him. "That looked like so much fun! Let's pick this up and then we can play a game with Mom!"

"Yeah!" said Isaiah.

When the game finished, Lucy turned to Mia. "Call any time for extra appointments. But remember, you are doing a fantastic job. This is really hard. Isaiah is processing huge emotions and navigating very serious topics that most of his peers are oblivious to. Luckily, he has a very supportive school. Sending him to the counselor, having him do breathing exercises, and letting him color—" She placed a hand over her heart. "That's all amazing. I wish more schools did that."

Mia nodded. "They're great. They're very supportive."

Lucy smiled and then asked, "What other support are you getting? I don't want to pry too much, but—I know sometimes as mothers, we tend to put ourselves on the back burner. Are you also going to therapy?"

Mia hesitated. "Sometimes."

She couldn't tell if Lucy believed her, but she just nodded. "Good. I'll see you guys next time. Take care of yourselves."

It was a stretch to say Mia attended therapy. Initially, she had tried, but she was never able to find a fit.

A few weeks after Austin had taken his life, she made an appointment at her primary care office. She wanted her normal provider, but she was unavailable. A new physician had joined the practice, and Mia reluctantly agreed to be seen by him.

Her stomach was roiling as she waited. The idea of bolting from the clinic was tempting. *But then I can never come back. And I like Dr. Lin.*

The unfamiliar doctor walked into the room and introduced himself. Mia was sitting on the exam table, hands underneath her thighs. He reviewed the chart and confirmed she was there requesting sleep medication. He asked her how long she had been struggling to sleep.

She stared at her knees, miserable. "I guess a few weeks."

"Are you having trouble going to sleep or staying asleep? Have you tried anything for this yet? Anything over-the-counter?"

Her eyes welled up, blurring the light brown lines that cut the floor's color into boxes. Hot, fat tears spilled down her cheeks. "I just can't sleep. I try. But then I wake up because—because I see him in my dreams."

She refused to look up, but could tell she had caught him off guard.

"Who?" he asked.

"My husband."

"Are these... nightmares?"

She almost couldn't speak. "He keeps dying. I know he's dead, but in my dreams, it's like it just happened. I keep forgetting he died."

"When—when did he die?"

She took a shuddery breath. "A few weeks ago."

The doctor set down the chart and sat on the rolling chair. He scooted over to her and touched her shoulder.

She looked up and more tears spilled. "He's dead because I killed him. Because I didn't know he was in trouble. I knew, but I didn't. And I didn't do anything. He—he shot himself with the stupid gun I bought him for his birthday."

She placed a hand over her mouth and sobbed silently.

The doctor was speechless for a moment. He looked worried. "I'm going to prescribe a gentle sleep aid, but I really need you to come back next week. Can you do that?" Mia nodded. He scribbled on his prescription pad and tore off the sheet. "This is for the prescription." He wrote something else down. "And this is a group that might be good for you. I think it would be a good idea to find someone to talk to."

She didn't go back to the doctor for a month, but she did take his advice and went to two of the counseling sessions. It was a group of women who sat in a circle, sharing their stories and their gripes about widowhood.

"We were married two days," said a middle-aged woman. "It's ridiculous. At least some of you had years with your men. But I didn't even find my poor Robert until I was forty and then life took him from me. He was the best man I ever knew, and now I get to be alone. That's it. He was my chance."

"Now, Jen," chided the counselor, "you can't judge how people grieve."

"Yes, I can! I got two days! I barely got to be a wife!" she snapped.

Someone else chimed in. "You're kind of right. I did have some magical years with my Vern. I'm very glad we were able to make a family and raise our babies before cancer decided to take him."

Jen's eyes grew wide. She looked at the counselor and pointed at the woman who had just spoken. "See!"

The counselor smiled politely. "Does anyone else want to share?"

Over the course of two sessions, Mia heard how cancer, car accidents, or a random work accident had taken their loved ones. Not one person had lost someone to suicide.

During the second session, Mia was invited to share her story, if she wanted, of course.

Shakily, she explained waking up to get ready for work and finding Austin's side of the bed empty. The house was eerily quiet, and she tiptoed around, not wanting to wake Isaiah. The entire house, minus her son's room, was vacant, and she walked out of the front door. Initially, she wondered if Austin had left for an early morning car ride. It wasn't uncommon for him to spend an hour or more driving after an argument. They had fought again the previous day. But his car was sitting quietly in the driveway. She looked down the block, trying to see if she could make out his silhouette walking in the early hours. There were no traces of people.

She wandered around the house again, dread building in her chest, until it dawned on her to check the garage.

As soon as she flicked on the light, she spotted him sitting against the woodworking table, body slightly slouched over. There was a disconnect between what she saw and what her brain deduced. There was a sensation of floating. The house held its breath. She watched herself walk over to him and touch his shoulder. "Austin?" she whispered.

He was cold. *I should get him a blanket,* she thought mildly. Lines of crimson blood fell from his nose and mouth in a shock of color against his pale skin and light blue t-shirt. The only thing she remembered thinking was, *No.*

She didn't realize she was screaming until she called 9-1-1. She barely remembered finding her phone and walking back into the garage.

"I need an ambulance; my husband is hurt. I live on—"

The dispatcher interrupted her, "Ma'am. I need you to calm down and speak slowly. I can't understand what you're saying. What is your address?"

Then, like a punch to the gut, she was present. She found herself sobbing; her heart was pounding. She took in his image, unable to leave, unable to get close again. When she heard the sirens, the spell was broken, and she ran outside. An officer caught her as she collapsed. He helped her to the couch.

"Is there anyone we can call?"

Camille arrived a few minutes before Isaiah came downstairs. She hugged Mia fiercely. Mia wailed and held onto her friend. "What am I going to tell Isaiah?"

They spotted him walking down the stairs at the same time. He held onto the rungs of the staircase, one little fist rubbing an eye.

Camille jumped up and forced a broad smile. "Hi, buddy!"

Mia hid her face.

Camille rushed Isaiah back upstairs. She fed him breakfast in his room and avoided questions about the commotion occurring on the first floor. She called Keegan, and he arrived not long after, having excused himself from work.

Mia thought she was spent of tears until Keegan stepped into the living room, his eyes glassy. She sobbed into his chest as he hugged her. Eventually, he made his way upstairs to retrieve Isaiah. He walked quickly down the stairs and out of the door, Isaiah in his arms and draped in a blanket so he wouldn't see any part of the scene. The police had initially advised keeping the child upstairs until after the body was removed, but delays made them reconsider.

When Mia finished her story, she looked at the group. They looked stunned.

"Oh my goodness. Bless you. And when was this? I don't know if I'd even be able to get out of bed yet," someone said. "You're so brave."

Mia never went again.

-Chapter 6-

September 2005

C amille dropped her hands noisily onto the table. Mia, who had been engrossed in writing flash cards, jumped. College had proved busier than they'd anticipated. They'd spent their senior year of high school poring over potential colleges and had eventually settled on a major in-state university. They were seeking different degrees and didn't share classes, but were able to share a dorm room and usually studied together.

"A few more years! Barely," said Camille. "It'll be worth it, though, right? Tell me it'll be worth it." They sat in an Italian mom-and-pop, popular with college kids despite the long wait times. Fake exotic plants adorned the interior.

Mia hissed. "You scared me half to the death! You know you're the worst to take out in public. This is a restaurant. Yes, it'll be worth it. Of course, it'll be worth it." She paused for a moment and considered. "And if not, we'll have our student loans to cry into."

"Oh, God, don't remind me." Camille laid her head sideways on the table. "Actually, if you wouldn't mind reminding me of one thing," she said, her voice slightly muffled. "Why are we doing this?"

"We want careers," replied Mia, scribbling more notes.

"Hi, my name is Austin. I'll be serving you today. Can I get you started with something? Maybe a pillow?" Their waiter stood expectantly next to their table. He suppressed a smile, and his eyes crinkled in the corners.

Camille straightened up and looked him over. "A double shot of whiskey."

"Oooh," he said in approval. "I'm a whiskey guy myself."

She laughed. "Yeah? I'm just kidding, though. I probably should study with a clear head. I'll have a sweet tea, if you don't mind."

Mia tilted her head. "Do you guys serve pie?"

"We do! Thinking about starting with dessert?"

"What kinds of pie?" she asked.

Camille shook her head. "If you have cherry pie, save yourself a few minutes and just bring her a slice."

Austin held Mia's gaze and smiled. She liked how it brightened his face. She noted a small beauty mark on his cheek.

Camille looked between her friend and the waiter. She let a breath pass. "Cherry?"

His smile fell for a second, and a blush creeped up his neck. "Oh, yes. No, I mean, no. We don't have cherry. We have peach, apple, and chocolate. Oh! And coconut crème."

Mia crinkled her nose.

He shrugged. "If I'm being honest, they're not actually that good. I would recommend their tiramisu, though. That with their espresso or latte is really good."

"Oooh," said Camille. "Fancy. Want to split it?"

Mia shuffled her deck of terms. "Sure."

Camille clapped. "Okay, cool. Cancel my tea and make it two lattes with a side of tiramisu."

After Austin left, Camille leaned in close. "He's cute."

Mia focused on her notes. "Yeah, I guess."

"Oh my God, stop being a prude. He's really cute. If I wasn't dating Nate, I'd probably have to ask him for his number."

Mia looked up. "Oh."

Camille sighed dramatically and flipped her hair. "'Oh,' she says. I guess the other problem would be that he seems to like you."

A blush settled on Mia's cheeks. She found her notes very interesting again. "I think you're reading into things."

Camille laughed. "You are literally the worst. This is why you end up dating shitty dudes, I swear. You can't tell when guys are into you. Otherwise, you would have never had that fling with Brandon or whatever his name was."

Mia shuddered. "I was drunk that whole relationship."

"Well, whatever you were, I'm glad it was short-lived. Guy was such a loser. No offense. Or maybe all the offense, if it means you'll raise your standards."

Mia had met Brandon in her statistics class. He was smart, albeit cocky, and laughed often. He was not traditionally good looking, with a nose that seemed a little too big for his face and a mouth that liked to dip into a frown, but he had an allure about him. People liked him and enjoyed his company. He was generous when taking people out, he'd help them or fix their cars, charging only the acceptable number of beers or pizza.

Statistics, a class she struggled with, seemed easy for him. He led a lot of class discussions and spoke with confidence. She liked conversing with him, and when he asked her out, she didn't hesitate to accept. He kept her laughing during their first few dates. When he offered to tutor her, she gladly accepted. However, as the class neared its end, so did his charm. The shift was subtle and hard to explain.

Eventually, she declined his help with statistics, saying he had helped her so much, she was confident she'd pass with a good grade. However, the truth was that he had grown increasingly condescending as their short relationship matured. It took Mia an embarrassing amount of time to realize he felt women were naturally weaker at math and, therefore, belittled them.

During their last week of classes, a female voice interrupted him in the midst of a class discussion. He turned to find their classmate, Karen, loudly disagreeing with him. The professor was very encouraging—toward her. Brandon was furious. He held it in well in class, but it soured his mood for a week. Mia took the brunt of it, and she allowed the abuse, unsure of how to respond.

They agreed to hang out at his place the following Friday, but her arrival time set him off. Brandon lived off campus in a small duplex he shared with a roommate. His bedroom was so small it barely fit his queen-sized bed. He had explained he preferred a larger bed, so he had no night stand or chest-of-drawers. His clothes were split between his closet and a hamper that was perched permanently outside of the Jack-and-Jill bathroom. There was no linen closet, which meant the guys had installed a towel rack that held the few they owned.

But the living room was spacious, even if it melted into the dining area. That's where Mia found Brandon, the back of his head visible over the sofa, the television displaying a first-person shooter video game.

She walked to the other side of the couch.

"Nice of you to show up whenever you want." His eyes didn't leave the screen.

Mia's head jerked back slightly. "I'm sorry, what's the problem? I didn't know there was a time you wanted me over. You said the evening. It's evening. It's not like we're going out."

"Oh, so that's why my time isn't a big deal to you? I'm not taking you out?" He finally looked at her. "Go figure. I take you out all the time, pay for everything. It's not the man's responsibility, you know. I thought you guys wanted equal rights and all that shit. But here you are, wanting to get into business, but not wanting to split the tab." His face was ruddy from the exertion.

"What?" She gasped. "I don't want to go out... I didn't say anything about going out."

"You just said we weren't going out tonight and that's why my time wasn't a big deal," he spat.

She frowned. "I didn't say—that's not what I meant."

"That's not what you meant? So, you did say it, you just want me to think you meant it in a good way."

"No. I—" She didn't know how to respond. "I'm sorry. I'm here now."

He sighed heavily and slumped onto the couch. He pressed a few buttons on the controller to get back to the starting page. "Yep, you're here now."

Mia watched him set up a new game, standing stupidly in the living room. "Do you want me to go?"

He ignored her for a moment, then sighed again. "I know you're sorry. It's okay. You're right. You're here now. You want to grab a controller?" He smiled and held one out to her.

Her head was spinning. Mutely, she accepted. Once she sat next to him, he stood up, grabbed a few beers, and sat back down. The more they drank, the more the tension eased from the room. They ended the night with sex.

Without meaning to, she spent the night. She woke with an upset stomach, mouth fuzzy from the beer she had drank. Brandon's snores pierced the otherwise quiet room.

She was naked and his arm was heavy on her abdomen. The urge to pee intensified. She looked over at him. Gingerly, she slid his arm off and tiptoed into the bathroom. The idea of quickly dressing and bolting crossed her mind. Her thoughts returned to his behavior the day he was outsmarted by one of the quiet girls in their class, then ended with his explosive temper the previous day.

He shifted in the bed and stretched. A sleepy eye opened slightly. He mumbled something unintelligible.

She forced a smile even though his eyes were closed. "I gotta go, babe."

He grunted in acknowledgement.

She dressed and found his roommate eating cereal in the kitchen. When their eyes met, her cheeks colored. He grinned; the look seemed swinish. She pressed her lips into a thin line and gave him a quick nod.

She drove back to campus. The walk back to her own dorm room felt long, and she prayed she wouldn't bump into anyone she knew, especially Camille. The idea of them guessing where she had been felt shameful. That's when she knew the brief relationship was over. It would still take a few weeks for her to find the words to end it.

Mia shrugged away the memory while shuffling her terms again. "Anyway."

"Yeah, anyway, here comes your hunk now."

Before Mia could quiet her friend, Austin arrived with the tray of lattes, waters, and dessert. He placed the tiramisu gingerly between them, handed them their drinks, and laid a small stack of napkins and two small forks by the plate.

"Can I get anything else for you ladies?"

Camille grinned. Mia suspected mischief. "Yeah, actually, if we could get —"

Mia kicked her lightly under the table.

"Ow, not nice. I was going to say I wanted the Mediterranean salad. What did you want to order, Mia?" Camille batted her eyelashes.

"This is great for me, thanks. I'll just steal some of hers," Mia said, eyes on Camille.

As Austin walked away, Mia glared at her friend. *You're the worst*, she mouthed. Camille winked.

After they split the dessert and the salad, they requested the check. By then, Mia felt bleary-eyed from staring at terms and theories.

"I'm going to the bathroom real quick and then we can bounce?"

Camille grimaced and nodded. "Yeah. I'm all notecard-ed out, if that's a thing."

Back at the dorm, Mia stood in their bathroom gently patting her face dry.

Camille hastily brushed her teeth and spat. "Ugh, I'll wash my face tomorrow. I'm so tired."

"That's how you get pimples."

Camille rolled her eyes and whipped out a facial wipe. She slid it across her forehead, cheeks, and nose. "There." Her face brightened. "Oh, yeah!" She bustled out of the bathroom and returned with a slip of paper.

Mia raised an eyebrow. "What's this?"

Camille waved her fingers over her shoulder as she exited the bathroom. "I might have had one more quick conversation with the cute waiter while you were in the bathroom. Goodnight!"

Mia picked up the paper. *I know a place that sells a good cherry pie. – Austin.* His number was scribbled underneath. She padded to her bed staring at the note, as if more words would appear underneath.

"Told you he liked you! Call him! I mean, not now, because you don't want to seem desperate. But tomorrow."

Mia felt butterflies in her stomach. She smiled at Camille. "You're the worst."

She looked smug. "You're welcome."

-Chapter 7-

August 2016

"That drawing is really sweet," said Camille. "And heartbreaking."

Mia agreed and took a sip of wine. The pair sat in the dining room, ensuring they had a direct line of sight into the living room. "Sometimes I feel like he's doing great and then sometimes I'm worried I'll miss some sign. Whenever he has a breakdown at school, I feel like maybe it's because I haven't been attuned to him and he's acting out."

Spaghetti night was a monthly tradition they took turns hosting. Neither remembered exactly when or how it had started but knew it was some time after both boys were born. After Austin had died, Camille showed up with Luca and spaghetti until Mia felt up to alternating locations again.

The boys were playing with Legos in the living room. Periodically, there was a crash and a round of giggles. Mia tried not to think about the disaster in the kitchen. She knew there were people who boasted they cleaned up as they cooked dinner, but that just seemed like a lie. Usually, she cooked and delayed the cleanup until right before bed. Sometimes, she would even wait until the next morning, but with Camille over, she had to make sure to finish before they left lest Camille clean it up for her, which made her feel like a failure in both domestic and hostess duties.

Mia looked down at Isaiah's drawing. He had drawn himself swinging on a swing set and Mia standing next to it. Flowers and green scribbles were etched across the bottom. A male figure with wings floated in the sky next to a yellow sun. A blue dotted line fell from each of the figure's eyes.

"That's Daddy," he had explained. "This is how he can watch me swing, because he's not here. He can't swing me like you. That's why he's sad."

Camille took Mia's hand and gave it a gentle squeeze. "I'm so sorry, love. That's so hard."

Mia pressed her lips into a smile and took another drink. "I think I panic too easily. I believe—well, try to believe—that processing grief is normal, crying is normal, and I want to extend that to Isaiah, but it feels like I'm failing. He has one bad day, and I'm calling his counselor. He sees a therapist twice a month, but I scheduled an emergency session, because it's like, what if he's struggling? What if I'm saying the wrong thing when I talk to him?" She sighed. "I don't know. It sucks."

"What did the therapist say?" Camille asked.

"She said it's normal for him to explore the idea of death. And that it's good for him to have an outlet like art." The picture was laid out on the dining room table, and Mia tapped it twice with her finger. "She loves how supportive the school is. In other schools, his outburst in class would have just earned him a reprimand. She was impressed with how they handled it. She's glad he's processing more of what losing his dad means. I guess Isaiah is realizing there's a lot of things he can't show his dad." Mia shook her head as if to clear it. "Well, anyway, how are you and Keegan? How's that going?"

Camille rolled her eyes and smiled. "Fantastic so far. Your comment about us being back together made me think hard about it all. I brought it up to him. Like, what are we, y'know? I think the question startled him a little bit. But he smiled, and I knew what he was going to say. So, yeah. We're official. We're back together. Might even change my Facebook status, but I'm going to make him earn that first."

They laughed.

"Well, good. I'm glad. Have you guys told Luca?"

Camille grimaced. "I still kind of want to wait. I mean, it's not like he fully gets what a romantic relationship is anyway. And I still am a little worried we'll be good for a while and then it'll all implode again. Keegan comes over just as often as before. Okay, maybe a little bit more. But overall, there's no big changes at the house." Camille paused. "I still don't let him stay the whole night."

Mia gasped. "Poor guy! You kick him out every night?"

Camille grinned. "No. Just the nights he stays past Luca's bedtime."

"Oh my God, same thing."

"Totally not."

Mia smiled. "You guys ever going to move in together?"

"Woah, hold your horses there, babe. We barely just got back together. I think this is working out for us. Maybe the problem we had before was moving too quickly. We didn't know what we wanted."

"What do you want?" Mia asked.

Camille paused. "Stability. Adventure. A good father to my son. Love. I want—I want what everyone wants, right? Companionship. Someone that makes you happy and excited, but also has your back. I don't know if that's real life, but—I really hope it is."

Mia nodded.

"I think when we first got together, we were just in it for, I don't know, a summer love or something. I thought he was gorgeous, the sex was great, but... I almost can't remember now. I don't think I was looking for a serious relationship, and he definitely wasn't. We just butted heads a lot. And part of me wonders if we were both scared of commitment." Camille sipped from her glass.

A commotion in the living room stole their attention. "Hey! Give that back!"

They looked over. Luca was holding tightly to a toy while Isaiah yanked on it, his little face turning red.

"Give! It! Back!" Isaiah's eyes were dark and angry.

Mia jumped up. "Woah, woah, woah. What's going on?"

Isaiah let go and turned to his mother. "He's stealing my truck! That's my special truck from Grandpa!"

Mia softened her expression. "Oh, I see. Luca, I'm sorry, that really is a special truck. But, Isaiah, if you don't want it played with, you should keep it upstairs."

"But I wanted to play with it."

"Okay, but it's a little bit rude to bring down toys that are off-limits and play with them in front of friends. It's nicer when we take turns."

Luca chimed in. "I wasn't going to break it. I just wanted to see it."

"But you can't!" yelled Isaiah. "Because it's mine." He took the distraction as an opportunity to yank the toy back.

"Hey!" snapped Mia. "That's not nice at all. Either, you share or you take it upstairs."

Isaiah frowned and held the truck close to his chest. "I want to play with it."

Mia closed her eyes and exhaled. "Then, you have to share."

"Luca," Camille warned. "There's so many toys down here anyway. You can play with everything else."

"No," said Mia. "Isaiah needs to learn to share or keep special things put up."

"Fine!" shouted Isaiah. "I don't want to play with Luca!"

Luca looked shocked and ran to the couch. He started to cry.

"Isaiah!" Mia cried out.

Her son stomped up the steps.

Mia turned to Camille, "Oh my God. I'm so sorry."

Camille went over to Luca and scooped him onto her lap. "It's okay, buddy. Isaiah is just mad, and sometimes we say hurtful things when we're mad."

"But what if he doesn't want to be my friend anymore?" cried Luca, his face pressed against his mother's chest.

"I'll go talk to him," said Mia. "I'll be right back."

"Should we go? Give him space?" Camille asked.

"No," Mia said quickly. "No. It's fine. I think he's just in a mood. And I don't want you guys to leave it like this. I'll be right back."

Camille nodded and drew Luca tighter against her body. His crying slowed, and he returned her hug.

Mia made her way up the stairs and gently tapped on Isaiah's door. She walked into the room. "Hey, there."

Isaiah looked at her and then threw himself onto his bed, facedown.

She walked over and placed her hand on his back. "You okay?"

Muffled sounds erupted from the bed, and she giggled. "I can't hear you when you talk into the pillow."

He turned his face toward her. "I said I'm a bad boy."

"Oh, honey, no. You're not a bad boy. Not at all." She picked him up and held him tightly. "Never think you're a bad kid. You're not. You're amazing. But you did hurt Luca's feelings."

"Do you think he hates me now?"

"No, I don't. I think he's afraid you don't like him anymore, though."

"I do like him," said Isaiah.

"I know. And I also know that sometimes when we're angry, we say mean things we feel bad about later. And we need to work on not saying those things, even though sometimes it's hard not to in the moment." Mia paused and looked at her son. She smiled. "But we're all human, and everybody makes mistakes. And that was a mistake you made downstairs. So, I think maybe you can say you're sorry to your friend."

"Because he's my very best friend."

Mia smiled again. "Yes, because he's your very best friend."

Isaiah rested his head on her chest. She thought back to all the time she spent nursing him, his little hand curled around a strand of hair or the edge of her shirt. So much had passed between his birth and the present. After a moment, his body straightened, and she loosened her grip. He stood and considered his toys. "I can let him play with my special truck. I'll just tell him to be careful."

Mia paused for a second and wondered if this was true reconciliation or if the truck would eventually spurn another fight. "Well, maybe, we can bring down other trucks. A bunch of trucks. And you guys can play with those. And once you've played with your special truck for a while, you can bring it out to share on a different spaghetti night, okay?"

He sniffed and nodded.

A few minutes later, the boys were playing again. Mia and Camille settled on the couch.

"I feel like he's so much angrier these days."

Camille shrugged. "I think he's a kid doing kid things. If he has a rough time here and there, totally understandable. But honestly, they're going to start fighting like brothers because of their age. Friends fight. It's fine. Plus, look at them now. Next week, Luca will be the one mad about something. It happens."

Mia picked at the fraying end of her shirt. "Yeah. Maybe."

∞ ∞ ∞

Mia sat on the couch reading a book while the television played in the background. Camille and Luca were gone, the kitchen was clean, and Isaiah was fast asleep. Mia was tired, but she needed the time to decompress. She felt departures more acutely now. One person was missing from their household, but with him went all of the background noise that made up the soundtrack of a family. All that was left was a loud silence and empty spaces.

She turned a page and frowned. Who was this new character? She flipped the page back and skimmed the content before sighing and giving up.

Mia knew she was luckier than a lot of other widows, even those who had lost their partner to suicide. After her trial with group therapy, she tried one grief counselor who talked more than she listened and then turned to social media for small groups that provided people who could empathize. In those forums, she read stories of people who had lost their loved ones to disease and now lived the nightmare of loss that left a bill. Very few had enough life insurance to cover the costs of all the treatments. In the worst cases, they had no life or health insurance at all.

Widows of suicide lived a much different ever after. In a lot of cases, secrets were discovered: giant loans, other women, drugs, and so on. There were posts from women who had felt blindsided, filled with rage or depression or embarrassment that they had not seen past the façade their significant other had constructed. Others felt guilt over the relief that had come, sometimes describing the abuse or drugs or turmoil that had existed in their relationship. And the majority fell somewhere in between.

Mia felt she was wedged firmly between the nightmare relationships some women had survived and those that sounded like fairy tales. She and Austin had fought constantly in the end. The arguments sapped all her energy. For both parties, the conflict was rooted deeply in insecurity and resentment. He was sliding deeper into a depression she didn't pay enough attention to, a depression he vehemently denied.

-Chapter 8 -

June 2014

A ustin filled a glass with a finger of whiskey. "I don't need a doctor, Mia."
They stood in the kitchen, the whiskey bottle open and dangerous on the
kitchen island.

"Baby, I just think you're—it's—I'm worried." Isaiah had been asleep for an
hour. She had read him his favorite bedtime stories and tucked him in while
trying to ignore the unease in the pit of her stomach. Unresolved conflict
always exhausted her, even as it robbed her of sleep. The kitchen vibrated
with tension when she walked downstairs, and she wished she had gone to
bed instead.

Austin's eyes met hers for a moment and then turned elsewhere, the
muscle in his jaw clenching and unclenching, the pulse of caged frustration.
"I'm fine. I'm—really, I'm fine. I'm just tired, and this 'not having a job' thing is
getting a little irritating."

"I get that it's irritating, but it's not that big of a deal. For now, we're
doing well. We're covering all the bills. I'm supporting us fine," she said. They
stood in the kitchen, him with his whiskey, her leaning against the wall, arms
crossed.

He took a sip. "You're supporting us. I know. I get it. I feel it every day."

She narrowed her eyes. "What the hell does that mean? You know damn
well I didn't mean it as a stab. Can you get over yourself? It's always this same
argument. God, I'm so tired of this." She rubbed her face.

"It's kind of funny how you're always talking about sharing feelings, and here I am, trying to talk, and now you're tired."

Mia took a slow breath as she felt fire surge in her belly. "I'm not saying you can't talk about it. I want you to talk to me. I just feel like you're acting like you need more than just *my* help."

He took a large swallow from his glass and laughed without humor. "It makes me feel a little bad that I can't support my family and that makes my wife think I need a shrink."

She wanted to pull her hair. "It's more than just the job! It's bigger than that! You know damn well if I were the one without a job, we wouldn't be having these arguments. It wouldn't bother you. I feel like maybe you need more control here than you think you do."

"Control? I'm controlling?"

"Not what I said. But this is what I mean when I say we need counseling. We keep misunderstanding each other. We're not communicating. I think you need a certain amount of control in your life, which is fine. Everybody needs that. My concern is that you get in these really deep, dark slumps, and I feel like I can't reach you. And I don't know what to do. If it's just not having a job —I don't know, it seems excessive."

He rolled his eyes. "Alright."

She threw up her hands. "And then you do that. Just wall, wall, wall."

"Oh, that's rich. Like you've never been mad before and kept me in the dark. Sometimes it feels like pulling teeth with you. You get into moods you swear you're not in. Then maybe—*maybe*—two weeks later you tell me. Or don't tell me and just get extra angry the next time because of shit I did last year that I still don't know about. But maybe that's my fault, too. I'm not good at telepathy. But apparently, you are and know exactly what I need. Well, congratulations. You're better than me. I'm so sorry I'm dragging you down with me."

"Grow up." Her muscles were tense. She felt the biggest urge to cross the room and slap him, hoping the sting of it would transfer the hurt she was feeling. Instead, she bit the inside of her cheek and forced herself to hold his eyes as he glowered at her.

He was the first to turn away but he did so to pour another finger.

"You're drinking more."

He cut his eyes at her. "I can't drink?" Before she could respond, he drained the glass, and this time it was her who looked away.

∞ ∞ ∞

Mia called Austin the day after he left her his number. Soon, he was around as often as Camille. Maybe more. Her favorite facet of his personality was the ease in which he laughed. It was as if the entire world was friendly and carefree. She was in awe of how he could strike up a conversation with anyone. It didn't matter if they had been friends for years or a stranger he'd never see again. In the end, he'd be remembered in the normal cliche: *He was always smiling.* But it was true.

Usually.

About a year after they started dating, Mia felt a shift. It was so slow that she didn't notice the beginning, wouldn't be able to pinpoint it except in hindsight. When his behavior changed enough she couldn't ignore it, she wondered if she was overanalyzing everything. He still hung out with friends, they still spent time together, and he still smiled a lot; but when he drank, he seemed to be drowning sorrows rather than celebrating.

She gathered all of her bravery one day and blurted out her concern. "What's going on with you?" They were sitting in his dorm room alone. His roommate was in a new relationship and almost never there on the weekends.

"What do you mean?" His eyes were glassy, his movements slow.

"Your grades are slipping, you're drinking more, you're—"

The room to his dorm opened suddenly, one of his friends appearing with a quick grin. He nodded at them and went straight to the minifridge. He grabbed a beer, saluted with two fingers, and left. "See ya."

"And what is that?" she continued. "People burst into your room, grab your alcohol because they know it's fully stocked, and then leave. Your fridge is always full. Like, this whole thing is just not healthy."

"What are you, my mother? I need to clear when I can drink with you? My grades are slipping... maybe not everyone is blessed with easy professors. Not all of us can get straight A's here," he said.

"Wait, what the hell? Are you kidding me? Fuck you and your tired ass assumptions. I can't get a good grade unless it's easy? I bust my ass for my grades!"

Austin sipped his beer, unperturbed. "You were just drinking with me yesterday and didn't say shit. Super convenient that if I'm covering the tab, you order your daiquiri and drink up with me. I didn't hear any complaints about drinking too much yesterday."

Mia felt stupid for bringing it up. She had no argument left. "You're drunk. Just—just call me when you sober up, okay?"

"What the—"

She didn't wait around to hear the rest and slammed the door as she left.

He wouldn't call for a week, but when he did, his voice was small. She suggested they drive out to their favorite park. They picked up tacos and two Cokes from a food truck on their way.

She spread their late lunch on a picnic table and sat. A lazy breeze played with her hair. After a moment, he took his place next to her. She took a bite of barbacoa to feign nonchalance. Her head was bursting with questions, but she kept them at bay by studying the activity at the park. The picnic area was situated next to the large pond located on the premises. Several geese softly landed in the water. A woman with her boxer jogged the paved loop that flanked the pond. A mother pushed a stroller, chatting with a man who presumably was her husband. Mia idly wondered why it seemed like there was an unwritten rule that women were the only ones who could maneuver them. Fathers, of course, pushed their babies in strollers all the time. But when was the last time she had seen a man do this when accompanied by a woman? Unless, of course, she was busy with two other children.

Normally, she would have brought up this question much to Austin's amusement. But more important things were on his mind, and she didn't want to give him an excuse to talk about anything else.

When he finally broke the silence, she was already eating her second taco. She set it down and looked at his face. His gaze was focused on the horizon. She noticed he had picked apart some of his food but hadn't really eaten any. "My great-uncle, my mom's uncle? He died. But I guess he's been dying a while. Bladder cancer."

She reached out and touched his arm. "Oh my God, babe. I'm so sorry."

He withdrew his arm and picked up his Coke. He took a sip and considered her statement. "I'm not."

She opened her mouth and then closed it.

"He can rot in hell for all I care." He studied the tree line. The chatter of squirrels sounded as they bounced from one tree branch to another. Birds called to each other.

A tear fell down his cheek. He wiped it quickly with his shoulder and took a deep breath. "That man abused me and my sisters every day for years. He—I can't even—I don't want to talk about what he did, really. We just—you know how old I was when I was introduced to porn?" His voice cracked. "He said they were games, but we knew it was all wrong—but he said—and I believed him. I was scared of him."

Another tear fell, and he wiped it with a fist. He took a bite of his taco, angry, and looked away.

"Oh my God. Austin," breathed Mia. She tried to hug him, but his body was rigid. She sat back and grabbed his hand. "Baby. I am. So. Sorry."

"For what?" he said. His eyes met hers, and she felt the anger emanating from them. "You didn't do anything." The tone was a challenge.

"For being so insensitive about you drinking and not—I don't know."

He studied his food. "I don't want you to look at me different."

She tried to catch his eye, aggrieved on his behalf. "Hey. Hey. No. I would never think of you differently. You are not responsible for anything an adult did to you. Ever. Especially as a child. I think of you exactly the same as I did before. Or, if anything, better. You went through something no child, no person, should ever go through. You're a survivor. This man... no, this child predator took advantage of you. And that's not a reflection of you. That's not a character flaw or something you need to be ashamed about. He is the only one at fault here. He's the only one that needs to be judged."

Austin's knee bounced. His head lowered. "My mom wants me to go to the funeral."

Mia blinked, shocked. "Does—does she know what he did to you?"

He met her eyes for a second. "Yeah."

Rage built behind her chest, and she clasped her hands together to keep them from shaking. "How can she know this and still—"

"She doesn't like to talk about it. It was so long ago anyway. And... we didn't really have a good relationship growing up. She caught my sisters and I—it's so awful, but I was five. She thought I was a monster. I think she regretted having me. The whole family thought I was going to end up in prison or something. It's still kind of a joke. People lost bets because I ended up in a dorm room instead of a jail cell. Plus, she didn't find out it was her uncle until we were teenagers. I think that broke everything. Sometimes, even if you're sorry, it's too late."

They sat there a while, their lunch strewn across the table and growing cold.

She broke the silence first. "Blame me."

"What?"

"Blame me. Don't go and say it's because I needed you for something. Something important. Then, it's not really your fault. And you don't have to explain more than that."

"I didn't say you can't drink, Austin," Mia said. "But you have to admit you're drinking a lot more often these days, and it feels like you're just leaning on it some. You get in these slumps. You don't talk to me."

"I said. I'm. Fine."

She let her arms drop, exasperated. "Then, why are you so defensive about this? Why can't you just go *talk* to someone—"

He slammed the glass down hard. Shards flew, and a ribbon of blood spread across his hand. "Fuck!"

"Oh—oh my God, Austin."

She pushed him to the sink and turned on the cold water. He winced slightly as the water flooded his hand. After she finished inspecting the wound and finding it free of debris, she grabbed a kitchen towel and wrapped his hand. He said nothing and stared at it. She was livid.

A small voice called from the hallway. "Daddy? Mama?" Isaiah's little form appeared in the kitchen doorway.

"Baby, what are you doing out of bed?" Mia asked gently.

"Noises." Isaiah stuck a finger into his mouth. He held his favorite stuffed bear by the leg.

She wanted to scream at Austin but instead took a breath and flashed her son a big smile. "Daddy just had an accident. Let me finish helping him, and I'll tuck you back into bed."

"I got it," Austin said, his voice hoarse.

"You sure? I just need another few seconds."

Shadows lined his face, and he refused to look up from his hand. "I'll finish and clean up the mess."

"Your hand is hurt. I can sweep it up."

"It's my fault. I'll do it. No big deal."

But it was a big deal.

After Mia coaxed Isaiah back to sleep, she walked into her bedroom and found Austin already in bed, his body curled into a loose fetal position, eyes closed.

She sighed, exhausted from the fight but too wired to feel drowsy. She slid under the covers. She pressed her body against his back and wrapped an arm around his middle. His breath was slow and even.

"I'm sorry."

It was a whisper, but it still startled her. "It's okay," she said. A lie.

"No. It's not. I'm sorry." A pause. "Maybe you're better off without me."

"What? Oh, babe. I don't want to separate our family. I think—well, everyone has hard times, right? Doesn't mean we need to get—it's just hard right now. We'll get through it. I-I'd really like it if we tried counseling."

He didn't respond, simply slipped his hand over hers. She knew he would never go. Deep inside, she wondered if he had a point. Maybe they would be better off separated, divorced even. She was exhausted from the fights. And if she were really honest with herself, she had contemplated that very thought before. Their future felt fragile. The thought felt ugly and traitorous and heartbreaking. She pushed it deep into the core of herself, hoping Austin couldn't sense the betrayal.

They lay like that for a while, but Mia knew one of them would eventually pull away; neither liked to sleep in that position. Who would let go first?

-Chapter 9 -

September 2016

Mia rummaged through her closet. She had no idea what to wear.

I don't care, she thought. *I'll just wear jeans and a t-shirt. No. A nice shirt and jeans.* She looked down at the 'no' pile she had created on the floor and chewed on a fingernail.

"Ugh," she moaned. "What the hell am I thinking?"

"Why are you in your underwear?" Isaiah had wandered into the closet.

"I'm getting dressed. I just don't know what I want to wear."

"Where are you going?" he asked.

"Uh, just out with Camille and some friends. Remember? That's why you're going to a little slumber party at Carol's."

"You're leaving all night?" He bit his lip.

"Oh, mi amor," she said. *Please don't do this. I really don't need this guilt trip.* "You're having a sleepover because I'll be out late, but I'll be picking you up early, okay? Plus, Luca will be there!"

"What are you guys going to do?"

She shrugged. "Just mom stuff. Go out. Talk. Maybe dance."

He considered the information. "Then, you should wear that dress." He pointed.

"The green one?" She frowned. "That might be a little too fancy."

"Nuh-uh. 'Cause if you're gonna dance, you're s'pose to look like a princess."

"You think so?" she said, smiling.

"Yeah. And Daddy liked it a lot."

Her smile dimmed. "He did, didn't he?" She ran a hand over the front of it. "It *is* a very pretty dress." She pulled it from its place and held it out arm's length. The dress's color was actually aquamarine, a color she loved because of how it looked against her skin. Its neckline plunged just enough to be provocative, but not so much she felt exposed. The fabric was smooth with a smart, creased gathering on its left side, which left an impression of a neat waist. It hugged her hips and tapered as it followed her thighs down to just above her knee.

Isaiah clapped. "Yeah! Wear that one."

She paired the dress with coral heels, added a smokey eye, nude lips, and gathered her hair up in a French twist.

"You look beautiful, Mama," Isaiah said when she modeled the look. He smiled and hugged her.

"Thank you so much, mi amor," she said.

Carol, Isaiah's occasional babysitter, was a middle-aged woman who lived about two blocks from Mia. Her morning dog-walking route took her past their home every morning. She was a divorcee that had never remarried, even after her three children were grown and had families of their own. Sometimes, Mia would join the family for dinner or a game night. Carol's children would sometimes gently encourage her to find someone to grow old with. She'd scoff and inform them all she was already old and assured everyone she loved the independence. For what it was worth, she did seem to thrive in it, though she wasn't entirely alone. She owned three dogs and a few indoor-outdoor cats.

"They make much better roommates than husbands," she often said.

Once Mia was ready, she ordered a cab to pick her up at Carol's address, and they walked over.

Carol lit up when she answered the door. "Oh my, look at you! You look stunning, dear."

Mia smiled. "Thank you. He's already eaten dinner and everything."

Carol turned to Isaiah, "Luca's here. We're playing some Chutes and Ladders."

"Really? Cool!" He disappeared into the house.

"Woah, hold on a second, Isaiah! You gonna say bye to Mom, at least?"

Carol moved out of Mia's way and chuckled. "Kids break your heart, don't they?"

Mia turned to her as she walked into the house, "Right? I'm chopped liver over here next to you guys and Chutes and Ladders."

She took a while to say goodbye, leaving only when the cabbie sent a second message asking if she had received the first; as a result, she was the last of her friends to arrive.

O'Connor's was one of the local spots that flirted the line between bar and club. There was a dance floor, a large seating area, and a stage for the contracted DJs or live musicians. Bars lined two of the walls. Mia noted there was a band playing tonight, which put her in a good mood. She always preferred live music to DJs.

High-pitched squeals caught her attention, and despite the butterflies in her stomach, she couldn't help but grin when she spotted the source. Camille and their friends Jessica, Lori, and Rochelle were waving at her from one of the tables. They all looked as though they were at least one drink in.

Their energy was contagious.

"Oh my God. Girl. You look hot!" Camille pulled her in for a hug and kissed her cheek.

"It's been forever! How are you? Look at you! Finally, out from under that rock! I've missed you," said Rochelle. She wore a fuchsia dress and loud, gold earrings.

"You guys look great, too! I'm—I'm good. I feel a little weird. It's been a while, I know, but I'm happy I'm here," said Mia. She was surprised to learn she meant it.

"You do look hot. All of you look hot, especially Jessica—and she knows it. You know the type of confidence you need to wear white shorts and heels? The kind that comes with abs," Lori said, laughing.

Jessica laughed in surprise. "I like these shorts. And I wish I had abs."

"Well, if you don't have abs, it's only barely. I'd kill for legs like yours," Lori said.

"You can come to the gym with me!" Jessica offered.

"Calamari?" said a voice. They looked over and noted the young waiter holding a tray with a few appetizers.

"Ooh!" said Rochelle. "That's me."

"Nachos?"

"Me," said Lori.

"And the O'Connor's martini?"

"That one is me, thank you kindly," said Camille.

Once everything was placed in front of the respective person, the waiter looked over to Mia. "Did you want to place an order?"

"Um, I don't know. I could start with water."

Camille cut in. "Could I get a vodka cranberry and a rum and Coke?"

"Sure," said the waiter. "Anyone else need anything?"

Lori was already eating her nachos. She answered for the group. "We're good."

"That vodka and cranberry is for you," Camille informed Mia.

She rolled her eyes and grinned. "Of course."

"Well, anyway," said Lori, shooting Jessica a dry look, "I only have time to complain about being fat. I have five children, Jess. Five. I would probably look like you from all the running around I do, but I stress eat."

They laughed.

"Girl, I got one. I can't imagine five," said Rochelle, shaking her head. "I had him and learned my lesson. Love him, but that little boy, whew! Let me tell you, he plucks my every damn nerve sometimes."

"Well, the offer is open," Jessica said. She looked around the table. "To anyone."

Camille stole a nacho and shook her head. "Don't do it. I went running with her once. It almost ended the friendship. That girl is hard-core."

"I am not!" Jessica exclaimed. She crossed her arms, grinning. "I just like pushing myself."

"I go with her once a month," Mia said. "But I do think that's probably the one time a month she takes it easy."

The group laughed.

"You know what?" said Lori. "Maybe I will. You're gonna have to push my fat ass off of the treadmill if I die, but that's fine."

Lori and Jessica clinked drinks. "Deal."

As food and drinks were passed around, Mia felt herself settling into the old routine of hanging out with friends. She laughed without thinking too deeply of anything. The women sat eating and drinking until the band started a cover of Rochelle's favorite song. She whooped, and they followed her to the dance floor.

Lori tapped out first. "I'm going back to the table."

"I'll go with you," said Jessica.

Not thirty minutes later, everyone else was ready to return to the table, and Mia excused herself. "I'm going to the bathroom real quick and then I'll head over."

"Want another drink?" Rochelle asked.

"Um, something with tequila?" she answered.

"Brave!" said Rochelle, laughing.

On the trip from the bathroom to the table, Mia felt a hand grab her ass; she ignored it and quickened her pace.

A man intercepted her path. "Hi there, gorgeous." He smiled and a dimple appeared. His blonde hair was gelled and well-styled. His eyelashes were a dark brown and framed his blue eyes really well.

She stopped and smiled. "Oh, uh, hi."

"Sorry, I saw you earlier with your friends and wanted to introduce myself, but you seemed busy."

Her smile turned polite.

"I'm Ian."

She hesitated. "Mia."

The band introduced their next song, which included a drum-heavy rhythm. "Mia! Beautiful. What are you drinking?"

"What?" She regretted the question even as it left her mouth.

Ian leaned closer, and she felt his breath, hot and wet against her ear. "I said, 'What are you drinking?' Can I get you a drink?"

She hesitated. "Oh, I don't really need a drink right now. My friends already have one waiting at the table."

"I really love your dress, by the way."

She glanced down. "Oh. Uh, thank you."

"That color really brings out your eyes."

"My eyes?"

"A guy could get lost in those eyes."

Oh no.

She laughed. "Oh, thanks."

He stepped closer, and she took a step back.

"Do you come here often? I've been a few times and don't think I've ever seen you."

She shook her head, still smiling.

"I thought so," he said. He flashed a pearly white smile. She was sure he was a regular and likely had a high success rate with the female patrons. He wasn't a bad-looking guy. She just knew the type: a little too suave, a little too confident, a little too pushy. He wore a silky short-sleeved button up, perfect for showing off strong, muscular arms. His cologne was a great choice, even if a little strong.

"I would have recognized you, I'm sure of it. A beautiful woman like you is hard to forget."

Mia was done with the conversation. She regretted the choice to go to the bathroom alone. "Oh, wow. That's so nice. I-I have to go. My friends—"

"Let me buy you a drink," he said. "Just one. I'm sure they won't miss you too much. And I promise I'll escort you back to your table myself." He gave her forearm a squeeze.

"I-I don't know," she said.

"A drink, maybe a dance? Make a man's night," he said, then laughed. After a second, he raised his eyebrows. "Oh, man, I didn't even think—you're out on a girls' night, huh?"

She smiled and nodded. He got it. "Yes," she said. "And I really gotta go back."

"And you probably have a boyfriend," he continued.

"Oh," she said, "no. No, I don't."

"Oh!" he said, surprised.

Shit.

"That's a little crazy. I'd think guys were always falling over themselves for you. You're just—"

She pressed her lips into a line. "Listen, I gotta go. I'm with my friends, and it's been a while since I've seen them."

"Mia!" a male voice called out.

They both turned.

"Hey, babe," he said and smiled at Ian. Mia had never seen him in her life, but she wasn't upset about the intrusion. He had a clean, casual look about him. The rust-colored shirt complemented his tanned skin and dark eyes. He had paired it with smart gray slacks. His dark curly hair was faded neatly on all sides. When he turned his gaze to her, she averted her eyes like she had been caught staring.

"Oh, bro, so sorry." Ian lifted his hands, showing off his palms and then left.

"I hope pretending to know you wasn't too creepy," the stranger said.

Mia gave a half-smile. She was both relieved and annoyed. Why did men only respect the boundaries set by other men?

"Camille told me to come rescue you," he explained.

"Camille," she echoed.

He extended his hand. "I'm Sean."

"Mia," she said, as they shook.

He grinned, and her stomach fluttered. "I know."

She blushed and smiled harder. "Oh, right."

They walked to the table together. Two other men, one of them Keegan, now sat with the group. Camille looked flushed and happy. Keegan sat next to her, their hands intertwined on the table.

"Hey, boo! I saw that loser harassing you," Camille said. "Sean is Keegan's friend. And you remember Sam, don't you? I know this was supposed to be a girls' night kinda, but they were out barhopping, and I figured I'd invite them over. But it was perfect timing anyway, because it saved that guy an ass whooping from your friends since Sean here volunteered to escort you back."

Mia laughed. "No worries. Thanks."

"He was kind of hot, though," Jessica said. She craned her neck. "Where'd he go?"

Rochelle laughed. "Aren't you dating someone?"

Jessica shrugged. "It was a casual thing, and it didn't work out. He was a little clingy."

Rochelle shook her head. "I'm so glad I'm out of the dating pool. I can't with men nowadays."

"Hey," said Sam, pretending to take offense. "We're not all bad."

"You're all various levels of frustrating," said Camille. Keegan made a noise in protest, and she laughed. They kissed.

Mia shook her head. "Well, he's probably hitting on someone else in a dress. I don't like pushy men. Or cheesy pickup lines."

"Noted," Sean said.

She blinked and looked at him. Butterflies again.

"Hey there! Got your orders here." A waiter appeared and passed out a few drinks. "The wings will be out soon."

Mia was very glad she had decided to accept the invitation. Her friends shared the milestones their children had met. Lori's daughters were all in band, one of her sons was in track, and the other had earned all B's on his report card. Rochelle texted her husband all night and shared his responses with the table. They laughed and tried to outdo themselves on the best responses. Keegan gushed about Luca while Camille beamed at him. Sam and Jessica were surprised to find out they had signed up for the same triathlon. They tried to convince the rest of the table to sign up, to which everyone declined except Lori, who agreed only if she was allowed floaties during the swim portion. Mia shared anecdotes about Isaiah.

When the group chatter died down, and a few left the table to dance, Sean turned his attention to Mia. "So, what do you do?"

"I work in finance. Kind of boring, I guess, but I like working with numbers. It can be soothing."

"Very cool," said Sean.

"Liar."

He laughed. "It's respectable."

"What do you do?" Mia asked.

"I work in marketing," he said. "Just as boring."

They laughed.

"Sounds more fun," Mia said.

He shrugged. "It pays the bills. Do you want to dance?"

"I would love to."

As the music played and the night progressed, Mia relaxed into her old self. She shared dances with Lori, Jessica, and Sam, but every time she found herself searching for a seat or a moment to pause, Sean was right there.

At the end of the night, they gathered outside the bar to bid each other goodbye. Clusters of people streamed from the entrance. It was nearing the end of September, and the light wind brought the promise of fall.

"Whew, it got cold!" exclaimed Rochelle.

Mia held onto her arm and grinned at her. "I'm just borrowing your warmth till you leave."

"We can go to the gym first thing in the morning," Lori told Jessica. Her words were slurred.

"Fantastic idea," Jessica agreed. "First you have to sleep off the booze."

"Oh, yeah. I might be a little bit of a cheap drunk, because I don't think I drank that much." She hiccupped, and the group laughed.

"Well, let's get you home," Jessica said. She wrote her number down for Sam. He blushed when she slipped it into his front shirt pocket. She laughed, winked, and escorted her friend to her car.

"She's a little direct, that one," Keegan informed his friend.

Rochelle's Uber arrived shortly afterwards. "Bye, guys! Mia, you need to come out more, girl. Live a little. I miss you." She hugged her tightly.

Mia smiled and gave her a kiss on the cheek. "I will. Let's get together soon. Maybe coffee or a playdate?"

"Do you need us to give you a ride? You can crash at my house, and we can ride together to Carol's in the morning." Camille said. "Sam's dropping us off. Or maybe he can make a detour to your house. Sorry, Sam, I'm volunteering you, if you don't mind."

"Nah, I'm good. I'm gonna grab a cab," Mia said.

"Okay, if, you're sure." Camille hugged her fiercely. "I'm so glad you came out. Sorry about the douche not getting the hint, but aside from that, I hope you had fun."

"I did."

"I, uh... I can drive you home, if you'd like."

Mia regarded Sean in surprise.

He quickly added, "I didn't drink much, so I'm good to drive. If you're worried."

"Well, we'll be on our way, then. Bye, you two!" Camille sang. Mia turned to her friend and saw she, Keegan, and Sam all looked amused. As they walked away, Camille took a moment to look back, grin, and wave furiously. "Have fun!" she yelled.

Mia looked at the ground, mortified. *Tomorrow, I'm going to kill Camille. The only question is where to hide the body.*

Sean cleared his throat. "Uh, sorry about that. I didn't mean for it—well, to sound like—some pushy..." He paused. "Line."

Mia just looked at him. Then, she burst out laughing.

He laughed, too, but didn't look like he got the joke.

"I'm sorry," she said, sighing. "I don't want to put you out. I'm okay with a cab."

"Oh," he said. "Okay. Um, well, have a great night. It was—it was really nice to meet you."

She smiled. "It was really nice to meet you, too."

Neither moved.

"I mean that sincerely," she added. "Not like, 'Nice to meet you,' because that's the automatic response. But it was just—nice to meet—" *Oh, my God, Mia, shut up.* She rubbed her forearm. "Anyway, it was nice."

Sean smiled at her, and she soaked in the moment. Then, it was over. "Well. I'll see you." He dipped his head once and started toward his car.

She felt abruptly off-kilter. The idea of being tipsy and alone in her house with her thoughts made her panic. "Actually!"

He paused and glanced back, startled. The orange glow of the parking lot lampposts highlighted his face, and she found him beautiful even in the unflattering light.

"Sorry. I didn't mean to be so loud. I just—" She closed the gap between them. The alcohol made her brave. "Is it too forward of me to say I want the night to be a little longer?"

Sean raised his eyebrows. "Um, no? I don't think so. I—did you want to go somewhere, or were you wanting me to drop you off?"

She shook her head in answer to the last question. She didn't want him to go to her house.

"Is there anywhere still open?" she asked.

He considered the question. "There might be another bar somewhere. But maybe just for another hour. Um, I guess there are some 24-hour diners I can look up. Are you hungry?"

She nodded. She wasn't.

"I do have some stuff at my apartment," he said, and his eyes widened. "Oh, God, sorry. I don't mean—"

"Okay," she blurted.

"Okay?"

"Going to a 24-hour diner full of drunks sounds like something college kids would do," she said.

He smiled, and a thrill raced through her. "Okay."

-Chapter 10 -

September 2016

S ean's apartment opened to a living room. It was neat and orderly, but not overly fussy. A loveseat sat across from the mounted television. A large bookshelf adorned one wall. It was mainly filled with books, but it also held stacks of DVDs, a few photos, and a small, pink teddy bear, which held a photo of an infant. It was an open floor design, which meant the kitchen and dining room blended together with a crisp floor divider separating carpet from tile.

He hung his keys near the door and told Mia she could set her things wherever she wanted, then walked to the kitchen cabinets and pulled out two glasses. She set her purse down on the counter and watched him fill the glasses with ice and water.

"I find drinking some water helps prevent a headache the next day." He walked over to her and handed her the cup. "Do you want to sit?" He motioned to the barstools.

"I didn't drink that much," she said, but she still drank from her cup. "And I'm okay standing. I feel like we sat a lot at the bar."

"You said you were hungry. Do you know what you want? I know I have some stuff here." He returned to the refrigerator and rummaged through it.

"I'm not very hungry." When he paused and looked back at her, confused, she felt blood rush to her face. "I mean—I guess I meant I was more snacky than anything."

He laughed. "Uh, okay. I think I have a few things." He rifled through his refrigerator and pantry. A few minutes later, he sat out a board with blocks of cheese, crackers, and strawberries.

"Geez, you entertain much?" she asked.

He laughed good-naturedly. "My family was in town, and I'm not much of a cook. You're just cashing in on the leftovers of my store-bought contributions." He raised his eyebrows. "Or maybe I just keep some things handy in case I find myself accidentally in the company of a pretty lady."

Mia bit into a cube of Havarti. "Mmm, that sounded like a line."

"It did! I'm sorry. That's my only line."

"That's what they all say."

"All men say they only have one line?" He looked amused.

"All men pretend they don't use lines. They pretend you're the only beautiful woman in the whole room, and that they were only ever drawn to you, and you are making their entire evening by gracing them with your presence and your conversation and your wit, when, really, they've been trying all of those lines and compliments and—and lines—"

"Hmm…"

"Yeah, I said lines twice." Maybe she had drunk more than she thought. "And all of those things were said to every woman who accidentally looked them in the eye, until they've whittled the field down to the one person who actually falls for the bullshit." Mia punctuated the air with a half-eaten strawberry.

Sean looked both surprised and amused. "If that's what you were talking about with the guy in the bar, no wonder he didn't leave you alone."

She sighed. "These are very good strawberries."

"You're very good at deflecting."

"You're very good at rescuing women at bars."

He chuckled. "I don't know if you needed rescuing."

"I wish I didn't," she murmured. She quickly ate the rest of the strawberry and wiggled her fingers in the air. "Do you have a napkin?"

He ripped a sheet off his paper towel roll. "Here you go."

"I just realized you haven't eaten anything, and I'm standing here stuffing my face."

He laughed. "I'm too busy shielding my poor male ego."

She grinned. "Whatever. You got the girl to go home with you in the end, right? I'd say that's a point for the ol' ego."

They smiled at each other, and Mia reveled in how easy the conversation felt. She had only met him tonight, but he already felt like a friend. She wondered if it was the alcohol at play or if she was simply enjoying not being alone.

"Well," he countered, "you were the one who asked to come over."

"You were the one who offered." She took a step toward him.

"Very true. But I didn't mean it like that."

He looked a little nervous; she loved it. She raised an eyebrow, a smile playing on her lips. "Like what?"

"Like," he paused. She was standing so close she could smell a hint of his aftershave. "I feel like this is where a line would come in handy."

She laughed. "This is probably where I say I never do this." She tilted her face upward, and he met her kiss. It was slow and gentle. His hand touched her waist and then slid to her back, finally resting near the base of her spine. He pulled her in closer, and she rested a hand on his shoulder.

The kiss ended, and she whispered, "I have done this, by the way."

He laughed in surprise. "I like you."

She kissed him again, but this time he met it with more heat. She undid his shirt as he kissed her neck. He returned his attention to her mouth, and she decided that if there was a moment she wanted to get lost in, it was this one. He undid the zipper on her dress, and it slid to the ground.

Don't think, Mia, she told herself.

She startled awake, disoriented. It was dark, and she heard someone breathing evenly next to her.

Sean.

Memories of the previous hours warmed her cheeks. Her body felt satiated, and her heart felt fluttery. Her stomach was in knots. She knew it wasn't logical to feel like she had cheated on someone, but it felt like she had cheated on someone.

She examined the shape of his body. His blinds were partially open and silver moonlight bathed his face. She felt a surge of lust and guilt.

She slid out of the bed and hunted for her underwear. It dawned on her that she didn't know his address. She wanted to call a cab, go home, sleep for another few hours, if possible, and pick up Isaiah.

Where was her dress? *Oh, yeah, the kitchen.*

It had been so long since she had awoken with another man in the bed. It made her feel both elated and uncomfortable. She wanted to crawl back under the covers and place her head on his chest. She imagined him half-asleep, shifting to accommodate her body, one of his arms wrapping around her. The longing was so strong, the image so domestic, it felt like a knife to the heart.

Her eyes filled with tears, as her breathing grew rapid. She was a caged bird, agitated, fluttering against the bars. She needed to leave. Immediately.

She spotted her dress and stepped into it.

"Hey." Sean's voice was warm and full of sleep. "You okay?"

Mia whipped around. "Hey." She said it quickly, afraid her voice would give away how close she was to crying.

He flicked on the hallway light, and she looked down, caught.

He rushed over. "What's wrong? Are you alright?"

She looked up for a second and nodded. "Yeah," she repeated, but her voice cracked. To her horror, fat tears started to fall.

"I'm—what's going on? I'm sorry, I'm a little bit confused." He hugged her, and the gesture made her fall apart. She started to sob.

"Oh my God," she said. She tried a few deep breaths. "I'm so sorry. This is so horrible. I'm—it's been a minute. I have to go home. I-I didn't mean—"

He let go and looked at her. "Did I miss—did I completely misconstrue—I thought—" He was holding her hand.

She wiped her face with the back of her free hand. "No, no, no. It's not you. It's just—well, my husband—" She started crying again.

He let go of her hand like he had touched an electric fence. "Husband?"

Goddammit, she thought.

"Can I get a tissue or something?"

He tore off a piece of paper towel.

Mia wiped her face and looked up at him. He looked both angry and confused. *I look crazy.*

"Don't worry. He's not—he died."

His eyes widened. "Oh."

She let out a short bark of laughter. "That sounds awful. He—he passed away a while ago. Over a year—I'm sorry. Wow, God, I'm so sorry. You don't need to know this. You were just trying to get laid, and I'm out here trying to be normal and—"

"Wait, hey, no. I was not just out trying to get—I—" He rubbed his face with his hands. He studied her for a moment. "You want some coffee?"

She shook her head. "No. I have to go. Maybe if I could have your address so I can call cab or something. I need to go home. I-I already messed this whole thing up worse than I could have possibly imagined."

"Woah, woah, slow down. It's okay. You don't have to go."

"I really do."

"Why?"

Mia paused. She raised her hand, palm up, and let it drop, deflated. "I don't know."

"I'm making coffee. You're sitting down. Go sit on the couch. It's okay."

Once the coffee was brewing, Sean came back into the living room and sat next to her. She wasn't sure if she was glad or offended that he had left space between them.

"You went out to be normal?" he prompted.

She pressed her lips together. "Yeah, I think that was the plan."

"Well, I went out to hang out with Keegan and Sam. There was no plan to get laid, thank you," he said.

She cringed. "Sorry. I didn't mean it like that."

He raised an eyebrow and gave a half-smile. "Like what?"

She laughed weakly, thankful. "I'm a hot mess."

"You lost your husband. You're supposed to be a mess." His tone was empathetic.

"Yeah…" She frowned, searching his eyes.

He looked away. "How do you like your coffee?" He stood and walked back to the kitchen.

"Oh, uh, some cream and sugar, thanks." She spoke to his back.

The coffee wasn't quite ready, so she took a few minutes to look around his living room. There were two large photographs of landscapes. One was of a small, one-story home sitting on top of a hill, a solitary tree to its left. Evening was approaching, and the colors of the setting sun blended into the light blue sky. The other picture was of a wooden bridge that crossed high over a rusting train track. Vague memories of herself and friends exploring the world they called home came back to her.

"Here you go."

Mia jumped slightly. "Oh, sorry, thanks. I was looking at the photographs. Those are really pretty." She blew on the coffee, took a sip, and set it on the coffee table.

He looked at the pictures and sat next to her again. "Do you like them?"

"Yeah," she said. "Makes me want to go on a weekend trip exploring some far-off countryside."

He laughed. "They're actually photos of places around here."

"Are they?" she asked, surprised.

"Yeah, maybe within an hour's drive at most."

"So, you bought these from a local artist, then?"

Sean grinned at her. "Not exactly." She felt she had missed something. "I took those."

She gasped. "Oh, wow! Did you? I really love them."

"Thank you. It's more of a hobby, but it does bring some fringe income every now and again." He studied his photographs for a few more moments. "You really don't have to go home. But I understand not wanting to sleep with a stranger."

She picked at a fingernail. "This is really weird, I know. I thought it'd be a little bit different now that it's been over a year."

She glanced at him and thought she saw an emotion flutter across his face, but it was so quick she wondered if she had imagined it.

"There's no real set time for this stuff. It's not like you reach year one and then everything is fine again," he said.

She looked at him quizzically.

"I think you should stay. It's almost morning anyway, then I can drop you off at your house. Or get you a cab if you really want, but I think sleeping a little longer might be a good idea. I can sleep on the couch, and you can take the bed."

"No, no, no. I don't want to kick you out of your bed," she said.

"You're always welcome in my bed," he said, then frowned. "Not exactly how I meant that to come out. Well, it's up to you. The bed, the couch, or, if you really want, I'll drive you home right now."

She didn't want to inconvenience him further. "I'll stay on the couch."

"No, you weren't supposed to pick the couch. I'll feel like an asshole. Plus, my mom raised me better."

She giggled. "I really am fine on the couch."

"Has anyone told you you're very difficult?"

She grinned wide. "Maybe once or twice."

"Mm-hmm." He walked to his bookshelf and picked out a DVD. "If you're insisting on the couch, then I have to do the gentlemanly thing and sit with you. And since we're staying up, we might as well do something productive like watch a movie. So, I hope you like terrible comedy, because according to a few people, that's my favorite genre."

After the movie started, he grabbed the throw that was draped across the back of the couch and spread it out on top of them. Mia felt herself relax. Eventually, she settled comfortably next to him. She felt herself blink heavily as the opening scene began.

When she woke again, she was back in his bed, but this time alone. The smell of coffee and cinnamon drifted through the air.

She hated that she only had her outfit from the night before, but at least the dress was mostly clean. She went to the bathroom and dug through his hygiene items. She washed her face and gargled with mouthwash. Her hair was a mess, so she pulled it down, raked her fingers through it, and pulled it into a ponytail.

Better.

She padded into the kitchen and he smiled. "Sleep okay?"

"You cheated," she said.

"Eh, you fell asleep and looked uncomfortable. Anyway, I'm out of eggs, so I made some oatmeal and coffee."

"You really didn't have to," she said. Her stomach grumbled. "But I appreciate it."

He smiled. "Well, it's also a little apology for rushing things with you yesterday."

"Oof, yeah. Sorry for the freak-out, but nothing I did yesterday was forced. Maybe the alcohol helped a bit, but I did want to come over."

He poured her coffee and added cream and sugar. "Well, that's a relief. Do you want me to grab you a shirt and some sweatpants or something?"

She took a large swallow of coffee and hissed. "Ow, that was dumb. That was hotter than I thought. And no, thank you. Let me do my walk of shame like a real woman. I still have my dignity, you know."

He laughed. "Okay."

It was a fifteen-minute drive to her house. They spoke very little, and by the time they parked, she felt sad.

She glanced at Sean. "Thank you." She wanted to say so much more but didn't know where to begin.

He smiled. "No problem."

The walk to her front door felt awkward. She never looked back, but she realized, based on the gentle noise of the motor, that he had waited until she was inside to drive off. He was a genuinely good person. The weight of the thought felt heavy around her neck. After all that had happened, did she deserve it?

-Chapter 11-

September 2016

Mia felt hungover from both the alcohol and the emotional outburst. After a shower, she walked to Carol's home, taking her time to soak in the morning air. This early in the morning, it felt like fall, but the cloudless sky allowed the sun to warm her body as she moved down the sidewalk.

She knocked on the door, and Carol appeared a few moments later. "Hi, dear! I'm so glad you went out and had fun!" She paused and called for Isaiah. "He did really good. Fell asleep just fine, but woke up early. He said he had a nightmare, but he didn't want to talk about it. He's already eaten breakfast."

Mia smiled and pulled out some cash. "Thank you so much. I appreciate it."

Carol waved her hand. "No, no, no. Camille prepaid for the night, and she told me to make sure not to accept any money from you, even if you insisted."

Mia laughed. "Of course she did. It feels weird just picking up."

"Well, don't feel weird. I love these boys," said Carol. "You know that. It's always a treat. Anytime you need some time for yourself, let me know, and I'd be happy to watch him."

Isaiah popped into view.

"You have fun with Luca?" Mia asked.

Isaiah nodded. "Where'd you go?"

"Just out with some friends, remember? You got your things?"

Isaiah lifted his backpack in response.

"Thanks again, Carol," Mia said. They waved good-bye and began the walk home.

"How come you stayed gone all night?"

She frowned. "I told you I'd pick you up in the morning. We stayed up way past your bedtime, and I didn't want to interrupt your sleep. Or Carol's."

A car rumbled down the street, its muffler complaining loudly. The smell of exhaust lingered.

Isaiah stole a glance at his mother. "You can pick me up late at night if you want to."

"What's going on, mi vida?"

He shrugged.

"Did you sleep okay?"

He shook his head.

"Do you want to talk about it?"

He shook his head again.

"Hmm, okay. But if you want to talk about it later, I'm all ears, okay?" She took his hand and squeezed it twice but he didn't return the gesture.

They walked the rest of the route home in silence.

Mia was allowed two weeks of bereavement leave. The days were filled with questions about decisions she felt were unfair to ask at the moment. Where would he be buried? What would be written in the obituary? What headstone did she want? Would he be cremated or buried? Where would the funeral take place? Mia hardly had a chance to sit down. She was numb, not truly grieving yet, operating under muscle memory. She pictured herself as a marionette under the control of an inexperienced puppeteer, her body making jerky motions as she finalized decisions.

The police conducted a short investigation. She was afraid of the toxicology report, though in the end, she was informed that he had been drunk and nothing else. Was it better or worse that he had numbed himself enough to pull the trigger?

It took Isaiah a few days to ask where his father was. Mia didn't tell him until the day before the funeral. Every time she opened her mouth, her voice disappeared.

Even then, Isaiah asked when his father was coming home for months. Death was a location, not a finality. In his mind, his father had gone away for an unexpected trip, a trip that would last a long time, but not forever.

When Mia returned to work, she found that although Isaiah didn't understand everything about death, he learned it was to be feared. It could take anyone from him at a moment's notice. She'd try to prepare Isaiah, but every drop-off went the same way. Isaiah would panic as soon as they walked into the daycare center. She'd pick him up, and he'd flail. Red-faced and out of breath, she'd burst into his designated room, smiling apologetically as he continued to scream. The teachers would gently coax him off her. Eventually, they'd loosen his grip, and he'd turn to his favorite teacher, gripping her as tightly as he had gripped his mother. He would give up physically fighting her departure and instead beg her to stay. His screams of, "Don't go, too, Mama. Don't go!" would follow her to her car.

Every drop-off, she'd try to outrun them and sit, body shaking, for a few minutes outside of the daycare before she could drive away. Every pickup, he'd jump up from playing, ecstatic, and hug her. "I thought you were gone forever!" Every pickup, she'd hug him fiercely, "I'm only at work, baby. I'm only at work. I'll always come back."

She negotiated time to work from home so she could spare Isaiah and herself the trauma of drop-off. As with all difficult things, time eased the burden. At some point, he accepted the fact that his mother would indeed return for him. The panicked drop-offs may only have lasted a month or two, but to Mia, they had felt eternal.

She made the mistake of telling her mother-in-law, Donna.

"Why would you go back to work, then?" she asked, appalled.

Mia stiffened, surprised. "Because I need to pay the mortgage."

"You got life insurance, didn't you? We didn't get a dime, and you don't see me complaining. If I got that money, I would have been staying home, caring for my baby. He's so small for you to be letting other people raise him."

Mia seethed inside, but said nothing. She figured Donna would die angry about her son leaving his money to his wife and child. She had heard whisperings from a few people, but suspected the leaked information was said to rustle up gossip rather than actual concern. Donna was not shy about insinuating that Mia had received a large sum of money, too large a sum, and was keeping it out of greed rather than necessity.

A month after the funeral, Austin's family and her own began to reach out. They offered their condolences, then discussed some financial hardship. Initially, she had offered money to cover small bills or car repairs. The life insurance had felt like blood money, a benefit she didn't deserve. She felt sick to her stomach whenever people called her lucky, though she knew in a way she was fortunate to have the financial help. Guilt outweighed any arguments to deny loans. At first. When the time came for them to repay, she realized no one had ever really meant to pay her back. They rarely answered her calls.

One day, furious, she learned how to say no to everybody. "This isn't my money to give. It's my son's. Austin left this money for his child. I can't help."

It was a win that increased the divide between her and Austin's family. She wanted to explain she had placed the same boundary with her own extended family, but in the end, she figured it didn't matter. Grudges formed in grief weren't rational, and she knew she was as guilty as them.

∞ ∞ ∞

"Can we play Legos?" Isaiah asked when they arrived home.

"Sure, I'll be up in your room in a second." Her offer was heavyhearted. She wanted nothing more than to curl up in bed and sleep away the morning. He ran off, and she plodded to the kitchen to start a pot of coffee. She scrolled through her phone as the coffee dripped, its rich aroma enveloping her.

"Hey!" She looked up, startled. Isaiah was pouting. "You said you were coming to play with me. I was waiting."

Guilty, she stuffed her phone into her back pocket. "Oh! I was just making a cup of coffee real quick. See, it's done brewing. Want to grab me the creamer?"

He ran to the refrigerator. "Okay!"

Coffee in hand, she followed him to his bedroom. There they played for about an hour before she felt like she had hit a brick wall.

Next time, I'm asking for a late pickup, Mia mused.

Her backside buzzed. She fished out her phone and saw the message. *Hey, it's Sean.*

Butterflies erupted, and she bit her lip.

She typed and deleted a text twice. Isaiah sensed the distraction. "Are you still playing?" She put the phone facedown. "Yeah. Just got a text."

A few minutes later, it buzzed again. *Hope you're feeling better.*

"Mom!" exclaimed Isaiah.

She looked up, surprised. "What?"

"You're just playing with your phone."

"Isaiah, stop exaggerating. I looked at my phone twice. We've been playing for a long time," she said, as fatigue pressed heavily on her shoulders.

He looked down, angry. "You don't have to play with me."

"I didn't say I didn't want to play with you. I just—"

"You don't like playing with me."

Her body tensed. "What? Where is this coming from? I play with you all the time!"

He started flicking the Legos in front of him. They landed around the table. He pushed her tower over.

"Isaiah," she warned. "Stop that."

He didn't look at her. Instead, he began to throw the Lego pieces.

"Isaiah! Knock it off! Pick up your Legos if you don't want to play with them."

He jumped up and ran over to his toys. One by one, he took them out of the bin and threw them. He started yelling. "I don't like these! I hate these! I don't like you!"

Shock turned into a rage so great it almost blinded her. She watched him, stunned, as his room quickly transformed into a mess. She thought of the cleanup effort. She thought of how tired she was. She felt disrespected. She was the parent. He was the child. She was supposed to give him directions. He was supposed to listen.

But he was not. He was yelling, throwing.

She was frozen and furious.

"I hate you!"

The words knocked the breath out of her. They were a slap to the face. And then, with just as much of a sting, came clarity.

He was drowning.

She knew this. She had him in therapy. It still felt like an epiphany. She had no idea what to do. He continued yelling as he threw his toys, and a wave of shame fell over her. How often had her first instinct been to discipline, to act as if he needed to behave appropriately? Had she ever allowed him space to grieve, truly grieve, in all its ugly forms?

"I love you, Isaiah. Do you know that? I love you. So, so, much. I am the luckiest mom in the whole world. And do you know why? Because I have you. You are everything to me. You are so special and so wholesome and so loveable. And every day, I wake up thankful I get to be your mom. I am so happy I have you. I love you."

She kept talking, not thinking, just feeling. At first, Isaiah was yelling so loudly, she didn't know if he could even hear her. But eventually, he stopped and watched her. She kept talking, encouraged, repeating phrases whenever necessary.

He kneeled in front of her, and she stopped. When their eyes met, he burst out crying. His sobs were so painful they caught her off guard. He collapsed onto her, and she gathered his crumpled body, holding him as tightly as she could.

She felt awful. Her first reaction, her first thoughts, were of herself, not her son. Her first impulse was to discipline, not investigate.

Emotions spent, he hugged her tightly around her neck.

"I love you, Mommy."

She squeezed him back. "I love you, too, baby."

"I had a bad dream." His body was shaking.

"What was it about?" Her stomach twisted.

"You were gone. You left me. And when I woke up, you were still gone."

She sighed. She knew that dream. "Oh, that's why you were so upset about me being gone all night."

"I thought you left me forever. Can you stay with me?"

She hesitated. "I think sleepovers should be fun for you again. But how about this? No matter what, I will always come back for you. If I'm not there in the morning, it's because I'm on the way, and I'll be there soon."

Isaiah let go of her and stepped back. "What about when you die?"

"I won't die."

"Never?"

"Well, everybody dies." *Shit.*

"What?" he asked, upset. "When?"

"When they're very, very, very, very old."

"Why did Daddy die? He wasn't old."

Wow, I'm terrible at this. "Daddy died because—because he was sick. Not like normal sick. He was... I don't know how to explain this." She paused to collect her thoughts. "I need some time to think about how to explain this. But I don't want you to ever worry about me. I promise I will live for a very long time. Okay?"

"How long?"

"Over a hundred," she said.

"Over a hundred!" He was impressed.

"Yes. Over a hundred. And you and I will be together the whole time, okay?"

He hugged her again. She prayed the universe wouldn't make her a liar.

Mia looked around the room. She didn't have the emotional energy to pick everything up. "Let's clean this later. Why don't we watch a movie downstairs, yes?"

Isaiah jumped up and down. "Yeah! With snacks?"

"Yes, with snacks. Just—let me take a shower really quick. Mommy's super stinky." She crinkled her nose. "Whew!"

He giggled. "Okay!"

"I'll just be like ten minutes. We can start the movie first," she said.

Once the movie started, Mia escaped to the bathroom. She set a ten-minute timer on her phone and stood under the torrent of hot water. Her tears mixed with the stream. She knew it was healthy for Isaiah to see her cry and process Austin's death, but she couldn't bring herself to let him see her break down. She was the safety net to his stability. How could she show him she was barely keeping it together?

-*Chapter 12* -

September 2016

M ia's stomach grumbled, and she realized her rushed breakfast wouldn't last her until dinnertime. She stretched and glanced at the clock on her office wall before gathering her things and walking to the nearest cubicle. "Hey, John. I'm stepping out for lunch. I'll be back by two if anyone is looking for me, but I'm also reachable by cell."

"Manager's meeting is at two," John said, not looking up.

"Oh, yeah, shoot. They keep adding those things. Well, I'll be back by 1:45, then."

"Alrighty."

Mia made her way to the local sandwich shop and got her usual, half of a loaded pastrami sandwich and a cucumber-tomato salad.

As soon as she picked up her sandwich and salad from the counter, she heard her phone chime. She sighed heavily and found a seat at a table. She took a few bites of her sandwich and then fished out her phone.

"They better not be moving the meeting up," she mumbled.

Hi there. The number wasn't a saved contact.

She tapped on the message, and her stomach sank.

It's Sean. Hope you're well.

She had never texted him back after the situation with Isaiah. Almost an entire week had passed, and she didn't know what to do, so she set the phone facedown and ate the rest of her lunch.

When she was done, she wiped her hands and opened the message. She had to go back to work soon. *Hey.*

The response was immediate. *How are you?*

Good. Eating lunch. You?

Working.

She smiled. *More like slacking if you're on the phone. :)*

No messages flashed for a moment, so she distracted herself by saving his number.

When his response came, she grinned. *Haha, good point. In an effort to not get fired, I should hurry and ask if you'd like to get together for dinner?*

She noticed the time on her phone: 1:45.

Alarmed, she jumped up, cleared the table, and hurried to her car. Before she drove off, she made sure to text back. *That sounds great. Call you later?*

∞ ∞ ∞

"Camille!" Mia was pacing her living room. Isaiah was in the kitchen finishing a grilled cheese sandwich.

"What's wrong?"

"Nothing's wrong. I'm just about to hyperventilate. I'm in a panic."

"About?"

"A date."

Mia heard a sharp inhale over the phone. "A date? Oh my gosh, that's so awesome! With who? Wait! Is it with Sean? Tell me it's Sean."

"It's Sean."

Camille squealed. "I knew it!"

"I don't know, though! We haven't really talked about it much. I have to call him in a little bit to figure out the day and—"

"I'll watch Isaiah if your dad can't," Camille said quickly.

"Camille. I don't know. I feel weird about it."

"Do you not like him? Don't force yourself to go out with someone just because he asks."

Mia smiled at the shift in her friend's tone. Camille was fiercely protective of her. "I don't feel obligated. I want to."

"Oh, good, because that man is fine!" A male voice said something Mia didn't pick up. Camille laughed. "What? I'm just saying. Make uglier friends, I don't know." A pause. "Oh, you can like girls on Instagram, but I can't say anything—Mia, I'll call you back. I gotta go get some ointment for some hurt feelings, but definitely make that date!"

Mia laughed and disconnected the call. She shoved the phone into her back pocket and walked into the kitchen to pour Isaiah a glass of chocolate milk. He smiled at her, and she kissed the top of his head. She blew out a breath and walked back to the living room, wringing her hands for a few moments before sitting down on her couch. She stood up, paced, and then sat again. *Just call him, Mia.*

He answered on the second ring. "Hey!"

"Sean? Hey, hi. It's Mia. I was just calling you back." She ran a hand nervously through her hair.

"Yeah. I'm glad. I have to be honest. I wasn't sure if you'd call, but it's nice to hear from you."

She grimaced. "Yeah. I—sometimes things get crazy around the house, and I mean to text back, but I don't."

"No problem. My friend Sam's the same way, funny enough. Man is terrible at communicating overall, though, so there's that." He laughed. "Plus, you have, what did you say your son's name is? Isaac?"

"Isaiah."

"Isaiah! Sorry, yes, Isaiah. Being a mom is a job in itself, so working and raising a person is a ton."

A smile played on her lips. "It definitely is. You know all about mom life?"

He chuckled. "Well, I appreciate it. My mom was a single mother, and she worked and raised me and my sister all by herself."

"She never remarried?"

"She's married now, but she didn't actually start seriously dating anyone until we were in high school. I have to admit I wasn't that nice to Mark in the beginning, but he's actually a good guy."

"Oh, good for her. That's awesome."

"It is. She deserves it. Especially for putting up with me for so long by herself."

Mia laughed. "Were you a wild child?"

"I had no fear. Which, I always tell her, comes from her. But I definitely contributed to a few of her gray hairs," he said.

"I appreciate fearless women. I always feel so shy and reserved," she said.

"Reserved? I don't know, you were pretty bold with your speech the other day."

Mia's brows knit together. "Oh! My rant about guys and lines? Sorry, I think that was pseudo-bravery from the alcohol. I'm usually a bit milder."

"Well, I'd love to find out," said Sean. He cleared his throat. "I was wondering if you wanted to come watch The Carolina Brothers play next weekend? I don't know if you know them?"

"Um, can't say I do."

"They're a really great local band! They do covers a lot, but they also write their own songs. You mentioned liking live music when we were at the bar. They play a lot of urban jazz. I don't know, it's usually a great show."

She smiled broadly. "I would love to. I just have to see if my dad is able to watch Isaiah. It shouldn't be a problem. He loves having him. What time would it be?"

"Um, well, you let me know what you have time for. The show starts at 8:30, so we should get there by 7:45. If you have time to spare, I can pick you up at six so we can grab a bite to eat first."

"That should be fine," she said. "The six o'clock pick up, I mean."

She could hear him grinning over the phone. "Great. It's a date. I'll see you then."

She hung up the phone and squealed. She felt giddy.

Isaiah walked into the living room. Crumbs lined the outside of his mouth. "What happened?" he asked.

Mia felt caught. "Oh! Uh, nothing. I just got off the phone with a friend, and we had a good conversation."

He smiled. "I like when you're happy."

"Oh?"

"You smile."

Mia tried not to let her smile disappear. "Do I not smile normally?"

"Not really."

She used a thumb to wipe a corner of his mouth. "You done with your sandwich?"

He pulled his head away and wiped his mouth with the back of his sleeve. "Yeah."

"You put your plate in the sink?"

He made a face and slunk back into the kitchen.

Mia shook her head. "You always put your dirty dishes in the sink, baby!"

"I know!" he yelled back.

She huffed. "If you know, then why don't you ever do it?"

"Mo-om," he complained. "I just did."

She rubbed her forehead for a second. "Anyway, next weekend I think you're going to see Grandpa. I just have to text him."

"Really? Yay! Are you coming, too?"

Mia sent a quick message asking her father if he was free the following

Saturday and if he could watch Isaiah. "Hmmm? Oh, um, probably for a little bit, but you guys will have some one-on-one time."

He frowned. "Are you going to leave for a long time?"

"Oh, no, baby. Just a few hours. I won't be gone all night. I promise, okay?"

He nodded.

"Plus," she added, "he's coming over this weekend for your grandma's birthday, and we'll all be here for that."

Her phone buzzed. *No plans. I'm watching him here or at your house?*

The idea of her father meeting Sean gave her heartburn. *Your place.*

Her father quickly agreed and she smiled, pleased. She slid her phone into her back pocket and walked into the kitchen. "Alright, buddy. Date is set. Bath time!"

-Chatper 13-

November 2005

Mia's study group ran a few minutes late. She burst into the Italian restaurant slightly out of breath. She heard a voice call out her name and spotted Austin toward the southwest part of the restaurant. He stood up, and they embraced when she got to the table.

"You made it!" he said.

"Yeah!" she laughed. "Sorry, study group."

"I get it. So, how's it been?"

"Good! Good. My final is next Friday, thank God. I'm so over this semester, it's not even funny," she said. Ever since Austin had scribbled his number on that torn piece of paper, they had been texting and calling each other. They had met once for coffee, Austin gifting her the promised slice of cherry pie, but schedules had prevented an actual date until today. "How are you?"

"I'm good." He smiled at her and then gave her a devilish look. "We eat dessert first here. I already ordered, because the food is decent, but the dessert is what sells this place. And I really wanted you to try it."

She blinked. "Oh, okay."

His look turned sheepish. "I'm not ordering your whole meal. Just dessert. Hope you're not on a diet."

Before she could respond, the waiter appeared with one plate. Two of the largest cannolis she had ever seen sat on it. He laid it gently on the table and asked Mia what she wanted to drink.

"Oh, wow. Um, I guess a water."

"Are you guys ready to order? I assume you need a few minutes?"

Austin answered, "Yeah, just a few if you don't mind."

Mia turned to him, wide-eyed, after the waiter left. "Dinner! I feel like this could feed me for a week!"

He picked one up and bit into it, the cream oozing slightly out of the other end. His eyes lit up and he smiled. "It's so good, I promise," he said, mouth full.

She studied hers for a second. "You know, I've never had a cannoli before. I don't think it'd be a dessert I'd automatically think to get."

"That's why you met me. So I can broaden your dessert horizons."

She looked up and grinned. She picked up her cannoli and took a bite. "Oof, it's definitely rich! Wow, that's really good. I'm not sure I'll be able to finish this bad boy, though. This thing is a monster."

He shrugged. "Not a problem. We can take it with us."

"Where are we going anyway? You said restaurant and a surprise. I don't think this is the real surprise, is it?"

He laughed. "Are you always in a rush?"

She opened her mouth in protest and let out a small laugh. "Yeah, I guess so. But you didn't answer the question."

"Hmmm, well, if I told you, it wouldn't be much of a surprise now, right?" He winked.

"Uh-huh. Well, if you plan on murdering me later, you'll never get away with it." She shot him a heavy-lidded look and took another bite.

The comment drew a burst of laughter from Austin. "Oh, really? How do you know I haven't watched a bunch of *CSI* or something?"

She shook her head. "First off, they always catch the guy because he's all cocky. Plus, I already told Camille that if I'm missing tomorrow, it's you." She winked back at him.

He drew in a breath. "Damn. I guess plan B it is."

"Which is?"

"Ready to order?" The waiter had returned.

Mia gasped. "Oh, no! I haven't even opened the menu. I'm so sorry. Just a few more minutes."

The waiter nodded curtly and walked off.

She grabbed the menu guiltily. "Let me see this thing before that poor man comes again for nothing. What's good here?" She nibbled on her dessert while pondering the options.

"I'm a fan of their seafood pasta. It has scallops, shrimp, lobster meat, everything."

The cannoli felt heavy in her stomach. "Maybe something a little lighter."

"The salads are okay if you're into them. Their tilapia is good."

When the waiter appeared for the third time, Mia ordered a salad and Austin the seafood pasta. Her eyes fell over his frame. "Where do you store all that?" she asked. And he laughed.

The dinner seemed to stretch indefinitely. Mia was lost in between the moments. He speared a scallop with his fork and stretched it out toward her. *Try it.* She took it gingerly with her teeth and nodded as she chewed. *It's good.* They talked about their classes, but also about their fears of the real world, the anxiety of stepping out of school and into that first real job that wanted a degree.

A chime sounded, and he looked at his phone. He looked startled, and his eyes darted around the restaurant.

Mia frowned. "What's wrong?"

"Oh, there he is, hey!" Austin waved their waiter over. "Can I get the check? Thanks." He turned to Mia and smiled. "It's time for the surprise. I guess it's nothing super special, but I found out you really like going to the botanical gardens."

Her eyes brightened. "I do! Who told you? Wait, we're going now? They're closed."

"Ah!" He stuck a finger in the air. "They're usually closed now. But not when they have their light display up. Camille told me you loved the place and mentioned their light show thing. They still somehow close earlier than I would have expected. Which is why we kind of have to hurry."

Austin paid the tab and asked for a box. Mia gently set her cannoli into the Styrofoam container. They gathered their things and went to their separate cars, the cannoli forgotten on the table.

"I'll follow you?" asked Mia.

"Sure."

The parking lot was half filled when they arrived. He hurried over to her car and opened the door.

"Oh," she said. She feigned surprise and touched her fingers to her chest. "What a gentleman."

"I aim to please," he said with a slight bow of the head. "I wanted to get here a little earlier so we'd be one of the first people but that's okay. Have you been here when they put up the lights?"

The wind picked up and carried the promise of winter. Austin slipped his hands into his pockets and she looped an arm through his, drawing herself close. Her light cardigan was no longer warm enough. "You know, I actually haven't. I remember hearing about it, but I've been so busy lately, it slipped my mind. Usually, I just come by when the flowers are in full bloom. Or to eat at their café."

"The café is kind of pricey," he said.

Mia shrugged. "I mean, I don't come all the time, but sometimes when I want a pretty spot to read a book and eat a sandwich, I'll swing by."

"Alright, money bags. Maybe you should have paid for dinner," he said and laughed.

She raised an eyebrow. "Okay? It's not that expensive."

He looked over at her. "I was just kidding."

She walked in silence for a moment. Then, a gasp. "Oh, damn it."

"What?"

"I forgot my cannoli at the restaurant."

He frowned. "Oh. Well, that sucks. I even thought about grabbing it for you, but I figured you'd remember when you were grabbing your stuff."

A flash of guilt washed over her. "Sorry."

"No big deal. Let's go inside."

They walked through the gardens, pausing at each light display. The cooler weather meant most of the vegetation wasn't flowering. The larger bushes stood alone with lit displays peppering the walk way. Mia smiled up at the lights that were threaded over a makeshift tunnel. Thin wire looped over their heads, and she ignored the urge to skip through with her hands outstretched.

They stopped at one of the tents that offered hot chocolate. Austin chose the classic flavor, and Mia opted for peppermint.

"This is the highest markup I've ever seen for store bought chocolate powder," Austin said.

"You're paying for the experience, though!" Mia's giggle was infectious, and Austin drank deeply from his cup.

"That's true," he said. "Especially if it's an experience with you."

She felt an explosion of butterflies when he turned his eyes toward her, and she averted her gaze almost instantly. She hid most of her smile by taking a sip of her own drink.

The trees that were closest to the walkway sported multi-colored lights.

She walked to one that was lit up with creamy oranges, cool blues, and fuchsia tones. The colors spilled onto her skin. "This is so beautiful."

She studied the artwork a moment and turned to see if Austin was still nearby. His eyes were trained on her, and she felt a blush creep up her neck. She hoped the dim light hid it well. He smiled. "You're so pretty," he said. He closed the gap between them and kissed her. When they pulled apart, he gazed into her eyes. She looked away first.

A gust of wind reminded her she was cold.

She hissed in response, and he pulled her close. "It's getting cold," she said. "It was nice with the sun out, but now it's gone, and all that's left is ice."

"Ice?" he asked.

"In the wind." Her hand danced around slowly, as if examining the air. "It's reminding us winter is around the corner."

He grinned. "I like how you explain things."

Water droplets landed with a soft pat-pat on her face. She pulled away from him and frowned at the sky. "Oh, man, is it starting to rain?"

"It sure is. I guess that's the end of the light tour! C'mon, let's go."

They ran back to her car as the random drops turned into a light drizzle.

"Thanks for tonight, rain and all," she said.

"Thanks for coming out." He kissed her again, this time longer. "You know, um, it doesn't have to end right this second. It's not that late."

She bit her lip and looked at the sky. "It's not, but I do have to get up early for work and then I have classes all day afterwards."

He kissed her again. "No one says you have to stay up that long."

She put a hand on his chest and pushed him away. "I feel like a few mistakes might be made if we extend the evening."

A smile spread on his face as he lightly gripped her waist. "I'm not opposed to a few mistakes."

She laughed. "I-I appreciate the offer of not staying up for a long time, but I really do have to get going. Plus, I'm freezing right now, and I think it's starting to rain harder."

"Are you sure? It's really warm in my room." He wrapped her in a hug.

She melted into his chest for a second and breathed him in. His cologne smelled amazing. For a moment, she was tempted. She did like him a lot. His hand started to wander, and she kissed him lightly on the lips. "I have to go."

He sighed and let her go. "Can't blame a man for trying. I'll see you later?"

"I'll call you," she promised. "Unless I die of hypothermia. I gotta start my car and get this heat going."

He laughed. "It's not that cold."

"I'm freezing."

"Why are girls always cold?"

"I don't know." She climbed into her car. After it roared to life, she blasted the heat. When she looked up, he was gone. Her phone chimed.

C U later beautiful

-Chapter 14-

September 2016

The doorbell rang as Mia pulled the lasagna from the oven. She wiped her brow and began coarsely chopping greens for the salad.

Isaiah raced to the door. "I'll get it!" She heard him shout when the door opened. "Grandpa!"

"Hey! There's my little buddy. How are you, mijito? Your mami in the kitchen?"

"Yeah," she called out. "Just pulled out dinner. Needs to sit a minute."

David appeared in the entryway of the kitchen, still holding Isaiah. He set his grandson down with a grunt. "'Ta pesa'o este niño, no?"

She nodded. "I keep telling him to stop growing, but he won't listen."

Isaiah frowned. "Stop talking Spanish."

"What!" David put his hands on his hips. "You need to learn Spanish. Tienes que aprender. You're Mexican! It's part of who you are! Mija, you need to do a better job of teaching him."

"You teach him! It's hard! He's half Mexican. All his friends speak English. His teachers speak English. The TV speaks English. Everything speaks English. You barely speak Spanish."

David conceded the point and tousled his grandson's hair. "Smells good in here."

Mia smiled. "That's what I thought. Thanks. I felt like Italian today, so we're having lasagna. And some side salads."

"Blegh," said Isaiah. "Salads are gross."

"They're good for you," chided Mia. She threw the chopped greens into a bowl, added slices of olives, tomatoes, cucumbers, and cheese.

"Plus," said David, "that's how you get some of Grandma's birthday cake!"

He pointed to the store-bought chocolate cake on the counter.

Isaiah crossed his arms. "I thought birthdays meant you could just eat cake and good food."

"Well, it's not your birthday," said David.

"I know, Grandma's birthday. I bet she would say I could have more cake and no salads."

David chuckled. "I think you're right, mijo. I think she probably would have spoiled you rotten."

"You think she's happy we do a birthday for her even though she's in heaven?"

Mia placed salad tongs in the bowl. "Yeah. I think she is. I think she's sad she doesn't get to play with you every day, but I think she likes that we still talk about her. I know she would have been very excited to play with you."

"Dad, will you give me a hand with these things?"

They moved the food over to the dining table and then settled into their spots. David took a few bites and smiled at her.

"This is really good, Mia. You got your cooking skills from your mama. I sure as hell don't know my way around the kitchen."

She smiled. "There's always time to teach you, you know."

David grunted. "Old dog, new tricks."

"You're not that old, Dad. I could teach you a thing or two. I'm not even sure how you manage on your own."

"Eh. I'm a simple man. But I do appreciate the occasional takeout, or when you cook."

"Well, thank you."

Isaiah chimed in. "Mom's the best cook! Except when she does broccoli. It's just wet and yuck."

"I think you just don't like vegetables," said Mia.

"You wanna grow up big and strong, right?" asked David. Isaiah looked skeptically at his grandpa. "That's right. Vegetables are what help your muscles get giant." He made a muscle. "Like your grandpa here. Might be old, but I'm strong as an ox."

They laughed together, and Mia felt her heart swell.

We're getting better, Mom.

Mia was a mama's girl from day one, and it never changed. Maybe it was that her father worked long hours, or maybe it was their similar personalities. Whatever the case, there was love and loyalty between them, but never closeness.

Gabriela was the glue to their little family. When a distracted driver took her from them, the family was destroyed. Sometimes Mia thought they would never be a family again, just people who knew each other. She didn't realize how much she had missed her family until Isaiah was born and provided another chance.

Dinner complete and Isaiah done with his cake, it was time to look through her photos. There was a ritual to her mother's birthday, one that had begun when Isaiah was two or three. It had started after Mia told Austin and her father that she was afraid of losing pieces of her mother, that she was afraid she wouldn't be able to pass along the essence of who Gabriela was to her son.

"Sometimes I don't even remember what she looked like until I look at her photos."

David's eyes went glassy. Abruptly, he had turned and walked briskly to another room. Mia thought he had left to avoid crying in front of them. He returned with a determined look and a large photo album. "Then, let's look at photos together." Thus, the tradition was born.

Now Austin's missing, too, Mia thought.

Isaiah pointed at a photo. Gabriela was facing the camera and smiling wide. Several necklaces of various lengths hung over her chest. Loud sunglasses were pushed up onto the top of her head like a makeshift headband. Her dark, wavy hair fanned out from a stiff breeze. Mia was young, no older than nine. Her smile was small, barely visible, but she looked content. She leaned against her mother, her eyes looking away from the camera.

Isaiah stuck a finger on the photo. "Is that you, Mom?"

He knew the answer, but still liked asking. Mia smiled. "Yes, that's me. And that's your grandma. She had the best laugh."

"Where were you?"

David answered the question. "Um, let's see. I think we were on our way to visit your grandma's parents, José and Teresa."

Mia remembered the trips they had taken to visit various family members. She enjoyed visiting family, but what she had always loved most were the trips themselves. It didn't matter how long the drive or how cramped the back seat, she loved the trip. It was a time of banter, small talk, road games, and as many snacks as she could con her parents into buying her. The rules were bent during road trips, limits were generous. Those were the moments in which she felt the safest, when they had felt most like a family.

"Gabriela! Vámonos!" said David. He was holding Mia's hand as his wife walked undecidedly around the gas station. "We still have six hours to go."

"Oh, calm down. We need to stretch our legs. Poor Mia has been in the car forever, haven't you, nena?"

Mia smiled, uncertain of what was being asked of her.

"Don't bring her into this. She's fine. She's gone to the bathroom," he said. "Just grab your soda and your chocolate bar. That's what you get every time, you just like to pretend that you're not predictable."

Gabriela let out a sharp exhale. She stomped over to the refrigerated displays, picked out a Coke, and swiped a chocolate bar on her way to the register.

"Happy?" she said when they were all in the car.

David glanced into the rearview mirror. "Mia, when you grow up, just own up to what your favorite snacks are. Don't hem and haw and drive your husband crazy." He exited the gas station parking lot and reentered the highway a few minutes later.

Mia sipped her juice and said nothing.

He glanced at his wife. "I swear all you women go through some course in high school on how to drag out decisions. Especially about food. Especially around men."

Gabriela swatted him. "Don't listen to him, Mia. Take your time, otherwise you'll end up regretting a rushed decision."

He scoffed. "Rushed decision. What else would you have got? You would have taken another half hour to feel better about the same choice."

She ignored him. "Oh, look, Mia! Cows!"

Mia put up the albums as her father taught Isaiah how to patch a hole in the drywall. That was also part of the tradition. She felt there was some innate drive inside of men that made them think the only way to express care or love was to fix, to save. Of course, she understood the need to feel useful. So, she would cook for her father, they would reminisce, he would fix something in her house that she left for him, and then he'd read Isaiah a story before heading for home.

Several weeks prior, Isaiah had angrily thrown one of his toys in the hallway. It hit the wall and made a small hole. She knew how to fix it, but left it alone, knowing her father would search for something to help with on the day of his wife's birthday.

Mia turned her attention to the dishes, her mind on her mother. It was funny, the memories that stood out to her. Most were from the mundane, the everyday. She missed the scent of her mother's soap. She knew the brand, but it didn't smell the same now as it had when she had her head rested gently on her mother's shoulder. She missed how her mother chopped vegetables, swiftly and efficiently. She missed her mother's coral-colored fingernails as they traced an invisible line under the words in her storybooks. She missed having opportunities to exist in the same room as her. And she regretted passing up on those chances.

Had I known...

Mia usually took the bus, even though her mother was an English teacher in her middle school. She explained that she liked sitting with her friends and that her mother left too early in the morning. Catching the bus meant lingering at home a few extra minutes. This was partly true, but mostly, it was because of the social shame she would have felt hanging out with her teacher-mother at a time when embarrassment was a personality trait.

"At least you're not in her class," said a boy named Logan. "If my mom were a teacher and I was in her class, I'd skip school every day. Otherwise, she'd probably pick me for all the hard questions. My mom's so mean."

"I think that would be illegal," said her friend Beth.

"It's not illegal, stupid."

"Don't call me stupid. I'll tell your mean mom. Jerk."

Mia smiled. "It's against the rules."

"See? That's what I meant." Beth smirked and stuck her tongue out at Logan.

He shrugged. "Whatever. I gotta go."

Gabriela chaperoned a few middle school mixers, which Mia sometimes tolerated. One evening, she and Beth got ready at Mia's house, experimenting with the makeup they had been gifted on previous birthdays. "If we put it all together, we'll have so many options," said her friend. "Trust me. I see my sister do this stuff all the time."

Mia opted for a sweater dress and boots that had a bit of heel. Beth decided on pants and a glittery shirt. "You look awesome!" they squealed to each other.

Gabriela drove them, but Mia begged her to let them walk in alone. "Maybe you could wait a few minutes?" Her mother made a face. "Mom! We're not little kids anymore! Please? Or we can go afterwards. I just don't want to look like you're babysitting us or something."

"Alright, mi tesoro." Gabriela had rolled her eyes and grinned. "Too cool for your mom. I get it. Run along. I'm only waiting two minutes." Mia beamed at her mom. A wave of guilt fell over her, so she hugged her mother before exiting the vehicle with her friend.

∞ ∞ ∞

The kitchen was clean, and Isaiah was in bed, courtesy of his grandfather. Mia gave her father a quick embrace. "Thanks for fixing the wall."

David shrugged. "Don't mention it. How'd it happen anyway?"

Mia shook her head, reluctant to tell on her child. "Isaiah was a little rambunctious with one of his toys."

"Ah. Boys. They play rough, don't they?"

"They definitely do."

A beat passed. "Your mother would be so proud of you."

Mia looked down and forced a smile. "I'm trying."

"You're doing great, kiddo. Life's dealt you a few hard hands. Some people would have given up by now. You're really strong."

She hated that line. What did 'strong' mean? There were plenty of days when she surrendered completely to chaos and left the house a mess. Or downed a bottle of wine by herself after tucking her son into bed. Or didn't move from the couch for the entirety of the day.

"Thanks, Dad."

"Well, I gotta get going. If you need anything—"

"I'll call. I promise."

They said goodbye one more time and then her father was gone. Mia locked the doors and checked the windows.

After brushing her teeth, she slid under the covers of her side of the bed and turned her back to the wall. Her thoughts turned to the night she spent with Sean, the heat that his body had provided and the security that his arms brought. The bedding felt cold. She felt an urge to call him and hear his voice over the phone, warm and low. She settled deeper into the bed, bunching the comforter around herself. Her phone was in the living room, and laziness trumped temptation.

Shortly after Austin's death, Mia's father was a consistent presence in her life. He taught Isaiah how to fish, acted as babysitter whenever he could, tended to the routine house maintenance, picked up her grocery staples, and mowed her lawn. He seemed genuinely disappointed whenever she didn't have a task ready for him.

They rarely spoke about Austin's death. Instead, they reminisced over shared memories or talked him up in front of Isaiah, but otherwise, there was no discussion regarding the grief left behind. In that respect, David was still David. Mia still retreated to a separate corner of the home to mourn her loss. Both losses. She rubbed her face hard with her hands and sighed.

"I miss you, Mom."

-Chapter 15-

March 1998

D avid paced the living room and tried the call again.

Mia bit her lip and watched him with her peripheral vision even as she pretended to do her homework at the coffee table. She sat on the floor, her body hidden between the couch and the table, feet growing numb. Her father's steps sounded heavier than normal. His face was lined with worry.

"She's never late." He tossed the cordless phone onto the sofa chair next to the small bookcase and ran a hand over his mouth. His eyes fell over the spines of the books, most of them unread and waiting for Gabriela's return.

Mia shifted from her sitting position. Pins and needles shot to her feet immediately. David's attention turned to her, surprise registering in his eyes. His mouth moved into a forced smile that looked like a frown. The muscles in his jaw worked for a moment. "Why don't you go up to your room and finish your homework? I'm sure your mom will be home any minute. I'll call you down when supper's ready."

She gathered her items and meekly exited the room, eyes on the floor. The quick clomps of work boot against floor resumed. Soft beeps sounded. She abandoned her school supplies on the kitchen counter and positioned herself behind the wall nearest the living room. Her breath was shallow. She strained her ear to listen.

"Hi! This is Gabriela's husband. Yeah. Hi. I was calling to see if she was working late today? Is she still in her classroom? Yeah, I'll hold."

The pacing continued for a while. When it stopped, Mia leaned her body a little closer toward the living room entrance.

"Mia!"

A prickle of alarm rushed through her body.

"Go. To. Your. Room. I will call you down when I hear something."

She raced up to her room. After a few minutes, she tiptoed back to the top of the stairs and sat, hands clasped tightly together, listening to the one-sided conversations her father had with family and friends. No one had an answer. David awkwardly thanked each one for their time and dialed someone else.

Finally, David's voice began to shake. He had called the police to report a potentially missing person. His voice rose as he argued that a day didn't have to pass for them to file a report.

"She's never late. Never. Not without calling. Something has happened. I just know it. I have my daughter here. Please. She's missing. I know it."

Mia leaned against the rail post. Her father's footsteps ebbed and flowed. Shadows grew in the house as the sun set. Eventually, darkness filled the home. A form materialized at the base of the stairs. "It's time for bed."

Her father's voice was flat, tired.

She nodded even as she wondered if he could see her in the darkness. There was no reaction from the figure; rather, it walked toward the kitchen, slow and heavy. This was when she knew something was wrong. Something had happened to her mother. She retreated to her room, its location on the opposite side of the house from the kitchen.

The moon was full that night. Its silvery glow bathed the room in harsh contrasts. The edges of her dresser and full-length mirror were razor sharp. Her closet door was ajar, and behind it, an inky black void. She was twelve years old. Far too old to believe in monsters, but young enough to know that mothers were superhuman. A nefarious presence must have taken her. That was the only explanation that could account for her absence. El Cucuy, a faceless boogeyman, older than time itself, hunting down unsuspecting women.

Mia got in bed and drew the covers to her chin, her hair a messy halo around her head. She tried to close her eyes, but found only images of monsters. She settled on staring at the ceiling. As she stared, she kept her breath as even as possible, lest she draw unwanted attention. Would the El Cucuy be back for her?

The house creaked with the weight of anxious thoughts. The ghost of an unanswered question shared her bed.

She heard a noise, a sharp rap at the front door. Low murmurs turned into something troubled. Then, they transformed into a wail. Her thoughts had given life to the make-believe monsters that occupied her head. Ice flashed through her veins when she realized the sound had not come from a monster. It was her father. The unwelcome question crashed into her mind, and she squeezed her eyes shut.

Did something bad happen to Mommy?

When the question wouldn't leave, she ran to the source and found the answer in the eyes of her father.

∞ ∞ ∞

Mia walked into school, eyes on the floor in front of her. Her backpack thumped her lower back as she shuffled to her locker. She was surprised to find she had kept the muscle memory of how to function at school, even after a lifetime had passed.

In the end, it was not El Cucuy that had robbed her of her mother, but a person who was made of flesh and bone. A person who, for reasons unknown, had lost control of their vehicle long enough to steal a mother. They had slammed their car into Gabriela's, forcing her into a tree, and then fled, leaving her mother to die by herself. No phone call. No last words.

Mia hated the image that it conjured. She had so many questions. Did it hurt? Was she scared? Did she think of them before she died? Could she have been saved had the driver stayed and dialed 9-1-1?

Her father had briefly explained what had happened. As he spoke, he focused on an area in the room slightly to her left. When he was done, he stood and made his way to the kitchen. She waited until the clinking stopped and then retreated to her room. On her trip past the kitchen, she paused and turned her attention toward him. The amber liquid stopped flowing into his glass, and he met her gaze. For a millisecond, they were trapped in a moment of what could be, of what-ifs. She imagined herself running into the kitchen, throwing the bottle away from him. In her mind's eye, she watched the bottle fly and hit the wall, heard the crystalline sound of glass exploding, its liquid contents wetting the nearby counters and cabinets. In her daydream, they held each other tightly, summoning Gabriela's presence to fill the room and their hearts.

Then, the moment passed. David continued to pour, and Mia left for her room before her father touched the glass to his lips.

After reaching her doorway, she paused and then continued down the hall. She made her way to the bathroom and picked through the dirty laundry. When she reached one of her mother's blouses, she withdrew it from the bin and pulled it over her head. Tears threatened to spill, but she waited until she was in the confines of her own room to let them fall.

She kicked off her shoes and crawled into bed. She pulled the comforter over her head and breathed in the scent of her mother.

Her father had just explained what happened. The most important person in her life had been murdered by another human being. A careless human being. But in her heart, she doubted that explanation. It made no sense. It couldn't be a person. Who could kill someone's mom without consequence?

She heard what the adults said, sensed their frustration.

"No one has been arrested yet."

"I thought they had the video from the ATM? Isn't that enough to see the plates?"

"You'd think this would be a priority."

As the gossip swelled, David retreated. It would be years before he could speak freely about Gabriela.

Mia was kept home until the Monday after the funeral.

That Sunday, David rapped on her bedroom door. He cleared his throat and cracked the door open. "Five minutes, then lights out. You got school tomorrow."

Mia tucked a loose paper into the book she was reading and set it on her nightstand. She lay back onto her bed and stared at the ceiling. When she awoke the next morning, she noted that her comforter had been pulled over her and the room's lights had been turned off.

At school, the counselor, Mrs. Jensen, was waiting at Mia's locker. She reminded Mia of her services.

"If you ever need to talk…"

Mia lowered her head and trained her eyes on the floor. Mrs. Jensen took a moment to pass along her condolences. She squeezed Mia's shoulder gently before turning to walk back to her office. Sharp clicks announced her path, and students absentmindedly parted.

She waited until she was out of sight before heading toward her first class. The bell sounded, and she was startled to find herself alone in the hallway.

When she entered the classroom, the buzz of twenty-plus voices dropped to a silence.

Normally, Mrs. Dillard, whose first name was Catherine, would have requested a note or explanation for the tardy entrance—even from Mia, the daughter of her best friend—just to prove she was impartial to all her students. That day, however, Catherine—or Mrs. Dillard, as Mia tried to think of her during school hours—only smile the forced smile she had begun to expect. The rims of her teacher's eyes were red, her eyelashes fluttering like the wings of an injured butterfly.

A flash of Catherine and her mother laughing in their backyard came to mind. Their husbands were swapping grill theory, pushing everyone to give feedback on whose slightly charred carne asada was better. Mia would deliver cold beer cans to whoever wanted one, her hands wet with condensation, secretly thrilled to handle such adult items.

She felt a compulsion to apologize to her teacher. *I'm sorry you lost your friend.* Why did everyone apologize over a death that wasn't their fault?

The moment passed, and her throat was too dry to speak anyway. *Maybe I'll never speak again.* She cast her eyes to the floor and made her way to her seat. Silence filled the room until it felt stifling. Chairs creaked as students shifted in their seats. She could hear the rushing of blood in her ears.

Mrs. Dillard cleared her throat. "Alright, class. Turn to page 84."

For weeks, people treated Mia as if death was contagious. No one else in the school had lost a parent. Her friends were nervous around her, afraid to say the wrong thing and deferring to awkward silences. Everyone else kept their distance. She was a ghost of her previous self, a ghost that everyone could see but was too afraid to acknowledge.

It was a loneliness she had never encountered.

Reluctant to prolong it, she began to talk louder, laugh quickly, and make jokes. The invisible barriers around her melted, and the world relaxed again.

"Do you want to come to my house this weekend? We're doing a movie night, and my mom said I can invite a friend or two for a sleepover," said Beth.

"Yeah! I need to ask my dad, but I know he'll say yes."

Beth grinned. "Awesome! I'll tell my mom."

For the sleepover, Beth invited Mia and their mutual friend, Laura. Beth's mother bought pizza and helped them make ice cream sandwiches with homemade cookies. Mia was a gracious guest. She laughed and smiled. They chatted about their crushes and lamented the amount of English homework assigned.

Long after midnight, the girls finally made it to Beth's bed. She and Laura fell asleep almost instantly. Mia moved to the premade trundle. She listened to the sounds of the house. The soft pat-pat of the cat's footsteps made her smile. The hum of an electrical unit began. An ambulance sounded for several seconds in the distance.

She turned to her side and closed her eyes. Tears formed, and she did her best to cry without making a sound.

-Chapter 16-

September 2016

"He ate a late lunch, but he'll probably be hungry soon," said Mia. She looked around her father's kitchen and noted the leftover pizza box, the dishes in the sink. "You want me to wash those for you real quick?"

David glanced over at the sink and made a face. "There's like three dishes there."

"Well, it's that much easier to get to."

Her father pressed his lips into a line and grunted. "I wait until there's enough to stick in the dishwasher. Don't stress me. Anyway, you look really nice. Going out with Camille?"

She hadn't disclosed the details of her date and was reluctant to share. She had tried to dress casually, as if she were meeting a friend—an acquaintance, even—but apparently a nice blouse and heels gave her away. "Oh, uh, no. Not Camille. Another friend."

Her father paused, but didn't press the issue. Instead, he addressed his grandson. "Ready to hang out with your grandpa?"

Isaiah nodded enthusiastically and hopped into the living room. When he spotted David's old beagle mix, he broke into a wide grin and rushed over.

"Eh! Eh!" Mia chided. "Gentle with Gus!"

Isaiah slowed his pace and softly patted the dog on the head, his eyes on Mia. "I am!"

She sighed.

David chuckled. "He's getting to that age where they just gotta push back, ain't he?"

"Six going on sixteen, I swear."

Her father watched her for a second. "Am I watching him overnight?"

She knew what he was trying to ask; she tried to look nonchalant. "Oh, no. I'm just going to a concert. Some local band is playing."

"Oh, do I know them?"

"Um, maybe? Probably not. They're called The Carolina Brothers," she said.

"Hmm… no, never heard of them."

"It's a local band." Mia rubbed her palms together. She was nervous. "Well, anyway, I gotta go. We're grabbing a bite to eat, then heading over to watch the show. I don't know when it ends, but I imagine I'll be back a little on the later side. At least, after his bedtime."

"Oh," said David. "Well, if you need him to spend the night, it's fine."

She nodded. "No, it's fine. I'll pick him up."

"Alright, tesoro. Have fun."

She made her way back to her house and waited for Sean. She checked her makeup three times before she heard her doorbell ring. He was early. Her stomach was in knots.

This is ridiculous. We've already slept together. What else is there to be nervous about?

His eyes lit up when she opened the door. "Wow, you look great."

She smiled. "You don't look too shabby yourself, sir."

"Thanks. I like to think I clean up fairly well."

They stood for a moment on her porch before she realized he was waiting on her. She locked the door behind her and made her way to his car.

He drove for a few minutes before breaking the silence. "Oh, I meant to ask, do you like seafood?"

Mia nodded. "I do! Except crawfish. I don't know why. Maybe it's that whenever people make it, it just looks like a bucket of bugs." She laughed and shrugged. "Other than that, I like it."

"Oh, good. I'm taking you to the best seafood place in town. The Pier? I mean, you might've been, but just wanted to double check my choice. And to warn you that if you venture too far off the seafood part of the menu, the quality starts to suffer a bit. They make a really dry chicken, for example."

"Noted. I actually haven't been, but have been meaning to go, so that's perfect."

Sean's shoulders dropped, and he nodded, relief clear in his smile. "Great."

People crowded the entrance of the restaurant, and Mia momentarily regretted not bringing a book along. Sean escorted her past the line and announced their arrival. He had made a reservation the day she had accepted his invitation.

The waitress arrived shortly after the hostess had seated them and took their order.

When the food arrived, Mia's eyes widened. "Wow. I didn't realize the portions were going to be so big."

He had ordered the surf and turf, a loaded baked potato, and an extra soup. She had ordered the rockfish with two vegetable sides. "It's pricey but worth it once you see how much they try and feed you."

"I see!" Mia said. "Can you eat all that, though?"

"What?" Sean looked over his plate. "Is that a challenge?"

"That's a ton of food."

He shrugged. "I'm a growing boy."

Mia laughed. "Ugh, men. I couldn't eat all that if I tried. And even if I did, my ass would expand two sizes by tomorrow. It's a little unfair if you ask me."

He laughed. "That doesn't sound like the worst thing."

"I mean, a little bit, right?"

He sent her a flirtatious look and lowered his voice. "You don't want me to answer that in a restaurant."

She felt a blush spread across her cheeks. The restaurant tried to mimic a candlelit atmosphere, and she hoped her pink face was hidden by the dimness. She speared a chunk of fish. "Anyway, how'd you find out about the band?"

"Oh, well, I appreciate all forms of art. Probably why I ended up in marketing to pay the bills and photography to feed the soul. I like to listen to music when I'm working by myself, especially from indie or local artists. One day, I stumbled onto their songs. When I found out that they play here often, I started to go watch them perform every now and again. And it's kind of a cool date."

"Ah, so you bring the ladies out to listen to jazz often?"

A corner of his mouth raised in a half-smile. "Maybe, but I can't disclose all the tricks of the trade. However, I do have to admit that I've also brought along Keegan and Sam."

"With other dates, or just like a guys' night out?" she asked.

A shadow crossed his face. "A little of both, I guess. What kind of music do you like?"

"Oh, um, I guess a bit of everything. That sounds like a cop-out, doesn't it?" she said.

Sean shrugged.

"Well, to be more specific, I like pop, cumbias, rancheras. I like R&B. Alternative rock. Hmmm, reggaeton, reggae. I feel like I'm just listing genres. Oh, you know what I really, really like? I love when different music genres mash up together. Do you know what I mean? When an orchestral piece is spliced in with hip hop elements. Or when people do hard rock covers with a violin. Or when pop fuses with country. Even though it's stuff we've all heard before, stuff that's familiar, it sounds so different and wakes up a different mood inside of you—"

Mia realized she was rambling and stopped. Sean had been watching her intently, a small smile playing on his lips. When her words ran out, he blinked. "Wait, were you finished explaining?"

She smiled, self-conscious. "Sorry, I was rambling."

He smiled, genuine. "You weren't rambling. And if you were, I liked it." A comfortable silence settled onto the table. "Well, I know what you mean. Which is great, because I think you'll really like this band, then. They experiment a lot with sound."

When they arrived at the venue, Mia found that it was the old theatre downtown. Her eyes widened. "I didn't even know this place was still open."

Sean smiled. "Yeah, it's a little well-loved, but sometimes appearances can be deceiving."

The inside opened to clusters of tables surrounding the dance floor. Though age had touched everything inside of the building, it was clear care was taken to ensure everything was clean and well-maintained. The stage was dimly lit and the band's members were chatting with each other, their instruments set up and ready for the impending performance. He found them a table and a waiter appeared.

Sean turned to Mia. "Do you want anything? They mostly sell appetizers and drinks."

"I'm not sure I have any room!" she said, her hand on her stomach.

He turned to the waiter. "Can we get two bottles of water? We won't be eating." After the waiter left, he informed Mia that there were no complimentary waters.

"What! Everyone has tap water."

"I'm sure they do, but you have to admit, they probably need the extra money to make sure this place doesn't fall apart. I usually try to order one thing," he said.

"I guess."

"Support what you love. Always."

He turned to face the stage, and she kept her gaze trained on the side of his face. She found she really liked the hint of beard, the sharp angle of his jaw. She blushed and looked down when he glanced her way. When she looked up, he was smiling, eyes shining with amusement. She felt more heat creep up her neck and wished she wasn't so easily flustered. People liked to ask what super power was most coveted; the answers typically ranged from flying to telekinesis. But if Mia were to answer truthfully, it'd be for her body not to give her emotions away.

Chatter in the room dulled as the mic squealed. The spotlight found the stage. An announcer's voice boomed through the room. "Gooooood evening, ladies and gentlemen! Welcome to the Avery Theatre in our beautiful downtown, where we highlight our local talents. Tonight, I am proud to announce our very own, very talented, Carolina Brothers!"

Sean found her hand and squeezed it twice.

The music, as promised, was impressive. Thirty minutes into the set, Sean stood and held out a hand. "Let's dance."

Mia sat firmly in her chair. "I don't know how to dance."

"What!" he laughed. "You were dancing when we met."

She looked away. "Uh, there was plenty of alcohol involved in that."

"Need me to order you a daiquiri or something?"

"Oh, man, no. Otherwise, poor decisions might be made."

"That sounds like a great reason to buy you a drink."

She swatted his hip. "I meant on the dance floor!"

He laughed again, but this time he succeeded in uprooting her from the seat.

The dance floor was full of couples laughing and dancing, or attempting to dance. One man held his drink up above his shoulder, shuffling his body from side to side. A woman danced in front of him, more for him than with him, smiling broadly. An older couple swayed offbeat.

"You're very good at this," Mia said, as they danced.

"You're being kind. I'm concentrating really hard on not stepping on your feet."

At the start of a slower song, Mia signaled that she wanted to sit down.

"I think you're a better dancer than you give yourself credit for," said Sean, as they returned to their table.

She laughed and shrugged. "I think you're better than you think as well." She lifted a foot in his direction. "See? No feet were harmed tonight."

He chuckled softly. "I'm glad you came out tonight."

"Me too. It's been a while. I know I was out with Camille when we met, but I normally don't accept so many invitations. In fact, if I'm being honest, I was going to decline it."

Her elbows were resting on the table, hands folded in front of her. He placed a hand on hers. "I'm glad you accepted."

Her cheeks warmed under his gaze. She looked away and wondered if other people had as much trouble with eye contact as she did.

"Really," he continued. "It's been fun. Plus, you're not the only one who's hard to get out."

"Oh?" She turned her attention to him. "You a homebody?" she teased.

He smiled. "Not quite. I just have times when I prefer being alone."

"I can appreciate that." She let a beat pass and scooched her chair closer to his. The band's music swelled and made it harder to hear conversation. "I'm not sure what my motivation is. I mean, don't get me wrong, I do like my alone time. I think every parent needs time to destress, but—sometimes I wonder if I'm still trying to block out the world. I don't know what I thought life would be after Austin, my husband… But sometimes I feel like I'm grieving too long. I should be a little bit better than right now." Her eyes widened. "God, that's depressing talk for a date. I'm sorry. Or maybe not, I'm kind of a mess. You should probably know that before you decide to invite me out again. Not that I'm saying you will or won't." She realized she was rambling again and bit her lower lip to stop the words from forcing their way out.

He smiled politely. "It's okay, it's fine. I get it. I really do."

Her head tilted.

He sighed. "Years ago, I was engaged. It feels like a lifetime ago or like yesterday, depending. Her name was Maribel. She was—she was the best. She worked at a hospital and picked up some night shifts. She was seven months pregnant with our baby."

Mia's eyebrows raised in surprise. She remembered the teddy bear she had spotted in his living room.

"I kept pushing her to cut back on her hours, but she said she couldn't sleep well at night most of the time anyway. Pregnancy insomnia or something like that. And, well, it's a what-if that I try not to dwell on." He paused and when he met her eyes, her stomach dropped. He smiled grimly in acknowledgement.

"On her way home from work, a drunk driver hit her car. It always seems like drunk drivers walk away from the wrecks unphased. I don't know, maybe their intoxication makes them less likely to tense, and they just go with the impact." Sean shrugged. "Doesn't matter, though. He walked away, and she ended up dying the next day in the hospital she worked at. They were able to do an emergency cesarean, but our daughter—I named her Danielle—only lived a week before passing in the NICU. She was too early. I was a wreck for a long while after that. A huge wreck."

Mia's jaw dropped. She took his hand. "Sean. That's awful. Did they catch the guy?"

He showed a quick flash of teeth in a humorless smile. "They did. He got ten years, served eight. But he probably could have served a hundred, and it wouldn't have made me feel any better." He frowned. "You're right. This really is terrible date talk."

She grimaced. "I'm sorry. I started it. Um, well—shit. How do I segue from this? I bring up Austin too much."

"You're fine. It's normal. I talk about Maribel often, but usually just with people who know the story. I don't try to sound like a sob story."

"Oh, gosh. I'm not looking at you like a sob story. Although, I am very sorry to hear that. You'd think I'd have something better to say than sorry, because I hate when people say that to me."

He gave a short laugh. "You'd think, but I never know what to say, either."

She frowned. "Weirdly that makes me feel better. Okay. Segue. Um, where have you always wanted to travel?"

"Oh, good one. Let's see. I'd love to visit Iceland one day. Also, Alaska."

"Yikes, all cold places."

"You don't like the cold?"

"I abhor the cold. I'd rather a summer heat wave than a midwinter day. I think I'd die if I lived in Alaska. Actually, I think I saw some reality TV show where they had to survive out there. Like, there's stores and stuff, but they use a woodburning stove to keep warm and grow a bunch of their food. No thanks. There I'd lay, frozen. Used as someone's lawn ornament." She shuddered.

Sean burst out laughing. "I didn't peg you for someone who liked reality shows."

"Oh, I'm sorry, do you know me? Let a man dance with you two times, and he has all your interests figured out." Her eyes flashed with amusement.

His look turned flirtatious. "You know what I really like about you?"

She shook her head slowly and waited.

"That mouth of yours."

She snorted. "You gonna ask me what it does?"

"I already know what it does," he said.

She gasped and swatted his arm. He laughed and leaned over to kiss her. She let herself fall into it.

"You said you only have childcare for the evening?"

Mia thought back to her father's offer to keep Isaiah overnight. Then, she remembered Isaiah's outburst after the last overnight. *Not tonight.*

She wrinkled her nose. "Yeah."

He grinned. "Just checking. Maybe next time we can order in."

An electric thrill rushed down her spine. "Maybe."

-Chapter 17-

September 2016

The air was thick with the promise of rain. Everyone took the threat seriously and decided to visit the park one last time. The cold front was fast approaching, and with it, the arrival of autumn. Halloween would likely be cold again.

Mia stood watching Isaiah play with Lori's youngest two. He didn't enjoy big crowds but didn't want to leave.

Or maybe I'm just imagining that he's uncomfortable in a crowd because I am.

Lori broke the silence. "He's doing so much better."

Mia glanced at her, brow furrowed.

"I remember when he refused to play with anyone. Even Luca."

Mia felt defensive. "Yeah, I guess. I think he just felt overwhelmed." If there was an edge to her voice, Lori didn't hear it. She simply nodded in agreement.

Lori looked around. "It's so crowded. I knew we should have gone to Luck Stone Park."

"They're enjoying themselves. And it's probably crowded there, too. I think it's supposed to rain forever after today." Mia shrugged off her oversized sweater. "This weather is weird. Cool enough to need a sweater when the clouds cover the sun, but warm enough to feel like I'm baking when it peeks through."

"Yeah, I'll be glad once this humidity is gone. As long as it doesn't rain on Halloween. The kids will be bummed." Lori snorted. "Actually, I'll be bummed because Mama don't do the rain. And in the cold? Forget it." She sat on the giant picnic blanket she had brought to the park. Her diaper bag and purse held down a side that liked flapping up with the breeze. "Sit down, you're making me nervous."

"You could always just drive through the neighborhood and let them run up to the houses." Mia sat cross-legged next to her and smiled conspiratorially at her friend.

"What? That's practically cheating! The true meaning of Halloween is walking ten miles for thirty pieces of candy your mom steals from you. It's tradition."

Mia giggled.

"If anything, I'll drive behind them while they walk the streets. What? Don't look at me like that. It's good for character." Lori grinned and fished around her large bag. She pulled out a small bag of dried fruits. She popped one into her mouth, then tilted it forward. When Mia declined with a shake of her head, Lori sat the bag next to her. "Are you guys doing Halloween this year?"

The previous year, Mia had skipped every holiday except birthdays and Christmas. Isaiah hadn't mentioned Halloween, and she gladly took advantage of his apathy.

Of course, she'd made the mistake of taking him to a store when the Halloween costumes were out on the sales racks. When he found out that Halloween was over, he threw himself onto the floor and screamed. Everyone within earshot, which seemed like the entire store, paused to stare. She felt herself turn red from shame and embarrassment. She knew what they were thinking: *What a spoiled brat. What a terrible mother.*

When she attempted to lift her child, he stayed limp and uncooperative. He felt surprisingly heavy. Eventually, she managed to grasp him securely and fled the store, her cart abandoned. She imagined everyone in the store felt relieved. He continued screaming and thrashing until they exited the building and was completely silent when they reached the car. She buckled him into his car seat, even though he could do it himself. He didn't protest, and she didn't question him.

Once he was secured, Mia slowly walked once around the car, attempting to slow her breathing before climbing into the driver's seat. She discreetly wiped the tears off her face, cleared her throat, and started the car. She tilted the rearview mirror downward and spied Isaiah looking blankly out of his window.

"Do you want some music?" Mercifully, her voice was even.

Isaiah looked at her through the mirror. She didn't wait for an answer and instead stabbed the power button.

She blinked back to the present. "What?"

"Are you doing Halloween this year?"

"Oh, yeah. He keeps changing his costume idea. He wanted to be a monster. Then, a ninja. Now I think a dinosaur? We'll see."

"Oh man. You need to hurry and get his outfit. Halloween is only a few weeks away."

Mia groaned. "I know. I'm always behind on a million things."

Lori sent her a sympathetic look. "I feel you. I always feel like I'm a chicken with my head cut off."

"I mean, you do have five kids. I can't even imagine. I have one and can barely keep up."

Lori shook her head. "It's all chaotic. If you have one or three or five, it's all the same difference. It's all hard. Plus, I have a partner. Jeff does a lot with the kids, and the older ones help with the younger ones."

Mia forced her lips into a smile. Why did that hurt so much to hear?

"Oh! A little birdie told me you went on a date?"

Mia relaxed at the question, and her smile turned genuine. "Maybe."

"Why didn't you tell me?" Lori said, feigning offense.

"I mean, it's been nice, but there's not much to tell. It was just one date."

"There's always a ton to tell. I live for first date stories. Jeff and I have been together for so long, there's barely any excitement. Don't get me wrong, I love that man to death, but the sexiness has completely worn off the marriage. I think that's what years of baby vomit and diapers get you. So. Tell me everything." Lori clasped her hands together and placed them over her heart.

"I mean, it's been really nice. We all met at the club, remember? Sean?"

"Oh, yes, I do remember him! He's a cutie, good job!" She nudged Mia in the ribs, and they laughed. "Where'd you guys go?"

"He took me out for dinner at The Pier. Then, we went and watched a local band play. The Carolina Brothers. I'd never heard of them, but they were really good! We danced a bit."

"Oh, nice! Did he ask you to spend the night?" Lori winked. "You're still smiling about him, so maybe?"

"Not that night. Isaiah gets a little panicky when I'm away for too long, especially overnight."

Lori's face sobered. "I can imagine. Poor little guy. I'm so sorry."

Mia realized she had spoiled the moment. The excitement had been replaced with an uncomfortable fog. The unspoken memory of Austin's suicide hung in the air. Aside from Camille, no one knew how to continue the conversation after his presence was introduced. He was a ghost that haunted so many conversations.

"But we're going out again soon."

Lori perked up. "Oh yeah? Where's he taking you this time?"

"Our next date is just a regular dinner and a movie. Might sound lame, but it's been so long since I've sat down and watched an adult movie in a theatre, I'm actually excited."

"That's not lame at all! What movie are you going to go see?"

Mia chewed on the inside of her cheek for a moment. "The one with—ugh, I forgot his name. The guy who—I think there's a bank robbery? Something like that."

Lori cackled. "That, my friend, was the worst description of a movie I've ever heard in my life. 'The one with the guy.' I cannot with you." She laughed until her face was pink and tears gathered in her eyes. Mia couldn't help but laugh along.

Nina ran to her mother. "I'm thirsty. Why are you crying?"

More laughter erupted from the women.

Nina wasn't amused. "I'm thirsty!" She dragged out the last vowel.

Lori wiped her eyes. "Okay, okay. Here, hold on." She dug through her bag again and produced a bottle of water. "There you go."

Her son, Xander, appeared, along with Isaiah. "Can I have some water, too?" Isaiah asked.

"There's a water fountain by the bathroom," said Mia. "We can walk there together."

Lori waved her hand as if shooing away the suggestion. "Oh, no need. I always bring extras. This bad boy has everything." She patted her oversized bag, then pulled out the extra bottle. "Here you go, baby."

Isaiah eagerly accepted the water and drank deeply. The children milled around the women, poking and teasing each other as they sipped from water bottles and shared some snacks. A few peeled-off sweaters and then they were off, laughing and running again, the edges of their hair damp from perspiration.

"I wish I were like you: prepared, collected, together. I'm always running around without any idea what's happening and a few supplies short."

Lori blew a raspberry. "I am not always prepared. More than one time, I idiotically brought a toddler or two to a whole day of errands without a spare diaper. And, of course, they pooped at the most inconvenient time. So, I have had to lug stinky, lumpy-butted babies through the aisles of Walmart to get a small pack of diapers and wipes. This thing might have everything, but it's no help when I accidentally leave it at home. I am a hot mess wrapped up in a chaos blanket. No, no, don't interrupt. I know everyone thinks I've got it together because I have five kids and haven't had a public nervous breakdown, but the idea of a perfect, flawless mother is a myth. You and me, we're doing the best we can, sister, and that's enough."

"I know. I just—it's hard to feel like enough sometimes. I don't want to play mom and dad." Mia smiled sadly at her friend.

"I know, sweetie. Life hasn't been very fair to you, has it? If you haven't heard it today, let me tell you: you're doing a great job. Be kind to yourself."

A scream stole their attention, and a little girl flew by, grinning, a few children close behind.

Isaiah and Xander were taking turns going down the tallest slide. Three little boys attempted to scale the slide rather than climb up the stairs. Isaiah looked cross for a moment. and Mia felt an impulse to run out to the equipment and deescalate a situation only she knew was there. But Xander jumped off the ladder and beckoned. They ran to the seesaw and continued their play there.

Mia relaxed and smiled at the image of her son playing. There was a time when she thought he'd never open back up to the world. Slowly, he had allowed Luca into his circle. Now, he was happy to play with more and more children. His angry outbursts were lessening.

Be kind to yourself, Mia, she thought.

"I'll try."

-Chapter 18-

September 2016

"How'd you like the movie?" Sean held the exit door open for Mia. The day had seen a series of scattered showers, and she had wondered if they'd be spending parts of their date walking in the rain. However, it appeared the clouds had held their breath until after they made it into the theatre. The parking lot was damp from the previous cloud burst, but the rain had subsided, at least for the moment.

She flashed him a smile. "It was good! Exciting. I like when a story makes you root for the bad guy a little bit. It's been forever since I've watched an adult movie, though, so that helps."

He grinned. "Well, I'm glad I could welcome you back out to the world of entertainment." They paused when they reached his car. He scanned the horizon before taking a breath. "Maybe one of these days we can go to a movie that's kid-friendly and Isaiah can tag along."

Her smile faltered. "Oh, um…"

Her thoughts wandered to a day on the playground a few months after Austin's death. Isaiah landed on the bottom of the slide at the exact moment a bright orange ball stopped to rest in the dip created in the wood chips by his feet. His little head cocked to the side, and he picked it up.

"Hey, there, buddy!" a male voice called out. A man with his son walked over. "Can you toss it this way?"

Isaiah's eyes lit up, and he tossed it. It went wide, and the father jogged over to meet it. Isaiah's smile dimmed as he watched the man toss it to his son. The father noticed.

"You wanna play with us?"

The three proceeded to toss the ball for a while next to the playground set.

Mia's heart felt like it had been stabbed. Austin's absence felt stronger in that moment. The back of her eyes burned, and she blinked quickly.

Sean's voice brought her back to the present. "Later on, I meant. Sorry. I don't mean to intrude." His fingers worked the hem of his sweater.

She rubbed her arm self-consciously. "He's just—sometimes he's a little weird around other people. And I feel like—I don't know. I'm not always sure how he's handling Austin's death. I hadn't really thought much about dating." She paused. "Well, I guess I did. Kind of. People brought it up—a lot. I think they mean well, but it sometimes feels like when people push me to date or find someone else, it's almost like they think I'm too young to be a widow. It doesn't compute for people. Like they think divorce is acceptable, but a dead spouse is unacceptable at my age. And maybe if I find someone, then everyone can just pretend it's over. They can pretend that I'm better. No more sad, lost Mia. She'll suddenly have her shit together."

Her voice cracked, but she pressed forward. "In terms of Isaiah, I'd like to get to know you a bit more before introducing him to you. He's been through so much. I'm not even sure if he'd understand. I don't have a concrete plan, but I figured if you met him, the first time would be..." She shrugged, unable to put words to her thoughts.

Sean took her hand and looked at her, his smile gentle.

She felt foolish and hoped he didn't feel sorry for her.

"I shouldn't have put you on defense like that. Sorry. And I get it. At least about losing someone and how opinionated people can get. For what it's worth, I think you're a lot more put together than you think."

"Yeah," she murmured. "So I've been told."

He gripped her waist, and he pulled her close. "You have a lot of great friends who care about you." He kissed her nose, then her mouth.

The noise in her head died down. "You know, Isaiah is sleeping over at his grandpa's tonight."

"Is that right? And where are you sleeping over?"

Mia smiled.

Mia bounced up the steps to her father's house the next morning. David opened the door before she could ring the doorbell.

"You're up early," he said. He turned and walked into the house. He was already dressed in a long-sleeved button-down and worn jeans. "Isaiah's still sleeping. I got a pot on. Want some?"

"I'd love some." She had declined coffee and breakfast at Sean's apartment, antsy to meet Isaiah as soon as he was awake.

"So," said her father, removing two mugs from the cupboards. "When do I meet him?"

She stopped short. "What?" Her father poured the strong black liquid into both mugs. He pulled out a little sugar dish and began spooning the contents into one of the steaming cups. "Don't put that much sugar in mine."

"That one's mine."

"I'm getting a cavity watching how much you're shoveling in there."

He grumbled. "Just like your mom. Okay, I'll wait till you're ready to talk about him."

She put a hand on her hip. "Just one teaspoon for me."

"Alright, alright."

She noisily pulled a barstool from the kitchen island and sat. "How are you?"

David grunted. "Can't complain."

"You eat yet?"

"I swear you turn more into your mother every day."

Mia smiled. "You're a little thin."

"Maybe more like my mother."

"Dad?"

He noticed the change in her tone and set his mug on the counter.

"Never mind. It's a weird question," she said.

"I'm a little more open to questions nowadays."

He stood looking at her expectantly, but instead of asking right away, she took a moment to drink from her mug and study the kitchen. A garlic chain hung next to the sink. Two small pots growing oregano and cilantro sat near a window. It was kept neat, with just enough clutter to let the observer know it was periodically used.

"Why haven't you remarried since Mom?"

David's eyebrows shot up. "Oh. Not what I was expecting." He eyed his coffee and frowned. "This is very sweet. I don't think I stirred it enough."

She studied his form, the aging hands cupped around the mug, the graying hair. He grunted a thank you when she passed him a spoon, and she watched him stir.

When she was a child, he was a giant to her, a superhuman who never cried and whose strong hands kept their house running smoothly. As she grew, she realized the stoic façade was not strength, but a role he was forced into by his own father. One more victim of the false narrative that men never cried. Gabriela's death had swept the legs from underneath him, and their fortress had crumbled. He sought strength from the bottle and learned it only hastened the destruction around him. Perhaps that had been his goal: chip away at everything until he was no more.

Mia was proud of him, though. He was six years sober and kept a dry house. His vices now were coffee and the ten o'clock news.

Right when she thought he would never answer, he cleared his throat. "Your mother was an amazing woman. She taught me so much about love. She set the bar really high. I don't want to compare someone else to her."

Mia considered the information. "I think she'd want you to be happy, though."

Little footsteps announced an arrival. "Mommy!"

She turned and smiled brightly. "Baby! Did you have fun with Welo?"

He threw his arms around her. "Yeah!" The word was muffled. "We played checkers, and I won every time! And then we had pizza. And Grandpa said I could stay up late, but then he turned on the news, which is boring, so I went to bed."

Mia laughed. "That sounds like a great time."

"I'm hungry."

"I got some pancake mix around here somewhere if I can convince your mama to cook for us."

She flashed her father an amused face. "Maybe if you say please." She stood up and rummaged through the pantry for the mix. She found some vanilla and nutmeg and an almost-empty tin of baking powder. "You have milk and eggs, right?"

David pulled the requested items from the fridge.

As Mia stirred the ingredients, she overheard her father finish their conversation.

"I am happy." He said it softly. She wasn't sure if he was answering her or convincing himself.

-*Chapter 19* -

Halloween 2006

Mia was a bundle of nerves. It was their first Halloween party as college students. She smoothed the green fabric over her body.

"You look hot, girl. Don't even worry about it. Poison Ivy was a great choice." Camille grinned at her.

"You should have been my Batman."

Camille scrunched her nose. "I liked the idea of being cute better." Her own costume idea had been a vampire queen. She struck a pose and batted her eyelashes.

"Batman could be cute."

"Yeah, I don't think so. But hurry up, you look great, let's go!"

Mia laughed. "Don't rush me!"

"I'm rushing! Let's go! It's almost 11! Plus, isn't Austin meeting you there? I'd definitely be in a hurry." Camille sent her a look.

Mia suppressed a smile. "Yeah, but not till later. He closes today."

"Oh, no wonder you don't care. Some of us have to make an entrance."

They held hands when they entered the house party. Music was blaring, and everyone was just arriving. Camille winked at Mia and ran over to the makeshift bar, which was really just a small table with a plastic covering draped over it. Bottles of cheap liquor and several containers of juice were bunched up on one end while red solo cups were stacked neatly on the other. Mia wondered how long the neat towers would last.

Camille returned with a gleam in her eye. "I don't think the bartender knows what she's doing, but it'll do the trick."

Mia took a sip and cleared her throat. "Yeah, I'd say."

The music played loudly, and the girls danced with a few of their classmates until around midnight. Camille's boyfriend, Ian, announced his arrival by throwing his arms around her. Her scream dissolved into giggles and then a gasp. Ian had scoffed at the idea of matching costumes but had arrived with fake blood smeared on the corners of his mouth and a black, collared cape.

"Awww, you dressed up like Dracula!" Camille kissed him on the lips.

He shrugged, looking pleased. "I did my best."

Mia excused herself after they attempted some small talk over the music.

"You're not a third wheel," Camille had said.

Mia waved her on. "I'm good. Go enjoy a dance or two."

"I'll be back in a bit," Camille promised.

A voice broke through the noise. "Hey!"

Mia turned. An attractive face smiled broadly. "I'm Derek."

She smile politely. "Hey."

"You here by yourself?"

She didn't like the question. "I came with my friends. I'm just chilling by myself for a bit."

"Oh, okay. How do you like it so far? I've never really been to one of these parties."

"Me neither. I think it's fine. It's good. You see the bar over there? I think the DJ is accepting requests."

He raised a red solo cup. "Yeah, I did. I just grabbed a beer. Do you need another drink?"

"Nah, I'm good."

"You sure?"

"Yeah."

"I haven't really seen you around, have I? Maybe I have. It's kind of hard with all the costumes. I like the Poison Ivy look, though. Very original. Sexy."

Mia pressed her lips together and nodded at the compliment.

"I'll go get you a drink—"

"No, I—"

He was gone before she could complete the sentence. *This is probably a good thing.* She retreated to a different part of the building and wondered when Austin would arrive. She looked around the room, locating all the people who were familiar and the many others who weren't.

There was a couple making out near the stairs. She averted her eyes as if respecting a request for privacy and spied a trio of girls clustered near a sofa. The one in the middle had her head bowed, and for a moment, Mia wondered if she had had too much to drink. When the girl lifted her head, Mia saw that she was crying, mascara already smudged.

It's a little too early for all that, girl, Mia thought and then felt bad for being judgmental. *Maybe I should go find Camille.*

Derek's voice broke through her internal thoughts. "It took me a minute to find you! I brought you a Coke. I figured you didn't want a beer or anything."

"Oh. Thanks." Her voice was flat. Mia took a small sip, and he launched into describing his days of homework and studying.

After answering a few questions, she finally blurted out she had a boyfriend.

He blinked and then grinned. "We're not doing anything but talking. Is this your way of saying get lost?"

She flushed. Did she read the situation all wrong? She felt snobby and presumptuous. "No. Sorry. Just didn't want to give off the wrong vibe."

He waved her words away. "No worries. Plus, I'm a complete gentleman."

"Oh, I've heard that before." She snorted, the previous drinks making her feel a little combative.

Derek laughed. "Ouch. What other guy would bring you a Coke, though, right? But maybe it was code. Did you want a real drink?"

"I've drunk enough for now, but thank you."

"So, who made the costume?" Derek traced his fingers along the decorative edges of her costume. When his fingertips passed her hips, she took a step backward. He stepped forward.

"I bought it."

"It's really pretty," he murmured.

She jerked her head back when he leaned in.

"Mia," said a voice.

She whipped around. *Austin.*

Derek looked startled. His face relaxed into a slow smile. "Hey, man. What's up?"

"He bothering you?"

"Nah, man. We were just talking. I wasn't trying to intrude." Derek shrugged. *You know how it is.*

"Mm-hmm, looks like it."

Derek raised his cup and walked away, melting into the sea of college kids.

Austin watched him retreat, then turned his attention to Mia.

She smiled without emotion. "Just in time, I guess."

"You okay?" His face reflected concern.

"Yeah. I'm fine. I guess I just don't know how to be rude enough."

Austin pulled her in for a kiss. "You should have told him you have a boyfriend."

She kissed him back quickly, then pressed a hand firmly against his chest. He dropped his hands, and she stepped backward, her face a challenge. "I did."

"Mm, well, I can't blame him for trying. You look amazing." He gently took her arm and pulled her close to him again.

She kept her face a frown but allowed herself to get close to him. He looked amused and kissed her forehead.

Camille bounced over with Ian. "Hey, guys! Did you just get here?"

Austin nodded. "Yep. Had to close at work, but I made it just in time to chase off some meathead."

Camille's eyebrows raised, and she turned to Mia.

Mia waved away the concern. "A guy wasn't getting the hint that I wasn't interested."

Ian laughed. "Shoulda told him you had a boyfriend."

Camille spoke before Mia had a chance to retort. "That doesn't work. They just say stupid shit like, 'Oh, I don't see him here. Where's he at?'"

The guys laughed. Austin put an arm around Mia's waist and gave it a squeeze. "Was that what he said, babe?"

Mia let out a short sigh. "No. He said we were just talking, like I was being presumptuous and conceited."

Ian let out a short laugh in approval. "Nice save."

Camille made a face and smacked his shoulder. "Hey, no. Not nice."

He laughed. "What? I'm just saying. It's a nice save for such a lame move." Camille glared at him. He cleared his throat. "Maybe not so nice now that I think about it."

Mia was done with the conversation. "Do you want a drink, babe?"

"Yeah, that'd be great. What do they have?"

Camille pointed. "There's someone playing bartender. I thought they were mixed a little funny, but I found out the more you have, the better they get." She giggled.

"She knows more about vodka drinks, so that's what I'd recommend." Ian winked and took a sip from his cup.

"I can go get you one," Mia offered.

Austin took her hand. "I'll go with. Keep you meathead-free."

Mia rolled her eyes. "Oh, my hero."

After the party, Austin followed Mia to her dorm. Ian was a senior and had already traded his dorm room for an apartment. At the end of the night,

Camille hugged Mia and let her know she'd be out for the rest of the night. *I'll see you in class.*

"Is it weird that I like that idea?" Austin spoke into her hair. They were in her bed, naked and wrapped in the sheets.

She noticed smudges of green makeup and glitter on the bedding and wondered how well it would come out in the wash. "What idea?"

"Keeping you safe."

Mia smiled broadly. "I don't think it's weird."

"I love you."

She lifted her head off his chest to look at him. His eyes were so intense and sincere she thought she could drown in them. An entire lifetime flashed in her mind at the sound of those words. It was too early to think of weddings and babies, she knew this. But her daydreams had drifted more than once to a future with him.

He had so many jagged edges, and she wanted to learn how to soften them all.

-Chapter 20-

Halloween 2016

The forecast predicted rain on Halloween, but to everyone's relief, it remained dry. It was overcast and slightly humid, which meant the darkness of night crept up a little faster than normal. Camille had the forethought of bringing along glow-in-the-dark wands and bracelets. The children were excited to use them and cracked the sticks to activate the illuminance far before daylight began to dim.

"So, is it getting serious?" Rochelle turned her attention briefly to her son. "Andre, slow down."

He and the children with him slowed at the warning tone, but only a little. There was a gaggle of superheroes, a fairy, a witch, a zombie, and a zombie fairy.

"They're about to hit the mega cul-de-sac, Mom. They're on a mission," said Lori.

Mia shrugged. "I don't know about serious, but we see each other regularly. Well, as regular as you can with a kid. My dad doesn't mind watching him, but I don't want to impose too much."

"Don't forget that I can watch him, too, if you want a getaway," Camille replied.

"I know, but Isaiah is still getting used to me being gone. Sometimes he gets a little cranky."

Rochelle's mouth dipped into a quick frown and then she nodded slowly. "Yeah, but, honey..." She paused. "You also have to live your life. Kids are resilient, but they're also notoriously narcissistic." She nudged Mia's arm with her elbow. "You know I love Isaiah, but you can't be his safety net forever."

Mia looked at the ground in front of her and blinked quickly. "Moms are supposed to be safety nets."

Camille took her hand. "Yeah, but we're also here to push our kids out into the world. I know you're thinking that you need to be around Isaiah as much as you can to make up for—well, to be there. But I promise he doesn't feel abandoned."

"Has Sean met him yet?" Rochelle asked. The group stopped at the mouth of the cul-de-sac to wait as the children made their way from house to house.

"No. I wanted to wait a while longer. I want them to meet at a group event, like a cookout or get-together or something. I want to ease into it."

Her friends nodded mutely.

They heard a whoop, and the kids rushed to their moms. "Look! They're giving out full-size candy bars at that house!"

Lori pretended to swipe the bag. "Oh! And you're coming over to share with your mom, right?"

The kids all laughed and screamed a variation of "No!" before darting toward the next house.

"It's nice out this evening. I was afraid it was going to be cold and rainy, but looks like that got pushed out a little," Lori said.

"Mosquitos are still out, though." Camille swatted at her arm. "Oooh, that front porch decoration is super cute. Did you ever put your stuff out like you wanted to?"

Lori snorted. "No. Not really. I took the kids to the pumpkin patch, let them all pick out whatever gourd they wanted. Then, I got too busy to do the carving, so I opted to paint them instead. They're kind of painted, but not very pretty because the kids lost interest about 20 seconds in. And they're still sitting in the mud room. Why? I don't know."

Rochelle shook her head, making a noise with each turn. "Mmm, mmm, mmm. See, this is why I don't even bother. One year, I thought I'd be super crafty and make a little cute fall display for Halloween. I left the pumpkin on the porch so long it rotted away. And we didn't use any of the stuff I bought to make decorations. I ended up donating them to the art teacher. The only thing I should have bought was the cinnamon stick broom, because it looked cute and smelled good without the effort. Just put it next to the door."

Lori sighed heavily. "At least you learned your lesson. I lie to myself every year."

"We made little oak leaves to stick on the windows," said Mia.

"Aw, that's a cute idea," said Rochelle.

"I just bake, because that's the only thing I can motivate my fat ass to do." Camille shot them all a grin.

Lori made a face and sent a dry look over to Rochelle. "Isn't it so annoying when skinny bitches say that?"

Camille stuck her tongue out. "Hater. It's not like I'm fit-skinny. I'm just skinny. With stretch marks."

"Girl, we all got stretch marks," said Rochelle.

Mia smiled. "And beautiful babies."

Rochelle sighed heavily as she watched the children laugh and trade candy. "Yeah. I guess."

They burst out laughing. After a few minutes, the children were done swapping candies and ready to find more houses. Without waiting for their mothers, they all bolted from the cul-de-sac, which earned them a few chastisements from their mothers. The children promised to stay within a certain distance from them and then promptly ran to the next house.

"Whatever," said Camille. "At least they're in our line of sight. Sort of."

"I think after this street, I'm calling it," said Mia.

"That's a good plan. My feet hurt," said Lori.

Rochelle nodded. "Remember when we used to go out in heels and be out all night? Ugh, we're old."

Camille shook her head. "That's because we could sleep until the afternoon. Staying up all night isn't the same when your kids wake you up at 7 a.m. demanding pancakes."

"Very true," said Mia.

They followed their children through the block and then informed them that Halloween hours were over.

"Awww, Mom. C'mon! We can do one more street!" Andre pulled on his mother's arm.

"Ain't nobody got anymore candy. Plus, we just completed the circle. If we keep going, we'll pass the cars."

"It all ends in five minutes anyway," said Lori. Which was a lie. Her children had given up asking to go to another house and were busy trading candy. "Do that at home, guys! You're messing up progress."

"What progress?" Isaiah asked.

"Progress to the car!" said Rochelle.

Luca glanced at his mother. "Can you carry me? My feet hurt."

"Oh my gosh, you're so dramatic. The car's like a block away. You're fine."

Once the children were all buckled into the cars, the women chatted nearby in a circle.

"You know what? I should have told Jessica I was doing leg day today. Then, she wouldn't expect me tomorrow," said Lori.

"Oh, you took her up on her offer?" Rochelle grinned. "I'm impressed!"

"Just every now and again. Whenever Jeff's available to watch the kids."

"Shit," said Camille. "We should probably have Jessica do Halloween next year with all the kids. This definitely counts as a workout." She pulled a candy out of her purse, unwrapped it, and popped it into her mouth. "With a great incentive at the end."

They laughed.

"This was fun. Tiring, but fun." Mia smiled at her friends. The sun was setting quickly, and darkness was enveloping the neighborhood.

The women hugged each other and got into their cars. Mia fell wearily into the driver seat and smiled at Isaiah through the rearview. A smear of chocolate was on his cheek. She chuckled and held her hand back toward him. He deposited a random candy onto the palm of her hand.

She sighed, weary but happy she was able to give Isaiah a normal holiday experience. When she shifted her car into drive, the rain began to fall, as if it had been watching and waiting, unwilling to ruin their fun.

-Chapter 21-

November 2016

"Sometimes I wonder why we want relationships." Mia propped an elbow on Camille's kitchen table and popped a pretzel stick into her mouth.

Camille looked up from her cup of tea, surprised. "Trouble with your new beau?"

"No, not what I meant. Everything is going well between Sean and me for now." Mia crinkled her nose and closed the pretzel bag. "I think these are stale."

"Uh-oh."

Mia frowned. "What?"

"'For now' doesn't sound like a great outlook."

Mia shifted in her seat. She and Isaiah were visiting for the afternoon. The boys were playing in Luca's room. Periodically, giggles erupted from behind the closed door.

"I didn't mean to sound so pessimistic."

Camille gave her hand a squeeze. "Sometimes our intuition points out issues before we figure them out."

"I feel like my intuition is broken."

Camille sat her cup on the table and waited.

Mia sighed and picked at fingernail. "I feel like I'm second guessing everything. Now with Sean, I'm worried that I'm dating too soon, but then I wonder what the appropriate time for dating someone new is. I mean, look at my dad. He's never really dated anyone for a long time. He obviously never remarried. And then I wonder if I'm missing a bunch of red flags because it's been so long since I've dated someone. I mean, he's a great guy, don't get me wrong. He seems almost perfect so far. He hasn't met Isaiah, and we haven't fought yet, so I can't completely judge him, but so far, it's been great." She looked up at her friend. "Or maybe I'm just self-sabotaging because I suck."

Camille clucked her tongue. "You don't suck. And Sean is incredibly lucky to have found you. But what did you say to me when I got back together with Keegan? Go slow. Take your time. Have a lot of amazing sex."

Mia laughed.

"Okay, maybe I was a little liberal with that last part. But I'm just saying. You're right. It's been a while since you've been in the dating pool. You're enjoying his company. Don't overthink. Don't overstress. Just enjoy. You deserve to be happy, and you look happy. And I think sometimes you feel guilty for feeling happy, which is really shitty of you to feel. Stop being so rude to yourself."

Mia groaned and put her forehead on the table. "Why am I like this?"

"Because you're trying to reach patron saint status." Camille laughed when Mia lifted her middle finger without raising her head. "Are you happy with him?"

Mia sat up and sighed. "Yes."

"Well, there you go. That's all that matters right now." Camille banged her fist on the table, startling Mia. "Sorry, didn't mean to make you jump. I almost forgot! My brothers and Selina will be in town, and we're having a get-together next Saturday. Party games, a lot of noise, and probably a lot of kids. Probably not enough booze, because kids. And you're invited. You can bring Sean along if you want to, even though you were just thinking about breaking up with him."

Mia laughed, surprised. "I wasn't thinking about breaking up with him."

"Sort of sounded like you were thinking of—"

"I wasn't."

"I'm telling him that he'd better step his game up, because you're—" Camille laughed as Mia swatted her arm.

"Go away, woman. You're absolutely the worst—"

"I'm the best."

"I want to ring the doorbell!" Isaiah hopped on one foot as he approached the front door.

Raphael showed a lot of pride in his outdoor aesthetics. The path leading to his home curved gently from the U-shaped driveway to the front porch. Large, decorative stones had been pressed almost flush with the ground around it. His lawn was well manicured. Medium-sized bushes dotted the boundaries. A large oak tree stood proudly in the center of the front yard, providing shade to a small bench and a few clusters of flowers. Eloise's influence was present in the wildflowers planted in the flower beds lining the house.

"Okay. Careful," Mia warned. Her hands busy balancing a side dish.

"I am careful." Isaiah hesitated before hopping up the four steps required to reach the porch. He grunted as he landed each time.

They hadn't seen Camille's entire family since the funeral, and Mia had butterflies.

The door opened almost immediately after Isaiah pressed the doorbell. Camille's brother, Theo, appeared in the doorway. He wore a cream-colored sweater and uncharacteristic slacks, but his dirty blonde hair was tousled in his signature style. He broke into a wide grin.

"Mia! I heard you might be making an appearance. And who is this giant man? Don't tell me it's Isaiah!"

Isaiah giggled. "Yeah, it's me!"

Theo held out his fist, and Isaiah bumped his own small fist against it. Theo winced and shook his hand. "Oh man! You're getting so strong! I bet you do a hundred push-ups every morning."

This prompted more laughter from Isaiah. "No!"

"Well, then how are you getting so strong?" Theo narrowed his eyes and crossed his arms.

Isaiah lifted his chin and shrugged. "I'm just strong."

Theo shifted his attention to Mia and winked. "Must be all of your mom's amazing cooking, right? I can take that." He took her covered dish without waiting for an answer.

Camille's voice rang out. "Theo! Is that Mia? Flirt on your own time, and let my friend in."

He laughed. "What? I'm being cordial." He stepped out of the way, and the pair entered.

Camille walked into view from the foyer and drew Mia in for a hug. She kissed her on the cheek. "Not everyone is here yet. Mom and Dad are in the kitchen if you want to say hi."

The house bustled with activity. A few people were sitting in the living room, but most were standing.

"Did you invite the whole town?"

Camille laughed. "Not quite. Most everyone here is family." She turned her attention to Isaiah. "Luca's upstairs with his cousins. I think one of them brought a game system, so they're taking turns playing video games."

Isaiah ran off without saying goodbye.

Mia smiled. "Well, okay then. Video games for the win." They walked to the kitchen. Eloise stood stirring the contents of a giant pot and Raphael was laughing at something his son Noel had said.

Eloise's eyes lit up when she saw Mia. She clanked the ladle against the pot before setting it on the stovetop, toweling her hands, and crossing the room to embrace her. "Mia! I'm so happy you made it. I was hoping you'd come. It feels like forever."

"Do you want a drink, Mia?" Raphael asked.

"Sure."

Raphael tilted his chin up slightly. "Theo! Get Mia a drink." He waved away Mia's protests. "He's already digging through the drinks. Might as well make himself useful."

"What are you wanting? Soda? Beer? Wine? Oh, there's also some of those seltzer juice drink things. Do you drink those? I don't understand the appeal. They taste like sadness with a cherry aftertaste."

Mia laughed. "Is there Coke or something?"

"Coke coming up."

Eloise touched her elbow. "Did you want a glass or ice for that?"

"No, it's fine from the can."

"Okay. If you change your mind, just ask." She touched Mia briefly on the cheek and smiled. "I'm so happy you were able to join us today! How have you been?"

Mia smiled, sorry she had let so much time pass between visits. "I've been good. Isaiah's in first grade now, which is crazy. I feel like for every year he ages, I age three."

Raphael laughed. "Yes! But imagine how much older we feel, with you little girls now grown with your own children. It goes by very fast. I'd love to have a few more days with my children as little ones again." He clapped a hand on Noel's back.

Camille beamed at her father.

"Really?" Theo asked. His eyes sparkled.

Raphael narrowed his eyes. "Maybe not you." He turned to Mia. "This one was a crazy one. I'm not sure how he survived childhood."

"That sounds like disappointment." Theo was grinning.

"What? Not disappointment. Just a statement. You were a daredevil."

Theo shrugged. "I'm adventurous, but also cautious."

Eloise shook her head and placed a hand on her heart. "All of your emergency room visits suggest otherwise."

"That was only twice. Okay, maybe three times. But those weren't from lack of caution. I just landed a little wrong."

Eloise looked at him mildly. "At least you're on your own health insurance plan now."

He made a face. "That does dampen things."

Raphael checked his watch. "Dinner is almost done. Is David joining us?"

"No, unfortunately. But he sends his love."

"Is Sean coming?" Camille stole a bite of the chicken salad.

Eloise fanned her hands as if shooing a fly. "That's part of dinner! Wait like everyone else!"

"Mom, this is really good." Camille stabbed a fork into the mix and took another bite. "You should try some."

Mia laughed. "Yeah, he should be here any minute, actually."

"Keegan's going to be here later, too." Camille scooped out more of the salad.

While Eloise was busy guarding the chicken dish from Camille, Theo crossed the room and spooned out a bite from the giant pot. "Sean?"

Eloise huffed. "Raphael, do something about your children."

Camille took another bite. "This is a compliment, Mom. Sean is Mia's new boo."

Theo looked at Mia with raised eyebrows. "Oh. That's great."

Mia felt her ears grow warm. She shrugged.

"Don't make it weird, Theo," warned Camille.

"What?" he said. "You guys are like my sisters. I have to screen people."

"I *am* your sister, you dolt."

"You know what I mean."

"Raphael!" Eloise relocated the chicken dish.

"Okay, children. Out. All of you, shoo, before you get me into more trouble."

Theo snagged a roll and fled the kitchen, laughing, his mother yelling at him in French.

The doorbell rang again. Mia heard Sean's voice, and her stomach erupted in butterflies.

"I feel so nervous," she said to Camille.

"Why?"

"I don't know. He gets to meet everybody. He gets to meet Isaiah. I thought a big, busy group would ease the pressure of a meet-and-greet, but this immediately feels worse."

Camille rubbed her arm. "You're overthinking."

"You're right." She took a big breath and rushed over to Sean.

His stance was rigid. When he spotted Mia and Camille, his shoulders dropped, and he smiled. "Hey. You said not to bring anything, so I brought some wine." He lifted a bag.

Camille grabbed it. "Thanks so much!"

Theo appeared. "Hi, welcome!" He thrust his hand out.

Sean accepted, and they shook. "Thanks."

"Theo, this is Sean," said Mia. "Sean, Theo."

Sean smiled. "It's nice to meet you."

"So," said Theo, popping the last bit of roll into his mouth, "what are your intentions with Mia?"

Sean's eyebrows raised, and he stole a glance at Mia.

Camille took her brother's arm. "Theo. Help me put this on ice."

"What? That's a red. It doesn't go on ice. I was—"

"Let's go. Right now. You heard Mom, she's stressed and needs help."

Mia suppressed a giggle as she watched Theo get shoved back into the kitchen and heard the subsequent protests from Eloise.

Sean cleared his throat. "He seems nice."

"I grew up with this family. Camille's brothers are like my brothers. They get a little nosy with our love lives."

"Good to know."

She kissed him lightly on the lips. "Let me introduce you to everyone. Well, everyone I know. There are a lot of people here that are new to me. Camille's family is loud and crazy, but they're also wonderful. Also, Keegan is arriving in a bit, so you'll have another familiar face besides mine and Camille's."

"Yeah, he had mentioned it."

Mia made the rounds and introduced Sean to Camille's parents and a few other guests. He soon began to work the room, and Mia found herself letting him take the lead on conversations with the people neither of them knew.

"I'm so jealous of people like you."

Sean looked at her quizzically.

"So sure of yourself. I feel so awkward in a room full of strangers. The only reason I agreed to this party was because I know so many people here."

Sean hugged her and kissed the top of her head. "You just have to fake it till you make it, right?"

"I think it's a little more than just faking it."

He shrugged. "Well, that and the fact that the part I'm actually nervous about is meeting Isaiah. The rest of this seems easy in comparison."

Mia smiled. "That's true. That's gotta be terrifying. What if he doesn't like you?" She made an exaggerated horrified face.

Sean barked out a laugh. "Oh! Thanks for the encouragement. I think I need another beer."

Eloise walked into the living room and clapped her hands. "Hi, everyone! Dinner is ready. Come help yourselves. I have the food set up on the table. It's kind of buffet-style. Sit wherever you'd like. The table seats a lot, but feel free to make yourselves comfortable anywhere."

Someone yelled up for the kids. A small stampede sounded as children whooped and called dibs on where to sit.

Isaiah spotted his mother and ran over. "I'm going to sit with Luca and his cousins, okay, Mom?"

Mia smiled at his excitement. "Of course, mi amor. But first I wanted to introduce you to... my friend, Sean."

Isaiah looked at Sean. "Hi." He ran toward his group of friends. "I can sit with you!"

Mia wasn't sure what she was bracing for, but it wasn't that. "Well. That was anticlimactic."

Sean laughed. "Yeah, I'll say. That's okay, though. That means he's excited to be with friends. Do you want me to grab you a plate?"

Keegan had arrived right before Eloise announced dinner. They sat with him, Camille, and the majority of Camille's siblings. Once she was full, Mia sat and watched her son laugh and interact with the other children. She remembered how healing it was to be with a family, albeit a borrowed one, after her mother died. She felt a stab of sorrow that her father hadn't joined them. He'd never been a fan of crowds, but she still felt like a piece of him yearned for connection. He just didn't know how to reach out or how to accept it.

"Maybe that's why he never remarried." It came out as a whisper.

Sean looked over at her. "What was that?"

Her eyes widened slightly. "Oh, I was talking to myself."

Isaiah appeared. "Can I have seconds of cake? Miss Eloise said I had to ask, even though I told her you would say yes."

Sean grinned. "That's a great selling strategy."

Isaiah glanced at Sean, then turned his attention back to his mother.

"Please." He drew out the word.

"I don't know. How big are the pieces?"

"Mo-om. Not that big. Very small. That's why I want another one."

Sean nodded. "I'm on his side. I definitely saw not-big-slicing going on in the kitchen when I got us more drinks."

Isaiah studied Sean a moment. He stood straighter and smiled. A grown-up was on his side. "See?"

Mia laughed. "Well, okay, but I need to point out, Sean, that you're not the one in charge of this little guy's bedtime later. But fine. One more slice."

"I'll go with him," said Sean. "And supervise the cutting. Want a slice?"

"I'll take a small one."

"You're right. He's a good guy," said Camille after the boys had left.

Keegan raised an eyebrow. "Of course he's a good guy. He's my friend. I have impeccable intuition when it comes to character."

Camille giggled. "Sure." She kissed him. "You're with me, so we know you choose wisely."

"Ugh, the ego." Keegan was smiling. "I actually think I want some cake, too. And I'll go make sure that Grandma isn't giving our son too much sugar. Mia made a good point about bedtime, and Eloise isn't one to say no to her own grandkids."

"Oh God, yes, you're right. Hurry! But bring me back a giant piece, please!"

"Giant piece coming right up!"

Camille sighed. "How's it going so far? He seems really comfortable."

Mia grinned. "That's because he hasn't met my dad yet."

"Oh, that's true. Meeting friends is different. And he found a way to score some brownie points with the kiddo."

"True, but hopefully there's not too much pandering."

"I say Isaiah should milk him for all he's got."

"Camille!"

She laughed and shrugged. "What? I'm just saying. That's what I would do."

"Because you're a brat."

"Who's a brat?" Keegan appeared with a slice of cake as large as the dessert plate it sat upon.

Luca was with him, pouting. "How come Mom gets a giant piece?"

Mia smiled and pointed. "See."

Camille graciously accepted the cake and took a big bite. "Hater." She turned her attention to her son. "Because Mom is awesome, and I know

Grandma probably gave you this much cake already."

Luca huffed, but said nothing.

Sean returned with three pieces of cake, each on its own plate. Isaiah bounced along next to him. "Here you are, madam."

"Mom! He let me eat a piece in the kitchen, and now this is my extra piece."

Mia raised an eyebrow.

Sean laughed. "Hey! I thought that was our secret. Guy code."

Isaiah looked offended. "I don't keep secrets from Mom."

Mia bit her lip and shook her head. "You totally got played, man." She had no doubts that Isaiah had sworn up and down that he'd keep a secret. She also knew her son was only bragging about another piece because he assumed she'd let him eat it anyway. And he was right.

"Noted."

Keegan tousled his son's hair. "These kids are criminals."

Luca batted his father's hand away. "Isaiah, let's go play."

Isaiah was busy with his cake. "In a minute."

Luca's lip jutted out for a moment. "I'm going with Tony." As he left, the group heard him grumbling, "Not fair I don't get extra cake."

Camille sighed. "That boy is never tired of sugar."

Keegan gave her a pointed look. "I wonder where he gets that from."

"Obviously, his father. Unless you mean because I'm so sweet." She fluttered her lashes.

He kissed her forehead. "You're impossible."

Isaiah pushed his empty plate toward Mia. "Here, Mom, I'm done." He ran off, presumably toward the noisiest part of the house.

The laughter and shrieking of the children increased a little until they heard Eloise clap her hands and raise her voice. The laughing continued, then ebbed away.

"Thank God for large backyards," said Camille. "For all our sakes, I hope they run off all the sugar."

After the children were ushered into the backyard, Eloise announced that she was starting a party game and anyone who was interested could join.

Camille stood and stretched. "Let's go. I know she made it sound optional, but Mom will be terribly disappointed if we don't join in."

Sean squeezed Mia's hand. "You're right. This is a great family. I'm having a blast."

She kissed him and smiled. Her heart felt full.

-Chapter 22-

November 2016

"**A**re you sure you don't mind, Dad?" Mia worried the hem of her blouse. "You know I'm not caught up on holidays." His voice was tinny, which meant she was on speaker. A short clatter rose over the phone, and she realized he was busy fixing something in his house.

"We're still doing Christmas here, just a little early. Austin's parents wanted to see Isaiah, and it's been a while."

David grunted. "They could also visit you instead of waiting for you to reach out, you know. It's a two-way street."

She sighed. "I know. I just—I don't know. It's been hard for them, too."

She heard dissent in the silence that followed, but she didn't say anything until he broke it. "Well, anyway, I don't mind if we celebrate a little early. No harm in that."

"Thanks. Isaiah is very excited about two Christmases this year."

He chuckled. "Well, what kid wouldn't be?"

"And then he has his birthday party before that. I don't know where I'm going to stuff all the gifts! Anyway, I gotta go, Dad. Love you."

"Love you, too, mija."

Mia set down her phone and rubbed the area above her eyebrow.

Her phone chimed, and she looked down. A text from Sean shone up at her. *Hey, beautiful. Bring your best Saturday.*

They had planned to run her favorite trail, and she felt a flash of competition through her veins. Embarrassingly, she wanted to impress him. But more than that, she simply looked forward to seeing him. She had expected the butterflies to calm after the first few weeks, but his daily texts and periodic gifts continued to excite her.

Once, he had sent her flowers at work. She hadn't let her coworkers in on her new romance, which meant office gossip was buzzing by the end of the business day.

"Don't do that again," she had said during a lunch date, but she was smiling.

Sean grinned. "I didn't realize we were a secret. Maybe I'm just trying to scare off the competition."

She laughed. "There's no competition, but it definitely had the office talking about me for a while. Nothing exciting happens there."

"I should have sent some to Camille's parent's house. Really show my intentions—"

"Oh my God, stop it. Theo is sweet. He means well."

"I'm sure," was the reply. She rolled her eyes, and he laughed loudly before promising another office delivery. She had narrowed her eyes and promised revenge. He called a few weeks later, laughing, promising her something even better than a singing telegram and chocolates. She found herself pledging a truce after a clown with a large gift box arrived during a team meeting. Even her functional manager, Bob, a man everyone said never smiled, laughed until his face turned bright red.

Mia picked up her cell and sent her reply. *Can't wait to see you.*

She arrived at the park a little after Sean. The gravel parking lot was half full, and she parked her vehicle catty-corner to his. She spotted him studying the posted trail map. After checking her laces, she jogged to him. He heard the crunch of steps approaching and turned. His face lit up, and he pulled her into an embrace.

He kissed the top of her head. "You excited? This weather is amazing for winter."

A stiff gust of wind penetrated the thin material of her outfit, and she pressed herself even closer to him. "Until the wind blows." She was wearing a long-sleeved athletic blouse and form-fitting jogging pants. "I should have worn my sweatpants."

"That'll feel nice once we start the run." Sean was in a regular t-shirt and basketball shorts.

"Hopefully. I'm not sure how you're not freezing in that getup."

He scoffed. "Because I'm a warm-blooded animal. But if it gets a little too cold for you, I know how to warm you up." He wrapped his hands around her and kissed her deeply. His hand wandered down her back.

"Excuse me, sir, there might be children present."

He looked exaggeratedly over each shoulder. "Hmm, I don't see any children."

She fanned her hand, dismissing his retort. "It's a state park. Keep it family-friendly, sir. Anyway, I thought we were here to run, no? Something about you don't think I'm as fast as I say I am?"

"What? I never said I didn't think you were fast. I just wanted to see you in action."

"Oh, in that case." Mia took off, laughing loudly.

"Wait! Cheater."

He caught up to her easily and nudged her elbow with his. She shot him a playful look and pulled away from him. Periodically, he'd fall a little behind, never lagging too far. Most of the trail was spent running side-by-side, their steps muted by the fallen leaves.

"Sometimes," she said, huffing as they made their way up a rocky hill, "it's nice to have someone behind you because it encourages you to go a little faster."

"I am always happy to support you from behind."

"Why you gotta say it like that?"

His laugh was warm. "What do you mean?" He increased his pace. "I'm a supportive guy."

"You were staring at my ass the whole time, weren't you?"

"The accusations."

She raised her eyebrows.

"Not the whole time. Just some of the time."

She laughed. "Shameless."

They turned at the sound of branches breaking. A white-tailed deer bounded away from them.

"Oh, nice," breathed Mia. "Deer are so pretty."

"Spoken like a true city girl."

"What?"

"They're kind of nice, but their appeal wanes quickly after living in the country a while."

"You live in the city, too." She stumbled over a root.

"Woah, careful." He caught her by the arm and slowed his pace until she assured him she was fine. "I live in the city now, but I grew up in the country. My parents live on the West Coast, but we're originally from New York—the state, by the way, not the city. I think most people forget the majority of the state is rural. Most of my family still lives there."

"I almost want to be offended that you assumed something about me, but I have to admit I immediately wondered why there were so many deer in New York City."

"See? Either way, deer aren't as majestic when they're all around you. And they're a little dumb." He groaned when he spotted another hill. "I hate this part of the trail."

She slowed on the ascent. "This is good for character. But I feel you. I hate these hills, too. I don't usually do them." She took a moment to breathe. "Deer aren't dumb."

"A deer once ran *into* my brother's car."

Mia snorted. "It did not."

"Yup. Right into the side of it. It was a small car, too, so it made a huge dent. That was a weird insurance claim."

She stumbled over another root. "Dang it. I can't run and laugh at the same time."

"We've been running a while."

"I know, but I really want to finish the loop."

"This is a really long loop."

She shrugged. "I missed a turn back there, but that's alright. It added a mile, which isn't bad."

"Well, if seven miles isn't bad, the hills are. I have to admit this is the longest stretch I've run all year."

Her eyebrows rose. "Really? I would have thought you were on top of your fitness."

"I mean, I like to toss some weights around, and I do run, but only because you can't have a good routine without running. But if I'm honest, I only run a few miles here and there."

"Interesting."

"I think I get most of my cardio when I go out to take landscape shots. I'm walking, but I have all my camera gear, and some places are hard to reach."

The trees thinned as they approached the mouth of the trail. The sun warmed their backs, and Mia was glad she hadn't worn anything thicker.

She stomped to a slow walk when they reached the sign marking the trailhead and wiped her face with her shirt. "What made you want to photograph landscapes and stuff?" She started stretching her arms.

A short wooden fence lined part of the parking lot to mark a stopping point for the vehicles. Sean threw a foot up onto the railing. "Maribel and I loved to travel. I always brought my camera along. Which also means I have a ton of photos and videos of her, of us. Not as many of Danielle, but I tried. After they were gone, I stopped all the travel. I didn't take out my camera anymore. I didn't want to go anywhere. There was no point, you know? Maribel is gone, my daughter is gone. It messes you up. And then, one day I guess I realized I needed to choose between drinking myself to death and rebuilding. And not that I would say I was an alcoholic, but I definitely wasn't choosing the best ways to cope with everything."

He switched legs and looked out at the trees. A squirrel bounded through the dead leaves and scurried up a tree. They watched it disappear.

Mia stopped stretching, not wanting to discourage him from sharing. She stood still, as if any sudden movement would shatter the moment.

Sean took a few even breaths, lowered his leg, and looked over. He smiled sadly. "Anyway, I didn't feel like traveling, but I wanted to pick up photography again. I was driving to my parent's house and accidentally took a wrong turn, which brought me by this amazing barnyard. I looked at it and immediately pictured it in black and white. That's kind of where it started, traveling specifically to capture views or architecture. And sometimes people, if you can believe it. I want every photo to be a story."

"You made your own sort of art therapy."

He mulled over the proclamation. "I don't know if it was therapy, but you're right that it helped."

Mia gave a half-smile. "Why are men so afraid of the word 'therapy?'"

He crossed his arms. "I wouldn't say 'afraid.'"

"I'm glad you got back into photography. I don't think I've seen a bad picture you've taken yet."

"Thanks for the compliment. But I only show you the best." He winked.

She took his hand and stared into his eyes, noting the amber flecks. Every new memory they created together was infused with death and grief, the ruins of their past lives. She wondered if this was creating a strong foundation or a cracked one.

She lightly touched her lips to his. "You want to take me out for a late lunch? I'm starving."

-*Chapter 23*-

Christmas 2016

Christmas Day started early for Mia. Normally, she loved a white Christmas, but since the morning and part of the early afternoon would consist of driving, she was glad it had been a dry month.

Breakfast consisted of pan dulce and small bottles of juice, but she had scheduled enough time to stop for a good lunch before arriving at her in-laws. The thought of the afternoon ahead made her stomach hurt. Visits always felt forced and awkward. She regretted accepting the invitation but felt guilty for not wanting to go.

This isn't about you. Isaiah needs this, she reminded herself.

The aroma of coffee filled the kitchen, and she lingered in the moment, dipping the concha in her beverage and then biting into the warm, sweet bread. She would forever associate the flavor combination with her father.

When she was a young girl, she'd sit in his lap, feeling very grown up for being allowed to dunk her pan dulce in his mug. Initially, she had disliked the bitter bite of the coffee, but she'd learned to love the contrast of its boldness against the muted sweetness of the bread.

She wrapped one of the sweet breads in a paper towel and grabbed a tube of yogurt and a small bottle of orange juice. She stuffed them into a small bag and sat it next to her purse. Isaiah had been bathed and dressed the night before. After he was coaxed to use the bathroom, she buckled him into his booster and started the car. She sat in the running vehicle for a few moments, counting and recounting the things she needed to bring along.

She took a breath and looked at her son through the rearview. He was asleep. "Alright, baby. I guess we're off."

The drive was relatively uneventful, and the idea of visiting Austin's family became less intimidating. The car's thermometer registered a drop in temperature even as she navigated south. When she arrived, the temperature was near freezing.

Her stomach flip-flopped when it was time to exit the car. She gave Isaiah a giant smile, hoping it looked genuine. *This is fun and exciting. We're happy to be here.*

He returned her smile, but she couldn't read it. With all she had brought, she couldn't hold Isaiah's hand.

"Press the doorbell for me, baby?"

Donna, Austin's mother, answered the door, her face arranging itself into a huge smile. "Hi, sweetheart!" She squeezed Mia tightly in an embrace. "You're so thin. Are you eating? And Isaiah! Wow! You're so big, it's been so long! You look so much like your daddy, oh man. Like déjà vu! Come give your grandma a hug!"

Isaiah shifted on his feet and searched his mother's face. Mia looked back, feeling as helpless as he did. They had seen Austin's family at the funeral and then two other times when Mia had decided to make the trip down to South Carolina.

"Oh, don't be shy. There's no being shy in Grandma's house."

Isaiah looked at his feet.

Donna turned to Mia for help.

Mia smiled politely. "He'll warm up in a bit."

Irritation flashed across Donna's face. Her lips thinned. "Well, let's get you in from the cold. No sense in warming up the neighborhood."

Mia's hands were full of presents for her in-laws and Isaiah. Isaiah held onto the bottom part of her shirt as he shuffled along next to her. He was so close she was afraid she'd stumble over him.

"Is this a bottle of wine?" Donna asked and plucked a package from her.

"Oh, yes, I—"

Donna tucked the bottle under her arm. "It's going to be a dry Christmas because Uncle Travis is here. I'll go ahead and hide it away before he sees."

Mia shifted uncomfortably. "Oh, I didn't realize—"

A voice thundered from the living room. "Is that my Isaiah?" Austin's father, Charles, appeared in the kitchen. "Nice to see you, Mia. Hope you're doing good."

"I'm well, thanks."

"Come give Pop Pop a hug!"

Isaiah blanched.

Donna shook her head. "He's shy."

"Oh, there's no being shy in this family!" He crossed the room and picked

Isaiah up.

Mia started and reached for Isaiah, the action almost making her drop a package. "Oh, I think—you don't need to—"

"Come meet some cousins." Isaiah's wide eyes met Mia's as he was carried out of the room. She wondered if other mothers were braver than her. She wanted to rush into the living room and rescue him but also didn't want to offend her in-laws. They were only visiting for the evening, after all.

"My sister's here this year, so I guess they're second cousins or something. Or is it once removed? I can't remember," said Donna and waved her hand, dismissing the thought. "Go ahead and set the presents down by the tree."

Mia rushed over to the Christmas tree and took her time placing the packages around the bottom. She stole glances at Isaiah. His rigid body began to relax as one of the older children showed him a video on his phone.

Donna's sister, Susan, spotted her and called out a greeting. She dragged her husband over for a quick welcome. Travis, Donna's uncle, sat watching the news, oblivious to the commotion around him. When he heard Susan yell out her name, he looked up, his facial expression changing from curious to pleased. He fought the reclining sofa into an upright position.

Mia hurried over. "No, don't get up."

"Bah! I might be old, but I ain't no cripple." He stood and gave her an embrace. The scent of alcohol and tobacco overwhelmed her. She pulled back as soon as she could without seeming rude.

When she returned to the kitchen, Donna waved her over. "Oh, there you are. Thought you got lost for a second!" She laughed. "Come help me get these potatoes done. They've been boiled, but I need them peeled and put into this pot. It's not too much because the girls aren't here this year. They're out traveling with their husbands and all that mess. I think one of them went to Florida for a warm Christmas. Who wants a warm Christmas? If anything, I'd go somewhere with snow."

Mia smiled politely at the potatoes she peeled.

"We're very glad you and Isaiah could come visit. It's a shame we don't get together more often."

Mia's smile froze. Her father's words returned to her. She used to call her in-laws more often until she realized she was the one initiating most of the conversations. Except for the funeral, Mia met with Austin's family either at their home or a place of their choosing.

Her jaw worked. "Do you have cream?"

"Cream?"

"For the potatoes."

Donna dismissed the request with a wave. "Oh, we can just use milk and butter." She began coarsely chopping a bunch of romaine lettuce. "I heard you started seeing someone?"

Mia let a beat pass. "Yeah."

"Oh."

Mia added milk, butter, salt, pepper, and some dried rosemary to the pot that held the potatoes.

Donna gathered the lettuce and threw it into a large salad bowl. "Well, good for you. No sense in living in the past." When Mia didn't respond, she added, "Is it serious?"

Mia focused her attention on the potatoes. "Not really. I mean, it's—we're taking it slow. It wasn't like I was looking to start dating again so soon."

"Right, well, life happens. Has Isaiah met him?"

Mia hesitated. "Yeah."

"Hmmm. Sounds a little serious if you're already introducing him. Unless you introduce him to everybody."

Mia forced a smile onto her face and looked at Donna. She held her gaze. "We're going slow."

Donna looked away. "I think my ham is about done."

"Where's your drinks again?" Susan walked into the kitchen and headed toward the refrigerator.

"I got them in the cooler."

Susan rummaged around and found a Sprite. She took a drink and watched the two women work. "I don't know why you insisted on a dry Christmas. Uncle Travis smuggled a flask in."

Donna gasped and marched out of the kitchen. "Pull out the ham!"

Susan glanced over at Mia, annoyed. "You'd think she's the older one from how bossy she is. Now, where is that darn mitten? Ah, here we go."

Susan pulled the ham out of the oven and gently set it on the stovetop.

Donna reappeared, flask in hand. "Ugh, stubborn old man. Oh, good. The ham looks perfect."

After affirming the sides were done, the women set the dinner table and called for everyone.

Isaiah sat next to his mother.

Charles sat at the head of the table and said grace. Mia kept her head bowed and peeked at her son from under her eyelashes. He was biting his thumbnail. She wondered if it was a sign that he was anxious and made a mental note to ask about his feelings later.

"Alright, guys, dig in," said Charles.

As everyone talked amongst themselves, Mia interacted as much as possible with Isaiah. She shifted her chair slightly to angle toward him, discouraging eye contact from anyone else at the table.

"So," said Donna, piercing through the chatter, "how's Isaiah doing in school? He's in first grade, right?"

Mia wiped her mouth with a napkin and looked up. "Yes."

"Wow, I can't believe it." Donna turned her attention to Isaiah. Her voice turned sing-song. "It feels like yesterday you were just a baby. And now you're six and in first grade."

"I'm seven," said Isaiah.

"Oh, yeah, I almost forgot! You just had a birthday. I wish we could've gone to your birthday party. Do you like school?"

Isaiah shrugged, and Charles laughed. "Yeah, your dad wasn't much for school, either."

Mia took an even breath.

Donna finished a bite of her salad. A small smear of dressing remained on the corner of her mouth. "Do you like your teacher?"

"Yeah. He's nice."

One of Susan's children interjected. "When are we doing presents?"

Susan hissed at him. "Shh. Don't be rude."

Travis snorted. "He's just saying what everyone's thinking. Donna, you got some dressing on your mouth."

"Oh! How embarrassing." Donna swiped a napkin over her mouth and chin.

Charles eyed everyone's plates. "Looks like everyone's finished. We can head over that way and get everything set up while the ladies clean up the kitchen. C'mon, kids."

Mia realized she was making a face when Susan nodded at her. "Exactly what I'm thinking. He's a little traditional in the way he thinks." She sighed and got up. "Alright, let's hurry, I guess."

Mia scraped leftover food into the trash and passed the dishes over to Susan. She rinsed them and loaded the dishwasher the best she could. Donna packed up the leftovers and shoved them into the refrigerator before pulling out a few pies.

"For after presents," she explained.

"Alright," said Susan, as they walked into the living room. "We womenfolk are done with our domestic duties. I think we're now allowed back in public."

Donna blinked and looked at her sister in surprise while Charles guffawed.

Isaiah sat on Donna's lap while presents were distributed and opened. After opening a gift, he'd turn and show both her and Charles his present, a big smile on his face.

Mia settled into the sofa a little easier watching him interact with his grandparents. It wasn't his fault that they didn't have a great relationship. Her personal feelings were irrelevant.

Even so, she didn't fully trust them. She wondered if some of their behavior was from remorse and apologies that were too late to ever utter.

As a complete family, she and Austin had only visited them on Christmas once.

"Christmas was never a big deal. Maybe for them, but not for me," Austin said once, as an explanation.

Mia frowned, confused. "What do you mean?"

"I just never got a bunch of presents or anything like that. It was always one or two. Which sounds horrible because I'm complaining about gifts. But I don't know. It was just weird."

She tilted her head. "I still don't understand."

Austin chewed on his cheek for a moment. "Once, we had a giant Christmas. We went to my grandparents' house because it was the biggest and everyone was able to join. The tree was piled high with presents. You could barely see the tree. Anyway, I was like nine or ten, I don't remember, but I was small enough to be excited. I couldn't wait. And then they started giving them out. My sisters' names were called. My mom, my dad, then my cousins. It took forever. And then finally. Austin! My name! I ripped it open, and it was a pack of white socks. I thought, 'That's fine. I'll see what else I get.' But that was it. It was the only gift I'd get that year. Later, my dad asked me what I got, and I just held up the socks. He said, 'Oh.' And looked away."

Mia's mouth dropped. "How dare they," she said, barely a whisper.

He shrugged and looked away. "I mean, gifts aren't everything. Plus, now we get to do Christmas our way." He turned toward her to smile, but it didn't reach his eyes.

All the gifts had been opened. Mia kept her eyes on Isaiah as he moved onto the floor and started playing with a remote-control car.

Donna clapped. "Wow! Look at how many presents you got!"

-Chapter 24-

January 2016

"I feel like such a bitch." Mia shifted in her seat. She and Camille were at an indoor play area. January had been mostly dry, but the current weekend was drizzly and overcast.

"Girl, you're a goddamn saint for keeping that relationship even a little bit alive. I'm lucky that no matter what, Keegan's parents are amazing and neutral. If we break up again for whatever reason, they'd stay committed and involved with Luca just like before."

Mia nodded, sullen.

Camille caught her friend's eyes. "But at the same time, Austin's parents were abusive, narcissistic assholes."

Another mother sitting near them cleared her throat and shot them a look. Camille smiled broadly at her. When the woman started scrolling on her phone again, Camille rolled her eyes.

"So then, is it wrong for me to go see them?"

Camille hesitated. "I don't think it's wrong, per se. I just think you don't need to be breaking your back to do it."

"I'm afraid if I close the door completely, Isaiah will grow up and hate me for it. They're all he has left of his father." Mia sighed and ran a hand through her hair.

"Oh, God, no. No. He is what he has left. Look at his little face. He has so much of Austin in him. When he looks in the mirror, he'll see pieces of his father. Austin is never really gone. I think what you're doing is beyond what you need to do. If you cut them off, or at least demand they meet you halfway, then that's fine, too. Have they even called since Christmas?"

Mia shook her head.

"See? As much as they try and guilt trip you over everything when you're around, they don't care in the moments in between."

Mia studied her folded hands and then pushed her hair out of her face. "Well, anything new with you?"

"I'm thinking about seeing if Keegan wants to move in with me."

Mia's eyes brightened. "Oooh!" she sang.

"Don't get too excited. I'm just at the thinking phase." Camille scrunched her nose.

Mia smiled, amused.

"Well, now he's over all the time. Luca loves it. And he hardly ever goes home. And it probably makes financial sense to consolidate bills and stuff."

"And?" Mia grinned.

Camille rolled her eyes again. "And maybe I like him."

Mia giggled. "Well, I'm happy for you. I'd say do it."

"That's because you're a romantic. How are you and Sean?"

Mia shrugged.

"Uh oh."

"No, it's fine. I'm just—"

"Spill it, girl."

"I'm mad at him. Maybe 'mad' is the wrong word. I am… irritated."

Camille raised an eyebrow. "What'd he do?"

"He came over for an early dinner with me and Isaiah. I think Isaiah was in a bit of a mood, and I should have cancelled, but I thought it'd be fine. Anyway, he was not on his best behavior. And to be fair, Isaiah does lash out when he's angry. But I think he has every right to be angry right now. Anyway, Sean snapped at him. Told him he was being disrespectful and to apologize. All that. But he just ran to his room." Mia held a hand up. "And I know he was right. Isaiah was being disrespectful. But it felt like… I don't know. You're not his dad, right? There's a line. Let me handle my own kid. We're not there yet." She dropped her hand in her lap.

Camille winced. "Yikes, that sucks. Keegan and I are always stepping on each other's toes parenting, and we're both Luca's parents. Did you tell him how you felt?"

"Yeah. But he said something like I feel too guilty over Austin's death and Isaiah is using that as a manipulation tactic."

"Kids are smart, but that's kind of a shitty thing to say."

Mia shrugged. "Well, I was also not nice. I told him he'd never been a parent, what did he know?"

Camille sucked in air through her teeth.

154

"Yeah. He left on a bad note. We've texted a little bit back and forth, but it's a little tense."

"You guys going to talk about it?"

"We have to. I still don't think he needs to be stepping in with Isaiah. Maybe I just need to take a few steps back from where we are. Like, no more evenings over. I think I'm just feeling territorial."

"Yeah, maybe that's a good thing. Overall, I like seeing you two together. Sean seems crazy about you. And you look happy when you're together."

Mia smiled. "Thanks." She sighed dramatically. "I'll call him later. Or something. We need to stop texting. It feels so passive aggressive."

"Because it is."

"Thanks, bitch. That's what I said."

Camille laughed, and the woman near them relocated to a different seat.

"Can we get juice?" Luca ran to his mother's side and shook her arm. Isaiah arrived a second later.

Camille looked at him in mock offense. "Hi, Mom. Love you. Thanks for bringing me to—"

Luca shook her arm again. "Thank you. Can we get juice?"

Her eyelids lowered, and she shot Mia a dry look. "I feel so appreciated. Okay, okay. I'll go grab a few juice boxes. You think they serve beer here?"

Mia smiled. "I think they're fresh out."

"Damn."

∞ ∞ ∞

"I love *Abuelita* hot chocolate. Especially when it's so cold outside," Mia said. She blew on the top of her mug. "My mother used to wait for it to cool, and she'd scoop up the skin that'd form."

She was in Sean's kitchen, barefoot and self-conscious, standing next to the island across from him. She had invited herself over, insisting they talk, and yet she found it incredibly hard to start the conversation.

The hot chocolate was an impulsive decision born out of the need to do something besides show up at his apartment just to talk about how he hurt her feelings.

The corner of his mouth lifted slightly in response to the story she shared about her mother. He had a hand wrapped around the mug of hot chocolate she had handed him, but he had yet to sample her offering. His eyes were trained on hers.

She looked away and took a sip. "I don't really like the skin, though. I like mine all stirred up. It settles quickly." She steeled herself. "I'm still a little mad at you."

He frowned. "Me? What the hell did I do?"

Her jaw tensed. The trip over to his place immediately felt like a bad decision.

He noted the change in her features and sighed. "I don't mean to snap. But honestly. What did I do wrong? I don't even understand what happened. One minute, everything's fine. Then, Isaiah says something really disrespectful, and I just said—"

"He's not your kid!" She yelled it out before she could stop herself. "Sorry, I'm just—" she stopped to take a deep breath. When she began speaking again, she purposefully kept her voice low and even. "He's not your kid. He's my kid. And he's struggling. And yes, you're right, he might be taking advantage of me or trying to get out of trouble. I think most people try to avoid trouble whenever they can, kid or not. But I constantly feel like I'm doing the wrong thing. And the last thing I want to do is to respond in a way that is harmful. I don't want him to feel like the only parent he has left is—"

Her eyes welled up, and she bit her lip. *Damn it.* She picked up her mug and held it in front of her chest, as if trying to create a barrier between them.

Sean stepped forward, and she took a step backward.

He exhaled and gave her extra space. "I know he's not mine. I know. And I know that I don't have any experience actually parenting someone."

"Sean, I didn't mean—"

"I just know I care about you, and Isaiah was being really mean and using his dad's death as—"

Her chest tightened. "Stop."

The warning came across clearly, and Sean paused, his eyes searching hers. "You've said before that he doesn't quite get death yet."

Mia stood rigid next to the kitchen island, bracing.

"So, he might not get that he's hurting you."

The mug made an ugly rapping sound when she slammed it down, her eyes blazing. Sean's eyes widened in surprise. "Isaiah is not someone you need to protect me from." Her voice was almost a growl.

He studied her face a moment, then looked away. He nodded, eyes focused beyond the wall of his home.

She thought about picking her mug back up and throwing it at him, imagined the dark hot chocolate painting the front of his shirt, imagined his surprise. She envisioned storming out of his apartment, leaving him, stunned and silent, forever.

As the silence settled heavily around them, Austin's loss pressed against her skin, drank in all the oxygen.

Not now.

She missed him so deeply she could barely breathe. She was in another man's home, discussing their son, and she wondered then if she was wrong. What if there was an afterlife? Was his essence watching the scene unfold? What would he think? Who would he side with? The floor threatened to give way.

She sat before her knees could buckle. Her mouth felt dry. "Isaiah needs me. It's not his job to grieve gracefully."

"Yeah, but it's also not okay for him to lash out like that. And it's not your job to be a whipping post. Grieving is one thing, but—"

"But why do you get to dictate how someone grieves?" She trained her eyes on the countertop.

"I'm not dictating!" He raised his voice again and blew out a breath. He pulled out the barstool next to Mia and sat. He took her hand. "I'm not dictating. I'm observing. And—"

"And I'm not doing this right." She bit her lip and looked away from him.

"No! No. That's not..." he dropped her hand and leaned back. "You're taking everything so personally."

The chair complained when she stood. "You know... I'm so incredibly tired of everybody giving me their opinions on what I should be doing and how. I am trying my absolute best and failing. And I don't know—I don't know how to do this." And with that, an ocean of grief crashed into her. She curled onto the barstool as best she could and clamped a hand over her mouth, afraid the wail of a mourning, guilty woman would bring down the walls.

"Mia." His voice was gentle, and the sympathetic tone killed her. She turned to run away, but he caught her by the arm and brought her close to him. She resisted for a moment and then gave in to it. He held her until her body stopped shaking.

Eventually, she felt the current of emotions ebb, and she shook out of his embrace, keeping her face down.

"Can you get me a tissue, please?" She wiped her face with a sleeve.

"You are a little snotty, aren't you?"

She choked out a laugh and thanked him when he held out a napkin. Her eyes felt puffy. "I'm a mess."

Sean made a face and a so-so gesture with his hands. "Eh." He grinned when she laughed again. "You're not a mess. Or at least, not more than allowable considering the circumstances."

Mia studied his face and walked to the pink teddy bear sitting somberly in its place on his bookshelf. It had stood out the first day she visited his apartment, but she hadn't thought about it then. After he had told her about Maribel and Danielle, he had taken her on a photo tour of his apartment. The toy held a small frame which housed one of the only photos of his daughter. A photo of him and a pregnant Maribel lived semi-hidden in his bedroom. His home office housed most of the other framed photographs. The loose photos were tucked into albums and shoe boxes.

"Sometimes I wonder if this is good or bad for us."

He followed her into the room. "What?"

"Bonding over loss." She shifted her focus from the photo to his face.

His mouth opened, then closed.

She sighed. "I'm sorry. All I wanted was to come over and talk about how I feel about you and Isaiah."

He shoved his hands in his pockets. "And how do you feel about it?"

She considered the question. "Territorial."

"Makes sense. I stepped on your toes. I'm sorry."

She smiled sadly. "But I lashed out. And I didn't think before speaking. And I hurt your feelings."

He bit his lip, and Mia felt a flash of desire. "It wasn't the best choice of words, no. But you're right. I've never been in your shoes. I've never parented a kid."

"Maybe we just need to take a step backwards."

He looked surprised. "What does that mean?"

"Maybe we're going too fast. I really like you. Like, really like you. I get excited when I come over. I'm happy when you come to my house. But I'm not ready to share parental duties or anything like that. I think maybe we just need more 'us' time and less..." she hesitated, "time that includes Isaiah. It's probably a little weird for him. He's adjusting to a lot."

He ran a hand through his hair. "Okay. If that's what you want, I'm good with it. I get it."

With that, the tension left her body. He felt the shift and pulled her into an embrace. This time, she met it.

"I love you, Mia."

Her head jerked back in surprise.

He smiled, almost in apology, and kissed her open mouth quickly. "You don't have to say it back. I've known I've loved you for a while now. Maybe today is a bad day to tell you, but I wanted you to know. I'll take all the steps you want, forward or backward, because I love you and you're important to me."

Her mouth, a circle of surprise, slowly changed into a smile. "I love you, too."

When he kissed her again, all she could taste was Austin.

-Chapter 25-

January 2017

Mia and Austin were lying in bed, their legs intertwined. The sheet lay tangled between them. The tension from their latest argument had dissipated, but she knew it was a momentary respite. A whisper of danger hung in the air. The fire was out, but its red-hot embers glowed maliciously in the shadows.

She massaged his chest with one hand. Austin's voice rumbled low. "That feels really nice."

He peeked at Mia from under an eyelid and added, "Surprised Isaiah didn't wake up."

She tapped his chest with a finger and grinned. "Yeah. You were a little loud."

He lifted his head slightly to get a better view of her. "Me? Someone's in denial. Unless it's a challenge for a second round?"

Her body was still tingling. "Oh? You got a second round in you?"

He settled back into the bed and closed his eyes again. "Yeah. Of course. Maybe. In... a while."

She laughed. "That's what I thought."

"Ouch."

"I don't have another round in me, either." She stretched her legs out and pointed her toes.

"I figured."

She slapped his chest, and he pretended it hurt. She studied the side of his face. His eyes were closed, and he looked relaxed, maybe even happy. The deep frown he had been wearing lately was gone. Age was starting to etch fine lines into his face, and she wondered what he would look like as the years passed.

As usual, she mused to herself about what a waste his eyelashes were. They were light brown, with one of his eyes sporting a few blonde ones. No one could appreciate their length unless they were intimately close to him.

Her own lashes were nearly black, but short. This meant Isaiah enjoyed dark, long lashes.

"Where do you see us in ten years?"

Austin's eyes opened, and he stole a glance at Mia. "What?"

"Ten years. Where do you see us?"

"Um, I guess here? Or in a bigger house, maybe."

"So, you do see us together?"

Austin propped himself up on an elbow and created space between them. His brow furrowed. "Where is this coming from?"

The red-hot embers had found their source of oxygen. She could have doused the embers with water, but she chose the wind instead.

What is wrong with me?

With it out in the open, she had to continue.

"I don't know. We've just been fighting a lot."

"Couples fight."

She sighed. "Sometimes I wonder what would happen if we were to… I don't know… just not be together. Would we split custody as well as Camille and Keegan?"

"What the hell, Mia?"

"I mean, would we?" The sunlight illuminating the room seemed to disappear. Lately, their relationship seemed as sturdy as a table that was missing a leg. Any bit of conflict was enough to topple it. They kept catching themselves, but just barely. She wanted to hear that they would all be safe, even after everything crashed to the ground. There was danger in the future; she felt it deep in her bones.

"Are you worried we'll split up because your best friend forgot to wrap it up and bounced once things got hard?"

"Why are you being such an asshole?"

"Why are we worried about Camille right now anyway?"

"We're not. I was just saying—"

Austin got out of the bed. He snatched his jeans from the floor and jerked them on. "Yeah. I heard. You don't see a future with me."

"That's not what I said." She sat up cautiously.

"Funny, because that's what it sounded like."

She buried her face in her hands and sighed, weary. Sorry she had brought up her doubts and terrified to know the answers. They were living in limbo, but only she was willing to point out the elephant in the room. Austin seemed content to ignore how choppy the waters had become.

When she lowered her hands, Austin was glaring at her. The hatred he emanated made her gasp and scramble backward in the bed. His skin was gray in the shadows. He was dressed in the clothes he had on the day she found him. The front of his shirt was drenched in blood.

"You killed me."

"What did you say?" It was a whisper.

His eyes were cold and hard. "This is your fault. You couldn't stand being married, could you? It was so hard to think about someone else except poor Mia, right? Your son is fatherless now because you couldn't get over yourself."

He was on her in an instant, hands around her neck. "Why was the neighbor's first thought that I killed us all? Mia!"

Austin was yelling at her, but his voice sounded distant.

"Mia!"

Her body felt like it was being shaken violently. Darkness came.

She bolted upright and looked around. Slices of fading light fell into the room through the window blinds. She startled at the shape of a person on the small sofa chair in the corner of the room. A blown-up canvas of a rocky stream hung on the wall next to the chair snapped her into the present. The "person" was a crumpled, knitted throw. She felt a hand on her back, and she turned quickly, realizing a heartbeat later she was in Sean's bed.

He was sitting up next to her, face drawn with worry. He rubbed her back. "You were kicking and gasping in your sleep."

Her heart hammered in her chest. She nodded quickly and took a deep breath.

"You want to talk about it?"

She shook her head and lay back onto the pillow. The sheets were twisted around her legs, and she kicked them off.

"Okay. I'll go get you a glass of water."

"No," she said. "No, I'm okay. I'm sorry. I didn't mean to fall asleep anyway."

He smiled. "Maybe you needed it."

"Apparently not." She gave a weak laugh.

He positioned himself on his side and rubbed her arm. "You want to try and relax a little longer?"

"No, it's probably a sign I need to get up and be productive."

"It's okay to be lazy sometimes, you know. Especially when your kid is off having a blast with his best friend."

Mia smiled and touched his cheek. He intertwined his fingers with hers and brought her hand up to his lips.

She rubbed her neck for a second, shuddering at the idea of Austin hurting her. "Yeah. I'm really bad at being lazy."

"I've noticed. You sure you don't want to talk about it? Sometimes it helps to get it off your chest."

A pregnant pause filled the room. "Did you have nightmares after Maribel?"

"Mm." He nodded slowly. "For a while, yes. Mostly, I had nightmares of watching her get hit by the car. Or nightmares of her angry that I let our daughter die."

She reached for him. "Oh, baby, that's not fair. It's not your fault in either case. There was a drunk driver. He caused both deaths."

He gave a humorless smile. "Same could be said to you. Austin's suicide isn't your fault. But it's hard to convince the subconscious about that, isn't it?"

She sat up and looked away. "Yeah, I guess it is." The room seemed too dark. She hated how winter robbed the world of light.

The bed shifted under his body weight as he climbed out of the bed. "It's hard, but eventually, the nightmares do start to go away." He walked to the other side and faced her.

She searched his face. "When?"

"When you start to forgive yourself." He kissed her forehead.

She closed her eyes, and a tear escaped. Her breath was a shudder.

He wiped the tear with a finger. "It's okay to cry, you know."

"Recently, my dreams about him have been awful. He's always angry in them. Or wants to harm me. Or does harm me."

Sean mulled it over. "What were your dreams like in the beginning?"

"Honestly, I can't remember if it was in the beginning or what. The beginning was such a blur. But I did have a period of time when I dreamt Isaiah had died along with him."

"That kind of makes sense. Losing someone rocks your world, and life feels less certain, less guaranteed. Why do you think they've turned to angry dreams?"

Mia chewed on her cheek. "I don't know. They make me feel guilty. More guilty than usual."

"I think that's common after a suicide, isn't it?"

"Probably. I feel like my head is always trying to mess me up. Anyway, I'm fine. It's fine. It was a bad dream, but the longer I'm awake the less I remember. So, let's talk about something else."

"Okay." Sean stretched next to the bed while Mia appreciated his naked form. "Are you hungry?"

"I could eat."

"Do you want pizza? Sam told me the new pizza place they just built across from the mall is pretty legit."

"That sounds good. As long as whatever we order has extra cheese."

"Extra cheese, check. I'm gonna go take a quick shower first. Do you want to take one, too?"

Mia sat up and frowned. "I don't have any clothes to change into. I guess I could put on my old stuff."

"I thought Isaiah was spending the night at Camille's?"

She threw off the covers and padded over to him, also naked. "Okay, first of all, yes, he is. But I wasn't trying to be presumptuous—"

He reached out and pulled her close. "You have my total and complete permission to always be presumptuous. Presume away, my beautiful—"

"Or," she said, laughing and batting him away, "maybe I just came over to yell at you and leave. Then, go home and treat myself to silence and a book."

"You could always just leave a change of clothes here, just in case."

Her smile dimmed. "Yeah."

Sean's apartment had no indicators he was dating anyone seriously. Everything—makeup, hair ties, and toothbrushes—were carefully packed into her little bag after any overnight stays. Once, he had joked she was the only woman he had ever dated that hadn't left the telltale warning sign via an abandoned bobby pin or travel toothbrush. She had responded with a shrug and smile and quickly changed the topic.

The few times he had visited her home, she scrubbed his existence away, as if the specters of her past wouldn't allow any trace of him to remain.

"Next time."

He flashed her a smile and looked away. "Yeah, next time."

-Chapter 26-

February 2017

Isaiah picked through the markers spread out in front of him on the kitchen table. An adult coloring book was opened and partially filled in. Someone had gifted it to Mia during a Secret Santa exchange her boss had hosted. Initially, she had only allowed Isaiah's involvement when she colored an adjacent page, but she learned it held his attention longer than those advertised for children, and thus, the coloring book soon turned into his special book.

As he filled in swirls and dots with oranges, reds, and blues, she studied his growing form. The soft edges of early childhood were turning into the slender lines of adolescence. Even his little fingers, once chubby, round things, were lean and long.

"You're so big," she said, smiling and tilting her head.

Isaiah looked up, pleased. He flexed his bicep, which made her laugh. He beamed, then returned his focus to his drawing.

Impulsively, she asked, "Do you like Sean?"

His brow furrowed, but he kept his attention focused on the page. "Yeah, I think."

"You think?"

"He's nice sometimes." He swapped an orange marker for a green one.

"When isn't he nice?"

"When he gets mad at me."

She bit her lip. "He only got upset the one time. Because you were being a little bit mean to me."

Isaiah set his marker down and turned to his mother, his brown eyes reflecting offense. "I wasn't being mean."

"I mean, it was—you were a little mean. I know that day you were having a tough time. And sometimes when I'm having a tough time, I get a little snappy, too."

"I wasn't snappy."

"What were you being?"

He shrugged, his attention back on his drawing.

"Were you upset?"

A purple marker rolled onto the floor as he picked up a new color. "No, I was just talking to you, and he got mad."

She crossed her arms. "No, you were being disrespectful, if we're honest about it. You weren't just talking."

He made a noise of protest and angled his body away from her. "Yes, I was. You just don't believe me." His voice dropped into a grumble.

She opened her mouth to continue the argument and then stopped. *What am I trying to prove?* She let a beat pass. "I'm making flautas tonight for dinner."

"Okay."

"Grandpa and Sean are coming over, too." After her argument with Sean, she hadn't allowed any Sean over unless she had a sitter for Isaiah. Similarly, any outing was adult-only. On a whim, she decided to keep the meet-and-greet she had scheduled with him and her father.

His eyes lit up. "Really? You think they'll play soccer with me? You can join, too! Even though you're a girl."

His enthusiasm pleased Mia. *He must like Sean if he's excited to see him.* She inhaled sharply and placed a hand over her chest, feigning offense. "Uh, excuse me, what do you mean, 'even though you're a girl?' Girls can totally play soccer. Who says they can't? Plus, your mama happens to be awesome at it."

"George."

"Who's George?"

"A boy in my class. Abbie wanted to play soccer with us at recess, but he said no because she was a girl."

Mia frowned. "Well, that wasn't nice. Why didn't you tell him she could play?"

He shrugged. "Because he's right. I saw Abbie trying to play soccer, and she can't kick the ball right. And then she gets mad and makes everyone play something else."

"Oh. Well, in that case, it sounds like Abbie isn't great at playing soccer. But not because she's a girl."

"But she is a girl." Isaiah had lost interest in the conversation and placed his markers back into their hard case. "Can I have chocolate milk?"

"Her being a girl doesn't impact her ability to kick a ball. Talent and practice does."

"Can I have chocolate milk?"

Mia sighed. *Well, that point's not being made today.* "Sure, mi amor."

As she mixed the chocolate syrup in with his milk, her thoughts wandered to the evening ahead. Her stomach churned nervously; she hoped it would all go smoothly. This would be the first time her father met Sean, and while she didn't hang all her decisions on her father, she realized his approval meant a lot to her. And so, dinner felt larger than just a meal. The apprehension hung around her neck like a yoke. Part of her couldn't wait until the next day because then this one would be over. Still, all three of the important men in her life seemed to be looking forward to dinner, and that was a start.

Shortly after their talk, Mia started a large pot of beans. Isaiah was excited to help initially, but halfway through the prep, he grew restless and decided to watch a movie. Mia was partially relieved, as his help tended to slow progress.

The aroma of the frijoles borrachos and seasoned chicken filled the kitchen. The doorbell rang as Mia squeezed a wedge of lime over her pico de gallo. Mia looked around the empty kitchen. She raised her voice. "Isaiah, baby? Can you get the door?"

Loud, hurried steps sounded. It always amazed her that such a small body could emit such loud sounds. "Hi, Sean! What's that?" She heard the bass of Sean's voice but couldn't make out the words. "Wow, cool!"

Quick, small footsteps sounded again, but with the addition of a muted heel hitting the floor. She knew it was Sean because of Isaiah's greeting, but had she not heard his name, she would have still recognized the confident, unhurried pace. Her pulse quickened at the sound.

"Look, Mom!"

She threw away the spent lime and looked up. "What's up?"

Isaiah proudly held up a Lego set. "It's for me, and it's not even my birthday!"

Sean was smiling as he entered the kitchen. He was dressed in a light blue button down and slate gray pants. "Wow, it smells great in here." He held a bouquet of wildflowers and a large, white box.

Mia raised her eyebrows and grinned. "Well, of course. Flautas, arroz, frijoles borrachos, and chiles rellenos because I think that counts as a vegetable. Prepare to be amazed."

"And she's modest."

She stuck out her tongue and pointed at his offerings. "Look at you trying to earn brownie points."

He crossed the room and set the box on the counter, then turned his attention to her. His kiss was warm and sweet. "Brownie points? Can't a man just be nice without ulterior motives? You look beautiful, by the way."

Mia laughed at the compliment and tilted her head. She had worried all day about what to wear. She didn't want her father thinking she was trying too hard but didn't want to look a mess, either. She had settled for her favorite skinny jeans and an oversized knit sweater. The colors complimented the coral lipstick she wore.

"Thank you. Let me wash my hands, and I'll grab a vase for those. We can set it on the dining room table for a centerpiece."

She turned and almost tripped on Isaiah on her way to the sink. "Can I open the Lego box now, Mom?"

"Oh my gosh, child. You stay in the way." He walked in a circle around her, and she bumped into him on her way to the stove. "Isaiah!"

"You didn't answer."

"Yes, you can play with it." She grabbed the towel that was hanging from the oven door and dried her hands, then dug through a bottom level kitchen cabinet. "Ah. A vase. Here you go."

She handed it to Sean as Isaiah popped the plastic bag that housed his toy. Legos spilled everywhere.

"Ay, Isaiah! Qué estás haciendo?"

Isaiah looked up and smiled sheepishly. "I was just trying to open it to look at it first."

"In the kitchen?" Mia rubbed her brow. "There's so much going on in here. When I said you could play with the Legos, I meant elsewhere. Not in the middle of the kitchen."

Sean grimaced. "Probably my fault. I should have waited to show him. Let me get this on the table and then I'll help pick them up."

She dismissed him with a hand. "Don't worry about it. I got it." Once all the blocks were placed back into their box, she told Isaiah to play in the living room.

"But no one's there," he said. "Will you help me?"

"I have to finish dinner stuff, but Grandpa is coming soon. He loves helping you build."

"I can help you, buddy." Sean had returned to the kitchen.

Isaiah mulled over the offer. "Okay."

"Oh! Before you do, try the pico." Mia spooned out some of the salsa and offered it to Sean.

He chewed for a second and coughed, smiling and blinking. "It's a little hot. How much jalapeño did you put in there?"

"Oh, is it? I tend to make a little spicier. I'll add more tomato. You know, my mom used to say that the way a woman made her salsa reflected her mood. When it was made too spicy, that means she's mad. Sometimes my dad would accuse her of making it a little spicier on the days she was irritated with him."

Sean laughed. "Are you mad, then?"

"Well, I almost always make it on the spicier side."

"Maybe that's because you're a little feisty."

She snorted. "Because I'm Latina?"

"Maybe."

She kissed him lightly. "That's a dumb stereotype."

"Well, you're definitely feisty when you get some alcohol in your system." He laughed when she swatted his hip again. "Alright, buddy, let's go set up in the living room so I don't mess up your mom's cooking."

"Finally," groaned Isaiah. "You guys take forever."

Sean winked at Mia as he and Isaiah exited the kitchen. "You'll get it one day."

"I'll never talk as much as grownups," Isaiah said, eliciting a chuckle from Sean.

Mia watched them enter the living room and then turned her attention to the food. The flautas had golden edges, and she smiled, pleased with the results. After laying them out on a serving platter, she sampled the rice and frijoles.

Perfect, she thought. She turned off the heat and threw the utensils into the sink.

Everything was cooked and prepped. She eyed the white box on the counter and gave in to the impulse to view its contents. She gently shimmied the top off. Red, vivid cherries peeked through the lattice pie crust. The tart fragrance brought her to another lifetime.

∞ ∞ ∞

"Look, babe!" Mia kicked off her sandals next to the front door. "Isn't this the cutest little outfit ever? And look! I bought a little giraffe that you can hang from the top of the car seat handle." She pulled a toy out of one of the bags she held.

169

She had just returned from a shopping trip with Camille, who was due with Luca any second and wanted to pick up a few last-minute essentials like diaper rash cream, a just-in-case tub of formula, and even more newborn clothes. Mia was easily swept into the excitement and returned home with baby mittens, more onesies, and a few infant toys.

She paused for a second and breathed deeply. "It smells amazing in here."

Austin appeared, his eyes sparkling in excitement.

She tilted her head and smiled.

"Close your eyes."

She set the bags at her feet. "What?"

"Don't question me, woman. Just do it."

"Okay, okay, okay."

Tentatively, she allowed herself to be led into the dining room.

"Okay, open!"

Candles adorned the middle of the table. Burgers, fruit salad, cut cucumbers with lime and chili powder, and a small bowl of spaghetti were set up around the candle display.

"All your weird, favorite, pregnant people food, all homemade. Well, to a point. The pasta is store bought, but I made the sauce from scratch. You know what I mean."

Mia laughed and kissed him.

Her first trimester was plagued with morning sickness that clung to her all day. Sometimes she knew it was likely because she had eaten too much or too little, or perhaps the wrong thing. Other times, a wave of nausea would hit her without warning, and she'd run to the bathroom, swearing off the idea of more than one child.

After her weight had dipped enough to earn a chastisement from the nurse, her doctor gave her a prescription for an antinausea medication, which she delayed filling after reading one too many horror stories online.

She wished fervently that her mother was around to give her advice. Gabriela had talked about her pregnancy with Mia before, but in the wistful way that mothers did when speaking to their children.

"You used to press your little foot out, right here!" She had told Mia, pointing to the left side of her stomach. "I would push back a little, and you'd kick back. It was like a little game between me and you."

But she had been taken years before practical stories needed to be shared. Mia couldn't imagine her father being of any help, so she turned to Donna. How had her pregnancy with Austin been? Had she taken any medicine? "Pregnancy isn't supposed to be fun, but it'll be over before you know it. Aren't you afraid of what the medicine will do to the baby?"

Mia's eyes turned glassy. She was afraid. But also knew she had to keep some food down.

After a brief silence, Donna continued, her tone softer. "I had bad morning sickness, too. I didn't throw up much, but I stayed so nauseous I could hardly stand it. What I found that worked for me was eating immediately after I woke up. Frozen grapes. I loved them. Maybe it was the little bit of sugar in the morning, but it helped a little. I'd eat some and then make an actual breakfast. It seemed to help. Maybe try that?"

At her following prenatal appointment, the doctor asked if she had started the medication after reviewing her weight. She called Camille crying, asking for her opinion.

"Forget everybody. I don't think your doctor went to med school for a decade just to prescribe dangerous medicines to women who throw up every time they turn around. You need to eat. You're growing a baby. Take the meds, eat whatever you want, and don't worry about it. This pregnancy thing is some utter bullshit. Everyone thinks they get an opinion on how you eat, work out, and walk around and then they think they can put their hands all over your belly like it's not still attached to your body. They can do whatever they want when they're pregnant. You do you."

In the end, she only needed to take the medication intermittently for a few weeks. Then, she crossed some invisible milestone, and it all ebbed away. As such, her appetite skyrocketed, and she ate whatever sounded good, which meant she mixed and matched without any reason except her whim.

"Wow. This is amazing."

"I figured you'd be hungry when you got back home. Save room for dessert."

After their meal, Austin walked out of the kitchen, a dish held out in front of him like a prize. He sat it gently in front of Mia. "Ta-da!"

The pie's golden crust was cracked and gave a hint of the red filling within. Her face lit up, and Austin grinned.

"Cherry."

"I made it myself. So, hopefully, it's good."

Mia's eyes teared up. "I already love it."

"You okay?"

Mia startled at Sean's voice. She covered the pie. "Oh, man, you scared me. Yeah, I'm good."

He gestured toward the pie. "I remembered you said your favorite dessert is cherry pie. I know a lady who makes desserts out of her home. It should be really good. It came highly recommended."

She smiled, hoping there was no melancholy within its edges. "That's really sweet."

"And your dad is here."

"Oh! I didn't even hear him come in." She rushed from the kitchen and found him in the living room with Isaiah. "Hi, Dad!" Isaiah was busy showing off his new Legos.

David stood and gave his daughter a quick embrace. He had dressed comfortably, but she could tell his shirt was ironed. His dark, curly hair had been tamed with a bit of gel. "Hi, mija. Smells good in here."

"Thanks. Did you already meet Sean?"

"Yeah, for a second."

She tilted her head toward the kitchen. "Well, let me actually introduce you properly. I didn't hear you come in."

Sean met them halfway, and Mia smiled at him, mostly trying to reassure herself. She wondered if they could hear her heartbeat from where they were standing. "Dad, this is Sean. Sean, my dad."

The men offered each other their hand, and they shook.

Sean smiled. "How are you, sir?"

"Oh, don't bother with 'sirs.' I'm David. I'm good. How are you?"

A hesitation. "David. Can't complain."

The conversation lulled. Mia looked at Sean, then her father. *Oh no.*

She clapped her hands together once. "Well, dinner is ready, if anyone's hungry."

Isaiah's head popped up. "Dinner? Yay!" He raced toward the dining room, and they all laughed.

The awkwardness melted as they loaded their plates with food. Isaiah crinkled his nose at the chile relleno. Sean coaxed him into trying a bite, which he did only to make a gagging noise. Mia narrowed his eyes and stuck her tongue out, which prompted giggles from her son.

The adults conversed about the changing weather and their summer plans. As they grew more comfortable, the conversation turned to a small celebration of new beginnings and old tales. David managed to talk about his late wife and his work. Sean, for his part, was a great listener and graciously answered any question sent his way.

Isaiah gingerly transferred the rest of his chile relleno to his mother's plate and stole a flauta. Mia pretended not to notice.

After everyone had eaten, Isaiah pressed his hands together as if praying and asked to play soccer in the backyard. The adults told him that was a great idea, which elicited an excited whoop.

Isaiah immediately chose Sean as his teammate. Mia pretended to be offended. *Traitor.* Isaiah laughed.

They set up two makeshift goals and took turns running the ball back and forth. David let Isaiah steal the ball from him and vowed revenge. Mia felt a surge of competitiveness every time Sean had the ball. She managed to intercept a pass meant for him and ran it to the goal. David gave her a high-five, and her son stuck his tongue at her. She scooped Isaiah up and gave him a big kiss on the cheek.

He pushed her away. "Mo-om! Stop! I gotta get the ball."

She set him down. "Okay, fine. Meanie."

Isaiah ran to the ball and picked it up. He placed it delicately next to the makeshift goal. His look turned determined, and he kicked as hard as he could. The ball went wide, and Sean jogged to it. Mia tried to steal it back but wasn't successful, managing only to step wrong and fall. The game paused for a moment as Sean fussed over her while she laughed.

And then on the game went, until the estimated score was in Isaiah's favor. Mia informed them that they could try for one more score and then it was time to go back inside. Isaiah frowned and rushed to the ball. Sean cheered him on while David ran close behind. Isaiah and Sean crowed in victory when the final ball landed neatly past the goal line. They all celebrated with cherry pie à la mode.

Night blanketed the world as they finished their desserts. Mia followed Sean to the front door for a final kiss. She returned smiling and blushed when she saw her father watching from the living room. Isaiah had turned on his game console and was showing his grandfather his latest game.

"What do you think?"

"He seems nice enough."

"That's a safe response." Mia placed her hands on her hips and grinned.

David shrugged and smiled. "You seem happy, and that's all that matters. Plus, he has a good job, and he plays well with Isaiah. What do you think? That's the real question."

"That's true. I'm happy. For now anyway." She sighed. "Can I ask you something and you give me your opinion? Like your real opinion?"

"Sure, mija." Her father patted Isaiah's shoulder and left the couch. They walked to the kitchen together.

"Do you think it's selfish of me to be dating already?" She leaned against the counter and drummed her fingers against the cool granite.

David frowned. "Selfish? Why would it be selfish?"

"I don't know. Is it too soon? I mean, look at you. You never remarried or anything like that."

"Just because I haven't remarried doesn't mean it's wrong for you to want marriage again."

Mia felt her stomach twist. "Well, I don't know about all that." She paused and debated her next question. "Why haven't you remarried? I don't even remember a serious girlfriend."

The kitchen filled with silence, and Mia stood still, playing emotional chicken with her father, knowing one of them would have to break the silence.

"Your mother's a tough act to follow." He looked out of the window into the inky darkness of the night. "Do I really get another chance? I don't know. I was kind of a bastard growing up. I'm man enough to admit that now. And in the beginning, your mom probably deserved better. But she loved me anyway, and I learned to work hard to deserve it. I never met anyone else that I wanted to spend my life with." He turned his attention back to her. "I'm really bad at all this. You're my daughter. I want you happy. If Sean makes you happy, I'm happy. If he doesn't, well, we won't talk about that so you're not forced to lie for me."

Mia laughed. "Dad."

"You shouldn't follow my lead on any of this. Your mom would probably deal better with all of this. She would have wanted you happy, too. But if you really want an answer to the selfish question... you're the least selfish person I know. You take care of me, of Isaiah, of everyone, before you even think of yourself. That's not my definition of selfish."

An excited squeal came from the living room. She flashed her father a gracious smile and left to inform her son that bedtime was approaching. He groaned until his grandfather promised two bedtime stories.

After her father had left, and Isaiah was fast asleep, Mia collapsed onto her bed, a smile playing on her lips. Dinner had been a success. Though she knew she'd regret it in the morning, she stayed awake, numbly scrolling through her cell phone. The following day was Sunday, and there were no plans.

A text message flashed. The number was restricted. *Don't trust him.*

-Chapter 27-

February 2017

W ho is this? Mia held her breath.

Her phone said nothing. Then, a chime. *It doesn't matter. Just know he's a liar. He'll promise the world and then pull the rug from under your feet.*

Cold washed over her. She wanted to throw her phone. *Who?*

You know who.

Mia was ready to scream. She hated the anonymity of the messages, the ambiguity.

Then, confirmation. *Sean*

WHO IS THIS. Mia stared and refreshed her phone for half an hour and finally threw it onto her nightstand.

An hour passed, and her mind was racing. She ripped back the covers and padded to the kitchen. She pulled out a bottle of Merlot and poured a generous glass.

I'm not going to respond. I don't care who it is. Mia's knee bounced as her mind raced. She poured another half glass and sipped. When she reached the bottom of the glass, she walked back to her room, bottle in hand. She retrieved her phone, ready to call Sean and demand an explanation. Her finger hovered over the screen and she took a deep breath. She pulled up her last text.

If you're going to make such a bold claim to someone you don't know, you could at least give a little more info.

The phone remained black and silent. Mia sighed, annoyed. She threw the phone on her bed and walked back to the kitchen. She corked the wine bottle and placed it in its appropriate spot. When she returned to her room, her phone was illuminated. An icon alerting her to a pending text message stood out like a bad omen. Mia felt a flutter in her stomach and she held her breath as she swiped open her phone.

It was a screenshot of the conversation between Sean and Restricted.

Restricted: *It's hard to trust you.*

Sean: *But u can. I miss u*

Restricted: *I know about Allison.*

Sean: *Allison is just jealous and can't handle a break up. You're it for me.*

Restricted: *Funny doesn't feel like that.*

Sean: *You coming over or not?*

Mia's mind was racing. The tone didn't sound like Sean even if his name was on the top of the screenshot. *When was this from?*

The response was delayed. *Does it matter?*

Mia frowned. *Yeah. It does. You're trying to destroy a relationship. Least you can do is leave in the date. Did he tell you this recently?*

There was a pause before the next message. *I'm not trying to destroy anything. I'm trying to warn you.*

Mia bit her lip so hard she tasted copper. *Why now?*

Didn't realize he was screwing someone else over.

Mia's heart fell and she felt tears forming. Could she be wrong about him? *Was this from a long time ago? I'm sorry he broke up with you, but it's not my drama.*

Cheaters never change. He was hanging out with another girl not long ago. Ask him.

Do you have proof? Mia paced the length of her room.

Restricted repeated her recommendation. *Ask him.*

Mia grit her teeth together. *You're real brave not even giving me your name.*

That was the last text of the night.

∞ ∞ ∞

Mia bumped her fist against Jessica's before they made their way into the gym. They met up at least once a month to work out together.

"I figure we'll run a little as a warmup, do some mobility, and then work on our lifts?" Jessica adjusted her gym bag. A piece of her auburn hair escaped her high ponytail, and she moved it behind her ear.

Mia nodded. "Sounds like a plan."

After they changed, they met on the indoor track and started a slow jog.

Jessica shot Mia a quick glance. "So, what's the whole story?" Mia had only vaguely mentioned the texts to her friend prior to scheduling their gym date. She had been reluctant to share because she was unsure if it would tarnish her friends' perception of Sean. Further, she didn't know if she was overreacting and needed to process. In the end, anxiety won, and the story began to make its rounds.

"Okay, this is tons of drama."

Jessica's eyes lit up, and she smiled, her hair bobbing in its ponytail. "You know I live for drama."

"About me."

She pursed her lips. "Well, maybe less when it involves you. I feel a little bit like an asshole for being excited."

Mia snorted. "I know you're a ho for drama. That's why I called you, so don't even worry." She waited until the man behind them ran past. "I got a text from some anonymous number saying not to trust Sean."

Jessica's eyebrows shot up. "Oh shit, really? He doesn't seem like the type to keep crazy exes in the closet. Or maybe that's why he doesn't seem the type. Most guys are all about throwing their exes under the bus."

Mia jogged to a cutout on the track and stopped. She pulled her phone from her pocket and opened to the messages. She offered the phone to Jessica.

Jessica skimmed the texts. "Damn." A pause. "Daaaamn."

Mia snatched the phone. "Okay, and what else?"

"Sounds like a salty bitch who's bored. Have you told Sean?"

"No. Not really. I don't even know what to say." Mia looked miserable.

"Um, how about, 'Hey, babe, what the hell is this?'" Jessica grinned. "Maybe not quite that in your face, though."

"Is that how you'd phrase it?"

"Probably."

They finished their laps and made their way over to the open floor space on the first floor. Jessica plucked two resistance bands from the wall and handed one to Mia.

"Let's do some mobility work on our upper body."

Mia mimicked Jessica's movements. "I don't know how to start the conversation. Or maybe I'm just worried about what he'll tell me. I feel all anxious about it."

"Or maybe it'll be someone from a million years ago who just found out he was dating someone."

"But what about the whole Allison thing and her being hesitant to take him back?"

Jessica blew out a breath. "Honestly? That sounds like a douche line after cheating on someone."

Mia sighed and switched arms.

"But." Jessica waited until she was facing her friend. "That doesn't mean he's doing something similar to you now. She didn't show any time stamps. This could have been ages ago. People change."

"Do they really?"

Jessica held up a finger. "I know I say people don't change, but I mean that they don't change while they're in a relationship. But they do grow between them."

Mia laughed at her mock serious look. "How do you know?"

Jessica leaned back. "Because I'm dating Sam. Exclusively."

"What!"

"Don't sound so surprised."

"I'm a little surprised."

Jessica shrugged.

"You look happy about it. Awww. That's so cute!" Mia squealed.

"And I'm happy for you. I haven't seen you this happy in a long time. I don't know if Sean is long-term material for you. But what he is, at the very least, is some good in your life. Do I believe this anonymous person? Eh. Guys are dicks. But this is hardly enough information to really figure out what's going on."

Mia groaned. "Why did she even have to text?"

"Do you have an idea of who it could be?"

"You know what? Now that I think about it, the only previous people we've talked about are Sean's late fiancée and Austin."

Jessica frowned. "Really? You guys never even swapped body counts?" They put back the resistance bands and headed for the squat rack. She pointed at the bar. "Let's start light as a warm up and then do a couple heavy sets, yeah?"

Mia made a face, and Jessica laughed. "Okay, fine. Can I start with the bar?"

"Whatever feels good, but when we go heavy, let's go heavy."

Mia let out a weak laugh. "Sure." She did a set and stepped away, giving Jessica space to load the bar with weights and get in position. "I mean, is it his business to know my body count?"

"I feel you there, but still, neither one of you got curious?" Jessica began her set.

"The past is the past."

Jessica set the bar onto the rack and then stared at Mia for a moment. "You guys have issues."

Mia laughed in surprise. "What? Because we don't quiz each other on exes?"

They finished their next sets before Jessica had a response. "Because you're both so unwilling to share with the other."

"We share." Mia frowned and thought back. "We share a lot, actually. He's shared a lot about Maribel, and I've shared a lot about Austin."

Jessica shrugged and smiled at Mia. "If you say so, but you're the one coming to me with so-called drama because of an omission."

"It's not Sean's fault. It's her fault for even bringing it up."

"So why are you mad at him?"

Mia chewed on the inside of her cheek for a moment. "I'm not mad at him."

"Okay. Upset."

"I'm not upset. Don't give me that look. Okay, maybe I'm a little upset. I don't know. This is all very confusing."

Jessica pointed to the carpeted area outside of the free weight area and they walked over. "Which part?"

"Well, not knowing who this is and why she decided to text at this point in our relationship. And late at night to boot."

Jessica laid out two purple mats that were set out for gym patrons to use. "Sounds like drunk texting. She might be regretting it at this point."

She modeled different bodyweight movements that engaged their core, and Mia mimicked. When they finished, Jessica suggested ending their workout with bench presses. They only got through one set before a man walked over.

"I know you guys aren't going really heavy, but I'm happy to spot. Light weight and high reps are good for women." He flashed his white teeth at them. The front of his shirt was damp enough to cling to his chest and abdomen, hinting at the defined abs underneath.

Jessica was adding a plate to the bar and shot him a heavy-lidded stare. "Oh, is it? We're just warming up. I think we can handle spotting for each other."

His smile brightened. "Oh, okay. My bad. I love badass women. You guys come here often? I don't think I've seen you around. I just moved here a few months ago, though. So, maybe that's why."

Mia smiled politely.

Jessica kept her face neutral and her tone flat. "We come when we come. Now, if you don't mind, I want to start on this set." She added more weight and laid back onto the bench.

The man stayed in his spot. "You don't think that's a little heavy?"

Jessica lowered and lifted the bar five times before Mia helped guide it back onto its resting position. She sat up and turned toward the man. "No. We're just warming up."

He frowned. "You guys trying to bulk up?"

"You afraid of women with bigger arms than you?"

"You're being a little rude, don't you think? Doesn't hurt anything to be polite. No need for the attitude."

Jessica's smile looked like a grimace. "Okay. Thanks for the pointers."

"Whatever." The man walked away grumbling to himself.

Mia waited until he was out of earshot. "I need some of these plates off."

"Oh, yeah, I went a little heavy." Jessica laughed. "God, he was annoying. I'm glad that doesn't happen often."

"You must really be into Sam."

Jessica tilted her head. "What do you mean?"

"He was cute."

"But also annoying. And patronizing. I can't deal with men that are afraid of some muscle on a woman."

"All good points."

"But, yes, I am also very into Sam."

As they left the gym, Mia pulled Jessica into another embrace. "I'm happy for you."

Jessica kissed Mia on the cheek. "Ask him about it."

"You don't think he'll lie?"

"Well, of course he'll lie. People always paint themselves in the best light. That doesn't mean he's wrong or doing you dirty. See what he says. And then let me know. And then we can kick his ass, if necessary."

-*Chapter 28*-

February 2017

Sean's eyes lit up when he opened the door. His smile irritated her, and Mia pushed past him. She turned around and held her phone toward him. "What is this?"

She hadn't meant to start the conversation with a harsh tone, but by the time she made it to his place, her anxiety was on red, which also meant she was pissed. The text messages were like a stone in her stomach. She started the drive to his apartment livid and ready to fight with everyone. Her thoughts teetered between wanting to end the relationship and wanting to start shit with Miss Anonymous.

How dare she, Mia thought. *What a coward.*

Sean glanced at the phone, confused. "What?"

They stood in his entryway. After a beat, he informed her the screen on her phone was black. She turned it toward her and saw it had timed out. Annoyed, she let out a huff of air and unlocked her phone. The text messages were still open.

His brow creased as he searched her eyes.

She raised her eyebrows and pointed. *Read.*

He frowned and took the phone.

Mia tried her best to assess his facial expressions as he scrolled, but he remained carefully neutral. *Maybe that's the tell.* "What is that?" she asked again.

"It's from a restricted number."

Mia exploded. "I know! Yeah! It's anonymous. I tried to get a name but couldn't. But this is all about you. So, who would take time out of their day to anonymously warn me about an awful person?"

"I'm an awful person?"

Mia spoke through gritted teeth. "No. A person decided to rob me of a whole night of sleep with crazy ass messages. Did you not send those messages to someone? Who did you send them to? And don't bullshit me."

He looked at the messages again. "I'm so sorry."

She let a beat pass. "About? Can we not beat around the bush?"

"I remember sending these texts, but it was so long ago." He ran his hand through his hair. A siren sounded in the distance. "You want to actually come in past the entryway, or are we going to stand next to the door the whole time?"

She exhaled sharply and walked to the kitchen. The barstool scraped the floor when she pulled it unceremoniously from its position at the breakfast bar. She sat and looked at Sean expectantly. "I'd love a water."

He studied her a moment before retrieving a glass from his cupboard. He filled it with ice and water from the fridge and set it on the counter in front of her.

Instead of drinking from it, she folded her hands together and set them on her lap, watching condensation form on the glass.

"Her name's Angie. She's an ex. We broke up a long time ago."

She lifted her eyes and trained them on his. "Okay?"

"That's it. That's all I got."

Her eyebrows raised, and she bared her teeth. "Oh! Oh, that's all. Well, thank God this is over. I was worried for a second because some girl decided to warn me about my boyfriend. But after that explanation, who could be worried?"

"Don't be condescending."

"No, you don't stand there and be condescending. Pinche desgracia'o. Me quieres ver con la cara de pendeja."

"I have no idea what any of that means."

Mia took a breath. "It means you're being an ass, and if you think I'm dumb enough to think that's the whole story, I'm just going back home." She stood, the stool screeching across tile.

"Wait, wait, Mia, that's not fair. What do you want to know?"

"What do you mean, 'What do I want to know?' I want to know why someone would be messaging me late at night telling me all this."

Sean barked out a laugh. He threw his hands up. "How am I supposed to know?"

"Well, what did you do to her? Maybe start there."

He frowned. "Why does it have to be something I did?"

"Did we read the same messages?"

He sighed. "I mean, there's two wrongs in every breakup." Mia moved toward the door. "God, Mia, just listen to me a second before you storm off."

"I'm not storming off."

"I don't know what storming off looks like in your world, but... okay, okay. I'm sorry. I think she's probably still not over us. I wasn't that great a man back then. When she wanted to break up, I guess I was still being selfish and asked for her back. But eventually, we broke up for good. Which was probably for the best because, clearly, I wasn't ready to move on from Maribel—"

Mia bristled. "Wait a second, are you blaming Maribel for how you treated your ex? It's her fault—"

His dark eyes filled with anger. "What?"

She balled her fists.

"I am not blaming Maribel for anything. She's not part of this, and I'd like for you to keep her name out of your mouth if you're just trying to get a rise out of me."

She lifted her chin, eyes flashing a warning. "A rise out of you? Are you kidding me right now? You think I just came over to yell at you because you have an ex-girlfriend?" She touched her fingers to her head and then pointed them to the ceiling in exasperation. "What do you think I'm upset about right now?"

He closed his eyes for a moment and took a deep breath. "I get it. That's a weird message. But you don't even know this person, and now you're mad at me because someone else decided to—I don't even know—start some shit because I wasn't a good boyfriend years and years ago."

Mia walked to the living room and sat heavily on his couch. She crossed her arms. "Can you call her and ask her what she's doing or something?"

He followed her but didn't sit. He shrugged. "I mean, she texted anonymously probably because she's not looking to actually face anyone. I haven't talked to her in years."

"If you guys haven't talked in years, then how does she know about us?"

Sean rubbed a hand over his chin, his eyes focused on the wall. "Well, I think she's still on my social."

"She has online access to you? Why didn't she message me right away?"

"Damn it, Mia! I don't know. Maybe she rarely checks my page? Maybe she got a little too drunk the other night and sent you a message? I don't know what she's thinking."

"Aren't you curious?"

He paused and blinked in surprise. "No. No, I'm not curious why a crazy ex would reach out years later to you instead of me."

Why are exes always crazy? Mia bit her lip and looked away. She took a measured breath. "What's the full story between you guys?"

He sighed in resignation. "I already told you. I have come a long way since I was younger. Especially after Maribel. Not that I'm blaming her for anything I've done. But I was a mess. I told you that. And part of that mess was..." He averted his eyes. "I guess being selfish. Angie was my first long-term relationship after everything, and I clearly wasn't ready for the commitment. It was probably a rebound, to be honest. She deserved better. The final breakup was a good thing. For me and her."

He walked over to Mia and pulled her off the couch. She let him embrace her, but she didn't return it. He laughed and kissed her forehead. "You're so stiff."

"Why is she crazy for being upset over a breakup?"

He grunted. "I'm not one to use crazy often, but she's the one texting you years after we broke up."

The corners of Mia's mouth pressed downward. "How many years?"

"Six."

"That's a long time."

"Are you going to hug me back or no?"

She laughed despite herself and wrapped her arms around his middle. "That better?"

"A little bit." He kissed the top of her head. "I'm sorry Angie dug up some drama. I'm sorry you're feeling upset. I could've treated her better, and I hope to think I've learned from my mistakes. She's—she's the type of woman who always needs someone. Do you know what I mean? Always dating someone. And I think that's why our final breakup was so tough. She really wanted it to work, and when it crumbled, it was a bit of a blow to her." He sighed. "Hopefully, she's gotten it out of her system."

The hug ended, and Mia took a step backward. "So, what does she mean about you talking to someone else the other day?" She studied his face for a reaction but all she saw was confusion.

"That, I don't know."

"Well, why would she text me that?"

He threw his hands up. "I don't know why she would text you, period! I have no idea." He stepped forward and held her hand. "I love you. I'm not doing anything to hurt you. I don't know why she's insinuating that I'm stepping out on you, but I would never do that."

"Why have you never told me about her?"

"I—well, because I didn't think I needed to. And it was so long ago. It's not like you've told me about all your ex-boyfriends."

"True. Has she ever been a problem before?"

He shrugged. "Initially, she'd ask around about who I was dating and stuff like that. But again, this was years ago. If I thought she was going to do anything like this, I would have warned you, or blocked her, or... I don't know. Something. But this is as surprising to me as it is to you. Mia. I love you. Okay? Just you. And I'm not talking to anyone else. But she's right to dislike me—hate me, even. I thought she would have moved on by now, but I guess I'm wrong. Hopefully, she feels better after this."

The discomfort in Mia's chest was relieved, but only a little. The silence between them grew. Sean's eyes searched hers, and she hoped they reflected the apathy of the ocean.

"You want to go out this evening?" He looked hopeful.

She crinkled her nose. "Not really. I'm a little tired."

His face dropped. "Oh. That's fine."

"Do you mind if we stay in?"

$$\infty\infty\infty$$

Later, after eating their takeout and curling up on the couch to watch a movie, Mia knew she loved him. The pit in her stomach had eased, and Angie seemed like nothing more than a random argument. Was she dating Sean or the opinions of his ex-girlfriends?

She tilted her head to watch him as his attention was turned toward the television screen. Fluorescent colors danced on his skin, and she found she loved his face in every hue.

Next time, she thought. *Next time, I'll leave an overnight bag here.*

-*Chapter 29* -

K id versions of popular adult songs blasted from the ceiling. Giant, multicolored inflatables adorned the floor. A huge foam pit was at the far end of the building, a line of children next to it. Squeals of laughter erupted periodically. Mia could hardly contain Isaiah as she checked into the birthday party group. His wristband was secured by the bored teenager working the counter and then he was off.

Mia watched him beeline to his friends. Andre, the birthday boy, appeared at the base of an inflatable slide and jumped when he spotted Isaiah.

"Ma'am?" The teen held up a different colored wristband when she looked his way. "You need the grown-up band so we can match you later when you leave."

"Oh, of course." She offered her wrist.

Rochelle met her as she walked into the main play area. She wore a red shirt with giant black polka dots and formfitting black jeans. "Hey! I'm so glad you could make it!"

They embraced. "You look so cute!" Mia said.

Rochelle gave a half-curtsy. "Thanks! I love this shirt. Even though Bryce, the hater, says I look like a ladybug."

Mia laughed. She loved the banter between Rochelle and her husband. "You guys are a mess. Well, you look like a *beautiful* ladybug." She held up a wrapped present. "Where do I put this?"

"Oh! I rented out a party room, so you can put it there. I'll show you. They get an hour and a half of play time and then we get pizza and cake."

After Mia was escorted to the room, she added the large, wrapped box to the pile of presents. The room had two long tables with folding chairs on all sides. The plastic tablecloth had cartoon drawings of superheroes. Party favor bags were gathered in the middle. A narrow side table was pushed against the furthest wall and on it were plates, cups, and cutlery.

"You know, I did mean it when I said no gifts necessary. He just wanted friends to play with at his party."

Mia smiled at her friend. "I know. But presents are always fun. Especially at this age."

"That's true. Well, I appreciate it."

Mia waved at the main group as they walked over. Different seating options for non-players formed a broken boundary around the area that housed the inflatables. Camille sat on a large pleather couch next to Keegan and Lori. A few unfamiliar people sat further away, chatting with Bryce. He noticed her approach and excused himself from the group to greet her. "Am I the last parent here?" she asked him. "I thought I was on time."

Lori laughed and stood to embrace her. "Nah, I'm sure there'll be stragglers. I'm waiting for the person who arrives right when the food is served. That person, I'll judge."

Rochelle shot her a look. "Look, man, that was one time. And you know why I was late."

Bryce chuckled. "She said it was my fault, too, but we all know what happened." He and Lori fist bumped.

Rochelle clucked her tongue. "Oh, it's like that? A'ight."

Bryce grinned. "I'm just stating facts, ladybug."

Rochelle pursed her lips. "Well, if you'd help get Andre ready and out the door..." She placed her hands on her hips, her chin tilted up slightly. Her voice was a challenge.

Camille's eyebrows shot up. "Oooh, shots fired." She sat straighter on the pleather couch.

"What? I help all the time!"

Rochelle raised an eyebrow. "Uh-huh. Help how? Who booked this?"

"Uh, who paid for this?" Bryce tapped a finger against his chin. He frowned to suppress a smile, but his eyes shone with amusement.

Rochelle sniffed. "That was my party planning fee." She began counting on her fingers. "I had to shop around. Make the arrangements. Send the invites. Do the headcount to make sure we bought enough pizza and party favors..."

"'We...'"

"But not so much that we overpay..."

"I'm hearing a 'we' again with the payment...."

"And then get our son ready for the day. Make sure he's clean, dressed, fed..."

Keegan shook his head. "Just stop while you're ahead, man. Trust me."

Andre ran over, dancing. "Mommy, I need the bathroom."

"Uh-oh. Emergency. C'mon. Why'd you wait till the last minute?"

Mia found a spot on a plush chair adjacent Camille, Keegan, and Lori. Relaxed in her seat, she periodically caught glimpses of Isaiah's smiling face as he and his friends moved from inflatable to inflatable.

After Andre was done in the bathroom, he beelined to his dad, coaxing him into being the monster outside a bounce house.

Bryce growled and stomped next to the mesh netting, pretending to try and rip through. The kids would scream each time, falling over themselves to run away. Eventually, the children tired of the game, and Bryce took a seat next to his wife.

Later, Luca asked his father to play a game of table hockey with Isaiah and himself, a 2-against-1 offer. Keegan grinned and pantomimed being deep in thought.

"Hmmm, I don't know. You guys are really tough now that you're seven."

"Please!" They said the word loudly and in unison. They grabbed his arm and pulled. Keegan let them struggle for a few moments and then made a show of being forced out of his chair. They cheered.

Mia watched them play the game and was grateful for Keegan's generous praises to both boys. Melancholy settled on her shoulders, and she held the moment carefully. The boys scored a point, and Isaiah hopped up and down in excitement. She had been reminded over and over by acquaintances, society, and Austin's family of the void a missing father leaves behind.

A boy needs his father.

In an unfair turn of events, Isaiah had no choice but to grow up without one. His was robbed from him too early in life, and by his father's own hand. Or, as Mia kept trying to remember, by depression. Suicide was an outcome, a lethal symptom, not a willful act. Maybe, had Austin not had access to a gun, he would have found an unsuccessful attempt as proof he needed intensive treatment. What if he had attempted by pills? What if she had never allowed guns in their home?

Stop with the what-ifs, Mia.

Camille cut into her thoughts. "They're so cute. You think they'll be friends when they're older?"

Mia smiled at the thought. "I'd like to think so."

"Me too."

Camille turned toward her friend. "Okay, so spill it."

Mia stared at her friend for a moment. "What?"

Camille stabbed her in the ribs with a finger. "You're gazing off in the distance. You're thinking of something, and I think I know what."

"Ow!"

"Stop being a baby. Did you even bring it up?"

The thought of asking Austin if he was suicidal two years ago made Mia feel dizzy. Fluorescent lights radiated down onto her, robbing her of any privacy. The room felt off-kilter. Why had she never asked?

Camille frowned. "You okay?"

Mia licked her lips. "Yeah, I think I'm a little dehydrated. Probably need some water."

"I'd feel a little off if I got random messages, too."

Oh, she's talking about Sean. Mia's lungs could expand again. "Oh, yeah. Um, I did bring it up. He's pretty sure it's one of his exes. Her name's Angie."

"Angie? Do we have a last name?"

"No, he didn't say, but I think he's still Facebook friends with her." Mia studied her friend's face and frowned. "Camille..."

"What?" She was smiling.

"Don't."

She pulled her phone out. "What?"

"You know what."

She ignored Mia and studied her phone intently, periodically scrolling and typing.

"Don't start looking up—"

Their children crashed into their laps. "Mom! Mom!" said both boys.

Mia grunted at the collision. "Oof. What? Que paso? Is there a fire we don't know about?"

Keegan followed behind, smiling. "I got my butt whooped by these little guys." He tousled Luca's hair.

Luca beamed at his dad and turned toward his mother, his face arranging itself into a look of concern. "Dad really sucks at that game."

Keegan laughed in surprise. "Excuse me?"

Luca shrugged. "If you can't handle the heat, stay out of the kitchen!"

Isaiah laughed generously and the boys ran off.

Keegan sat heavily next to Camille. "Guess that's what I get for letting them win."

"You're a sucker, baby. You gotta whoop their butts mercilessly. Let them know who's in charge."

Keegan raised an eyebrow. "Oh, yeah? Then, how come you let Luca win last time?"

"I didn't. I actually do suck at that game. This was your chance at defending my honor. You blew it."

Rochelle walked over. "Hey, ten more minutes and then they're going to want us in the party room. We get thirty minutes to eat and all that."

After everyone relocated to the party room and the children had their pizza of choice, Camille scooched closer to Mia. "Okay, I think I found her on Facebook."

"Camille!" Mia flicked her friend on the forearm.

"Ow! Is that how you treat a concerned friend?"

"Nosy friend, more like it."

Rochelle leaned over. "Nosy friend? I like where this is going. What is happening, and how can I get involved?"

Mia sighed.

Camille showed them her phone. A selfie of a smiling woman beamed at them. She had a floral headband, and though the background was a bit obscured, one had the impression she was part of a bridal party.

"Oh, she's pretty," said Rochelle.

"This is the psycho that was sending Mia weird messages about Sean."

Mia started. "I never said psycho."

"Ohhh. She's not that pretty," said Rochelle.

"What am I missing out on?" Lori's children were all busy with their pizza, and she was able to join the huddled women.

Mia crossed her arms. "We're also not insulting her."

Rochelle rolled her eyes. "I'm not insulting her. I'm just saying you're prettier."

Lori's daughter Nina approached them. "Who's prettier?" Lori waved away her question, and she shrugged. "Anyway, can I have more Coke?"

"Are you going to stay awake all night like last time?"

Nina smiled brightly. "Of course not! Why would I ever do that?"

"You can have Sprite."

"Ugh, fine." Nina stomped away from the group.

The text messages had only been vaguely explained to Lori and Rochelle, so Camille generously filled in the missing information.

"Oh, this is juicy," Lori said.

Mia protested searching her profile until they stumbled on the few pictures of Angie and Sean.

"Okay, fine, let me see."

Camille cackled. "I knew you were curious."

"Only because it's right there."

Lori hummed as her eyes skimmed the phone. "Is she dating anyone? Recent breakup? That would explain suddenly being interested in Sean again. Kind of sucks it's mostly locked down. Is she still friends with him on here?"

Camille nodded. "Yup. That's how I found her, and that's why I block all my exes. Guys are idiots."

Mia frowned. "Why would she reach out to me if she has free access to Sean? Why did she wait so long?"

"You even blocked Keegan?" Rochelle asked.

Camille took a giant bite of pizza. "Only for a few years." She clicked on the messenger icon. "Those are all great questions, Mia."

Mia drew in a sharp breath. "No! Don't message."

"Why not?" Rochelle's eyes sparkled.

"I don't want to start drama." Mia chewed on a fingernail.

Rochelle raised an eyebrow. "If some little hoochie," she lowered her voice into a whisper for the last word, "started messaging me about Bryce, I'd totally let her have it. Don't mess with me, don't mess with my man."

Mia shrugged. "Well, Sean did admit he was an a-hole to her. He didn't admit to cheating, but I'm assuming that's what he meant."

Camille nodded absentmindedly. "Guys are dicks—oops, sorry, Rochelle—guys suck sometimes, but people change. And I still say she's psycho because of how she messaged you. It's super shady."

Lori verbalized her agreement. "It's been like six years. Her obsession just started grade school."

Keegan's voice broke through their circle. "You guys planning world domination without me again?"

They all jumped and laughed. Camille kissed him. "Of course not. You're gonna be my second-in-command, remember?"

Rochelle glanced at her watch. "Oh, dang. It's almost time to wrap everything up. Did everybody get cake and their little goodie bags?"

∞ ∞ ∞

Bedtime was a breeze after Andre's party. Isaiah didn't even protest brushing his teeth and was asleep before Mia was finished reading his favorite book. A new moon meant night felt darker than usual, and sleep called for her as well. However, after getting in bed, curiosity kept her from falling asleep.

Eventually, she gave up trying to fall asleep and sat up, groping around on the nightstand to find her phone. Blinding light pierced through the darkness when she swiped at the screen. Her eyes squeezed shut involuntarily. She forced them open a sliver and dimmed the screen. Spots danced in her vision, and she blinked hard several times.

Once her sight was restored, she opened Facebook and typed a name in the search bar.

Angela Chapman.

The familiar smiling face looked up at her.

I should really leave this alone. Angie hadn't texted her since the initial barrage of anonymous texts. Sean had explained his involvement with her. And yet, doubt lingered.

She pulled up messenger and typed, deleted, and typed again.

Her thumb paused over the send arrow. She set her phone next to her and lay on her back. Had she never been sent the text messages, there would be no nagging questions, no doubt or confusion.

She debated with herself. *Sean has never done anything to imply he's cheating on you. You wouldn't even be wondering who he's around if a crazy lady hadn't said he was talking to someone else. But what does "talking" even mean? And he's allowed friends that aren't guys. I have guy friends.*

Mia bit her lip. When she was a little girl, she used to find it magical that grass and flowers could grow through the sidewalk. She understood how they could squeeze their way through the spaces between concrete slabs, but what fascinated her were the plants that pushed through the middle of the rock-solid walkway. Flowers were so flimsy and frail. And yet.

Then, she grew up and learned it was the slow rate at which they grew, the elements that assisted, and the weaknesses of the seemingly impenetrable material that allowed the sidewalk flowers to crack something so much stronger than itself. In the end, it boiled down to which material was most determined to make it.

She mused over the materials of her relationship with Sean. Their friends seemed to think it was solid. A question echoed in her mind. *Is this good for us? Bonding over loss?* There were moments when they lay in bed, wrapped in each other's arms, talking about their missing loved ones, laughing over memories and caressing each other when the pain was too great.

Mia picked up her phone and hit send. Then, she tossed it to the foot of the bed, hoping it was devoid of messages in the morning.

– Chapter 30 –

February 2017

M ia walked down the expansive hallway. Generic paintings adorned the walls. A small tree sprouted in her peripheral vision. She smiled as she turned toward it. Isaiah hung from its branches.

"Look, Mommy! I'm climbing so high!"

"Be careful, mi amor."

"Do you think Daddy would be proud of how high I am?" Isaiah's smile disappeared. He made his way to a lower branch and lay down on it. The leaves and flowers obscured her vision, and it looked like the tree's branch had curled itself around the small boy.

Mia frowned, confused. *Where is Austin?*

She continued down the hallway until she met a doorway. Behind it was a stairwell, the interior walls cold and gray. She ran up the steps two at a time, willing herself to go faster. The upper level gave way to their home, and she rushed to her bedroom, panic building in her chest.

Maybe he's in here.

The room lay barren, with only a neatly made bed and a dresser. Each wall held a door, and she frantically threw them all open. They led to Isaiah's bedroom, the kitchen, and the garage. Each room was empty. Her chest felt as if it held a frantic bird, its wings batting against her ribs, struggling to get out. Something was wrong.

Where's Austin?

She snapped awake. Early morning light filtered through the blinds. She turned to her side and slid her hand over the cold side of the bed. Recently, the voids in the house had felt smaller, but this morning, the weight of the missing was crushing.

She pulled a pillow down to her chest and hugged it, burying her face into it. Hot tears began to spill from her eyes, and a sob broke out. Austin was gone forever. She had heard that humans couldn't fully appreciate large quantities. There is a struggle to grasp how much a billion is, a disconnect when explained the distances between stars. And so, the concept of forever felt both obvious and confusing. She knew he was dead, knew death was permanent, and yet she found herself periodically surprised when her search for Austin yielded nothing.

The sun continued to rise and increased the brightness around her. The cheery light belied the feelings within her bedroom. The tears continued until she felt like a husk of a woman. She hated her life. She didn't want to be a young widow, cursed to a lifetime of nightmares, struggling daily as a single mother, and tainted for future loves.

She rolled onto her back and stared blandly at the ceiling. A deep frown cut into her face.

Why me?

She turned her head and inspected the crumpled pillow. It was wet with tears and snot.

"Get over yourself, Mia," she said. *The pity party is over. Get up.*

She sighed and threw the covers back, her body feeling impossibly heavy. It was another moment before she sat up and rubbed her eyes. She pulled off the pillowcase and threw it in the hamper on the way to the bathroom.

The cool shower was unpleasant, but it rinsed off the uneasiness of the dream and hopefully lessened the puffiness around her eyes. At times, Isaiah would notice the marks leftover from grief. He'd point out the reddened nose, puffy face, or glassy eyes. She'd fake a smile and wave him off. *Go play.*

His therapist had said several times that it was healthy to let Isaiah see sadness and grief. It was important to model feelings for him. But Mia didn't know if how she was handling Austin's death was healthy. She kept putting off seeing a therapist. Of course, lack of providers with availability or who took her health insurance didn't help, either.

As she rinsed her hair, a rapping sounded on the shower door. "Hold on."

"I'm hungry." Isaiah's pixelated form shifted from side to side.

"I said hold on. I'm almost done. No, don't open the door! Water will get everywhere. Just wait a minute!"

A small noise of protest came from the blurred figure.

She turned off the water and opened the door. "Hand me the towel." She wrung her hair as Isaiah obliged. "Thank you, baby."

"I want cereal."

"What? You can get the cereal by yourself. You don't have to wait for me." Mia riffled through her hair products and found a bottle of leave-in conditioner.

Isaiah pouted. "I know, but you always say not to because I pour too much milk."

She raked her hands through her hair to distribute the conditioner. "Oh, yeah. Okay, well, give me a second, and I'll make us both cereal."

After she dressed, the memory of the impulsive message to Angela returned to her. "Go ahead and go to the kitchen, I'm right behind you."

The phone was still on the base of the bed, the black screen pointed toward the ceiling. Gingerly, she picked it up and illuminated the screen. There was one message notification from Sean. She pushed the guilt aside and went to her Facebook messages.

It was marked unread. Who was Sean hanging out with?

Mia exhaled slowly. She felt better, but also dishonest. She knew Sean thought the incident was behind them. Overall, it was, but she needed to know. The lack of response felt like an answer in itself. Maybe her friends were right. It had been a series of drunk texts from a jealous ex-girlfriend who was lashing out in hurt.

She tapped on her text messages and responded to Sean's greeting. She said nothing about her message to Angie.

∞ ∞ ∞

"You think I should tell him?" Mia worried her nail against her teeth. She sat on Camille's stiff couch, one leg crossed under the other.

Spaghetti night had spontaneously turned into grilled salmon night at Camille's request. It was her turn to cook, and Keegan was craving fish. After dinner, he escorted the boys to an upstairs room to play video games while Mia and Camille chatted.

Camille drank a sip of white wine and shook her head. "You really need to stop biting your nails. And no, I don't think so. What's there to tell?"

"I don't know. It feels a little dishonest, even if only by omission." Mia shrugged and frowned at her glass.

Camille stood and stretched, careful not to spill the contents of her cup. She disappeared into the kitchen and returned with another bottle of white. She poured generously into Mia's empty glass. "Eh. He'll get over it. Plus, it's not like she had your best intentions at heart. I hate bitches that have nothing better to do than stir up drama."

Mia drank deeply from her cup and set it on a coaster. She slumped backward and dramatically threw her hands in the air. "But I want to know!" She dragged out the last word and laughed. "Ugh, it's so very annoying, but there's this little, tiny feeling that won't leave me alone. I feel like it's crawling on me, or maybe right underneath my skin."

"That's the most disgusting metaphor ever." Camille shuddered. "Listen, that's called anxiety. And we all have that nagging little doubt in the back of our head. We want to trust our partners wholeheartedly. We do. But we also don't want to be idiots, right? I trust Keegan, but if I feel like something isn't adding up, I'm going to start investigating. Why wouldn't I?"

Mia nodded solemnly. "You're right."

"I know. I'm always right."

"So, do you think I should keep investigating?"

Camille considered, tapping a manicured nail against her wine glass. The sharp sound punctuated her thoughts. "I think you should follow your instincts."

"What if they're broken?"

"Do you trust Sean? Has he ever made you feel like he's hiding something?"

Mia shook her head and noted that Camille's glass was now empty. She found the wine bottle and filled the cup halfway.

"Thanks. Okay, see? I think there needs to be a certain level of trust in relationships. If you don't have that, then the foundation is broken. You're not going to last. If I didn't trust Keegan, I wouldn't be with him right now. It's not worth it."

"You're right."

"Plus, whenever I get any paranoid feelings, I just take a quick scroll through his phone to make myself feel better."

Mia burst out laughing. "What?"

"Shh!" Camille laughed, too. "Don't judge me. If that man didn't want me in his phone, he wouldn't have given me the passcode."

"I've never gone through Sean's phone."

Camille pursed her lips. "Maybe you should. Just real quick. Make yourself feel better."

"You're a mess. Ugh, did we really drink almost an entire second bottle?"

"Hmm. So, we did. You're not good to drive now."

"I have work in the morning."

Camille topped off their glasses with the rest of the wine. "Go home in the morning. It's going to be Friday anyway. It's almost expected for everyone to be slightly hungover. I have spare toiletries. You guys can crash in the guestroom. Or Isaiah can bunk with Luca, and you can get the bed to yourself. However you want." She sighed. "God, remember our twenties? We'd drink until four a.m. and then show up bright-eyed and bushy-tailed, like cracked out squirrels. Those were the days. Now, a little bit of wine, and we're ready to go to bed by eight."

"We're getting old," Mia said with a grin.

"I think kids age you quicker. That's got to be it." Camille looked at Mia, a gleam in her eye. "Keegan and I are talking about having another baby."

Mia gasped. "What? That's incredible!"

"I know there'll be a big gap between Luca and the next one, if there's a next one, but that's okay. I've talked to other moms with big gaps between kids, and they've said it's worked out just fine. In fact, sometimes it's better because you're not dealing with a newborn and a toddler at the same time. That said, I do worry Luca will be more jealous. He's been the only kid for so long."

"I think whatever you choose will be fine," said Mia. She squealed. "This is so exciting."

"Well, I'm not pregnant yet. And we haven't decided whether we're going to actively try yet or not."

"Okay, well, not to bribe you into having another baby, but I will totally throw you a baby shower this time around."

Camille snorted. "We both know Aislinn would kill you if you took that from her."

"That's true. Does she know you guys are trying to have a baby?"

"Oh my God, no. We even talk about it in hushed tones so her grandma senses don't start tingling."

They laughed.

"Can you imagine? She'd be knocking at our door and blowing up our phones asking everyday if I was pregnant yet. If it happens, I'll tell her then."

"This is so exciting," said Mia. She sighed happily. "A baby."

A thundering noise sounded. They looked up, startled, and found the source to be two very excited little boys running down the stairs.

Keegan followed behind, his face a grimace. "They don't even weigh that much."

Camille laughed.

"Can we spend the night, Mom?" Isaiah pressed his hands together like he was praying and bounced with excitement.

Luca hopped onto his mother's lap. Wine spilled over the lip of her glass and onto her shirt. "Please, Mom!"

"Party foul, boy," Camille said, placing the glass of wine gingerly onto her coffee table.

Luca frowned. "What party?"

"Never mind. Yes, Isaiah can spend the night."

Keegan eyed the two empty wine bottles on the coffee table and their flushed faces. "Did you guys already plan the sleepover before the boys could ask?"

Luca squeezed his mother around the neck. She squeezed him back and positioned him next to her on the couch. She reclaimed her glass and raised it as if giving a toast. "We're nothing if not prepared." She tilted her head up, and Keegan leaned down to kiss her.

"I'll go ahead and throw these away," he said, collecting the bottles.

Mia watched the exchange and felt happy for her friend, though it felt bittersweet. Isaiah crawled into her lap. As she wrapped her arms around him, the dream image of the tree wrapping its leaves and branches around her son came to mind. She wished Austin was around to complete the nest. She'd heard a triangle was the strongest shape. Its simple design was wedged into architectural works like bridges, rafters, and domes. What happened, then, if the triangle was destroyed?

She knew Camille would be announcing a pregnancy in the following months, regardless of how much she insisted she was debating the decision. There was always an air of hesitancy in her words, and most people viewed her decisions as rash and impulsive because of her back-and-forth. But Mia knew better. The decision had already been made; Camille was just testing reactions.

Mia wondered if they'd have a boy or a girl and sat holding her son until he finally pushed her away, eager to play with his friend. Images of Isaiah as a newborn rolled through her mind. She wondered what the future would bring her, but every time she tried to imagine it, she found herself wandering the hallways of her memories alone.

-Chapter 31-

March 2017

Mia was in her office chewing on a pen cap as she finalized the quarterly profit projections. The room was small, but it had a window, which made her happy. She had outfitted the two available walls with an abstract art piece and a blown-up photograph Sean had gifted her. Her door, as usual, was wide open.

It was only Tuesday, and she already knew the week was going to be crazy. An upcoming audit was on everyone's mind, and leadership had sent an unspoken message that urged everyone to complete their normal tasks days ahead of schedule.

"Done," she said. "I need a coffee."

"Or a beer." Brian, one of her coworkers, stood next to her desk holding a binder. He laughed when she gasped. "Oh my goodness, sorry. I thought you saw me walk up."

"I was too into this workbook, I guess."

"Apparently. You need a break, my dear," he said.

She smiled graciously. "I do. I might just take off after lunch. Drive away and never come back. Go visit Cancún forever."

Brian laughed and waved the binder. "Let me drop this off on Bob's desk, and I'll join you."

"Oh? Yeah, let's do it. Run away and elope."

"Absolutely. You'd be a stunning bride. And I'd be an even more stunning groom. Sean might get a little sad, though."

She shrugged, smiling. "He'll get over it."

"Although, you know, he'd also be a stunning groom."

When Mia blanched, Brian laughed. "Well, now I know your thoughts on the topic. I'd run away with him any chance I got, though. The man is gorgeous. Unfortunately, I'm not his type." He sighed. "Anyway, don't work yourself to death, sweetheart."

She laughed. "Okay. You either."

He grinned. "You know I'd never." With that, he was gone.

The main office was mostly empty. Lunch was taken at everyone's discretion, but most people left around the same timeframe. Usually, Mia ate at her desk. Sometimes, tired of staring at screens, she'd leave the building and grab a quick bite at a nearby deli. Sean had joined her a handful of times, but their work schedules didn't allow for much visitation.

She saved a copy of the workbook on her desktop and uploaded the final version to the shared drive. With a slow exhale, she leaned back into her office chair, eyes closed. Something buzzed against the desk, and her eyes opened. The phone was facedown, so she answered without looking.

"This is Mia."

A strangled cry sounded in her ear.

She sat up quickly and checked the caller ID. Camille.

She returned the phone to her ear. "Hello? Camille? Hello?"

"Mia," said a hoarse voice, then all she heard was crying.

"Camille, is that you? Are you okay? You're scaring me."

There was a small cough. "Yeah, it's me. I'm okay—but it's not okay. My dad—" Her voice broke, and she began sobbing.

Mia stood quickly, pushing her office chair backward roughly. "Camille?" She realized her voice held a note of panic when Brian rushed over to her desk.

"Everything alright?" His eyes reflected worry, and Mia could see herself within them. She shook her head and shrugged, helpless.

There were muffled sounds like the phone had been dropped or transferred. After a moment, Keegan's voice came on the line. "Raphael's been in an accident. We're on the way to the hospital." Then, a pause. "I think it's bad. But we don't know all the details. I just know he fell doing something on or near the roof. Eloise's distraught, of course. I know he's in surgery."

"Oh my God, I'll meet you there."

"You don't have to—"

"Yes, I do. I'll be right there. Tell Camille I'll be there as soon as I can." She tapped on the end button and met Brian's eyes, stunned. "Um, I gotta go. Family emergency. Can you tell Bob? I'll—I'll be in tomorrow, but I have to go. The projections are done and saved. He can look them over whenever he wants."

He nodded mutely.

She gathered her things, her hands shaking and clumsy.

"Are you okay to drive, dear?"

"I'll be fine." Her tone was curt. "Sorry, I didn't mean to snap. I'm fine. I just—I have to go."

Brian walked over and gave her a quick squeeze. "Okay. Be careful. Text me. I'll see you tomorrow, but if you need more time, I can cover for you."

"I appreciate it. But I should be in tomorrow."

Brian headed toward Bob's office, and Mia rushed from the building. She called Carol and explained the situation. She graciously offered to pick up Isaiah from his bus stop. Mia worried he'd think something bad had happened to her, and Carol reassured her they'd call so Isaiah could hear his mother's voice and know she was safe. Mia agreed with the plan and promised to update her as soon as she knew more about Raphael's situation.

The drive to the hospital was a blur. Before Mia realized it, she was turning left at the Emergency Department sign. Her phone buzzed. Assuming it was Camille, she pulled her phone out on the way into the building.

It was Angie. She had read Mia's message. The response was a photo of Sean embracing a red-haired woman.

Mia's pace slowed for a second and then she threw her phone into her purse. There was only room for Camille and Raphael. Sean was a vague memory.

Her heels clacked urgently down the sterile hallways, announcing her advancement toward the waiting room. She spotted Camille and Eloise in the bright room; their bodies were huddled together on a cluster of cushioned seats. Keegan stood behind Camille's chair and rubbed her shoulders. Noel paced the floor, wringing his hands.

Camille looked up as the sharp sounds of Mia's shoes grew louder. Her eyes widened. "Mia!" Her face crumpled, and she began to cry.

Mia ran and gathered her friend in her arms. Camille sobbed into her shoulder as Keegan looked on, his face tight with worry.

Spent, Camille collapsed into her seat. "I'm sorry. I didn't mean to have you leave work early."

"You know family is first for me."

Eloise took Mia's hand. "We appreciate you being here." Her eyes were red and puffy.

"What happened?" Mia asked.

"Raphael wanted to fix one of our exterior lights. The one that's situated on that weird crease in the roof."

"He should have called me," said Noel, his steel blue eyes darkened in anger.

Eloise ignored him. "He was halfway done with replacing it when the ladder failed. Or maybe he overextended himself. I wish I was outside; he does so much work by himself. But," she waved away the thought, "it's too late for anything but regret. I was inside. And I heard a horrible, horrible sound. I knew—I knew what it was. I knew he had fallen. He fell in the most terrible way. His head had hit the walkway. At first, I thought he had died, there was so much blood. But then he started moaning. It was a terrible sound. I can't stop thinking about it—but at least I knew he was alive." A sob escaped, and she pressed her hand over her mouth.

Noel rushed to his mother and sat. She leaned on him and cried.

He caressed her hair, not unlike how she used to when they were children. "I wish you would have told me you needed something fixed."

"You know your father—"

"And now look! He needs to get over his pride, his fear of being dependent —"

Camille shifted and touched his arm. "Noel, please."

Mia recognized the sorrow behind his tone. It was strange, how the fire of anger could soothe the rough edges of worry, as if its heat could lap away the pain. He met his sister's eyes, his mouth turned down into a frown. He blinked back tears and nodded, then kissed his mother's forehead. "He'll be fine. You'll see."

"Mom!"

Everyone turned toward the voice. Theo slowed to a stop. He stood, breathing hard, his eyes wild. His hair was disheveled, and he raked a hand through it. He studied everyone's faces, trying to assess the situation without asking questions, as if afraid of the answers.

"Theo."

His mother's voice pierced through his uncertainty, and he rushed to her. He landed on his knees and took her hands. "You okay, Mom? Do we know anything?"

Eloise pressed her lips into a smile. A tear fell. "He's in surgery. I think we'll get updated afterwards. They think he has a concussion, but we haven't been updated with the severity yet."

Theo kissed her hand. "When's the last time you've eaten?"

Her eyebrows furrowed, and she looked around, confused. "Oh. Eat? I don't know. Lunch, maybe? It's been a blur. I'm not really hungry."

"You still need to eat. I can get you something."

Mia turned to face Camille. "Have you eaten? Keegan?"

Camille's face looked blank. "Um?"

"I'll go with you, Theo," Mia said. "We can get something for everyone."

She gave Camille's hand a squeeze and stood. Theo shot her a grateful look, and the two of them walked in search of the vending machines. She knew he needed to feel useful, and feeding everyone was the easiest way to find something to do.

After they found the machines, they stood side-by-side, weighing the options. Mia glanced at Theo. He stared intently at the selection of chip bags. She took his hand. "You okay?"

He turned quickly, as if surprised to see her. His voice cracked, and he cleared his throat. "Sorry, yeah. I'm fine."

"It's okay if you're not." She released his hand.

"I know." His eyes were glassy. "I wish we knew more about his condition. I know he's in surgery, but I'm worried about the head injury. I hope the concussion isn't bad. The shitty part of all this is I know what spot he was on. Had he fallen the other way, he would have landed in bushes and probably only had a bruised ego and some scratches. I heard his arm is broken, so the surgery is probably to set it. That's gotta be good news, right? If his head injury was severe, they wouldn't be in surgery already, right? We'd have even less information?"

Mia forced a smile. "I think you're right. It's a waiting game right now, but I think he'll surprise everyone. Raphael is anything but weak. If anyone can bounce right back from an ugly fall, it's your father. And he'll probably be back to doing his own house repairs and pissing Noel off in no time."

A tear rolled down his cheek as he let out a short burst of laughter. "That's very true." He wiped his cheeks with the back of his hand.

She fished out crinkled bills and quarters from her purse. "Let's grab some snacks for everyone. You included."

"No, I got it."

"I wasn't covering for you, mofo. Just adding. There's gonna be a lot of you out in the waiting room soon."

He gave her a wan smile. "I appreciate it."

She fed bills into the machine and pushed a few buttons. "Of course. You guys are my family." A Snickers bar fell into the slot.

He pulled her close, and they embraced. She laid her head on his chest. His heartbeat was steady and loud.

During high school, she had developed a crush on Noel. His chiseled features and stoic demeanor made him seem like a Greek god, someone who could only be worshipped from afar. And so, Mia quizzed her best friend as nonchalantly as possible about which brother was due for a visit. Unfortunately, Camille picked up on her amateur detective work and pointed out the obsession. After very little interrogation, Mia confessed her infatuation.

On the other end of the spectrum lay Theo. His hair was as wild as he was, and he always seemed to be coming back from some adventure or another. Mia thought he was funny, but they were quick to shoo him away. His antics always seemed to involve something flammable or dangerous, and they wanted no part in the post-mess cover-up.

She giggled.

He stepped back. "What?"

"I was just remembering the time you tried to make a short film for one of your college classes. Some war reenactment? You did like zero research, so it wasn't even accurate. But you bought those little chain firecrackers. The ones that go off like a machine gun or whatever."

He groaned. "Oh my God, Mia, what the hell? I had almost forgotten about that." He made a few selections from the vending machine.

"And ground spinners, right? Something like that. And you were trying to tell me and Camille to keep an eye out for your parents, but we were so caught up in all the flashes and smoke, we didn't hear them pull into the driveway." She walked over to the drink machine and began paying for an assortment of sports drinks and sodas.

"I learned never to trust you guys for anything."

"Hey!"

"You have to admit you were terrible lookouts."

"That's fair." Mia's eyes welled up at the memory of Raphael's face. She let out a short laugh. "They were really mad."

Theo's own eyes were glassy. He shrugged. "I did mess up the lawn a little bit."

"A lotta bit."

"Agree to disagree."

She laughed again and looked at what they pulled from the machines. "We should have enlisted Keegan for some help carrying this. I think we were just feeding money into the machine and punching buttons. Well, shall we go back?"

They returned to see a few other people had joined the family. Camille stood and helped ease the load of snacks and bottles. She began passing the items around. She pulled a Snickers and a sports drink for her mother. When Eloise shook her head, she took on a motherly tone.

"You need to at least take a bite and drink something. You're no good to Dad if you pass out from low blood sugar." Eloise cracked a smile and nibbled on the candy bar. Camille didn't leave her alone until she drank from the sports drink. "That's better."

"Mrs. Laurent?"

Everyone turned. In front of them stood two men. One was a tall, lean man dressed in light blue scrubs. Fine wrinkles were etched on his forehead and near his eyes. His tone was curt, but not unkind. The other man stood a few inches shorter. He had thick, dark eyebrows and a generous belly.

"I'm Dr. Lange, from neurosurgery. This is Dr. Reddy. I know you were told we'd have a more in-depth conversation about surgery that involved more than the arm before it started, but we felt it was important to start right away."

Camille gasped and touched her fingers to her mouth. "Neurosurgery?" It came out a whisper. Keegan wrapped his arm around her.

"Tell me," said Eloise. "How is my husband?"

-*Chapter 32*-

March 2017

"Why does he need a neurosurgeon?" Noel asked. Mia stole a glance his way and found him looking very much like Isaiah did when recounting a nightmare.

Dr. Lange met his eyes. "Your father fell a considerable distance and onto a very hard surface. It's lucky his head didn't hit first, but he still had a skull fracture that required urgent surgery. The surgery went very well, and he's in recovery."

"His arm was broken and also required surgery. He had a plate, screws, and a few pins placed to make sure it heals correctly. They will be removed at a later date," said Dr. Reddy.

Dr. Lange turned to Eloise. "The most concerning injury is the skull fracture and concussion. We're going to admit him into the ICU. I don't anticipate he'll stay there for more than two days, but of course, I don't make any promises. Afterwards, he'll be discharged from the ICU and stay in the hospital for another several days, maybe a week. It depends a lot on how he's recovering. I know that's a lot of information in a short amount of time, but do you have any questions?"

"Can we see him?" Camille's chin quivered.

Dr. Reddy nodded. "Once he's been transferred to the ICU, he's allowed up to two visitors. However, he'll be pretty groggy today, maybe even confused. Don't be alarmed if he sleeps a considerable amount of time, today especially. Someone will come out and let you know when you can see him. You'll get a lot more follow up information from his care team, as well."

Eloise nodded. "Thank you."

With a humorless smile, Dr. Lange dismissed himself and his colleague.

"I want to see him with you," Camille said to her mother, a note of desperation in her voice.

She embraced her daughter. "You'll all see him." She faced her children. "He's going to be fine. He's injured, but recovering. You all know your father, so you know a successful surgery was a given. The doctors explained what will happen. ICU, then a hospital stay, then home." The line of her jaw lifted, reminding Mia of royalty.

Her children responded in various ways. They smiled, crossed their arms, or set their shoulders. Hope entered their circle like a warrior. Raphael had to pull through. He'd prove his wife a liar if he didn't, and everyone knew Eloise was not used to disappointment.

On their wedding day, when he had begun to say "...till death," she had interjected with, "No, until one hundred years." Everyone, including the priest, had laughed. She had smiled, eyes shining, daring him to prove her wrong, as if she had already peeked into the future and seen them happy for the next 75 years.

A few hours later, a nurse appeared to announce his admittance to the ICU. Two people were now allowed in the room. Eloise and Camille went first. They disappeared for about an hour and eventually Camille returned, her face blotchy from crying. One by one, her siblings joined their parents. Each returned a little shaken.

Noel went last. When he returned, he nudged Mia. "Your turn."

She blinked. "Are you sure?"

"You're family. Plus, you want to see him. Otherwise, why stay here so long?"

Mia hesitated.

He smiled. "Don't be shy. Mom appreciates your company." He embraced her. "We all do."

When she crept into the room, Raphael was asleep. A nurse fussed over the IV machine.

Eloise raised her head and smiled, her eyes red-rimmed and tired. "Mia, thank you for always being there for us."

Mia smiled, surprised. She wondered if they understood how much their family kept her going through her last year in high school and after Austin's death. "Do you need anything?"

"Oh, no, love. But I appreciate the offer."

"How is he?"

"In and out. He was awake a bit ago, but I think a little confused. His words are a bit slurred sometimes. I think it's the pain meds. And probably the concussion."

"I'll be back in a little while," said the nurse. "Use the call button if you need anything before then."

Eloise smiled and nodded.

Mia watched Raphael sleep for a few minutes and saw a black eye was developing. His hair was slicked to the left, revealing a large, shaved area. A bandage covered most of it. A variety of tubes ran from his body. She could name the blood pressure cuff and IV, but otherwise, the equipment was foreign to her.

She walked up to his bed and stroked his arm. "You are amazing. You'll be home so quick, it'll surprise the staff."

He stayed unresponsive. His chest rose and fell methodically.

"It's scary to see him like this," she said and looked back at Eloise.

"He's a very strong man." Eloise squared her shoulders. "It is strange to see him with tubes and a cast. But I know he will be okay. Because he's my Raphael."

"He's a stubborn, strong man. He'll be out of the hospital and home in no time."

Eloise nodded approvingly. "Yes."

They sat next to each other for a while, the silence periodically punctuated by beeping machines or the ICU staff. Mia stood and walked over to Raphael. He hadn't stirred since she had walked into the room. Tenderly, she leaned over and kissed his forehead. "I'll see you soon," she whispered. "I have to get going."

Eloise smiled. "I appreciate the time you spent with us. We'll keep you updated. They said he should be more alert tomorrow."

"Make sure you keep yourself hydrated."

"Oh, don't you fuss over me, too."

Mia chuckled. "I have to. It was the rule as soon as I became an unofficial family member."

"Oh, well, in that case."

She grabbed the large plastic hospital cup and held it up for Eloise to see. "I'm going to go fill this up for you and then I'll be off."

The waiting room had thinned slightly since everyone had arrived. Camille sat on a large plush bench seat, her arms hugging her knees to her chest. Her head laid on her knees, blonde hair tumbled over her arms, and Keegan sat next to her, stroking her head. Her eyes were red and swollen from crying, but she was spent of tears. Theo sat diagonal to her, his head tilted back as he studied the tiled ceiling. Noel was on the phone, pacing.

"Hey, guys. I'm going to take off."

Camille sniffed and rubbed her sleeve over her face. She stood, and they embraced. "Okay, be careful on the drive home."

Noel walked over. "Selina is getting on a plane tomorrow." A few of their siblings lived close enough to drive, but their sister had relocated to the Midwest.

"Oh," said Theo. "Is she bringing everybody?"

He shook his head at his brother's question. "No. She thinks it's better if she leaves Antonio and the kids behind. It's faster."

"Keep me updated," said Mia.

Noel squeezed her arm. "We will."

The sharp rap of her heels sounded even louder in the hospital after hours. She wondered who else was sitting, terrified, waiting for news that their loved one had made it out of surgery successfully. She imagined sometimes the worst of news was shared, like with Sean's fiancée. A man and woman with white coats passed her, talking amongst themselves. Had they recently informed a husband or wife, a mother or father, that someone they loved more than the world itself had passed on?

She thought of the nights she had spent wailing, feeling like the physical embodiment of grief. When she was young and her parents took her to church, she loved listening to the Bible stories. They were larger than life, and though they terrified her, she was enthralled. Stories of angels with four faces visiting prophets, stories of fathers almost sacrificing their beloved sons, stories of angels of death swooping down and slaughtering firstborns. As a child, she shuddered listening to the story about the plagues of Egypt, especially when the Angel of Death visited every firstborn child. The imagery of a country full of weeping mothers and the collective gnashing of teeth horrified and fascinated her. As an adult who had been visited by that very angel twice, she knew the city not only wept, it raged. That's why they ground their teeth together; they had to channel the anger somehow.

And so, as she walked, she didn't dare pray, lest the angel hear and swoop down yet again. Instead, she willed images of Raphael, laughing and healthy, to remain in her mind.

Frigid, winter air blasted her at the exit, and she wrapped her arms around herself. Hints of spring were edging their way into the daytime, but it was barely March, and nighttime temperatures still liked to plunge into the high 30s.

As she neared the parking garage entrance, she heard her name. She looked around, startled. A deep, male voice shouted her name again.

She whirled around and then laughed in relief. "Oh my gosh. Don't do that. I was wondering who the hell would be calling my name in the middle of the night."

Theo smiled apologetically. "My bad. You know, you walk really fast."

"Why are you out here?"

He lifted a hand to show off a set of keys.

She gasped and looked in her purse. "Dang. I didn't even realize they had fallen out. Okay, my wallet and phone and stuff are still in there."

She held out her hand, and he passed the keys. He shivered. "It's cold out here. You don't have a jacket?"

"I left it in the car. It was nicer in the daytime."

He chuckled. "I think it's a rule that women have to leave their jackets everywhere but where they're accessible." He unzipped his leather jacket and started to remove it. "Here, you can use mine."

"Oh, no, no. It's okay. I'm parked on the second level, so it's not that long of a walk."

"Well, you can wear it until we get to your car."

Mia raised an eyebrow. "We?"

"You seemed spooked when I called your name. I figured maybe you wanted the company. I can fight off any weirdos lurking in the shadows." He paused. "Unless they're bigger than me, then you're on your own."

Her laugh brightened his face. "Oh, thanks!"

He shrugged and pulled off his jacket. "Don't worry. I'll call 9-1-1 from behind the cars. I'm nothing if not a gentleman."

The jacket was warm from his body heat and smelled like him. She zipped it up and dipped her nose below the stiff collar, partly to keep warm and partly because she could enjoy the blend of worn leather and his spicy cologne.

"See? You already look warmer." He shoved his hands into his pockets.

"You look colder." Her voice was muffled by the jacket. She held onto his arm. "Here, we can share."

They walked in a comfortable silence until they reached her car. "I really need a remote start for this thing." She slid off his jacket and handed it back. "Ugh, now it feels even colder."

He chuckled and pulled her into a hug. "Thanks for being here for everybody."

"Of course."

He pulled back slightly and looked down at her. She noted a few yellow flecks within the light-blue of his eyes and wondered why she had never noticed before.

When he leaned forward, she closed her eyes and felt his lips meet hers. There was heat behind it, but she only felt the warmth of comfort.

Bonding over grief again. Sean's face flashed into her mind, then the image of him embracing a woman. The thought jerked her back, and her elbow connected with the car window. She gasped in pain.

"Shit. Sorry, sorry. I don't know what I was thinking."

Mia rubbed her elbow. "It's okay. It's been a weird day for everybody. I think—" She paused and bit her lip. "I think sometimes we're drawn to what's familiar."

Theo's eyebrows furrowed, and he increased the space between them.

"When we're in pain or afraid, we look to the people we connect with as a source of comfort and love, even if we don't mean it."

He rubbed the back of his neck. "I didn't really have a plan to come out, and, well—but it didn't feel like a forced... thing. I..." He looked away and sighed. "Sorry. Maybe you're right. I got a little caught up and wasn't thinking straight."

The air felt tense between them, and she wished she hadn't forgotten her keys. She reached a hand out to touch him, but aborted at the last second.

"Thanks for walking me to my car." The words sounded lame in her ears.

He smiled, but it looked sad. Maybe even regretful. "Yeah. Anytime." He saluted with two fingers. "Okay, well, I'll see you."

Mia watched him walk a few paces. "Theo?" He turned his head. "If Raphael wakes up before I'm back, hug him for me?"

"Yeah. Of course. I will." He swallowed. "Bye, Mia."

She opened her car and sat with the engine off, barely registering the cold. When she didn't see him in the rearview anymore, she started the car and began the drive home. It was late, but she sent Carol a message.

If you're still up, I can swing by and pick up Isaiah.

To her surprise, a message chimed back. Carol was awake. She altered her route, and twenty minutes later, she was greeted by the smell of chamomile tea and lemon.

"There's nothing a cup of tea can't cure. Or at least make a little bit better." Carol smiled warmly, offering Mia a seat at her kitchen table. "Isaiah's sleeping in the living room. I pulled out the sofa bed and let him fall asleep to a movie. Don't worry, though, he didn't make it much past nine o'clock."

Mia smiled. "That's okay." She accepted a cup and took a sip. "Thank you."

"Ah, it's nothing. Just thought you needed a minute to sit somewhere that wasn't a hospital before going home."

"You're amazingly astute."

Carol dipped her head in appreciation. "When you get to my age, you pick up on a few tricks. You, my dear, have been through more than most. So, you understand that empathy comes from experience. How is he?"

Tears filled Mia's eyes, and she blinked quickly. "Honestly? He looks awful. He hit his head so hard he fractured his skull. He wasn't even awake when I saw him. He's just this bruised thing with a million wires coming from him."

Carol placed a hand on top of Mia's. "He'll pull through. Anyone who knows that man knows he's too stubborn a person to be set back by a fall, of all things. How's everyone else?"

"Eloise is trying to be as strong as she can. They're all worried, of course. I think, as the days go by and he becomes more responsive, everyone will feel a little better." Theo's kiss flashed into her mind. "I think everyone's doing the best they can while living in limbo. There's a bit of uncertainty in the air."

Carol just nodded.

They sat the rest of the time in silence, sipping on the warm tea.

When she was done, Mia placed her cup in the sink. "Thank you."

"Don't mention it."

She walked to the living room and took a moment to appreciate her son's sleeping form. Isaiah let out a long sigh and shifted. When he settled again, she gently scooped him out of the bed. He stirred and turned his head toward her chest. The nostalgia of nursing a baby settled into her arms alongside her son.

His eyes opened when she placed him into his booster seat.

"Mommy."

She shushed him. "We're going home."

He blinked heavily in response.

The drive only spanned a few blocks, but he was fast asleep when she opened the door to collect him. He woke enough to stumble into the house.

"Can I sleep with you?"

"Sure, baby."

She locked the door behind them and picked him back up. He laid his head on her shoulder. His warm breath tickled her neck as she walked up the stairs into her room. He stretched his arms when she set him on Austin's side of the bed and then curled into the fetal position. She walked to her side and slipped under the covers. The sheets were cold and made her shiver, but she knew with both bodies under the comforter, it'd warm quickly.

Isaiah's soft snores made her smile.

She opened her phone and brought up the picture Angie had sent her. The picture had been taken from across a room and left a bit to interpretation. The large potted plant in the background made her wonder if they met at a restaurant or the nearby mall. Was one location more incriminating than the other? The heat from Theo's kiss returned to her and settled into the pit of her stomach. She placed her phone on the nightstand and laid back onto her pillow, one hand holding onto her son's arm. When did her love life get so complicated?

-Chapter 33-

March 2017

T heo sat in the deli looking more like a boy who was just called in to see the principal rather than a friend. It made Mia giggle. He gave her a lopsided smile in response.

"You look so tense."

He shrugged. "We kind of left things a little awkward, and now you want to talk about it."

"You didn't?" Mia flicked a piece of her hair behind her shoulder.

He made a face. "I was okay pretending it never happened."

She felt a stab of disappointment. "Oh."

"But we're here now. So..." He looked at her expectantly.

Color rose to her cheeks. "I just—I didn't want to leave it weird, I guess. You know I love you and your family. And we've always been so close. I didn't want to ruin it all."

Theo smiled again, but it was polite. "Ruin it?"

"Our friendship."

He exhaled and nodded. His eyes wandered around the table. "Okay."

"I—"

"Hi, there! Who had the Rueben?" The waiter appeared holding a tray with two dishes.

Mia raised her hand.

"Impeccable timing," said Theo under his breath.

"I take it you have the BLT?"

He nodded and gave a wide smile.

After the waiter took his leave, they stared at their food. Mia cleared her throat. "I don't want it to be weird between us. I feel like—well, like enough is weird right now. For me anyway." She paused. "My brain is already messed up enough. I feel like I can barely make normal, day-to-day decisions. I'm always second guessing myself. Half of the time, I fall into bed exhausted, and the other half, I lie awake. And then I don't even get a break sleeping."

Theo looked at her quizzically. "What do you mean?"

Mia poked at her sandwich and shrugged. "I feel like… like I don't even dream unless it's about him."

Theo frowned. "You mean Austin?"

The back of her eyes felt hot. "It's been a year and a half at this point, and I still dream about him like I don't realize he's dead. Until recently, every single dream has been a nightmare. It's been him choking me or hurting me or wanting to hurt me. I'm so scared of him. He's accusing me of killing him or —I don't know."

She bit her lip hard, but a tear still slipped down her cheek. She brushed it away hastily.

Theo took her hand. "It's okay. Hey, look at me. It's okay. Did he ever hurt you?"

She lifted her chin. "He was a good man."

"I know. I know he was. But you told me before he was different in the end."

His eyes searched hers, and she broke eye contact. "Once." Her voice faltered. "One time, he slapped me. Hard. Only one time. We were arguing. And I don't even know what I said, but it set him off. He never hit me before or after that."

She glanced up and saw Theo's face change. Her eyes fell onto her plate. "I don't want your opinion of him to change because of that. He was different at the end. He wasn't himself."

"Men that love you aren't supposed to—"

"I know." Her voice was hard. She pulled her hand away.

She heard Theo shift in his seat. His voice pierced the fog in her head. "Austin was a good person and a damaged person. Both things can be true. Sometimes we do things we regret and can never take back."

"One of our neighbors," she said, her voice a whisper, "came over the next day. She was more his friend than mine. She said when she saw the flashing lights—" Mia's voice failed her, and she swallowed. "She said when she saw the flashing lights, she thought he had—he had killed everybody." Mia met Theo's eyes. Hot, fat tears fell. "What kind of man did I marry? What did other people see in him that I didn't?" Her lips tugged down into a frown. She regretted their meeting place.

He considered. "I think your neighbor was scandalizing real life. You know how nosy people can get. Bad events are like train wrecks. People can't look away. And some people need things to be dramatized for their own entertainment. If she thought that, it was probably because she watches way too much true crime and was wondering if she was going to be interviewed."

A short laugh escaped her, and she raked her fingers through her hair. "That actually makes me feel a lot better. And now that I think about it, it makes sense. She pushed for a lot of info and then stopped coming around when I didn't really answer."

"See?"

"I just—I don't know. I still don't trust myself, I guess. I feel so guilty. Guilty and angry and victimized. I don't know." She sighed and rubbed her forehead. "God. Sorry. I didn't mean to dump on you."

"It's okay."

"It's really not." She looked at him again and smiled. "But I appreciate you."

He set his clasped hands on the table. "Thanks."

"I really do."

"Well," he said, shrugging. "You really are like family." He made a face. "That I decided to kiss. Okay, that's not a good comparison."

She giggled. "I guess not. But I do want to stay close to you all, including you."

He took a large bite of the BLT sandwich. "This is a terrible breakup. But the sandwich is really good."

She laughed again. "Breakup? We didn't even date."

"You should try the sandwich. It'll make up for the fact we've never dated."

"You're a mess." She bit into her sandwich. "You're right. I'm still glad we've never dated."

"You had to add 'still?' Man, you're mean. Thank God I ordered double bacon." After finishing another bite, he lifted the sandwich slightly. "I like to eat my feelings."

A piece of corned beef flew from her mouth when she laughed and landed between them. She clamped a hand over mouth and snorted. They both laughed until they cried.

"You're disgusting," he said.

She nodded, wiping her eyes. "Apparently."

The rest of their lunch was spent talking about family and Raphael. He had recently woken enough to say a few words and register the children who had come to visit. Selina had arrived and was keeping her mother company in the hospital.

Theo held the door open as she exited the deli.

"Thanks for meeting me."

He smiled, but it didn't reach his eyes. "Any time."

They embraced. "Give Raphael my love. I'll be by this weekend."

"Of course." And then he was gone.

Mia walked to her car, sat in the driver's seat, and started it, blasting the heat to warm the interior. She flipped her phone open once again to the image of Sean and the other woman hugging. Initially, it felt like a stab, a crumb of deceit in an otherwise innocent gesture. There was something to Angie's claim, even if she didn't know what. And there was something missing to Sean's version of their relationship.

Theo's kiss had provided a clarity that surprised Mia. She had felt the pull of attraction, but only in the offhand way one does when walking through a group of people and spotting a handsome face. There was no intent behind her reception of the quick gesture, and she refused to consider much about Theo's intentions. She just needed him to understand they were simply friends. Had someone snapped a photo of them right then, it'd be difficult to explain.

The photo was low-quality. She could only see a glimpse of the woman's face. She could have been anywhere between twenty and fifty. Mia was sure the woman wasn't one of Sean's family members because they all lived on the West Coast and rarely visited, but other than that, it could be anybody from friend to coworker.

But it bothers you. Why?

Mia chewed on the inside of her cheek. She felt herself flush and realized she hadn't turned down the car's heat. She threw her phone onto the passenger seat, lowered the heat, and headed home. Lunch had lasted longer than she had anticipated, and even though she was working from home the rest of the week, there were end-of-business deadlines she needed to meet.

Just focus on your work, Mia.

-Chapter 34-

March 2017

It was Friday, and the day was unusually warm for the season. Isaiah was spending the night at his grandpa's house, which meant Mia could relax until it was time to go to the hospital. Raphael had been transferred out of the ICU, and they were all going to visit on Saturday. Camille had called, giddy with relief, the day he was transferred. No communication from Theo had arrived.

Mia was lying on her back on the couch, legs hanging over the arm. She held the book she was reading up away from her face.

The door opened, and she heard Sean's voice call for her. She flipped the page and continued reading. The floorboards creaked in the familiar spots as he walked toward her.

"You know, you should probably lock your doors more often."

She flipped another page. "I knew you were on the way, and laziness won."

"What if a serial killer had walked in instead of me?"

"You'd have an awkward time explaining to the police that you weren't the killer. They always suspect the love interest."

He scoffed. "Is that what I've been reduced to? Love interest?"

She giggled and dog-eared the page. She pushed herself off the couch and set the book on the side table. "Speaking of awkward things... we need to talk."

His lips pressed into a line. "I'm not terribly surprised. You've been a bit distant lately."

"Have I?" She frowned. "I mean, it's been crazy between work and Raphael's accident."

"Well, for one, you'd usually kiss me by now."

Mia gave a half-smile and kissed him.

He held her around the waist and kissed her forehead. "Well, now you're just pandering."

She shoved him back playfully with her hands. "Anyway." She turned for her phone, searching her couch cushions. The screen illuminated, and she scrolled to the photo. "Here."

"What—" His mouth dropped. "What is this?"

Mia sighed and rubbed an arm. "Angie sent a photo."

His jaw worked as he looked over the photo again. He handed her the phone. "Okay."

"What do you mean, 'okay?' No curiosity behind why she would send this?"

"I thought we talked about this," he said and crossed his arms. "No. I'm not curious. I don't—this was so long ago. I don't understand why she would send you a photo of me meeting someone."

"The photo was a long time ago?"

"No, Mia." His voice rose a notch. "Angie was a long time ago. This was about a month ago or so."

She frowned. "Wait, is she following you?"

"How should I know? And why would she send this—"

Her ears burned. "I kind of know." When she realized he was waiting for more, she rushed forward with the explanation. "It was me. I asked."

"What?" The word was an exclamation.

She retreated to the other end of her living room and started pacing. "I know! I know. I'm sorry! I couldn't help it! It was bugging me so much. I just wanted to know what she was talking about. And at first, she didn't even say anything. She didn't read it, although now I think it's because we're not friends on Facebook."

"You reached out on Facebook? How did you even—"

Mia batted the question away impatiently. "You said you were still friends with her, which is probably how she found my phone number. After you told me her name, it was easy to find."

Sean laughed and rubbed his brow. "I can't believe it. I should have blocked her. You know what? Let's just get to the end of this conversation, because to tell you the truth, I'm a little sick of it."

She bristled. "What?"

He held his hand out, and she handed him her phone, her adrenaline spiking. He sat on the couch, and she followed suit. When he pressed the speaker button, she realized he was calling someone.

A woman's voice sounded from her phone. "Hello?"

"Hey, Angie."

There was a pause. "Sean?" The voice held a note of incredulity.

"What's up?"

"I—nothing. Why are you calling me?"

His laugh was humorless. "Oh, I don't know. Maybe because you're trying to start shit between my girlfriend and me."

The pause was so long Mia thought she had hung up. Sean pressed on.

"Angie?"

"What?"

"What are you playing at?"

"I'm not playing nothing. You know what? Screw you and your girlfriend. I was just trying to do the girl a solid and warn her about your bitch ass promising all sorts of things and asking for second chances—"

Sean jumped off the couch. "A solid? Christ! It's been six years! People change—"

A bitter laugh sounded from the phone. "No, they don't."

Mia stood from the couch and took care not to get in his way while he paced the living room.

"People change, and even if they don't, it's not your problem to deal with anymore."

"You're damn right."

"So, leave it alone. Why do you care so much?"

"I don't! She's the one that asked." Electronic static distorted Angie's voice for a second. "I don't care about you or her."

"Is that why you're taking pictures of me?"

"You know what? I don't need this."

The call ended.

He sighed and stared at the phone for a moment. Mia realized her mouth was open when he turned to face her.

"Well." She frowned.

"When we dated, I wouldn't have pegged her for someone who would stir up drama years later." He made a face. "Actually, maybe a little."

Mia's eyebrows rose.

He shrugged. "Honestly, that's probably what attracted me to her. The wildness, the chaos. She was so fun and ready to tell you what was on her mind. Never afraid to tell you how she felt. And she was always down for the next adventure."

"Why'd you cheat on her?"

Sean looked surprised, and he took a moment to respond. "Sometimes people do things they regret later."

"That is the most bullshit response ever." Mia crossed her arms.

His eyes widened at the rebuke. "Okay, yeah. That's bullshit." He clenched and unclenched his fists. "I cheated..." His voice faltered and he looked down at the floor. "I cheated because I wanted to, because I felt like it. Because I was using her."

Mia's eyes were wide when he paused and looked at her, gauging her reaction.

When she didn't respond, he continued, his body agitated. "Not intentionally. I didn't ask her out knowing I would be unfaithful. But we weren't looking for anything serious, neither one of us. And I think I was just in this dark place where I needed the distraction. I didn't think about it like that at the time, but there's a crazy period where you just do things that distract you from real life. I didn't want to be the man who had lost his fiancée and baby all within a few weeks. I wanted to be married. I wanted to be a father. Or someone else entirely. It felt like the whole entire world had said, 'fuck you,' so I said it back. And I hurt someone. Apparently, more than I initially thought. I can't take it back, but I don't think it defines me. It just makes me human. I've never stepped out on someone before then or since."

"Who's the woman in the photo?" The words reverberated like an accusation.

He looked up at the ceiling and took a deep breath. "You know what, that's fair. She and I used to work in the same nonprofit together back in the day. I went out to pick up some takeout from a new Peruvian restaurant, and I happened to see her with her husband. She's a hugger and was excited to see me because it'd been a while."

The fight drained from her. "You know what I realized? Angie knew what I looked like. When she realized you weren't hugging me, she snapped the photo." She frowned. "That's kind of weird."

"You think?" His voice was sarcastic.

She ignored the tone. "Do you think she's stalking you?"

"I don't think she's following me. I think it was a crime of opportunity."

She giggled. "Crime's a little harsh."

"You know what I mean. Either way, I think she'll stop now."

Mia picked at a fingernail. "I have to tell you something." She didn't meet his eyes when she told him. "Theo kissed me."

"What!"

She shook her head. "Don't yell."

"I'm not yelling, I'm just—please don't walk away, Mia," He grabbed her arm roughly, and she felt the color drain from her face. He probed her eyes, and she tried not to let her knees buckle. "What happened?"

She regretted the confession. "It was quick, and I pulled away, but I just wanted you to know because not telling you felt like lying."

He scoffed and let go of her arm. "Thanks."

Free from his grip, she retreated to the sofa chair, her eyes filling with tears. "Yup." She tucked her bare feet under her bottom and hid her face.

"Why do you do that?"

She willed herself to breathe evenly. After wiping her eyes on a shirt sleeve, she turned to face him, her jaw set. "Do what?"

His eyes searched hers, frustrated. "Hide."

"I don't hide."

"Yes! You do. You hide all the time. When someone doesn't react the way you want them to, you just run off and hide. In another room, behind work, behind Isaiah."

She burst out of the chair, livid. "What are you talking about? If I wanted to hide from things, I wouldn't have even said anything about Theo. You weren't there. It's not like you would have known. I wanted to be transparent and let you know. And then you're sarcastic about it."

"Well, I don't know what reaction you wanted when you're telling me the guy you described as a brother kissed you. And then! On the same evening you wanted to talk about a picture of me hugging someone."

"It's not like it was just a picture. You had an ex-girlfriend sitting there telling me you were unfaithful and about to be again. You have to admit that's extra fishy."

Sean let out a breath that sounded more like a growl. "Okay, I get why that would raise some concerns, but that was years ago. At some point, the statute of limitations is reached for mistakes. At least, I'd hope so." He crossed his arms again. "So, what did Theo do when you pulled away?"

She shrugged. "He apologized. I called him later, and we talked about it. He hasn't talked to me since."

"Oh, I bet."

Mia's nostrils flared. "Can you just stop it! At least when there was another woman telling me not to trust you and that you were stepping out on me, I wasn't a complete bitch about it."

He sighed. "I'm going to the hospital with you this Saturday."

"Oh, no," she said, shaking her head. "Visitors are already limited, and you escorting me just because you're jealous isn't a reason you should be going."

"I don't have to go into the room—"

Mia exploded. "Then, why go? Just to claim your property? And when

Raphael almost fucking died from a head injury. Yeah, I think not. Get over yourself. I don't even know if Theo will be there. And if he's there, it'll be fine. We already talked about it."

"Gee, it seems you already talked about being spoken for the day he and I shook hands."

Her chest felt tight with pressure. "Oh my God. I wish I had never told you. I haven't even told Camille because it's not an issue."

"Then, why bring it up now?"

"Because maybe I wanted full transparency, and obviously, that was a mistake!" Her hands were balled into fists, and they both stared each other down inside of her living room.

"Is this why you don't let me around Isaiah anymore?"

The question surprised her, and her mouth formed a small 'o.' She tilted her head. "What?"

"Ever since we talked about slowing down, I haven't been allowed over to your house if Isaiah was there. Minus the time I met your dad. It's like you allowed one extra dinner together, and that was that. We don't go out except when you have a babysitter. You haven't brought him over to my place even once. I'm not allowed over if he's here."

She crossed her arms. "That's what slowing down is. It's taking a step back."

"But for how long? There's not even a trace of you at my house."

She almost laughed. "What?"

"There's no trace of you. I've never dated someone who hasn't left something. I mean, you don't leave a toothbrush, a hair tie, nothing. Less than nothing. You make it a point to not leave anything behind."

Mia shrugged, her brain failing her.

"Really? That's all I get? A shrug?" He pressed his lips into a line. "Is Theo the reason you don't want to go any further with us?"

She barked out a laugh. "Really? That's what you think? You think me wanting to go slow is because of another man? You really are full of yourself. It can't ever be because a woman wants to take it slow, can it? It's gotta be another man. It *must* be another man. Theo kissed *me*. I didn't kiss him. And I told you because I thought people in relationships were supposed to communicate. My mistake."

"Now who's being sarcastic?"

"And now you're bringing up shit that hurt your ego."

Sean's face was a challenge. "Any person would be mad about their partner kissing someone else."

"I didn't kiss—"

"You got mad over a hug and shit I did years ago, so don't sit there on your high horse acting like I'm the issue. I'm the one taking this slower than I want to because of you. I'm respecting your space. I'm trying my best not to step on your toes over Isaiah. I'm listening to you when you talk about Austin. At what point are you going to look forward to your own future?"

Mia felt the question like a slap. "What?"

"You live in the past, Mia! When are you going to start looking forward and at what's here and now?"

This time she bit down hard on the side of her cheek to stop the tears. She would not cry. Not now.

"What do you see when you look forward to the future?" When she said nothing, he pressed her. "Do you see a future? With me?"

Her mouth opened, but words failed her.

He waited a full minute before smiling. His eyes were glassy. "Okay."

Ice ran down her spine. "Okay?"

"You're an amazing woman, Mia."

"Wait..."

"But I don't know if I'm what you need right now."

The tears she held at bay began to fall down her cheeks. "What are you saying?"

"I think you need to figure out what you want. Am I what you want?" He sighed. "Don't answer right now. Think about it."

He walked over to her and pulled her close. She held onto him, eyes wide, like she was afraid he'd disappear forever if she let go. He kissed the top of her head and loosened her grip on him. "I'm going to go. I want the best for you, Mia."

"Sean," she said, her voice a prayer.

He walked out of her house, and she watched, wanting to throw herself at his feet. *Please don't go. Don't leave me alone.*

And then he was gone.

That night, she dreamed she lived in a house filled with rooms, hallways that led everywhere and nowhere, and beautiful furniture. She wanted to feel grateful and happy to live within such privilege, but it felt empty, without. She walked through its interior, running her fingers over the creamy wallpaper, pausing briefly to admire enlarged photographs of landscapes. A spark of recognition existed within the photos, but she couldn't place them.

The hallways curved, and the curtains were drawn. She couldn't find an exit, only more rooms or stairways.

Why did she feel so alone?

The memory of Austin slammed into her, and she panicked. She hadn't seen him in what felt like a lifetime. Where had he gone? Where was he? She picked up her pace and began seeing glimpses of someone turning around a corner. This went on so long she started to think she was seeing a ghost.

Maybe he's outside.

She ran, struggling and failing to find a door. Finally, she turned to a window and yanked down the curtain. The sun blinded her, and she blinked several times before pushing the split window outward. She leaned her body out over the frame, squinting.

A man's form slowly walked away from the building.

She yelled out his name, desperate to get his attention, hoping the sound would carry through the distance. "Austin!"

The man stopped walking and looked back. It was Sean.

-Chapter 35-

April 2017

The hospital felt less menacing with Raphael out of the ICU. Soft light streamed through the tinted floor-to-ceiling windows, somehow muting the harshness from the bright overhead lights. The weekend proved to be a busy time. People littered the hallways, and a line formed around the semi-circle Patient Services desk. Hospital staff bustled down the halls, some laughing with each other.

Isaiah held Mia's hand as she and her father walked past the busy interior to the elevators. She let Isaiah press the number three once they entered the elevator. He grinned up at her, and she smiled back, crinkling her nose. She wondered when buttons would lose their appeal, but for the moment, she was glad he felt the magic of childhood behind the mundane.

Looking around the waiting area as they approached the reception desk, she wondered if Theo would be present. The thought revolved between relieving and anxiety-inducing.

They checked in with the charge nurse.

"He's in room six."

God, I hope he's not there.

They thanked the nurse and made their way to the room. Mia's stomach tied into a knot right before they entered the room, but once it was in view, only Eloise and Raphael were present. Eloise rose to greet them. Flowers adorned the corners of the room, and a large stuffed teddy with an oversized card lay crooked across the windowsill.

Mia gave her a squeeze. "Wow, look at all the love in this room."

When Eloise smiled, it reached her eyes. "Yes! I wasn't expecting such a response, but it's been so lovely."

Mia turned to the bed and found a groggy Raphael. "Hi, you! You scared everybody! How are you?"

"I'm good, I'm good." His words were slow and groggy. "Happy to be here now. Looking forward to my own bed, though."

Eloise clasped her hands together near her heart. "I'm so glad we're out of the ICU. It's so busy there. The nurses are constantly coming in and out. Not that they've been anything but lovely. But still, sometimes you just want some peace. I'll be happiest once I can take him home. Did you all want something to drink? I was just about to go grab him some juice."

David shook his head. "Oh, no. Don't worry about us. Thank you, though."

"Do you want some company?" said Mia.

"No, no. Enjoy your visit. I'll be right back."

David tipped his head as she left the room and then turned toward Raphael. He grinned. "I heard you got your ass kicked by a ladder. How'd that happen?"

Mia elbowed her father in the ribs, but Raphael chuckled, wincing a bit.

"Did it hurt a lot?" Isaiah walked tentatively over to the hospital bed. He pointed to the bandage on Raphael's head.

"I don't really remember the fall. But right now, it hurts a little bit. The doctors are giving me medicine to help with that."

"Luca said you bumped your head. You hurt your brain?" Isaiah's eyes were wide.

"Oh," said Raphael. "Yes, I did bump my head. Kind of hard. The doctors helped fix that, too. When I go home, I'll have to be really careful. Especially when I climb things. I think I'm a little too old to do everything around the house."

"Mm, okay." Isaiah walked over to a chair and sat, studying the fallen teddy bear.

David smiled at his friend. "Old age is rough. A young man probably would have bounced. By the way, you still owe me a rematch from the last time we played cards, so I hope you don't stay cooped in here for too long."

"Still nursing a sore ego after I schooled you on how to play?" Raphael paused every few words, as if speaking taxed his body.

"One extra point. Not sure it's anything to brag about."

"A win is a win." Raphael shrugged and grimaced.

"Oh, what's wrong, mon coeur?" Eloise had returned in time to see the pain contort her husband's face. She hastily dropped the drinks on the small side table and rushed to his side.

"Nothing, nothing. No worries. I was just trying to move." He glanced sheepishly at everyone in the room. "You'd think bruises wouldn't be so painful."

David walked to the other side of the bed. "Do you need some help?"

"Maybe with shifting this pillow behind my neck. A little bit."

Once Raphael was settled again, he grinned at his wife. "David here says he's coming over to get his butt kicked at cards again."

She laughed. "Is that right? Just let me know, David, and I'll make sure to have dinner prepped for you."

David laughed heartily. "I appreciate it. Just let me know when you're ready, amigo."

A noise stole Mia's attention, and she turned to see Isaiah tug on a large arrangement of sunflowers.

"Don't do that, baby."

"I was just looking. These are ugly." He tried to tug on a petal.

Mia suppressed a laugh. "Don't touch them. That messes up the flowers. They're not ugly. I love sunflowers."

"Well, then, you like ugly flowers."

"Shoo, mijo. Go sit down."

Isaiah rolled his eyes and stomped over to a seat. Mia raised her eyebrows. *Man, I'm in trouble when he's a teen.*

She crouched next to him and cut him a look. "Don't act so ugly, Isaiah. What's wrong?"

"Nothing," he said, looking cross. "I wasn't doing anything."

"Is he thirsty? I got some apple juice for him." Eloise stood near them, smiling, the bottle of apple juice already in hand.

His eyes lit up. "Ooh! Yeah!"

"What do we say?"

"Thanks!" Isaiah struggled with the lid for a moment before it finally gave. The motion sloshed juice onto his shirt. He frowned. "Oh man."

Mia found a wipe and cleaned him up. "No biggie. Don't forget to cap it when you're done with it." She kept him within her peripheral vision when she turned back toward the group. When she noticed he was fidgety again, she pulled out her phone to give to him.

That can't be good long-term, she thought mildly. Before she rejoined the adults, she watched him play one of the many games she had saved on her phone for him. The activities in the room were now lost on him. *But it gets the job done.*

∞ ∞ ∞

Isaiah stared out of the window on the drive home. Mia glanced at her son a few times, but never caught his eye. Her own thoughts were tumultuous. She wondered if Sean was thinking of her.

"Do you want hamburgers for dinner?" She glanced back and saw him shrug. "Burgers it is."

When they arrived home, he ran to the living room and turned on his favorite show. Mia threw some ready-made frozen French fries into the oven to cook while she seasoned the pre-formed patties. Anxiety had suppressed her appetite, but after skipping breakfast and having a bottle of juice for lunch, the aroma the patties made when placed on the skillet made her mouth water.

She uncorked a bottle of cabernet and poured a generous amount into a coffee cup. The alcohol hit her system quickly, courtesy of an empty stomach. She checked her phone between flipping burgers. A few spam notifications urged her to take advantage of new daily games. She had two new emails. No messages.

The coffee cup was half empty when she smelled the fries.

"Shit." Hastily, she opened the oven and flipped most of them quickly. The bottoms were past the recommended golden hue. She turned off the oven and shut the door. "Oh, well."

Once the burgers were done, she plated their dinners. "Isaiah!"

"It's almost over!"

She marched to the edge of the kitchen. "Now!"

Isaiah sulked into the kitchen and took a seat. The television was still on, but Mia decided to leave it alone.

"Eat and then you can go finish your show. Bedtime is early today." She took large bites from her burger.

"Oh man, why?"

She frowned. "Because I said. And I'm tired."

"Then, you go to bed early."

"Hey," she snapped. "You don't talk to me like that. I'm your mom. So, what I say goes. If bedtime is a little earlier, then bedtime is earlier."

He glowered and ate a few fries. "Fine, I'll go to bed right now."

"That's not what I—"

He stormed out of the kitchen. She heard him stomp up to his room.

Music played in the living room, and she realized the show had looped. His burger hadn't been touched. He'd be hungry before nightfall, and she wanted to drag him back down to finish, but her energy was depleted.

Her own burger was almost finished. She popped a fry into her mouth and stood. She dumped the contents of her plate into the garbage before refilling her coffee mug with more wine.

Isaiah was still in his bedroom when she finished cleaning the kitchen. She had left the television playing to see if he'd slink down to watch, but he had stayed in his room. His lone plate sat on the table. She bagged his burger and put it in the fridge, then scraped his fries into the trash. They didn't tend to reheat as well.

The burger and wine felt heavy in her belly. She rinsed out the last bit of wine that remained in her mug and placed it in the dishwasher, then corked the bottle and put it away.

She turned off the television and made her way to Isaiah's room. She rapped on the door lightly before pushing it open. He sat on the floor working on a small Lego figure.

"Hey, papa. What are you working on?" She sat on the floor next to him, cross-legged.

"I'm making a zombie."

"Oh, nice. Creepy."

He smiled. "It's not that scary because there's no Lego blood."

She made a mock surprised face. "It needs blood to be scary? I don't know, man. Something that eats brains is scary, with or without blood."

His movements faltered. "Mom?" He looked up and waited for an acknowledgement before continuing. "Luca's grandpa hurt his brain, right? He bumped his head so hard it hurt his brain? That's why he has to stay with the doctors."

"Yeah. He did. But the doctors were able to help him. He should be going home soon, and he can rest there until he's all the way better."

"How come the doctors weren't able to help Daddy?" He burst into tears, and she felt taken aback. "His brain was hurt, too, right? How come the doctors didn't fix him?"

Mia never knew how to explain depression, let alone suicide, to a child. She didn't know when to tell him his father had taken his own life, but she knew eventually she had to.

Once, she mused to Carol about keeping it a secret.

"I don't know how to explain this to him. He's so little! If he was going to die, why couldn't he have died from cancer or a car crash? Maybe I can just lie about how? Or never talk about it? Because why suicide? Why did he leave us?"

Carol had held her while she wept and stroked her hair in a motherly fashion. "My dear, I'm so sorry. I wish I knew what to say. I don't know how to explain it, either. I guess that's why there's professionals. But you can't hide it from Isaiah forever. He's not going to be 70 years old and not know how his dad died. It's probably best if he learns it from you and not from rumors or by overhearing someone."

It made sense to Mia, but so far, all she had explained was that Austin was in a severe depression. The terminology had confused Isaiah.

"It's like a brain sickness," Mia had said. "It wasn't his fault. People sometimes get this type of brain sickness, and it's not too bad. Like a small cold, and they can get help and get better. Sometimes it's like a serious sickness. You need medicines and doctors. And sometimes, it's too much, and people die from it, even though they fought really hard to stay healthy."

She knew it made sense to question why one person's brain injury was fixed while another's was not. In Isaiah's mind, the doctors had failed his father. She pulled him close and willed herself not to cry.

His tears wet the top portion of her blouse. "I want Daddy."

And with those three words, the fight to contain her grief was lost. "I know, baby, I know." Tears spilled down her cheeks. Some landed on Isaiah's hair. Her voice was shaky. "I'm so sorry, mi amor."

Several minutes later, he turned his head, wiping his face on her shirt. It made her laugh.

"Gee, thanks."

His face was blotchy. "Mommy?"

"Yes, mi amor?"

"I'm hungry."

Mia blinked. "Oh." She felt like she had been hit by a tornado, and now he was hungry.

"Can I have some cereal?" He looked expectantly at his mother.

The untouched, leftover burger came to mind, but she anticipated a fight and didn't have the energy to argue. "Sure. *He can have the burger tomorrow.*

She put on a movie and let him eat in the living room. When it was over, she announced the arrival of bedtime, and Isaiah was happy to comply. He drifted off to sleep almost as soon as she started reading his book of choice. She remained sitting at the base of the bed and read it through, just in case.

When she stood, her body felt heavy and achy.

"Good night, mi vida."

Later, in her bed, Mia opened her phone. She sent two texts. Both made her cry.

To Camille: *When will this stop hurting?*

To Sean: *We should probably talk about how we left things.*

-Chapter 36-

April 2017

T he sky was a beautiful teal, broken only by a wisp of cloud here and there. There was very little wind, which meant the shining sun gave the day a preview of spring. Isaiah and Luca were playing with a soccer ball in Mia's backyard. Luca wound up for a kick and ended up slipping in the grass. The boys shrieked with laughter.

"Did you see me, Mom? Did you see?"

Camille laughed. She and Mia were sitting on the back patio. "Yeah! Good recovery!"

She shifted and turned her attention to Mia again. "I'm sorry it's been so hard for you. I can't imagine having to explain death—and the death of his dad, of all things. You're doing so great."

"I don't feel like it most of the time."

Camille smiled sympathetically. "Because you're too hard on yourself. Isaiah feels comfortable enough to ask you hard questions and go to you when he's scared or hurting or confused. That's the goal. We can't shield them from everything."

Mia crossed her legs and watched their sons play. Luca had stolen the ball and kicked it down their makeshift field. Isaiah frowned, a competitive gleam in his eyes. At the last second, he kicked the ball away. It danced across the grass into a bush.

"Foul!" said Luca and took off toward the bush. Isaiah was close behind.

"I know," said Mia. "I just wish it would get better faster." Her knee bounced. "Sometimes I wonder if it's me."

"What do you mean?"

"I hate feeling like this. I don't want to be Austin's widow. I just want to be me. I'm so angry that he chose suicide. I know it wasn't a real choice, but it feels like it sometimes. I hate that Isaiah has to deal with this. I want to be able to spare him the hurt, y'know?" She took a shaky breath. "But on the other hand, I feel so guilty. So incredibly guilty. I was the closest one to Austin, and I failed him. Sometimes I feel like I deserve all this, the pain and the grief. Not Isaiah, of course, but just me. And here I am, dating Sean and can barely function like a normal girlfriend, because it's always tied up or overshadowed by Austin. A part of me wonders if I even deserve a second chance."

Camille's eyes watered. "Oh, Mia. Don't say—"

The faint sound of the doorbell sounded, and they both turned toward the noise. "Oh, the Chinese," said Mia and rushed to the front door.

She set out the food on the dinner table as Camille coaxed the boys back inside. They smelled of grass and earthy sweat. They shoveled rice and pieces of orange chicken into their mouths.

"God, what is the food bill going to look like when these guys are older?" said Camille with a half-smile.

"It's okay. I'm planning to take it out of his student loan fund." Mia winked, and the women laughed.

The boys finished their meal and ran back outside.

They tidied the kitchen and returned to their previous places to supervise. The boys had abandoned the soccer game and were now swinging on the playground set that had come with the house.

"Maybe..." Camile said, and her voice faltered. She cleared her throat. "I mean this in the best way possible, but maybe it's time for therapy." Mia chuckled, but Camille pressed on. "I'm serious! You take Isaiah to someone a few times a month and say it's really helped. Maybe you need that, too. Someone who can give you a fresh perspective."

"Yeah, you're right. I'm just so busy and—"

"And you constantly keep yourself on the back burner. Do you think you're not going because you don't think you deserve the help?"

Mia blinked.

"You just said you feel like you deserve the grief and pain and all that. You know therapy works because you send Isaiah. If you don't think you need it for your sake, do it for Isaiah's. He needs a mom who is happy and who forgives herself. They're astute little things. They can tell when something bothers us. Sure, he might not understand the complexities of your feelings, but he can tell you're not at your best. You've told me before he's mentioned that you don't laugh a lot. You deserve to be happy. I know it. Isaiah knows it. Now you just need to know it."

Mia's eyes filled with tears. She smiled. "You do make sense."

"Oh, God, don't cry. Then, I'll cry. I wasn't trying to be mushy, just truthful. This mascara isn't waterproof." Camille fanned her face.

Mia laughed and sniffed. "Sorry, sorry."

"It'll get easier." Camille rubbed her arm.

"When, though?"

"Look, Mom! Look how high we can go before we jump off!" Luca grinned. Once he reached the peak of his swing, he pushed his arms in front of him and leaped out. His body arced out and forward while the swing went the opposite way. He landed in a crouched position and jumped up, crowing in triumph.

"C'mon, Isaiah! Your turn!"

Isaiah eyed his friend, then his mother. He smiled, nervous, and looked at the sky. It took him two full swings before he finally looked ready to take the leap. Mia wanted to tell him he didn't have to jump, that he could slow the swing to a stop. She knew his cautious nature stemmed from her. Likewise, she knew his stubborn streak came from her, and he might do the opposite of what she suggested.

It's up to you, mijo.

His eyebrows knitted, and he looked forward, ignoring everyone in the backyard. He pumped his legs out one more time, and when he reached the top, he let go.

-Chapter 37-

April 2017

Mia sat cross-legged on Sean's couch. He sat across from her, looking amazing in a powder blue V-neck shirt and slacks. She averted her eyes.

Since their last argument, they hadn't shared more than just text messages and a few brief phone calls. Each short conversation was loaded with unspoken feelings and created a tension Mia hated. The elephant in the room crowded out any space for conversations that contained more than niceties. Finally, she suggested an evening in his apartment.

"We need to talk."

He let out a small laugh. It held a nervous edge. "Yeah, I figured. I want to take the easy way out and ask you what you want, but I think you've been following my lead."

She forced herself to look at him. Her thoughts raced. The front door looked enticing. *Stop being such a chickenshit.*

"I started therapy," she said. *Coward.*

"Oh," he said, his eyebrows raised. "That's—that's good."

Heat rushed up her neck. "Well, almost started. I made an appointment. But—well, I guess I wanted to say I need therapy."

He smiled politely.

Oh, he's not touching that one. Smart man.

"I guess what I mean is I've been putting off therapy. You didn't make me realize I needed it, per se, but you're right. I'm stuck in—I'm not over Austin's death. Worse, I don't feel like I can get past it. I feel like I deserve to grieve forever. I mean, why do I get a second chance at everything? It's not just unfair that my husband killed himself. It's unfair that he died and I lived. I didn't realize he was struggling so much. I failed him. I feel like I killed him and now am living with the guilt of it."

Her words hung in the air.

Sean shifted in his seat. "I don't know what to say to that."

"You don't have to say anything." The room felt awkward. Leading with needing therapy forced their issues aside. As per usual, Mia had brought up Austin. The ghost of his memory was both a problem and a safety blanket. She'd been haunted for so long, she didn't know what it was like to be alone, only lonely. The realization slammed into her like a cold wave, and she knew then Sean had been wrong. He left her house wondering if he was wrong for her, when it was her who wasn't able to give him all he deserved.

She had heard of people meeting the right person at the wrong time and never understood the predicament. The clarity crushed her.

Sean broke the silence. "You'd think after Maribel I'd know what to say, but I don't. I never do."

"It's okay."

"Your life after Austin isn't a second chance," he said. "It's just your life. It continues. It's just different than what you planned. That I do know." He closed the gap between them and lifted her chin so she met his eyes. "His death isn't your fault. You didn't kill him. People have troubled marriages all the time, and they either fix it or get divorced. That's not a crime. This isn't a second chance, because you didn't do anything wrong."

Mia's face crumpled, and she covered her face with her hands. She felt his arms wrap around her as she cried and leaned against him. Here he was, so present and solid and real. Her body was ready for the security he provided, but her mind lived with ghosts.

She took a shuddery breath and stood, heartbroken over what she was going to confess. "This is unfair for you."

He stayed on the couch, his eyes meeting hers, confusion plain on his face.

"This. Me. Comforting me every single time we mention Austin. Not able to talk about what we really need to talk about because I start some pity party by accident."

His jaw worked.

"It's so messed up. You've gotta admit that much."

He shrugged. "Austin was a huge part of your world. He's the father of your son. You're allowed tears."

Mia let out a short laugh. "God, you're too perfect sometimes. Maybe that's why I fixated on the whole Angie fiasco. I thought, 'Oh, here's the red flag.'"

His head tilted. "You're looking for red flags because you don't see any?"

"I didn't say it was logical or anything." She stood and began pacing the living room. "It's probably just more proof I'm the crazy one." She gasped. "Maybe you're the one that needs to be looking harder for red flags."

He let out a short laugh. "You're something else, but I don't think there's any red flags."

She stopped pacing and looked at him, taking in the angles and curves of his face, the color of his eyes. Nights consisting of pleasure and talking ran through her mind. Even after all the time they'd spent together in his apartment, he was right, there was no trace of her left behind.

"You deserve better than me."

His eyes widened. "Did you come over to break up with me?"

"You want a future, a family. And I'm still trying to figure out how to plan more than a week at a time."

"Mia." His voice was low.

"You told me to think about what I wanted—"

"And what do you want?"

She bit her lip, her eyes studying the floor. What she wanted and what she deserved were two different things. She didn't know how to explain it. "The last dream I remember having was one where I was in this huge house, a mansion, I guess. And it dawned on me that I hadn't seen Austin in forever. I ran through the house in a panic. I didn't know where he was. I opened a window and saw someone, so I yelled out his name. And it was you."

When she looked up, it was Sean's turn to look away. His eyes wandered to the bookshelf. "I don't know what that means."

"Sometimes I feel like I'm cheating on him."

"Wow. Ouch." He closed his eyes and crossed his arms. Mia felt a wall forming between them.

"I'm trying to be honest."

"That doesn't mean you can just say things like that and expect me to take it with a smile. Damn it, Mia. What do you want me to say?"

She dipped her head. "I know. I don't know. That's not—I'm sorry. I guess I'm trying to say that I can't let go of the guilt. And everything I do that is for *me* makes me feel guilty. Dating you is part of that. Probably worse than that, because it's me moving on."

"You're right, you need therapy."

The hard edge in his voice irritated her. "Yeah. I know. That's why I made an appointment."

He ran a hand through his dark hair and made a frustrated noise. "Well, what now?"

She barked out a laugh. "You just said I need therapy, and now I'm making decisions about us?"

"You said it first, and you're the one who said you feel like you're cheating on someone. And I'm the other guy. So, yeah. I don't know what to do with that information." He rubbed his mouth and chin with one hand and then threw his hands up. "I don't know."

"Maybe I need to know I'm okay on my own first." The words were out before she could measure the implication behind them. She stiffened, wishing she could pull them back from the air. The idea of being alone again hit her in the gut.

He stared at her a moment. "Well. There you go."

Tears threatened to return, and she bit the inside of her cheek hard. When a tear escaped, he walked to the kitchen. More ran down her cheeks. Quickly, she wiped her face and turned to collect her purse from the coffee table. She pulled the strap over her shoulder and rushed to the front door, anxious to collect her shoes and flee the apartment.

Sean intercepted her and pulled her toward him so hard she gasped. He embraced her, and she leaned her head against his chest, listening to his quickened heartbeat.

"Screw it. I don't know. Maybe you're not ready to take it to the next level, but I'm not in a hurry." He held her out in front of him. "You want to know what I want? You. Just you. We all have shit to work on. I mean, look at me with ex-girlfriends coming out of the woodwork." He grinned to show her he was joking. The corners of her lips tugged downward. His smile fell. "Okay, maybe not the best time for jokes. But I love you, Mia."

"I love you, too. That's why I know you need someone better." Her chin quivered. Before he could stop her again, she pushed her way past him and out of his apartment, determined not to look back. She didn't think she'd let go the next time he held her.

-Chapter 38-

April 2017

Mia ran from Sean's apartment, her pulse thundering in her ears. She felt shaky, uncertain. Mostly, she felt selfish.

He called her before she was even halfway home. She turned off her phone and visited her dad. If he noticed her agitation, he didn't mention it. Instead, they made coffee and sat talking about everything and nothing. Before she left to collect Isaiah from Lori's house, she cooked her father a large dinner, portioning out the extra in small storage containers.

"There," she said. "Now you have a week's worth of good meals." She kissed her dad on the cheek and promised to visit soon with Isaiah.

The next day, she texted Camille about the breakup but refused company. *You need to focus on your dad. I'm fine. Promise.*

On Monday, she buried herself in work. It was three days before she found the nerve to answer his calls.

"So, that's it, then?" Sean asked, his voice angry. "My feelings on this don't matter?"

Mia let a beat pass before responding. "They do, but that's why this is right. You asked me what I wanted, but it's not about what I want. It's about what is best for us. If there's anyone who has the privilege to get what they want, it's you. I can't give you what you want."

"What do you know about what I want?" His voice was angry but also dejected.

"Sean," she sighed. The call ended, and silent tears began to fall.

He called again that weekend. "Come over." A pause. "Please."

The desire to see him outweighed her caution. After Camille agreed to watch Isaiah for the evening, she drove to Sean's apartment, her thoughts tumultuous. "We just need to talk. Break ups are hard. We'll talk about it, and maybe we'll both feel a little better," she murmured to herself.

But the idea of just talking fled her brain as soon as he opened the door. Desire flashed through her, and he reacted to it like kindle to a flame. When he pulled her inside, he kissed her hard. All she wanted to do was lose herself in him. She bit his lower lip, and one of his hands found its way to her lower back. His mouth traced a line from her mouth to her collarbone.

"I love you," he whispered.

"I love you, too." With that, he carried her to his room.

Afterwards, tangled in the sheets, he began to talk. She silenced him with a kiss.

"I have to go get Isaiah. Camille could only watch him for a little bit."

Sean's face darkened, but he didn't argue. She collected her clothes. When she left the room, she didn't look back.

He called her that night. "What was that?"

"What was what?"

His tone was thick with irritation. "Don't play dumb."

She knew he had the right to be angry, but the order still made her defensive, and she ended the call. Before he could call her, she turned her phone on airplane mode and slept fitfully. The next day, she was briefly disappointed to find he hadn't tried to call or text her back. *Maybe that's for the best.*

∞ ∞ ∞

Mia sat in her office, her door closed. Lunch had been a salad that left her hungry an hour later. Her stomach grumbled, but she didn't feel like the trek to the deli, nor did she want to order something for delivery. Brian had shot her one too many curious glances, and she knew she was acting differently. She wasn't ready to explain her breakup to him yet. In a sense, the breakup didn't feel final or concrete; it felt ambiguous. And so, aside from Camille, there was no one she had mentioned it to.

That didn't mean she was acting like herself. Which led her to avoiding the people she knew would ask questions. But, of course, that also meant it spiked her friends' curiosity that much more.

She sighed, annoyed she couldn't feign apathy better.

A buzzing noise broke through her thoughts, and she glanced at her cell. It was Camille. Raphael was set to be discharged from the hospital. Eloise was throwing a very small welcome home reception.

Mia gasped, overjoyed to hear the news. There had been a small setback that delayed the predicted discharge date.

She texted back. *That's great! What should I bring?*

Camille assured her nothing was expected, but that Saturday, Mia arrived with ready-to-eat meals. She and David carried the boxes inside of the house, Isaiah trailing shortly behind.

Raphael was positioned carefully on the couch, his children gently fussing over him. Mia wondered if it would be a little awkward to interact with Theo after their last meeting over lunch, but all he did was jump up and help her and her father offload the boxed meals in the kitchen. The environment was festive, even if a little hushed to ensure Raphael didn't feel overwhelmed, and it pleased Mia to feel like everything was headed back to normal.

David gifted Raphael a new set of playing cards. "For next time."

Raphael chuckled in appreciation. "Thank you, Dave. Don't think I'll let you win, even with a bribe."

This elicited laughing from the pair, and they launched into good-natured ribbing. Eloise clasped her hands in approval, and her eyes shone with gratefulness.

She turned toward Mia. "Thank you for coming. I'm so glad David could join."

"He wouldn't have missed today for the world," Mia said.

Isaiah was reintroduced to Selina's children, as the rest of her family had finally made the flight to visit. He was a little hesitant until Luca started a game of hide-and-seek tag. Eloise quickly shooed them into the backyard, afraid they'd accidentally hurt Raphael.

Unperturbed, the children raced out into the outdoors, and Eloise shut the screen, leaving the sliding glass door open. Periodic peals of laughter and shrieks punctuated the adults' conversation. The only time the noise bothered anyone was when it all fell to silence, broken only by a loud wail.

Selina dashed outside and returned with her youngest son, Sebastian, his top lip bubbling with blood and already starting to swell. She and Eloise tended to the small wound, applied some ice, kisses, and hugs, before he decided he felt better and needed to rejoin the backyard fun.

"Okay, but be careful!" Selina said.

"He'll be fine," Theo assured her, and she cut her eyes at him. "What? I'm just saying. A fat lip builds character."

"Mm-hmm. Figures you'd be the one to say that. He reminds me a lot of a certain uncle."

Theo grinned. "That's why he's my favorite."

Selina snorted. "Well, don't go giving him any ideas. He's rough and tumble enough without encouragement."

"I thought kids needed encouragement to grow and—"

"Theo!" Selina yelped.

He laughed, and Camille swatted his shoulder. "You're incorrigible."

After a simple dinner, Raphael was tired and helped into his bedroom by Noel. Mia picked up their plates and was quickly joined by Theo.

"I don't want you cleaning up by yourself," he explained.

"I appreciate it," she said with a smile. Her back pocket buzzed. After rinsing off the plates and setting them in the dishwasher, she fished out her phone. It was a message from Sean. Guiltily, she stuffed it back in her pocket. She avoided Theo's gaze and started washing the pans.

"Oh, I got that." Camille had wandered into the kitchen.

Mia shrugged. "Eh, don't worry about it. I don't mind."

"Well, we can do it together, then." Camille pivoted on her heel slightly. "Theo, go grab the rest of the dishes."

"You know," he said, mildly, "for a little sister, you're quite bossy."

Camille's lips thinned.

"I'm going. I'm going."

She turned toward Mia. "How are things with you and Sean?" she asked, her voice low.

Mia shrugged, scrubbing one of the larger pans. "I mean. I don't know. Some days, I think it's over—completely over, and we're both better off. And then other days I wonder if maybe I made a mistake. Sometimes, he calls and I can't wait to head over. And sometimes, we ignore each other. And other days, I text him things that I don't need to be texting him. I almost can't help it."

Camille nodded and toweled off the pan. "Break ups suck. Especially when it's more like... it's just not working out for some reason. You know what I mean? Like, it'd be better if he had cheated. Then, the breakup would feel more... justified."

They both paused to work on the dishes. Mia turned toward her friend. "You talking about your breakup with Keegan?"

Camille exhaled a laugh. "Yeah, I guess I am." Another pause. "But sometimes it's right. You know? The breakup. But then... maybe after a while... when you're ready..."

"Ready for what?" Theo's voice startled both of them. He was balancing a stack of plates.

"For more dishes," Camille said.

∞ ∞ ∞

After a tense conversation with Sean, she had conceded to a late-night visit at her house. The decision was against her better judgement, but selfishness won in the end, and she found herself in bed with him again, this time in her own house.

Afterward, they laid next to each other, their naked bodies left a sliver of space between the other. Mia had one leg crossed over the other. Sean was next to her, breathing evenly. Neither reached for the other. It was then she knew they were ready for the truth.

"We need to stop doing this," she said, eyes on the ceiling.

He took her hand, and her heart dropped. "I wish things were different."

"Me too." She wasn't sure if she had said the words loud enough for him to hear.

"I could wait for you, you know."

Mia bit her lip. Her body felt dried up, unable to cry. If there was any sorrow to be had, it was spent.

"That's unfair to you." He began to speak, and she cut him off. "And to me. I need to make sure I'm okay by myself. I need therapy to work this all out. And if you wait for me, there's this weird pressure to get over Austin. And—well, I don't need that. And you don't need to be waiting on a woman who's still hung up on another man."

When he removed his hand from hers, her heart shattered, but she forced herself to turn her head and meet his eyes. "You're living with ghosts, Sean. I can't let you do that. Please don't wait for me."

-Chapter 39 -

August 2017

Mia stepped into her therapist's office building, regret washing over her as soon as she crossed the threshold. Goosebumps erupted on her skin, courtesy of the enthusiastic central air of the building. August was in full swing, which had inspired her to put on a business casual dress for work.

I should have brought a sweater.

Any hope for a warmer room was dashed the second she was called back to Sandra's office. She took her place on the cold pleather couch, her arms and legs crossed for warmth.

Sandra smiled apologetically. She sat on the chair opposite Mia. "It's a little cold in here."

"I thought it was a little chilly last time, but now it feels like the a/c is set on Arctic. But maybe it's the temperature difference. It's crisp in here and muggy outside. I think it's supposed to reach a hundred today, no?"

"I think you're right." Sandra smiled broadly. "So, what's on your mind today? It's been a while, huh?"

"Yeah. I meant to schedule earlier but—I didn't." Mia fidgeted in the plush chair, feeling not unlike a student in the principal's office. Sandra had recommended bimonthly visits for the time being, instead, two full months had passed since the last visit.

Sandra nodded. "Life can get busy. I understand."

Mia sighed. "Yeah. I told Isaiah about how his father died."

"Oh?" Sandra folded her hands in her lap. "How'd that go?"

"I mean, as good as it could." Mia played with the strap of her purse. "I think his therapist disagreed with me about telling him his father completed suicide."

"What do you mean?"

"I guess she just seemed taken aback. What do you think?"

Sandra hummed a flat note. "I don't think it matters much what I think. Or what Isaiah's therapist thinks. Every situation is a little different. And you know your son much better than either of us. We're here to support."

"But also to give advice, no?"

Another hum. "What do you think?"

Mia used to bristle at the questions framed as responses. However, she'd learn to appreciate the pauses.

"I don't know. I guess it's too late to take it back now."

Sandra scribbled a note on her pad and looked up. "Yes, I suppose it is. How'd Isaiah react to the news?"

"Um, I guess he was shocked, confused, angry. I regretted it almost right away. But at the same time, I think he was starting to guess. I couldn't give him concise answers when he asked questions. He wanted to know what type of illness his father had, how often he had gone to the doctor, why the doctors couldn't see what was wrong with him. And I think the deciding factor was his fear that I would die the same way. What if a doctor couldn't help me? Or him, for that matter."

Sandra nodded. "He's a very bright kid."

"Too bright, sometimes," said Mia with a sad smile.

"And now that he's had time to process it?"

"He's still mulling it over. I think he still has a lot to process." She recounted the day he had failed a spelling test. His teacher offered to let him retake it, but Isaiah was devastated. He refused to study, terrified of taking the test again. Eventually, he was forced to redo it, earning a C, but it was the first time she had noticed perfectionist behavior.

It was difficult to say whether this was part of his persona or a reaction to the news of his father's suicide. He'd had a tendency to take any failure hard, but with school becoming more technical, grades were beginning to reflect effort, a reflection Isaiah had begun to measure against his self-worth.

"Life is all about learning from failures. Failure is not a bad thing. That's the only way to learn," Mia had said, Isaiah curled up in her lap. She wrapped her arms around him and gave him a squeeze.

Isaiah had melted into the embrace for a few minutes, then roughly shoved her away. "I know," he said and fled to his video games.

The ticking sound of the clock's second hand reverberated around Sandra's office. Muted footsteps made their way down the hallway outside of the room. The unintelligible murmur of a man's voice made its way in through the door, his words drowned by the white-noise machine situated outside of the room.

"It's not uncommon for children to blame themselves for their parent's death, regardless of circumstance," said Sandra.

Mia nodded, her face a mask.

"Transparency, though, is never a bad thing."

She slumped back in the chair. "I know. But maybe it was too soon to tell him."

Sandra inclined her head. "Maybe."

"I thought you were here to make me feel better about my decisions," said Mia, turning her attention to one of the paintings on the wall.

"I'm here to offer some guidance and a safe place to talk."

"Do you think I told him too soon?"

"Well." Sandra paused. "What makes you think it was too soon?"

"Ugh." Mia covered her face with her hands. "I don't know why I thought you'd answer any differently." She sighed and removed her hands. "I guess... he's just so young. And now he feels like if he had behaved better, his dad would still be here."

Her therapist smiled sympathetically. "Well, I don't see pediatric patients, but I do counsel a lot of adults who have lost a partner and who also have children. And I can assure you, most deal with their children blaming themselves. Even when the death is due to illness or an accident. And that's because grief is complex, and they're struggling to process death at a time when death itself is barely a concept. Some kids wonder if they had gotten straight A's, maybe God or the universe or the powers-that-be would have spared their mother from cancer."

Mia's stomach flipped. "Oh my gosh."

Sandra dipped her head in agreement. "I know. And I'm not saying Isaiah isn't going to struggle with the concept of suicide—even adults struggle with that—but I think you need to trust your instincts. You saw your child needed more information. And you responded to that need. There's no manual for this. And even if there was, there's no way for it to be one-size-fits-all."

"Thanks. It's just hard."

Silence enveloped the room while Mia thought of Isaiah.

"Is there anything else on your mind?"

"I saw Sean a few weeks ago. I guess that's not that big a deal." Mia fidgeted in her chair. "Okay, maybe a little bit of a big deal. I know the breakup was dragged out a bit, but when we finally agreed it was time to step away, it felt like a good decision. Then, I see him at a gelato shop, and—it was surprisingly painful. We made small talk, and that was it." Mia made a face. "It's weird to say a breakup hurts when I'm here talking about my husband. At least no one died, you know? Sean's healthy and alive. He's going to find someone else if he hasn't already, and I should be happy about it."

Sandra shrugged. "There's no cosmic scale that weighs one type of loss against the other. A broken leg hurts a lot more than a stubbed toe, but that doesn't stop people from saying they both hurt."

Mia smiled. "You're great at analogies."

"I try my best."

When the time allotted for the appointment expired, Sandra prompted her to schedule the next appointment. As always, Mia paused as if imagining her calendar and promised to call and schedule soon. As always, Sandra smiled and accepted the lie.

Mia collected her purse and paused. "Actually. Let's make an appointment for next week."

Prioritize yourself, Mia.

Heat blasted her face when she pushed the front office door open and made her way to the car. On the drive to work, she mused over an end-of-summer vacation for herself and Isaiah. The idea of creating new memories together made her smile.

-Chapter 40-

May 2018

M ia huffed up the stairs, a stack of premade dinners in her arms. She made a mental note to schedule more gym dates with Jessica. May had arrived with bright, cloudless skies, and she felt a trickle of sweat run down her back. "Baby, ring the doorbell."

Isaiah bounced up the stairs two at a time and smashed the doorbell several times.

"Not that many times! What if the baby's sleeping?"

He glanced back at her, looking sheepish. "Sorry. I forgot."

She narrowed her eyes at him in response for a moment and then smiled. He flashed her a grin and turned toward the door, bouncing on the balls of his feet.

Keegan opened the door and smiled in greeting looking happy, even if a little tired. "Hey, you two! Oh man, what is all that?"

"Dinners for a while!"

"I see! Let me help you." He relieved her of the dishes, and they made their way to the kitchen.

"I figured you wouldn't mind some easy meals while you get used to having a baby all over again." Mia winked at him.

He sighed and smiled. "Thanks. We appreciate it. I forgot how involved it is to have a newborn! All they do is sleep, but somehow, we don't. Camille's in the bedroom."

"Oh, are they sleeping?"

"No, they should be awake." He turned to Isaiah. "Luca's playing video games in his room."

Isaiah was off in a flash, and they laughed.

"Is he adjusting well to the baby?"

Keegan tilted his head, thinking. "Yeah, I think so. Maybe it helps that she's a girl. Either way, he's been really helpful with grabbing diapers and making himself sandwiches when we're tired."

"That's good. How are you doing?"

"Oh, me? I'm good. Sleeping better than Camille anyway. Delilah is a fussy thing sometimes, so I'll get up and walk around with her. But most of the time, Camille has the night shift because I can't really breastfeed."

"Men and their useless nipples," said Mia, prompting laughter from Keegan.

"I do make sure to let Camille nap during the day since I'm going to be home for a little while."

Mia made a faux stern face and wagged her finger. "Good. I was gonna say."

He chuckled.

After more pleasantries, she excused herself and made her way to the master bedroom. She lightly rapped against the door.

"Come in!" Camille's voice was muffled through the door.

The curtains were drawn, which gave it a twilight feel. Camille sat on the bed surrounded by pillows, a tiny bundle held against her chest. Her hand made rhythmic passes over her baby's head.

"Oh," said Mia, her voice hushed. "Is she sleeping?"

"Nah, she's nursing." Camille pulled gently on a tuft of her baby's blonde hair. "I think Luca's hair already had hints of red in it at this age, but I can't remember. The pictures of him as a newborn don't really do his hair color justice. Of course, I could also be remembering it differently, because I could have sworn he had so much more hair when he was a baby, but the pictures show he barely had peach fuzz." Camille pulled another piece to its full length. "Does she have a lot of hair?"

Mia made a so-so gesture with her hand.

Camille clucked her tongue. "Dang. Okay. Maybe my memory's just shit. Well, either way, I think she'll end up with my hair color, not Keegan's. We'll see."

"I think she looks like you."

Camille sat straighter. "Really? That's good. I can't do all the work for two kids and not get at least a little bit of credit."

The baby nursed from both breasts and was gently burped. Both women sat and watched the newborn's subtle movements. Heavy-lidded eyes blinked, and her mouth opened slightly.

Mia smiled. "She's milk drunk. I forgot about that."

"Do you mind holding her while I take a shower?"

"Oh my gosh, of course I don't! Let me go wash my hands real quick."

When Mia returned, Camille gently transferred her daughter. The baby stirred for a moment and then settled. When she didn't move more, Camille stood and stretched, her belly still swollen in postpartum.

She rubbed her stomach. "I think I snapped back a little faster last time."

Mia shrugged. "I think you look great. Your body is going to take as long as it needs."

"Yeah, I know. Still annoying, though." She laughed. "I'm sure being older is also factor. Anyway, I'll be quick about it."

"Take your time," said Mia, gazing at the sleeping baby.

After a few minutes, she heard the shower start. She traced the baby's brow. "You do look just like your mama."

Delilah sighed, and the smell of her milky breath took Mia back to Isaiah's infancy.

Mia had made it a point to pat Isaiah's back after every feeding. He didn't always burp, which meant Austin thought it was pointless. Once, very late at night or very early in the morning, depending on which perspective was preferred, Austin had scooped up their extremely alert infant. Mia had drifted off to sleep and awoken moments later to the sounds of gagging and spitting.

Austin had held up their son only to receive a shower of spit-up, some of which landed in his smiling mouth. When Mia realized what had happened, she sat up laughing. He thrust the startled baby into her arms and ran to the bathroom, still retching, his stomach not yet accustomed to parenthood.

"What are you smiling about?" Camille was fresh out of the shower, dressed in pajamas, her hair twisted up in a towel. "Sorry that took forever."

"Never be sorry for letting me hold your sweet baby." Mia kissed Delilah on her head. "She smells so delicious! I was kind of laughing to myself because I remembered once when Isaiah was a baby, maybe a few months old, Austin made the terrible mistake of holding him up higher than his head right after he nursed. And he hadn't burped him."

"Oh no!" Camille started giggling.

Mia laughed along. "I know. It was so funny. Spit-up everywhere. I mean, at least it was just breast milk spit up and not solid food—"

"Oh, yuck, you're right!"

"—but Austin wasn't ready. He practically threw the baby at me and ran to the bathroom. It was hilarious."

"Guys are so helpless at first, aren't they? Keegan's a lot more helpful this time around." Camille smiled contentedly and looked down at her baby. "So, how are you doing?"

"I'm good. Work is work. Isaiah's excited summer vacation has started."

Camille made a face as she removed the towel from her head. "Yeah, I could have timed this baby better instead of waiting until I didn't have school as a break." She tossed the towel onto the chair next to the small writing desk across from her bed.

"You're welcome to send Luca my way any time."

"Oh my gosh, don't tempt me. Do you want him for the summer?" Camille laughed. She grabbed a brush and pulled it through her hair.

"Well, maybe not any time. Call first."

The women laughed, which startled the baby. She stretched in Mia's arms, her little arms reaching upward, her fists barely clearing the top of her head.

"Oh, did I tell you? Sam proposed to Jessica!" Camille's eyebrows rose, and her mouth opened, as if pantomiming the image of surprise.

Mia smiled in apology. "She told me a few days ago."

Camille's shoulders slumped. "Damn. I really thought I had some hot gossip. Well, either way, isn't that exciting? I legit never thought she'd settle down. I guess Sam's really the one."

"Must be."

Delilah began to fuss, rooting at Mia's chest.

"I swear that baby is already going through a growth spurt," said Camille. The doorbell rang again, and a loud, male voice sounded at the entrance. "Oh. Sounds like Theo just got here. Mom and Dad are probably right behind. I think everyone else is coming over this weekend, minus Selina. She'll visit next month if you want to see her."

"Of course. Just let me know."

Mia held the baby as they walked down the stairs. Camille gave her brother a quick hug and kissed her parents before settling onto the couch. Mia handed her the baby and asked everyone if they wanted refreshments.

"Hey," said Keegan. "You're putting me out of a job."

She laughed. "Well, I can help."

After Delilah had had her fill of milk, she was dutifully passed around to the new grandparents and uncle.

"She looks just like Camille!" Theo's eyes twinkled mischievously. "Poor little thing."

"Hey!" Camille feigned throwing one of the small decorative couch pillows. "You're lucky you're holding my baby, or I'd kick your ass. Postpartum or not."

Keegan intercepted. "Hey, careful, babe. The doctor said you needed to take it easy for a bit when you got home."

Camille glared at her brother. "It might be worth popping a stitch."

Theo frowned, confused. "A stitch?"

"My poor hoo-ha. You think that big head can come out without tearing anything?"

"What?" Theo's face visibly paled, and Camille burst out laughing. He glanced at his niece, eyes wide.

Keegan turned away from the group, shoulders shaking from laughter.

Eloise frowned and stood to collect her granddaughter. "Oh my goodness, you two. I swear."

"I'm going to go get the drinks," said Mia, throwing Theo an amused look. Keegan followed her, and they grabbed everyone's requests.

Conversation started again when the two of them returned, and Camille turned toward Mia. "I heard Sean started seeing someone." She winced. "Sorry, Keegan told me the other day, and I just thought about it."

"That's okay. I'd already heard anyway." A stab of envy pierced her side. She straightened her shoulders. "I hope she's great. I'm happy for him."

Camille raised an eyebrow.

"No, really. He's a great guy, and he deserves to be happy."

"So do you."

"I know," said Mia. "Don't look at me like that. I mean it. I feel like—I'm finally able to think back to Austin without feeling as guilty or awful about it. I don't have nightmares about him anymore. Now, when I dream, it's almost like we're friends. It's kind of weird, but my therapist says it's progress."

Camille smiled genuinely. "I'm really glad you started going. You seem— lighter. I don't know if that's the right word to use, but that's what it seems like."

Mia thought back to the feeling of trudging through the weeks and months after Austin's death. Every step had felt like a struggle, her feet weighed down by the shackles of guilt. Grief had felt like drowning without the ability to give in to its finality. She had no idea how deep the ocean could be, and it worried her as she sank. The guilt and anger hung around her shoulders like diving weights, pulling her down as the pressure to move on increased. But somehow, with time—and likely the therapy—the weights had slowly shed. It was easier to navigate through the day-to-day.

Camille's living room was full of life and love. The boys were hiding away playing video games, likely to emerge only when they realized snacks were being distributed. She looked at all of the important people in her life. Theo caught her eye and smiled. The new normal everyone had promised her had crept right up to her, surrounded her, without announcing itself.

This was living: breakups, new births, friendships, and future plans. The loneliness that had haunted her was finally gone. She hadn't noticed its departure, but maybe that's why it was finally free to leave. It was no longer held prisoner by her grief.

"You know what?" She smiled at her friend. "I think you're right."

Resources

As of 2020, the CDC estimates one person in the United States dies by suicide every 11 minutes. The number who attempt suicide is even higher.

The World Health Organization estimates that more than 700,000 people die due to suicide every year. It is the fourth leading cause of death among 15 to 29-year-olds.

If you or someone you know is considering suicide, please reach out for help. Below are a list of resources in North America.

Resources for the United States

Suicide and Crisis Hotline: Call 988
(please note, the previous number, 1-800-273-TALK, will continue to work indefinitely)

Crisis Counselors for LGBTQ+ courtesy of the Trevor Project:
Text 'START' to 678-678
Phone: 1-866-488-7386

Veteran Crisis Line:
Call 988 and select option 1
Text: 838255

Resources for Canada

Talk Suicide Canada: Call 1-833-456-4566
Text: 45645 (4 p.m. - midnight ET)

Kids Help Phone Line: Call 1-800-668-6868
Text: 686868

Hope for Wellness Help Line: Call 1-855-242-3310

Online chat available on the website

Quebec Residents can call 1-866-27-3553

Resources for Mexico

Suicide Hotline: 01800-713-43-53

SAPTEL: Call 5259-8121 (Ciudad de Mexico)
Call 01-800-472-7835 (resto de Mexico)

Acknowledgements

First and foremost, I have to think my fiancé, Timothy Lucas, for all of the love, support, and encouragement he's shown me along the way. Though this book is my debut, it may likely be the most difficult one I'll write as it draws heavily from my personal experiences. There were many difficult chapters that had me needing space and time to process afterward. He held space for me during those times and I cannot thank him enough.

He was also the first one to lay eyes on the very early drafts of the book. Thank you, mi amor, for believing in me even when I felt like it was too difficult a story to pen.

Huge thanks, hugs, and besos to my children who were my personal cheerleaders (and first promoters!) throughout this entire process. Thank you for your patience when I had to rush off after dinner to finish a chapter, for your love when I needed to be lifted up, and for just being you. You all are my stars, my entire universe. I know you think I teach you a lot about so many topics, but you all teach me new things all the time! I am so lucky to be able to call myself your mother.

I want to express my gratitude to my cover artist, Frina. Thank you so much for all your patience when I was going back and forth with what I wanted for the cover. Especially because I gave you so little to work with. I think I just gave you a quick blurb about the book and said I wanted the ocean as a background. The cover you provided is better than I could have imagined.

Also, a million thanks to Lota Erinne and Whitney Morsillo for editing this manuscript. There is no way I could have polished their story to this degree without you both.

Special appreciation to everyone who volunteered to be alpha and beta readers for this manuscript. Your feedback and critique helped immensely.

And lastly, thank you to everyone who decides to give this book a chance. I truly hope you enjoy the story and its message.

About The Author

Gloria Lucas

Gloria Lucas is the author of several short stories, including 'The Man Who Turned into a Mountain,' available in Palaver Journal, and 'Un Cafecito at Midnight,' which is part of the Fiesta Nights romance anthology.

She is a Navy veteran and holds an MBA in Healthcare Management. In the Navy, she worked as an Aviation Electrician on F/A-18 A-F aircraft. After leaving the military, she transitioned to a career in healthcare and has worked in home birth midwifery, in nonprofit clinics, and now in pharmaceuticals.

She began writing as a child but wouldn't start publishing her work until 2019. 'How Deep the Ocean' is her first novel.

When she is not writing or reading, she enjoys spending time with her partner and children, hiking, and perusing art museums. Less often, one might find her at a divey karaoke bar.

Made in the USA
Middletown, DE
02 November 2022

13891498R00156